DORINDA TRAPPER OF RED RAPIDS

Fergus P Egan

Dorinda Trapper of Red Rapids

Author and Publisher: Fergus P Egan

ISBN: 978-1-9993941-9-6 (Paperback Edition)
ISBN: 978-1-7776037-1-7 (Hardcover Edition)
ISBN: 978-1-7776037-0-0 (Electronic Book Edition)

Email: FergusEganPublishing@gmail.com

Story Development: Aisling Egan
Editor: Andrew Niall Egan
Cover Photo: Fergus P Egan

Disclaimer

This book is a work of fiction. For authenticity, iconic streets and buildings are accurately identified. However, the interior of these buildings and their occupants are the products of the author's imagination and are used fictitiously. Any resemblance to actual persons or events is entirely coincidental.

ISBN: 978-1-9993941-9-6

<u>*SHADOW*</u>

More than nothing...

Less than something...

A shadow on the street.

Drinking something...

Thinking nothing...

A shadow hide-and-seek.

Someone's falling...

Something's crawling...

A shadow without feet.

Less than something...

Less than nothing...

No shadow on the street.

LIST OF CHARACTERS

<u>**Investigation Team:**</u>

Jack Doyle – private investigator

Okwaho'kó:wa – First Nations activist

<u>**Trapper/Cool Family of Red Rapids:**</u>

Dorinda Trapper – member of Cree Red Rapids Reserve

Amy Trapper – mother

Mark Trapper – brother

Kokum Cool – grandmother

Jim Cool – uncle

Rose Cool – aunt

<u>**Toronto:**</u>

Ken Andrews 'Jamaica Man' – club owner

Misty Morning – club personnel manager

Monique – sex worker

Colin Clark – bank inspector

John Maxwell – bank credit manager

Pete Harvey – bank office manager

Alex Crouse – police detective

<u>**Elliot Lake:**</u>

'Grouchy Man' – owner of rural roadside convenience store

'Greasy Man' – Nathaniel 'Nate' Carson – junkyard owner

Stan Wilcox – police detective

PROLOGUE

Rose Cool enters the 51 Division Metropolitan Toronto Police Station at 51 Parliament Street to report a missing minor. She gives the information to a desk sergeant. The sergeant summarizes the tendered information into the record sheet:

> Dorinda Trapper, age 15 (niece of complainant, Rose Cool of 435 Jarvis Street, unit 206) – picture not available.

> Disappeared on the morning of Tuesday 04 April 2017 – last seen at noon in the *Eaton Centre*. No foul play witnessed.

> Note: Subject ran away from home on 03 February 2017 from Red Rapids First Nations Reserve.

The sergeant regards this as one more tragic runaway. In Canada, over 40,000 children are reported missing each year. Of these, most return home or are quickly located within two days. But after one week, 8% remain unaccounted for. These young runaways, approximately 2,500 children, seldom turn up. In Dorinda's case, she left of her own volition and no foul play is evident. Therefore, there is no 'crime' to investigate – just be on the lookout for one more runaway minor.

DORINDA TRAPPER OF RED RAPIDS

CHAPTER ONE

JACK DOYLE

Jack Doyle glances around his office one more time. This is his final day at U.S. Immigration and Customs Enforcement in Buffalo, New York. He is dressed appropriately in the standard black-shirted ICE uniform. He is thirty years old and has been an officer in ICE since 2003. His dark-brown hair is beginning to recede and turn grey, but it still imparts a reddish tint when the light is right. He is particularly skilled at ferreting out information and in conducting investigations. It comes as no surprise that as of tomorrow, 01 September 2010, he will commence duties with the newly-formed Homeland Security Investigation division (HSI). HSI is a critical investigative arm of the Department of Homeland Security and is a vital U.S. asset in combating criminal organizations. Jack's new posting will be at Toronto Pearson Airport as a special agent investigating an array of cross-border criminal activities – money laundering and bulk cash smuggling, human smuggling and trafficking, and narcotics and weapons trafficking by transnational gangs. At Pearson, he will share office space with the Canada Border Services Agency (CBSA), in an arrangement that facilitates USA/Canada cooperation in joint operations. Jack holds dual citizenship, an advantage that affords him a greater degree of movement in either country.

Jack is satisfied that his office is cleared and ready for the next occupant. The room is windowless with solid walls. His framed awards are removed from the now-bare walls. Thus, the sparse office appears more austere than usual. The solid door is fully open. This gives a spacious feel to the room but, more importantly, it assists the airflow from the air conditioning system. Jack looks at his personal effects laid out on his desk. He checks through his things and prepares to place them in his attaché case, thus ensuring that no personal belongings are left behind after his departure. He places his Visa statement and bank statement to one side as his reminder that the credit card payment is due within the week. And he smiles at the picture in his Ontario driver's licence. It is a much better picture than the one in his Canadian passport. Jack is feeling good and is looking forward to *Tim Hortons* double-double coffee and a maple-dip doughnut at work on the following day. He checks his watch and determines that he will knock off work in an hour. This gives him sufficient time for a quick good-bye to his Buffalo colleagues in U.S. Immigration and Customs Enforcement.

Jack is unexpectedly interrupted by a voice at his open door. "Jack, we have a bit of a nutcase out at the front counter."

Jack looks up as Chuck Nolan sticks his head through the doorway of his office. Chuck is a colleague in immigration and customs enforcement and is one of Jack's social buddies. "What is it, Chuck, that you can't handle it out front?"

Chuck twists his mouth as he formulates his answer. "It's a pedestrian from Canada. He walked across the Peace Bridge and here he is with no papers – no passport, no driver's licence, no citizenship card, no nothing."

"So deport him back to Canada. You can handle that, can't you?"

Chuck twists his mouth again and steps inside the office. "I sense that this is more than a pedestrian who has simply wandered in here in error. You have a nose for these things, Jack. I'd like you to take a look at him for anything sinister."

"Sinister? Okay, Chuck. Send him in here for an interview." Jack is impatient to be done with his duties. However, he expects this to be some confused person that needs to be returned across the border. Deported pedestrians require an escort, but this is a simple task that Chuck Nolan can coordinate with the Canadians. But if the person is mentally challenged it requires delicate handling. Jack glances at his watch again and determines that the pending interview ought to take no more than five minutes or so.

Moments later, Chuck Nolan ushers a man into Jack's office. Jack gestures to a vacant chair. "Please have a seat." Jack sizes up the visitor in a glance. Male, late twenties, 5' 10", tanned complexion – not just tanned, his colour and features reveal his indigenous identity. His straight black hair is pulled back into a ponytail that falls to below his shoulder blades. Yes, this is a First Nations man. He is sporting a tan leather western-style hat, pulled down to shade his eyes, even though he is inside and is out of the sun's glare. It is clear that this is the hat's normal fit of comfort. Added to this apparel are a buckskin jacket, jeans and delicate hand-stitched deer-skinned moccasins. The clothes are clean and well cared for, but not crisp-new. His belt matches the hat and is fastened by a large silver buckle. The jacket is open to reveal a red-and-white check shirt, unbuttoned to the waist, thus revealing a bronzed chest with a partial view of a tattoo. Jack understands that the man's apparel is too heavy for late summer, especially for walking, hence the reason why the shirt is unbuttoned and open. There is a thin mist of perspiration on the man's brow and his outfit imparts a strong smell of leather.

Notwithstanding the distinctive clothing, the most striking characteristic of the man is in his bearing – noble and commanding. The man's movements are unhurried, yet deliberate. He is well proportioned and fit. As Jack watches the man take his seat, he realizes that 'fit' is not an apt description, perhaps 'lithe' is more appropriate. Sitting thus face to face, and having spoken not a word, the man appears to have assumed control of the meeting. This is unexpected. Jack understands now how Chuck sensed something sinister in the man.

Jack coughs and addresses the man. "I understand that you are from Canada and that you wish to enter the United States. Is this correct?"

The man renders a statement, not as an answer but as a correction. In a soft commanding voice, he makes it clear that Jack's question is deficient. "I am from Mohawk First Nation on the Grand River; I am journeying to visit my kin at the Oneida Nation at Te-o-na-ta-le ('Pine Forest' in Haudenosaunee)."

"So you are travelling from the Six Nations Reserve in Ontario, Canada, to the Oneida Reservation at Verona, New York? Is that what you are saying?"

"No. That is what **you** are saying."

Jack is unsettled by this response. He waits for an explanation. The man is silent. He fixes his eyes on Jack. Jack senses that he is examining the room with his peripheral vision. Jack curses inwardly as he remembers that his personal effects are still lying on the corner of his desk. He opens a drawer and casually slides his personal papers into the open drawer – his New York bank statement, his Visa statement, his Ontario driver's licence and his Canadian passport. He covers his discomfort by recommencing the interview. "To enter the United States you are required to identify yourself and provide documentation for entry. First, what is your name?"

"Okwaho."

"Just 'Ogwaho'?"

"Okwaho'kó:wa."

Jack is unable to grasp what is being said. "I need you to produce written identification confirming your name."

With that, the man, Okwaho, pulls open his shirt to display a tattoo. To Jack, the tattoo depicts a dog walking over a bundle of sticks. Okwaho remains silent; his eyes still fixed boringly into Jack.

Jack is getting annoyed. He gestures angrily at the man's bare chest. "What is this then?"

Calmly, Okwaho responds. So far, he has not blinked nor moved his penetrating eyes off Jack. "First, you asked me regarding my journey. I spoke truthfully, but you did not like my answer. Perhaps you did not understand it. Next, you asked me my name. I told you my name. And then you asked for written confirmation of my name, and this I displayed to you. If that is all you require of me, I shall continue on my journey." Slowly, Okwaho rises to his feet.

Jack barks at him, "Remain seated!"

Okwaho freezes but remains standing. His eyes continue to bore into Jack. Jack is uneasy. Okwaho looks like a wolf preparing to spring. Jack moves his hand to the gun in his belt in a clear demonstration that he is prepared to use force if necessary. Okwaho does not flinch.

Jack is put in mind of the 'Oka Crisis' in which a group of Mohawk people had a land dispute with the town of Oka, Quebec in 1990. There was one fatality. God, he does not want to start a crisis here today. Jack rises and addresses Okwaho with all the authority he can muster. "I said 'sit down'! If you refuse to cooperate, I have the authority to detain you! And use force if necessary!"

"Ah, 'force'," Okwaho responds calmly. "Indeed you have force – you have a firearm. So too do your fellow officers back there. And you have alarms, high walls and detention centres. But do not confuse 'force' with 'authority'. Be warned, you have no authority to prohibit the free movement of indigenous peoples in our own lands."

Jack shouts for assistance. "Officers! Here!" Immediately, two border enforcement officers arrive at Jack's office.

"Escort this troublesome Indian back to Canada. He attempted to enter the country illegally. If he resists, arrest him."

Okwaho delivers a parting remark. "Onyare, I know that you are deaf. But are you blind also? For over a thousand years we have walked this land here. Then you came to claim these lands. Treaties were made; treaties were broken. So by what right do you lord over us? Note this. I came here peacefully today; now I leave peacefully. The next time we meet, Onyare, who will have 'authority' and who will exercise 'force'?" Okwaho surrenders himself quietly to the two officers who escort him arm-in-arm to a van. Thence, they deliver him across the Peace Bridge to Canadian Border Services.

*   *   *   *   *

Jack is relieved that the troublesome Indian is out of his hair. Deporting him back to Canada is less onerous than detaining him for unlawful entry. Detention would have entailed procedures requiring more of Jack's time. As it is, he is behind schedule. Jack gathers his belongings into his attaché case, bids farewell to his colleagues and drives home to his house at 169 Tracy Lynn Lane, West Seneca.

Tracy Lynn Lane is a pleasant suburban neighbourhood of mostly upper-middle-class and professional people. Every lawn is manicured. A few windows display *Neighborhood Watch* signs as evidence of the responsible people who reside there. Jack enters his two-car driveway and parks. He notices the 'for sale' sign posted at the sidewalk. Mary Liz, his

Canadian-born wife, will remain here until the house sale is completed. Thereupon, she will join him in a new home in Canada. Early tomorrow, Jack Doyle will travel 100 miles to Lester B Pearson Airport Toronto to his new assignment. 100 miles? No, 160 kilometres.

*   *   *   *   *

On Wednesday 01 September, Jack Doyle exits his house at 6:00am. He is singing as he throws his attaché case and overnight bag in the trunk of his *Ford Fiesta*. Okwaho and the unsettling incident of the previous day are furthest from his mind. He is eager to sink his teeth into serious investigative work and is looking forward to a two-hour drive to Toronto.

Once seated in the driver's seat, he notices a card stuck in his wiper blade, probably a business card from the real estate agent. Opening the driver-side door, he stretches his arm around the windshield and grabs the card with his fingers. It is a simple white card with black markings. It displays a snake in a striking pose – a strange logo for a real estate agency. He flips it over to read the other side. He shivers upon seeing it. It is a picture of a dog running over a bunch of sticks. On closer examination, he establishes that it is not a domestic dog but a wolf. And the 'sticks' symbolize a woodland environment – a timber wolf. With sudden clarity, Jack realizes that the 'troublesome Indian' of yesterday revealed his name by displaying this same picture tattooed on his chest. 'Okwaho'kó:wa' is the 'timber wolf'. This disturbing man was in his office yesterday and was here at his house this morning. Jack glances around the street. There is

8

no one in sight, certainly not Okwaho the wolf. He flips the card over and attempts to decipher the pictograph. What is the significance of the snake on the card? Unable to come up with an answer, he slides the card into the breast pocket of his shirt and proceeds with his journey.

CHAPTER TWO

JACK DOYLE IN CANADA

On Wednesday 01 September 2010, Jack Doyle is driving on the Queen Elizabeth Way (QEW) from Fort Erie to Toronto. He has decided to dress in his standard-issue black-shirted ICE uniform for his initial visit to Homeland Security Investigation division at Toronto Pearson Airport. Henceforth, he will operate in plainclothes as an undercover investigation agent. It has taken him less than half an hour to travel from Tracy Lynn Lane to the Canadian border via I-90 N and I-190 N. Even allowing for the time it would take to park at Pearson, he expects to reach his destination by 8:00am. He is approaching Exit #74. He checks the time and decides to exit on Casablanca Boulevard to avail of a *Tim Hortons* coffee and a maple-dip doughnut.

Minutes later, Jack is sitting at a table in the coffee shop. His mind is on his recent jolt from discovering the disturbing card on his windshield as he was about to leave home. He removes the mysterious card from his breast pocket and repeatedly taps it edge-up on the table – flipping it over to read both sides alternatively. It is peculiar that, although the snake depicted on the back of the card is in a detailed striking pose, it has no eyes. Are the eyes closed? Or is it a mistake by the artist? Jack neglects his 'double-double', permitting it to get cold, and dwells on the visit by the sinister Indian 'Wolf-man' of yesterday. Who is Okwaho? Is he a threat to him or his family? And how was he able to find Jack's private house? Jack surmises that he must have read the papers on his desk. After all, the bank statement has his address displayed with the account name. But how could the troublesome Indian have been at 169 Tracy Lynn Lane, West Seneca, last night if he had been deported to Canada a few hours prior? And him walking? Jack resolves to look into the matter as soon as he is settled into his new job. As a HSI officer, he is well equipped and authorized to investigate the unlawful entry of a Canadian resident into the United States. Having made this decision, Jack stands up and places the card back into his breast pocket. His coffee and doughnut are still on the table. He leaves them both unconsumed and continues on his journey.

*   *   *   *   *

Jack Doyle takes to his new assigned duties with dedication. His resolution to track down Okwaho is still present but is low on his list of priorities. A year has elapsed since his encounter with the 'troublesome Indian'. In that time there has been no mention of Okwaho and there have been no threats to his family, now settled at Huron Park in Mississauga, Ontario. Okwaho, it would appear, has vanished off the face of the earth. Furthermore, Jack is faced with more pressing assignments that demand his undivided attention. But Okwaho is not entirely forgotten. Jack is left with a bad taste in his mouth for all indigenous people and an unshakable distrust of all Indians. His opinion is reinforced by his investigative work. Jack's focus is on the contraband activity of Indian bands. Drugs, tobacco and alcohol are moved around with impunity through the Indian communities straddling the US/Canadian border. Recently, there has been an increase in firearms smuggling. And a new alert is issued to investigate possible human trafficking. Investigations are encumbered by the administrative confusion of overlapping authorities – band councils adhering to traditional chiefs vying with elected band councils in opposition, provincial legislation and federal ministries, state and national authorities. Jack is impatient and takes risks in his investigative practices. He bypasses official channels and employs reckless shortcuts. He operates, often alone and unauthorized. In working around these obstacles, he penetrates the 'Indian Warriors' through contacts and informants. Thus, Jack's investigations result in a high rate of success. But it also exposes him to personal danger.

Friday 09 December 2011 is a damp evening. Wet snow is falling at Queen Street & Spadina Avenue, Toronto. Jack Doyle is sitting in *The Horseshoe Tavern* listening to the husband and wife duo of Raven Kanatakta and Shoshona Kish of *Digging Roots*. Jack is dressed in *Mark's Work Warehouse's* best – blue work shirt over dark-grey cargo pants and snow boots. A *Blue Jays* baseball cap conceals his receding hairline, and his gunmetal-green parka is flung open to hang from his shoulders. He is too hot dressed thus. But he decided to wear boots rather than shoes because of the slush on the ground. And the parka contains his cell phone and conceals his sidearm. He shifts his weight and remembers that his handgun is not on his person. As per the required protocol on carrying firearms whilst off duty, Jack's gun is under the driver's seat of his car. He is drinking hot black coffee. HSI agent Jack Doyle is officially off duty. But Jack is reckless. He has arranged, off the record and unauthorized, to meet a covert informant. This is a new informant, one assured to be trustworthy, and he needs to stay alert. Therefore, he foregoes alcohol. He peers out through the window at the moist pavement on Queen Street West. A westbound streetcar stops and passengers disembark. He studies them. Maybe 'Tom' is one of the disembarking people. It is just gone 7:30pm, the agreed meeting time. The tavern is filling up. Jack hears the clink of a cup on his table. He studies the reflection in the window. He observes a man standing behind him at his table. Jack remains looking out the window. "Hello, Tom," he says quietly and distinctly. This should elicit the confirming response.

"Hello, Coach." The contact utters the correct response.

'Tom' remains silent. Jack continues. "Are you going to sit? Or is this a quick meeting?" Jack swivels around to face Tom and asks, "So, why the meeting?"

Tom's bald head is uncovered and is moist from newly-melted snowflakes. His tan raincoat is buttoned up to his neck and is dripping rainwater past his mukluks to pool on the floor. Like Jack, Tom is also drinking black coffee. The informant stares past Jack and focuses on the streetcar as it moves away on the green traffic light. He speaks. "The next streetcar to stop here will have a white van behind it. Enter the van by the back door." Tom drains the remaining coffee and places the empty cup on the table. Thereupon, he walks away and disappears into the crowd at the stage. Jack could easily follow him but he spots another streetcar arriving at the stop.

Jack exits the tavern. People step off the motionless streetcar and new passengers are lining up to enter. Jack looks intently up the street. Just as he was informed, he observes the white van, now stationary, behind the streetcar. Cautiously, he walks past the line of people and steps off the curb to the van. The driver is a young woman, or maybe a young man. He is unable to tell due to the glare of the street lighting. Jack hesitates. The doors of the streetcar are closing. He must act now or fail to make contact. Indecision is the worst decision. Jack must either enter the van or walk back to the curb. Jack acts. He opens the rear door of the van and enters. The van moves forward as Jack slams the door shut. The interior of the van has two rows of seats running lengthways. There are no seatbelts. Perhaps the 'seats' are deliberately installed as low shelving for carrying goods, but Jack knows that this is a common mode of unlawful transport for farmworkers and labourers.

The driver speaks. "You are lucky to have found parking off Sullivan Street."

The driver turns her head slightly as she checks the van's blindside. Jack catches a glimpse of her face and deduces that it is a teenage girl and wonders if she is old enough to hold a driver's licence. There is no front passenger seat. In its place is a stand of pigeon-hole compartments. It is likely a delivery van. Jack is standing in a hunched position in the moving van. He asks, "Where are we going?"

The young driver surveys Jack in the rear-view mirror. Since there are no windows in the rear of the van, the rear-view mirror is positioned to view the interior cargo. She speaks. "Just have a seat. I'll drive you back to your car when we are finished."

"Finished what?"

"The meeting. That's what you were told. Yes? Just sit down. It is not safe to stand in a moving van."

Jack asks more questions but the girl concentrates on her driving and is uncommunicative. This is not the first time Jack has experienced this manner of meeting. It is risky and is certainly not approved. Nevertheless, these clandestine meetings have previously garnered many favourable outcomes for Jack. He relaxes and waits out the journey.

Jack attempts to establish the route from his restricted view of street lights and tall buildings. South on Spadina, west on the Gardiner Expressway, 427 north. Shortly, the van exits the 427 and travels on a twisting road. From this point on, Jack loses his sense of location and direction. For almost two hours he is unable to distinguish any visible landmarks. Eventually, the van comes to a halt. Jack checks the time displayed on his cell phone. It is 9:17pm. He notes the warning message displayed at the bottom of the screen – 'no cell connection'. Wherever this is, it is too remote for cell-phone service.

The underage driver turns to Jack and speaks. "We're here. Follow me to the longhouse."

Jack exits the van and walks alongside the girl. 'Longhouse' suggests that he is on a reserve, but he has no inkling which reserve this might be. It is dark with snow falling. No other buildings are visible. 'Underage Girl' enters the porch of the building. She places her cell phone and bowie knife on the small table at the side. This elicits a nod from the quiet man standing guard nearby. The quiet man puts Jack in mind of the 'troublesome Indian' he encountered in the previous year. What was his name? 'Okwaho'. This man is burlier. Perhaps he is Okwaho's brother?

"Weapons and cell phones are not permitted in the longhouse," Underage Girl informs him. "Place your gun and cell phone on the table here, and remove your cap."

Jack places his cell phone and cap on the table and says, "I don't have a gun." Whereupon, the man frisks him with expert ease. Satisfied that Jack is not carrying a weapon, he is directed into the building with Underage Girl. The room is arranged in theatre style with chairs in rows facing a head table. Three elderly men and one old woman are seated randomly in the chairs, presumably waiting for a meeting to commence. Underage Girl directs Jack to a chair in the front row, to the left of centre. They sit here side by side. A man in buckskin clothes and moccasins enters from a side room and takes his place in the front row, right of centre. Thereupon, three men enter from a back room and proceed towards the head table. Suddenly everyone rises.

A distinct aroma of sage wafts in with the entrance of the three men and blends in with the underlying smell of oak and leather. The three men range in age from thirty-something to sixtyish. All are dressed completely in buckskin. Jack surmises that this must be some uniform or traditional attire. The three men sit facing the assembly, whereupon all people in the room resume sitting. Jack wonders why he is present at a tribal meeting and what relevance it might have. As if on cue, the three men place red-and-blue patchwork-weave headbands on their heads. The centre man's headband contains three erect white feathers, of which the centre feather is red-tipped. The headbands of the men on either side contain two erect white feathers and one erect white feather respectively. 'Elders', Jack deduces. He turns to Underage Girl to enquire and he sees that she too has donned a similar headband, but her single white feather hangs down beside her left ear. He opens his mouth to speak, but she signals him to remain silent.

'Three Feathers' speaks. Jack fails to catch what is being said. 'Front Man' stands and responds. Three Feathers nods. Front Man resumes speaking. Jack whispers to Underage Girl, "What are they saying?"

"It's Haudenosaunee", she whispers back.

He scrutinizes the feather hanging in her long black hair behind her left ear. Jack wonders if this denotes rank or formal position. "So, what is your role here at the meeting?"

"I am your defence council. Now, be quiet."

Jack opens his mouth and closes it again. He is speechless and he needs to put context on what is happening. Just then, Underage Girl stands up and commences to address the head table. The three elders look at Jack and nod. Underage Girl ceases speaking and resumes her seat. The elders converse quietly together. Jack decides that it is time to leave. He readies himself to stand up and glances at the exit door. The burly doorman is standing with arms folded staring intently at

Jack. There is no mistaking his message – 'stay seated and remain quiet'.

The girl nudges Jack and whispers, "Stand up. The chief is addressing you."

Jack stands up – anything to get this over with. His temper is rising. The chief speaks a few words. Then all three elders remove their headbands and rise from their chairs. Concurrent with this, the entire assembly stands. The girl whispers to Jack, "Congratulations. You have been found 'not guilty'. You are free to leave. However, it is courtesy to thank the elders for their wisdom in exercising fair judgement."

Jack glances around. Everyone is standing, awaiting his expression of thanks. Puzzled, Jack asks the girl, "Not guilty. Not guilty of what?"

"'Disrespect to the Nation'."

Thereupon, Jack's Irish erupts. He addresses the elders in English. "Disrespect? Do you consider this primitive meeting to be 'respectful' in any way? How..." Too late, Jack bites his tongue.

Everyone looks at Jack in shock. The elders resume their seats and likewise the entire assembly – except for the doorman who hovers over Jack. Jack sits contritely in his chair. He regrets his loose tongue. The elders don their headbands and confer for a few moments. Once more, the girl prompts Jack to stand. The chief addresses Jack a second time. After a few words, the elders remove their headbands, stand up and hurriedly exit the room. The assembled band members file out of the building slowly, each one pausing briefly to cast a derisive look at Jack in passing. Jack and Underage Girl and the doorman are all who remain standing in the meeting room.

The girl removes her headband. She looks at Jack and shakes her head and says, "Stupid."

Jack is contrite and embarrassed. "Okay, okay. It was stupid of me. So, what now?"

"For disrespecting the nation, you are sentenced to wear the mark of 'Onyare'."

Jack feels relieved. Still, this is a lost night of futile activity for him. He has achieved nothing of merit. And now he must wear some Indian symbol. Jack envisages a disk hanging from a leather necklace. "All right," he sighs in resignation. "Let's get this over with."

The doorman directs Jack to a room off the main meeting room. A man is standing inside at a desk with his back to Jack. His long hair hangs fanlike to below his shoulder blades. He speaks. "Remove your anorak. And present written identification."

Jack complies. It is hot in the room and his parka is heavy. He removes it, holding it upright lest his car keys fall out of the pocket. The doorman (the 'bouncer'?) assists him. The doorman stares at Jack, waiting. Jack understands. He reaches into his pants pocket and removes his wallet. He flips it open to reveal his I.D. The doorman grabs the entire wallet from him. This is not good. A HSI officer must maintain possession of his credentials and prevent them from falling into unauthorized hands.

'Longhair' is holding what looks like a curling iron for hair, only in his case, it is probably a hair-straightening iron. There is a dish or shallow bowl on the desk. He appears to be examining it. 'Longhair' speaks. "Sit." The doorman directs Jack to a lone chair in the centre of the room.

"Onyare,' Longhair addresses him, "who will have 'authority' and who will exercise 'force'?" Longhair slowly turns around to face Jack.

"Okwaho!"

"Ah, you remember me." Okwaho-Longhair turns briefly towards the bowl on the desk. He dips the tip of the curling iron in the bowl and turns and approaches Jack.

Jack is puzzled, almost amused, that this long-haired Indian will attempt to groom the HSI agent's thinning hair. Suddenly, Okwaho presses the tip of the iron to Jack's exposed forehead. It happens so fast and unexpectedly, that he fails to react immediately. He realizes that what he perceived as a curling iron, is an electric branding iron. Jack recoils in surprise, and a second later he feels the burning pain. He suppresses a yell. Then he looks to Okwaho for an explanation.

"Now, Onyare, you have the mark of Onyare. So shall you

henceforth be known. This is your written identification. Indigenous people will look at you and know that you are disrespectful and, therefore, undeserving of respect in return. Now leave. You are not welcome here; not now; not ever." He addresses the doorman. "Escort this man back to Canada."

The doorman thrusts the parka at Jack and escorts him to the van. Jack notes the license plate – NEW 859. This will assist him later in the subsequent investigation he intends to execute. Jack enters the van. The doorman passes his baseball cap to him and shuts the van door. The van moves off. Jack attempts to put this incident into perspective and take stock of his situation. The loss of his I.D. is his primary concern now. There will be hell to pay when he reports it missing. And worse, it will reveal Jack's unauthorized activities in acting alone in his investigations without the consent of his department and the cooperating legitimizing assistance of local law enforcement. And the burn in his forehead is stinging. There is a second occupant in the van. He is sitting opposite to Jack. Jack ignores him, assuming that this is his 'escort'.

'Escort Man' speaks. "Here. Take this. It is a plaster for your wound." He passes a band-aid to Jack.

Jack unwraps it and sticks it to his head with an 'ouch.' "Thanks."

"There is a big shipment of drugs arriving."

Jack is jolted by this unexpected statement. "A shipment of drugs?"

Escort Man reads the surprise on Jack's face notwithstanding the faint light in the interior of the van. "What? You thought the requested meeting was solely about your lack of respect for First Nation people? You are still a crude piece of dirt, but you **are** an investigator for HSI nevertheless."

Jack leans forward to clearly catch the man's words over the rumble of the tires on the wet gravel road surface. "So, tell me."

"You know that drugs pass through the border concealed within tires."

"Yes. Sometimes."

"The drugs originate in Colombia; they are transported to Mexico and from there to the USA. Some shipments from Mexico enter via Canada."

Jack nods. He is aware of this, but the traffic is small.

The man continues. "You know *Quest Transport* in Aberfoyle?"

"In Aberfoyle, Ontario? Never heard of it."

"Yes, you wouldn't, would you? It's a nothing transportation company. They have a company truck stop off the I-90 in Cheektowaga."

"Yes, I remember it now in the context of Buffalo. It is a wreck of a place." This is beginning to sound very interesting to Jack – an insignificant trucking company in Aberfoyle with a rundown truck stop in Cheektowaga.

The man continues to speak. "*Quest* sends trucks across the border with low-revenue cargo – or should I say low-revenue **declared cargo**. Some, not all, of the truck tires contain drugs. And not on every truck either."

"And in Cheektowaga, the 'defective' or 'recalled' tires are replaced with 'clean' tires? I see. And the driver may not even be aware of the true nature of the cargo he is transporting." Jack has encountered this form of smuggling in the past. "And you know this how?"

"Ah. Never underestimate a 'stupid Indian' doing grunt work. But here's the thing that should interest you. What if you could nab the mother lode before it reaches *Quest* and before the tires are installed on cross-border trucks?"

"How?" The HSI agent is keen to learn more.

"A cargo of cocaine, worth between ten million and fifteen million in street value, is about to enter Canada by air from Mexico."

"Are you sure?" Jack wonders how reliable this information is.

"A cargo of truck tires, manufactured in Mexico, is cleared to arrive in Hamilton Airport on flight PR 2090. That's what I learned today."

Jack considers this information. If this is true, then it is not part of the 'Indian Warriors'. This sounds like an unwelcome competitor attempting to muscle in on their established territory. 'My enemy's enemy'. The Indians want HSI to stamp on the competition. 'So what?', thinks Jack. A bust is a bust. And this could be the biggest seizure ever in Ontario. "So when is flight PR 2090, with its precious cargo, due to arrive at *John C. Munro Hamilton International Airport*?"

"6:05 tomorrow morning."

"Six o'clock tomorrow morning? That's, that's..." Jack struggles to locate his cell phone. He needs to check the time and contact HSI.

"That's in seven hours' time. It is now after eleven."

"I need to contact..."

"You will be reunited with your car and your belongings by one o'clock. That gives you five hours to get your agents' feet on the ground. That is more than enough time. If you act too soon, and there is unusual activity at the airport in the off-hours, the pilot may get tipped off and turn the flight around. Don't launch your hit team until the flight has passed the point of no return, the point where he has insufficient fuel for a return flight to Mexico."

Jack considers this advice. The joint operation with The Canada Border Services Agency (CBSA) needs to be poised and ready, well outside the perimeter of the airport, by 4:00am. And local, provincial and federal police services ready at 5:00am – staying well out of sight until the plane lands, and then... Jack is anxious. His mind is off his wound and he is unable to sit still.

At 12:47am the van stops at the curb on Sullivan Street. Jack exits the van and it immediately drives off. They did not return his possessions to him before driving off – wallet, keys, cell phone. He scans the adjacent parking lot. His car is the sole vehicle visible on the lot. He sees it covered in snow. Jack is relieved to distinguish footprints from the street to the car, and back again. This means that someone was here since the recent snowfall – within the past few minutes. He runs to the car. The door is unlocked and the snow is disturbed. He opens the door wide and holds his breath. There, on the passenger seat in full view, are his missing belongings. He checks under the seat and confirms that his gun is still in the seat holster. He starts the engine to warm up the car. Then he punches a phone number into his cell phone.

A block away, the van stops and 'Escort Man' peels off the white-and-blue tape from the license plate. 'NEW 859' in blue lettering on a white background is removed to reveal 'TZ 45327' in black lettering on a white background. Within seconds, the commercial van drives off to complete its mission.

The top story in Sunday's news is a report on a major drug seizure by Canada Border Services executed on the previous day. Local police forces assisted in the arrest of twenty-two people in Hamilton. This is Canada's greatest haul of illicit drugs to date. The Border Services acknowledge the valuable contribution of U.S. agencies that cooperated in the cross-border operation. As part of a related operation, a further three people were arrested in Buffalo by U.S. authorities.

Jack Doyle is sitting in his living room. He is half awake as he recovers from the hectic events of the past few days. Mary Liz, his wife, is attentive to the news report on TV. She turns to her dozing unshaven husband on the couch and asks, "Is that the operation that you were on? When I hadn't seen you for three days?"

Jack opens his sleepy eyes and responds, "Yeah, that's the one." He does not elaborate. Some things are best concealed. Mary Liz has not yet seen the burn on Jack's forehead. It is healing, but Jack has placed a fresh band-aid on the wound. He considers using his wife's facial makeup. He could apply it to the scab to hide it. Or, he could wear his baseball cap in the house. Yesterday, he inquired into the van's license plate number – NEW 859. That number was retired when the legitimate plate was surrendered in 1985.

Mary Liz is still speaking. "Well, I hope that big drug bust puts an end to your late nights. Do you know how anxious I get when you disappear all of a sudden with no contact and no forewarning? I don't know if you are alive or dead when you are off like that."

Jack groans in agreement. But he refrains from openly expressing his feeling of apprehension. Regardless of how he feels, he does not expect things to ease up. With the Mexican competition subdued by the recent drug bust, the Indian Warriors will be emboldened to greater activity. In the inevitable fallout, Jack expects to scale up his future investigations. He fingers his wound to remind himself that he has good reason to agitate the troublesome Indians.

*   *   *   *   *

For the next seven years, Jack continues in his investigations. He gains a notorious reputation. And he is a constant thorn in the side of First Nation smugglers. His persistent investigations result in numerous arrests, although nothing as significant as the Hamilton Seizure of 2011. Jack is content in knowing that his activity is a significant deterrent in curtailing otherwise large-scale smuggling.

In 2018, Jack's relentless harassment of First Nation smugglers comes crashing down suddenly and unexpectedly. In pursuing members of the Black Hand Warriors of the Mohawk Nation at Akwesasne, in a suspected migrant smuggling operation, Jack's boat collides with a Warrior boat under the international bridge at Three Nations Crossing at Cornwall Island. Both boats are travelling at high speed at the time of the head-on collision. Jack suffers two broken legs, three cracked ribs and a concussion. The Warrior boat, although crippled and taking on water, succeeds in reaching shore on the island. The occupants of the Warrior boat evade capture.

Later, in hospital, Mary Liz insists (yet again) that Jack retires from his dangerous line of work. This time, he gives in. Although he is offered a desk job in New York, Jack resigns from Homeland Security Investigations and cuts ties with US Customs and Immigration.

Okwaho the 'Wolf' continues to be active. He protests against the infringement of indigenous rights – blocking rail passage in Ontario and halting oil pipeline construction in British Columbia. He is not hesitant to use the threat of violence to press his causes, but he councils against actual violence except as a defensive last resort. He is stalwart in the face of injustice, but not aggressively hostile. Victories are few and slight. Yet, he is committed to enduring the struggle. In 2018, his attention is focused on the dismal living conditions in neglected remote reserves. These conditions, he believes, are the primary cause of young people 'disappearing' from reserves.

CHAPTER THREE

THE TRAPPERS

Dorinda Trapper watches her teacher board the skiff – a flat-bottomed open boat with a sharp bow and square stern, capable of accommodating eight people. Brenda Cheechoo, having concluded her day's task teaching the primary students, is returning to where she lives on the 'A' section of the reserve. As Brenda enters at the bow, a group of six, four boys and two girls, disembark at the stern. Dorinda waves at the group of youths, giving special attention to her brother Mark. Dorinda lives in the Red Rapids Reserve 'B' section. She is 14. Next term, she will join her brother in attending the internet high school across the river in the 'A' section. Mark is a year older and, at 15, is old enough to obtain employment as a guide for the hunters who come here in summer. Dorinda is impatient for her brother to extricate himself from the group.

Dorinda looks up to her brother. He is protective of her; he is a good hunter who provides fish and meat for the family; he is knowledgeable and amuses her with descriptions of the world outside the reserve. Mark has even trekked off the reserve, having once travelled as far as Elliot Lake. But recently, Mark has been spending too much time with this cluster of friends. They are a raucous group that treats all serious matters with flippancy. Dorinda regards their behaviour with disapproval. She witnesses one of the boys stamp forcefully on a muddy puddle to splatter one of the girls. The mud-splattered girl retaliates by swinging her school satchel at him in an attempt to strike his head. He ducks. Mark grabs her swinging satchel and dislodges her books. They spill to the ground and suffer a muddy fate. Thereupon, the entire group empties the contents of their satchels onto the wet muddy ground and laughs at the damaging results. Dorinda fails to understand what is amusing in this performance. Mark is smart, but he behaves stupidly when in this pack. When involved with the group, he does not want his younger sister around. So, Dorinda waits for the crowd to disperse.

While awaiting her brother, Dorinda muses. She clips shut the zipper on her olive-green polyester jacket but leaves it unfastened, not because she is cold but to prevent it from flapping in the breeze. She is comfortably warm in her red woollen cardigan which, out of habit, she wears closed at her throat. Her jeans are baggy to accommodate her penchant for stuffing her pockets, and they sit crumpled where they rest on her once-white bootee runners. She wears her black hair long and permits it to flow in the wind. She secretly wishes that she could dye it midnight-blue just like Penny McGilvery did.

Today is Monday, 20 June 2016. Tomorrow is *National Aboriginal Day*, a holiday from school. Instead of classes, there will be a celebration at the community lodge – the *June Pow-wow*. Perhaps the pow-wow council elders can explain why the reserve is entitled the 'Red Rapids Reserve'. The river is not rapid – except in the spring run-off from the melting snow. And that ended two weeks ago. Most of the snow has disappeared by now and the river is flowing placidly. It flows into Red Fox Lake. That's probably why the river is named 'Red Rapids River'. The water itself is not red at all. It is a dark-grey blue with a hint of green. The river splits the reserve into 'A' and 'B' sections. This is the 'B' side, the poorer side. The band council lodge and the reserve administration buildings are in the 'A' section. The 'A' section has two hotels. They are called 'hotels' because the buildings are double the standard length and they can accommodate a total of ten guests apiece, hunters and fishermen who come here in the summer. Dorinda does not see much of these white visitors. They never come to the 'B' section of the reserve. She is aware of their arrival and departure from the floatplanes she observes.

Dorinda proceeds to walk slowly along the gravel road, slow enough to permit her brother to catch up. Why is it called 'gravel' at all? – she wonders. Most of the time, it is snow-covered; afterwards, it is muddy like today. Sometimes it is dry. That is when the grey dust clings to her clothes and blows into their home. She continues to walk slowly, choosing her steps carefully to avoid the mud puddles. Once, before her time, there was a margin at the side of the road, separating it from the properties. It is impossible to see any demarcation today – the mud of the road encroaches over the property lines and the mud from the properties seeps onto the roadway. No one cares about this – there is the road and there are the houses, and the mud is all over. Of course, there are no legal property lines in the reserve; people just claim a bit of personal space in front of their homes. She walks past the noisy generator. It provides electricity to the 15 wooden houses in the 'B' section. The generator is a blessing and a curse. It shuts off when it runs out of gasoline, which is often. The residents steal gasoline by siphoning it from the generator's gas tank. Dorinda knows that her father obtains his gasoline this way. There must be four containers of stolen gas stored in their house. No one bothers to hide it. The price they pay is in the absence of electrical power during the generator's downtime. Frequently, days elapse before the generator's supply of fuel is replenished.

Dorinda reaches her house ahead of Mark. Mark is still with his friends, shoving and laughing loudly. Her house is a wood-frame uninsulated hut on concrete struts. It is a one-room abode with a mudroom-porch constructed at the entrance. Inside, a plywood partition gives the illusion that it is two-roomed. Paul Trapper, her father, is asleep on the couch. An empty whisky bottle lies beside him on the floor. It is hunting season. Paul ought to be employed as a guide for the short season. But he was fired yet again. Amy Trapper is not at home. Dorinda's mother is employed in housekeeping duties in a hotel in Niagara Falls. That's a long way away. Dorinda understands that it is somewhere near Toronto. Amy sends money orders home to the reserve almost every week. Paul picks up the mail at the administration building and deposits Amy's money orders into the family's account at the reserve's credit union. Immediately thereafter, he walks across the hallway to the general store. An arrangement is in place that authorizes the store to charge the Trappers' purchases against their credit union account. Depending on the availability of funds, Paul purchases a mixture of household essentials and whisky – sometimes, just whisky. He considers Amy's contribution as adequate income for the family. Consequently, he has no motivation to work.

Dorinda checks for food in the house. All she finds is pancake mix. There is sufficient milk available to mix up a batter. She prepares enough to feed the three of them. She hears Mark enter the adjoining room. Judging from the racket, he has brought his friends along. Dorinda is annoyed. There is not enough batter to make pancakes for everyone. She enters the adjoining room and confronts her brother. Mark and his friends are smoking cigarettes and sniffing gasoline. The four boys and two girls declare that they should get high, high enough for a gang-bang.

Dorinda is distressed. She slaps Mark hard on the shoulder and berates him. "Mark, get serious!"

She attempts to say more, but she is drowned out by the group's boisterous laughter. "Mark, do as your goody-goody sister says!"

In frustration, she runs sobbing to the comfort of Kokum (grandmother) in the neighbouring house. Kokum's hut is smaller than Dorinda's. There is one room. Kokum, who is partially blind from drinking contaminated river-water, is sitting in her rocking-chair.

Kokum is not surprised at seeing Dorinda. She frequently visits her grandmother. Kokum greets her in Cree. "Nôsisim, are you here to check up on me?" Dorinda makes no response. Kokum senses that she is upset. "What's the matter, Nôsisim? You can tell your Kokum."

Dorinda expresses her frustration. "It's Mark. He is being stupid. He and his loud friends are in the house now."

"And they don't want you around. Right? Don't you mind them. Spend a while here until they leave. Then Mark will return to being himself." Dorinda accepts Kokum's counsel.

Kokum Cool is minding three of her pre-school grandsons. All three are lying on a mattress on the ground in a corner of the room. The same corner is heavily stained black with mildew. The plywood wall has rotted at the base and dampness permeates the entire space in a musty smell. Dorinda glances at the three youngsters. She recognizes the effects of the wet mildew on them – red eyes, runny noses and wet coughs. There is no way Dorinda could spend the night here with Kokum. She decides to wait until things quieten down at home and then return to continue with her pancakes.

Dorinda is concerned for Kokum. She is unable to care for three small boys. And the smallest boy, Jeff, stares at her with sorrowful pleading eyes. This is Rose Cool's little boy. But Auntie Rose is far away, working in Toronto. If Dorinda had a phone, she would phone her mother in Niagara Falls and phone her aunt in Toronto. But the only available phone is in the administration building in the 'A' section. She resolves to place the calls on the following day when she attends the pow-wow. Kokum rocks, and croons a song to comfort the sick boys. Dorinda sits on the edge of the mattress and sobs quietly into her hands. She is overwhelmed by the helplessness of the situation.

Dorinda awakens with a start. She had dozed off momentarily. The sound of an explosion woke her. Or did a disturbing dream startle her awake? She is unsure. Then she hears panicked shouting emanating from outside. She rises from the mattress in Kokum's house and rushes out to investigate. Flames are reflected off the buildings. The source is her own house now engulfed in fire. The cause is instantly clear to her. Mark and his friends had been sniffing gasoline and smoking in the room where Paul Trapper's stolen gasoline is stored. There is noisy activity from 20 or more band members fighting to contain the fire. Dorinda is unable to discern any order in the apparent chaos. Beset by the tragedy and her own helplessness, Dorinda rushes back to Kokum and buries her face in her grandmother's lap. She fears that all are dead in the burning house. She attempts to block out all sound and sight in a vain attempt to reject reality.

Later, she is nudged by a hand. She is lifted off Kokum's lap. The band chief is here. He holds her shoulders and gives a brief account of the tragedy. "There was a devastating blaze at your house. A bucket brigade brought the fire under control before it spread to other houses. But the Trapper house, your house, is gutted. Six youths were rescued. They are burned, but not seriously. They had quickly run out of the burning house at the first signs of fire, some short seconds before the explosion."

Dorinda reacts to the chief's account. "The explosion. It must have been the stash of gasoline in the house."

"What? Paul Trapper had a stash of gasoline stored in the house? That explains the source of the flaming eruption."

"So Mark is alive?"

"The six youths were peppered in burns, most of which had

not penetrated through their clothing. Acting quickly, their band neighbours wrapped them in blankets and doused their smouldering burns."

Kokum comments, "We all know that fires in wooden houses are a constant threat in the reserve."

The chief continues. "True. Fortunately, the residents know how to react promptly when such an emergency arises. The six youths are lucky. Currently, they are at the first-aid centre in the administration building where they are receiving treatment by the reserve's paramedic. If their injuries prove to be serious, they will be transported to Sudbury Hospital."

Dorinda nods in understanding. Then she asks, "What about Opâpâmâw? He was in the house. What happened to him?"

The chief softens his voice to impart the saddest news. "Alas, Paul Trapper never made it out of the building. Paul Trapper is dead."

Overcome with grief, Dorinda collapses.

On 21 June 2016, National Aboriginal Day, a floatplane arrives at Red Rapids. Doctor Kathy Wesley is here in response to the report phoned in by the reserve's resident paramedic. The doctor determines that the six injured youths can be adequately cared for by the band's medical staff. The council meeting room will serve as a temporary medical ward until they are sufficiently healed to return to their homes. The band chief requests the doctor to visit Kokum Cool. In yesterday's visit, the band chief observed the poor state of her house and the sick children lying on the mattress.

The doctor visits Kokum Cool, accompanied by the band chief. The doctor forthrightly condemns the house as unfit for human habitation. She scolds the chief. "This is deplorable. I insist that you immediately move the old woman and the three boys to healthy living conditions." She questions Kokum in English. Kokum turns to Dorinda to interpret.

"How long have you been living in these conditions?" the doctor inquires.

"What? The damp and the mildew? For more than five years now."

"How can that be?" She turns again to the band chief. "Are not funds sent here to maintain healthy housing conditions?" She knows, of course, that 40% of reserve homes are in need of major repair, but she suspects that in the 'B' section of the Red Rapids Reserve the number could be as high as 100%.

Kokum understands enough English to follow what is being said. She interjects to explain to the government doctor. "I was promised a new house three years ago. And again two years ago, and then it was last year. And now... I don't believe any new house is coming. This house will rot and collapse over the next winter with me inside it."

The chief is anxious to interrupt Dorinda as she relays Kokum's account to the doctor. He states, with more emphasis than truthfulness, that funds are received and are allocated by the band council according to priorities. Not enough funds are received from the government to meet the entire needs of the reserve.

"Priorities?" the doctor asks. "What priorities could those be? Perhaps a government inspection is in order at this point."

"No, no. That will not be necessary. Considering that the Trapper house is burnt down and this house is collapsing from rot, I am confident that funds will be provided to accommodate the Trapper family and Kokum Cool in one spacious two-room house. Have no fear."

"When?" the doctor asks sternly.

"Today. It is the top priority as of today." 'Today' could mean 'next year'. Even with the immediate allocation of the necessary funds, lumber cannot be trucked in and delivered to the reserve until the ice road is formed in February.

The doctor examines the three boys. "This boy here, the smallest. He is coming with me to Sudbury. I suspect that he is suffering from pneumonia. He could die without treatment. Is there an English-speaking member of the family who can accompany him?"

Immediately, Dorinda volunteers. "Me! I can go with Jeff."

"And you are family?"

"His cousin from next door."

The doctor looks at the chief and at Kokum. They nod in

acceptance. "Okay then. Jeff, is it? And..."

"Dorinda. My name is Dorinda Trapper."

"Okay, then. Jeff and Dorinda are coming with me to Sudbury. Now, who can sign the consent document?"

Shortly afterwards, Jeff and Dorinda join the doctor in a four-seat floatplane. Dorinda has not had time to visit Mark. She did not have time to phone Amy or Rose. They do not know about the death of Paul Trapper. She wonders if Mark has been informed. She resolves to contact them at the first opportunity. This is Dorinda's first experience in a plane and her first time to leave the reserve.

Dorinda's ride in the plane is at first unnerving, but it is promptly replaced with exhilaration. She senses the shift in her body weight as the plane accelerates on the lake water and rises quickly into the air. The hum of the engine is like the purring of a mighty beast – powerful, yet at ease. Everything about the plane is new – it looks new, it smells new. And for Dorinda, this is a new sensation. She strains against her seat belt to look out the window. She studies the ground below. She easily identifies Red Rapids Reserve and the blackened scar of the scorched ground that had once been her abode. As the plane continues to rise, the reserve diminishes in size until it is an insignificant patch in the vast boreal forest. For the first time in her life, Dorinda realizes how small her home community truly is. From up high, she picks out and identifies the conifers in the landscape – black spruce, white spruce, jack pine, balsam fir, tamarack and white cedar. Of course, the hardwoods are easily distinguished – the fast-growing poplar and the distinctive white birch. She peers intently in an attempt to spot wildlife – black bears, wolves or lynx. She is satisfied when she observes a lazy moose at the edge of a lake.

The doctor periodically checks on Jeff's condition. He is hot from fever. He coughs and rubs his eyes. For the moment, the experience of the plane ride distracts him from his discomfort. Dorinda settles back in her seat and looks forward to her visit to Sudbury in eager anticipation.

She is going to miss the pow-wow.

CHAPTER FOUR

DORINDA TRAPPER OFF THE RESERVE

Dorinda sees Elliot Lake coming into sight. The plane lands smoothly on the water and the pilot navigates it skilfully to the dock. "Is this Sudbury?" she asks.

The doctor smiles at her. "No, pet. This is Elliot Lake. I came here in my hospital service vehicle. We drive from here to Sudbury."

Dorinda gazes around at the wondrous novel sight. She scans the lakeshore area from Spine Beech to Flat Rocks to Spruce Beech to Westview Park and all the way to Timberock. "Are there no hospitals here? Elliot Lake looks like a really big place. And there is no hospital?"

"St Joseph's Hospital is an excellent hospital here in Elliot Lake. But I am taking you to Sudbury where I am attached to *Health Sciences North*. Jeff is going to the *Children's Paediatric Care Department*. It's a special place to treat children."

Dorinda attempts to take it all in. The roadways are wide and the surfaces are solid even though it is summer. In the reserve, the ground is not solid like this until it freezes. En route to Sudbury, she is fascinated by the number of cars and trucks plying the highway. She wonders where everyone is going.

It is early afternoon when they reach their destination.

Dorinda gapes at the immense four-story building. The hospital building is larger than all the buildings on the reserve combined. She asks in amazement, "How many people are in there? More than a hundred, I bet."

The doctor laughs. "There are 3,900 employees. And there are 462 beds for patients. And that does not include 515 physicians like myself and over 600 volunteers."

Dorinda attempts to picture the number of people represented in these statistics but gives up. The number is too high for her to grasp. This is more than she has ever seen at a pow-wow.

Dorinda and Jeff follow the doctor into the building. Jeff clings tightly to Dorinda's thigh, so she lifts him and carries him. Inside the building, the entrance hall is vast. It is spacious enough for great owls to fly around unimpeded. Even though it is the middle of the day, thousands upon thousands of lights illuminate the interior of the building. From all the activity she perceives, Dorinda deduces that it is always bright and busy here, day and night, winter and summer.

They are escorted to a waiting area where they are instructed to sit until called for. There are many people around. Some are sitting in chairs and getting up and sitting down again in apparent confusion. Dorinda sits with her head down, staring at the floor beneath her feet. She focuses on a small area and examines the mottled pattern in the tiles. This is all she can do to settle her bewildered mind. Jeff, on the other hand, sits beside her. He gazes up at the high ceiling and observes everything that his eyes behold. His curiosity far outweighs his apprehension.

"Jeff Cool and Dorinda Cool, is it?"

Dorinda looks up. She is being addressed by a candy-striped volunteer. Dorinda understands that this is who they are waiting for. "I'm Dorinda Trapper. This is my cousin Jeff Cool."

"Well, I'm Carmel. I will look after you and show you where to go. Doctor Wesley is signing you in. You, Jeff, are now a patient in the hospital. Let me get you a set of wheels so you don't have to walk..." Carmel the volunteer continues to talk. First, they follow a green line on the floor to the elevators. While waiting for the doors to open, she grabs one of the wheelchairs parked alongside. She places Jeff in the wheelchair and they enter the elevator. This too is a novel experience for Dorinda and Jeff. The sensation of the rising elevator is similar to taking off in a floatplane. They exit the elevator two floors up. This time they follow a purple line on the floor. "And here we are. Room 322."

There are two beds in the room. Jeff's bed is next to a large window. Between the bed and the window is a pull-out chair. Carmel demonstrates how this converts into a cot. Dorinda may remain with Jeff for the duration of his stay in the hospital. Carmel explains that the other hospital bed is for another patient – two patients per room.

Jeff is diagnosed with pneumonia. The doctors will wait for two clear days to determine if he is responding favourably to treatment. Then, if all is well, he will be discharged on 24

June to recuperate at home.

Dorinda encounters new delights during the three day's stay. She learns how to order at *Tim Hortons* in the cafeteria food court. And Carmel takes her for a short car trip around Sudbury. She is thrilled to see planes take off and land at the airport, amazed that one plane holds 90 passengers. She even learns its name – 'Dash 8'.

During the three days in Sudbury, Dorinda puts Red Rapids out of her mind. Sudbury affords her a means of denial – no fire, no tragedy, no reminder of life on the reserve – and mostly, no reminder of death on the reserve. On Friday, she and Jeff make the return trip with Doctor Wesley. From the plane, Dorinda identifies the reserve as it comes into view. When she beholds the blacken sight of her devastated home, she is jolted back to the reality of her situation. Upon landing, she enters the administration building and phones her mother in Niagara Falls. As usual, Amy Trapper fails to pick up, but Dorinda leaves a brief explanatory message. After that, she phones her Aunt Rose in Toronto. Rose answers and is surprised by the tragic news. It appears that no one in Red Rapids had the presence of mind to advise either of them of the death of Paul Trapper and the loss of the family's house. Dorinda feels the burden of responsibility weighing heavily on her young shoulders.

Meanwhile, the doctor visits the first-aid centre and consults with the resident paramedic. She delivers instructions on the procedures for Jeff's ongoing recuperation treatment. Thereafter, she visits the chief and ensures that the Cool boys are housed in better living conditions than hitherto, albeit with more cousins. As a result, 12 Cools and Trappers are obliged to reside in a single uninsulated unit. This is gross overcrowding, but in First Nation reserves, some units accommodate 20 people. Dorinda reluctantly accepts the new situation. Having concluded her health inspection, Dr Wesley returns to Sudbury. But for Dorinda, her visit to Sudbury has afforded her an understanding of the world outside the reserve.

On Sunday 26 June 2016, Paul Trapper's wake commences. Dorinda slips into depression. She is unable to grieve for her father and is weighed by guilt. For almost a year prior, Paul Trapper progressively withdrew into himself and ignored his family. At first, he became morose, then brooding, and finally non-communicative. At the time of the devastating fire, Paul Trapper no longer resided within his own body. His spirit had already departed. No one knows how or why he lost the will to live. Dorinda grieved the loss of her father many months earlier. Today, his charred remains are concealed under a blanket. The Cree believe that the spirit of the dead continues to be with us after death. Alas, Dorinda cannot find it in her heart to believe this – at least not as it pertains to Paul Trapper. She feels emptiness rather than grief. Furthermore, it is the custom for the women members of the family to prepare the wake. Dorinda has not the will and Kokum has not the strength. The neighbouring women undertake the task. The menfolk are tasked with hosting the ritual. Mark's hands are still bandaged. Thus, he is prevented from performing his duties. Only Jim Cool and other men of the Cool clan are able to cope. The wake falls short of the required ceremonial rituals.

When Amy Trapper learns of her family's tragic events, she immediately attempts to take a leave from her job. The last week of June is high tourist season in Niagara Falls. The hotel refuses to give her time off. The most they offer is to stagger her shifts so that she has two successive days off. This is insufficient time to travel to Red Rapids and back. In desperation, Amy pleads with her fellow workers for help. Many of them are sympathetic. Fortunately, Amy benefits from the support-camaraderie of the group. She successfully trades shifts. Twelve of Amy's hours will be worked by others. She will pay them back by working subsequent shifts in their names. The hotel does not approve. Nevertheless, they turn a blind eye. 'Shift swapping' occurs in the industry, in which the credited worker is not the one who fulfills the shift. Upon her return, Amy will work a 52-hour week followed by a 48-hour week, but she will be credited for two standard 44-hour weeks.

Amy arrives at Red Rapids Reserve on Wednesday night, in time for Paul Trapper's funeral on Thursday 30 June. Rose Cool fails to attend. Amy views the burned-out remains of her previous home. In looking at her family's situation, she is more determined than ever to send financial support. She returns to Niagara Falls on the following day with renewed determination to send money home weekly.

On 02 July 2016, Dorinda Trapper turns 15. She has aged more than one year in the past 12 days. Weeks pass. She recovers from her grief and effectively undertakes new responsibilities. She manages to use her mother's funds wisely. Although she has no authority to withdraw cash from the credit union, she is authorized to purchase family necessities from the store to be charged against the account. She pushes this to the limit. She purchases goods in excess of the available credit and is obliged to remove items from her shopping basket. At first, this flusters her. Then it becomes part of the routine of shopping. Notwithstanding, their diet substantially improves. Mark recovers quickly from his burns. He and his friends are brought before the band council to answer for their actions.

This is the reserve's court of justice. The reserve has no jail, and fines are futile. The elders insist on restitution and rehabilitation as appropriate punishment for offences. In practice, in Mark's case, this amounts to a scolding and a 'don't-do-that-again' sentence. Mark teams up with his uncle Jim Cool and embarks on hunting. Thus they provide the family (now an extended family) with an adequate supply of meat. Dorinda worries about other necessities that are outside the budget for basic food. For one thing, Mark needs to obtain a hunting rifle of his own. Furthermore, the family snowmobile was destroyed in the fire and needs to be replaced. With the approach of winter, Dorinda is concerned about the adequacy of the wood-stove and the increased need for cooking gas. She visits the reserve's clothes-exchange program where she obtains clothes for the growing children. But the adult clothing will require stitching and patching to last another year. At 15, Dorinda is 'mother' to the 11 other residents of the unit, including Kokum.

Dorinda requests more financial help from the family members that live off the reserve – from Amy Trapper and Rose Cool, her mother and aunt. She frequently contacts her mother from the phone in the administration building. Her mother never picks up while at work – a rule on employees' use of cell phones. Instead, her mother returns the calls. Consequently, Dorinda is required to set a time to be present in the administration building to accept the calls. She phones her aunt, Rose Cool, Jeff's mother. Rose almost always picks up. But she is busy working on the streets in Toronto and is financially stretched. Dorinda wonders what work it could be. Is Rose cleaning streets in Toronto like her mother cleans hotels in Niagara Falls?

Dorinda gauges the family's needs against the meagre supply of incoming funds. She decides that she should find work off the reserve and send her earning's home. To avoid causing unnecessary worry to her mother, she determines to go to Rose in Toronto for work. She keeps this decision secret from her family lest they take steps to prevent her from embarking on her mission. From her visit to Sudbury, Dorinda knows what route to take. She knows how to travel to Sudbury, and Toronto cannot be that much farther. Dorinda's concept of distances between places outside the reserve is sadly deficient. She pictures the school-atlas page that displays the province of Ontario. Sudbury and Toronto appear on the same page, so how far can that be? The first reference-point on her journey is Elliot Lake. However, since she cannot afford to fly by floatplane, she will embark on foot. And that means waiting for the winter frost to harden the ground.

There is a road from the reserve to the outside world. But it is seasonal. It is a 'gravel road', but the gravel washed away years ago. In reality, the 'road' is a passageway through the forest to connect the reserve with a highway some distance away, but it is only serviceable as an ice road. Dorinda waits for the arrival of winter before embarking on her mission. The first snow arrives before the hard frost freezes the ground. And when the snows first arrive, the drifts are too deep to traverse. Dorinda waits for the snow to settle and harden sufficiently for walking. It is February before the ice road is traversable.

On 01 February 2017, in the early morning predawn, 15-year-old Dorinda Trapper steps out from the family unit and commences her journey to Toronto. It is -40° Celsius under a clear bright starlit sky. The snow shimmers in the starlight. Uncle Jim's mukluks are too large for her, so she accommodates them by wearing triple socks. Fortunately, Kokum's parka fits well. She has no money. Dorinda never has any money and never had. To sustain her on her journey, she brings a little dried meat for a snack. There is food in the house, but taking any more than this would leave the family short.

She secures the string to fasten the fur-lined hood well over her head and closed at her neck. Thus, she breathes without the risk of freezing her lungs. Next, she places her hands into the warm mittens dangling from the sleeves. She is filled with a feeling of trepidation. She hesitates for a moment. But the urgency of her mission emboldens her to advance. She crosses the frozen Red Rapids River to the 'A' section of the reserve, walks past the administration building and proceeds to the ice road. She is unable to look behind due to the enclosing hood. She would need to halt and turn around in order to look back, but she is intent upon maintaining her steady pace uninterrupted. Her feet crunch the hard snow. In the silent stillness of the night, the sound of her footsteps echoes through the reserve. She shuts her eyes and prays that no one hears her, or at least chooses to ignore the sounds of a walker in the night.

The young Cree girl vividly remembers the flight from the Red Rapids Reserve to Elliot Lake. The trip took less than half an hour. At this rate of walking, Dorinda expects to make the trip within five hours. Alas, her understanding of air travel is unsound. In viewing the ground from the plane, she grossly miscalculated the travelling speed due to her misperception of elevation. Four hours later, in the predawn, she consumes her supply of meat. Dorinda is not experienced in hunting or tracking. Otherwise, she would know that meat at dawn in the boreal forest in mid-winter is an inviting signal to wolves for miles around. Within minutes, a timber wolf comes sniffing at the spot where she had consumed her meal. The wolf is a shrewd hunter, and it is hungry. It quickly tracks and locates the tramping Cree girl and stalks her, not by following in her footprints, but by loping stealthily alongside her within the cover of the forest. The wolf is joined by a second wolf and a third. At this point, Dorinda senses that she is in danger. She glimpses movement in the forest and, although she never gets a clear view, she knows that it can only be a predator wolf – or wolves. Dorinda realizes that in choosing suitable apparel for her journey, she neglected to bring a weapon. She maintains an even pace. If she stops, the wolf will pounce. If she runs, the wolf, which is hard-wired to pursue, will surely catch her within a few steps. By maintaining her present rate of walking, the wolf will choose an appropriate time. Regardless of which option she chooses, the wolf will attack, sooner or later.

The wolf shows itself – and a second one, and a third. This means that the attack is imminent. Although the frightened girl knows that it is futile to run, panic takes over and she races ahead. She stumbles in Uncle Jim's mukluks and falls to the ground. She buries her face in the snow and waits for the predictable assault. She is startled by the unexpected noise of a gunshot. Holding her breath, Dorinda hears the sound of the wolves running away. She peers tentatively around and beholds a large timber wolf lying bleeding a mere metre away. The animal is still breathing, but it is disabled by the wound in its chest. It struggles to breathe and looks at Dorinda with deep dark eyes. For a brief second, it appears to be appealing for help. And then, it goes limp. She rises to her knees, still too shaken to stand upright, and looks around. A hunter approaches. Surely she recognizes the familiar gait. It is her brother, Mark.

She rises to her feet and rushes to him. She leans her face on his chest and sobs in relief. "I'm sorry, Mark. I'm sorry that I ever thought bad of you. I'm sorry that I blamed you for the fire. I'm sorry that I cannot do enough for the family. I'm sorry, I'm sorry, I'm sorry."

Mark, still holding the smoking rifle, rests his free hand on her shoulder. He gently moves her back so that he can look into her face. He studies her for a moment with a questioning look but he remains silent.

"But, how did you find me, Mark? How did you know?"

Mark glances down at Dorinda's mukluks – actually, at Uncle Jim's mukluks. Then he casts his eyes back along the ice road towards the reserve. Of course, he followed her footprints after he noticed that she and Uncle Jim's mukluks were missing from the house. Mark studies the ice road for a moment. Then he turns 180° and peers into the distance where the ice road meets the horizon. The unspoken question is whether to return to the reserve or continue onwards.

Dorinda composes herself and, with stubborn resolve, she recommences her journey. This time, Mark walks beside her. The determined girl is confident that she will reach Elliot Lake safely with a protector at her side. Mark does not ask her, but she tells him anyway. "I'm walking to Elliot Lake," as if that explains it all. Mark just shrugs and accepts it without question.

After ten hours of walking, Dorinda asks, "Where is Elliot Lake? We should have reached it by now. We can't have gone the wrong way. There is no other way but this." She is tired but, with Mark at her side, she maintains a steady pace.

Mark responds factually. "We are not yet halfway to Elliot Lake." Thereupon, he returns to his preferred state of silence.

She wonders if Mark is just saying this to dissuade her from her journey. Dorinda doggedly continues. After 22 hours of walking, she is tired and hungry. The only available drinking water is snow, which she consumes at intervals. She considers if it would have been more prudent to have made the journey in summer. She assesses the difficulty in navigating through the waterways alone, in a canoe, not knowing the route and not knowing the places for portage. That would have been an impossible undertaking for her. No, the winter walk is the only viable option.

"There it is, Highway 639 ahead." Mark's unexpected voice startles her. These are the first words spoken by him in eight hours.

"What is Highway 639? Is that Elliot Lake?"

"It is the road we take to Elliot Lake. We are not there yet. Another seven hours of walking, maybe a bit more."

Mark and Dorinda enter Secondary Highway 639. It is an unpopulated route in winter. From its termination – or, for Mark and Dorinda, its starting point – it is 30 kilometres to Elliot Lake.

"Look!" exclaims Dorinda. "There are tire tracks on the road." True enough, there are tracks of vehicular traffic in the packed snow of the road surface. But if Dorinda expects to see traffic here, she will be disappointed. The most recent tracks are a day old. All the other tracks are much older.

Dorinda and Mark recommence walking. They walk in the hard tire tracks in the snow, Dorinda on one side and Mark on the other. After seven hours, Mark stops and sits on a large stone at the roadside. He points ahead and speaks. "There ahead is Timber Road. See the sign?"

Dorinda looks ahead and sees a cluster of low buildings and a green road sign in the distance – 'Timber Road' – with an arrow pointing right. She hears the distant sound of traffic. A car travelling east on Timber Road passes by the buildings and disappears from sight. Judging from the sound, it turns right and heads south. This must be the outskirts of Elliot Lake. She looks at Mark. He remains immobile sitting on the rock. So, this is as far as Mark comes. From this point on, Dorinda must proceed on her own.

She looks at her brother and longs for the intimacy of her family. If Mark asks her to change her mind and return with him, she will follow him. But Mark remains silent. Dorinda resumes her journey to Elliot Lake. After ten steps, she looks back at Mark. She waits, expecting him to wave, to beckon to her, and then she will run back to him. Mark remains immobile. She continues onward. She is almost at Timber Road. She turns once more. She sees her brother in the distance. He has not moved. He is still sitting on the rock. If only he were to stand or even move, she would run back to him. Dorinda sighs and walks around the curve in the road. This time, when she looks behind, the rock is no longer visible. Fretful, she runs back. It is not too late to change her mind and return to the reserve.

When the rock comes into view, Mark is no longer there. She dashes to the rock. She is panting hard when she reaches it. She looks back up the highway from whence she came. Mark is nowhere to be seen. She looks in vain for his footprints in the snow, but if he walked in the tire tracks there would be no prints. Dorinda throws herself on the rock and sobs. She is weary and hungry. She is loath to venture back through the ice road for fear of the wolves. She realizes that she has crossed the point of no return and must continue onwards regardless.

She wipes her tears and walks as far as Timber Road. From this point on, the road is clear of snow. There is a garage at the corner with a sign – *Winter Windshield Washer For Sale*. She enters the garage.

The mechanic is surprised to see a First Nations girl enter. He did not hear a car drive up, so he guesses that she is walking. The mechanic wipes his hands on an oily rag and speaks. "Hello, little girl. And what can I do for you?"

Dorinda does not regard herself as 'a little girl', but maybe this is how they speak here. "Is this Elliot Lake?" she asks.

"Elliot Lake? No. But you are close. It's just down the road a bit. If you are walking, well, it's half an hour to the centre." He points her in the direction. "Be sure to shut the door tight as you leave. It's damn cold today."

It is about noon when Dorinda reaches the centre of Elliot Lake. She recognizes *Tim Hortons*. There are a lot of food stores in Elliot Lake. The smells assail her nose, and her mouth salivates in hunger. But, having no money, she continues walking. She passes *McDonald's*, some banks, and a place selling cars. When she reaches *Foodland*, she stops to take stock of her situation. There is a van delivering bread to the store. The driver is about to shut the rear door when Dorinda approaches. She addresses him. "Hello!"

The driver looks at her and responds "Hello!" expecting her to say more. Since she remains silent, he shuts the rear door and proceeds to the driver's door.

Dorinda gets the nerve to speak again. "Can you take me to Sudbury, please?"

The driver turns to her and asks, "And why do you need to go to Sudbury, Sugar?"

This is unexpected. Dorinda is not prepared to answer questions. And why did he call her 'Sugar'? This is not her name. She devises a story on the fly. "My brother is three. He is in the children's hospital in Sudbury. He has pneumonia and got burned in a fire. I am going to visit him." Dorinda swallows, hoping that this sounds like a plausible reason to go to Sudbury. Then to press her urgency she says, "And I will let you kiss me if you take me there."

The driver looks at her in puzzlement for an instant and then laughs. "So a drive to Sudbury for a kiss? Well now, Sugar, let me tell you. You shouldn't be offering kisses like that. You are much too young and it might land you in trouble."

Dorinda's face falls. Her ploy has failed.

The driver looks at her expression of disappointment and at her attire. "Tell you what, Sugar. I'll drive you as far as the Trans-Canada Highway. That's as far as I'm going. You have a good chance of getting a ride from there to Sudbury. And you won't have to kiss me, or anyone else besides. Now, hop aboard."

Minutes later, they are driving south on Highway 108. Dorinda learns that he addresses all girls as 'Sugar'. And that he delivers bread to food stores. His last delivery of the day is to a store on Highway 108 just north of Highway 17 (Trans-Canada Highway). The driver is incredulous at Dorinda's story about visiting her brother. He suspects that she is a runaway. He has seen it before. Perhaps she has good reason to run away.

Twenty minutes after leaving *Foodland*, they reach a roadside store. There is no name on the store, just a sign that reads 'Gas and Hot Food'. This is a gasoline station with a food store attached. It is a large wooden building not unlike buildings on the reserve, but much larger. Dorinda did not see any buildings like this in Elliot Lake. The front parking lot is snow-covered, but the snow is packed down hard to accommodate cars. There is a sole beaten-up pickup truck parked at the side. There are no other buildings around. *Gas and Hot Food*, if that is its title, faces a vacant snow-covered parking lot on the opposite side of the road, large enough to accommodate 18-wheeler trucks. Judging by the tracks in the snow, it is used frequently. 'Bread Man' drives up to the front door of the store.

"This is my last delivery of the day. This store is run by a cranky old man with a cranky old wife. I think they still live in the eighteen-hundreds – except for the no-name gasoline they sell." He points to the two gas pumps near the roadside. "He doesn't even have a till. He just puts the money in a drawer and scribbles a note to record receipts. And no credit cards either. The store stays open in the evening for as long as the man is awake – sometimes later, if he falls asleep in his chair." Bread Man laughs. He exits the van and shouts back to Dorinda, "C'mon, Sugar. Help me carry in the bread. I'll introduce you to 'Grouchy'."

Dorinda assists Bread Man in stocking a shelf with ten loaves of wrapped sliced bread. Bread Man removes the previous day's unsold loaf and goes to the counter to settle the transaction. He directs Dorinda to sit at a small table by a window overlooking the gasoline pumps. Shortly, he joins her at the table.

"Now, Sugar, I am going to eat. How about you? You look as if you could do with a bite yourself."

The hungry Cree girl nods. The store serves all-day breakfast. Bread Man orders bacon & eggs (over easy) with home-fried potatoes, white bread toasted, coffee and orange juice – for two.

"So tell me, Sugar, what is the real reason you are running away from home? And what is your name anyway?"

"My name is..." Dorinda hesitates. "...'Sugar'. As of today, my name is 'Sugar'."

The man regards this as amusing. "But why run away in winter?"

Dorinda tells him about the fire, and Jeff, and 12 people living in an uninsulated single-room hut, and the wolf.

"And you think you will be better off in Sudbury?"

Dorinda nods her head, but she does not reveal that Toronto is her ultimate destination. They both concentrate on their breakfasts. Bread Man sees that the 15-year-old girl is truly hungry. While eating breakfast, she looks around the store. There are shelves stocked with potato chips, tinned food – and bread, of course. There is one other table in the store. She did not notice it before. It is obscured by the food shelf. A scruffy man is sitting quietly at the table, nursing a cup of coffee and staring out the window at the vacant lot. He is dressed in a greasy boiler suit and is wearing an oil-stained black baseball cap. Is he a mechanic, perhaps? Dorinda wonders what is of interest to him in the vacant lot that holds his attention. She considers that his attention might be focused on her conversation with Bread Man. She moves in her seat to face away from him.

'Grouchy Man' walks to 'Greasy Man's' table with a coffee pot. "A fill-up there, Nate?"

Nate (Greasy Man) looks at his cup. He places it on the table and shakes his head. "Naw, I'm done for the day. Phone me if any trucks park there tonight."

Grouchy Man nods and returns to his station at the counter. It is apparent that each man knows the other man's routine and they have an understanding that is communicated in silence.

Dorinda is aware that Bread Man is speaking. "Sugar, I don't believe that Sudbury is the place for you. Once you get there... well, it may not be as welcoming as you expect. You could be disappointed and wish to return to the reserve. And in the meantime, while you are there, what will you do for money?"

Dorinda screws up her nose in response.

"Ah, you don't have any money. I thought so." With that, the man fishes some bills from his pocket. He determines what is owed for breakfast and slaps money on the table loud enough for Grouchy Man to notice. Then he slips a twenty-dollar bill towards Dorinda. She is about to grab it when he snaps it back. "No. Not a twenty. How about four fives?" With that, he selects four five-dollar bills. He passes three to Dorinda and goes to Grouchy Man to change one five-dollar bill into coins.

At the counter, Bread Man inquires of Grouchy Man "So, who is Nate? A friend of yours?"

"Nate, a friend? Nate has no friends. He just tries to milk money out of people without actually working. See that lot out there?" – pointing across the road. "That was his junkyard until a few years ago. It was an eyesore so they made him move it out of sight. He lives alone amidst his junk and tires. But you can't see it from here. Like I said, it's out of sight. The old lot is empty now, so he lets trucks park there for a fee. He checks on it once or twice a week. If I spot a truck parked there, I phone him. Well, that's Nate – a right pain-in-the-ass."

Bread Man smiles at Grouchy Man's opinion of Nate. He turns and gestures to Dorinda that it is time to depart. When they leave the store, the Cree girl is holding $20, more money than she ever held in her hand at any one time. Dorinda is baffled. Then she remembers to say 'thanks'. She asks, "Why are you doing this? You don't know me."

"Sure, I do. You're 'Sugar'." He smiles at her and slaps her playfully on her shoulder, "Now, I return to Elliot Lake. But first, I'll drive you to the intersection." He points to the Trans-Canada Highway about 100 metres away. "Look. Do you see that long low building there on the highway? That is a truck inspection station. A lot of trucks travel the Trans-Canada Highway, travelling great distances. But trucks seldom stop for a hitchhiker. The trick is to go where they are already stopped. That inspection station, there," pointing, "is where eastbound trucks pull in for inspection. Afterwards, they all go to, or through, Sudbury." True enough, Dorinda hears trucks rumbling along the highway and is convinced that his advice is sound.

Bread Man drops Dorinda at the intersection. He makes a U-turn at the termination of Highway 108 and drives back to Elliot Lake. Dorinda, now 'Sugar', crosses over to the south side of the Trans-Canada Highway.

CHAPTER FIVE

SUGAR

Sugar, previously Dorinda Trapper, crosses to the south side of Highway 17. She walks the short distance to the truck inspection station and stands at the exit ramp. An 18-wheeler has just cleared inspection and is inching slowly off the scales. Sugar walks towards it with the intent of intercepting it before it builds up speed. She remembers Bread Man's advice – 'trucks don't like to stop'. She waves timidly at the driver. He stops the truck and shouts out through the open passenger-side window. "What's up, kid? Are you in trouble?"

This emboldens Sugar to speak. "No trouble. I need to get to Toronto."

"Toronto? No can do. I can bring you to Sudbury if you like. Your chances for a ride to Toronto are better there."

"Sudbury's okay." Sugar regards Sudbury as a major step closer to her destination.

"Well, hop up quick. I can't stop here, blocking the exit."

Sugar climbs up to the passenger door. It is like scaling the side of a hut and it's just as high. The truck is actually moving as she struggles to open the door. The door is heavier than she expected. She gives the handle one strong tug and the latch disengages. She opens the door a fraction and squeezes in. She flops down on the passenger seat as the door swings shut from the motion of the truck. "Thanks!" she shouts over the noise of the accelerating engine.

The driver is looking over his left shoulder to gauge his speed to merge with east-bound traffic. "Fasten your seat belt!" He looks over at Sugar and fingers his own belt to indicate the process. Sugar fumbles due to the hindrance of her bulky parka and hood, and eventually succeeds in fastening the belt.

The man glances over a second time. "You'll be too hot dressed like that."

The driver is dressed in a navy-blue shirt and matching pants. His jacket is lying in the floor-space behind him. Although it is -22°C outside, the interior cab of the truck is at +22°C. Sugar releases the seat belt and removes her parka and places it behind her seat. She unzips her jacket and reattaches the seat belt. She slides her feet out of her hefty mukluks and settles in for the 90-minute drive to Sudbury. The driver is busy speaking to his hands-free cell phone mounted on the dash. Sugar is amazed that he can concentrate on his driving – shifting gears and checking for blind spots – while maintaining a conversation on his phone. In addition, he directs sporadic attention to her.

"You don't mind if I smoke? Do you?"

At first, she is unaware that the driver is addressing her instead of his phone. Why on earth would he require her permission to smoke in his own truck? "Sure. Go ahead."

The driver strikes up a conversation. "You know that smoking in the workplace is prohibited in Ontario. When I am alone, no one is going to report me. But you are here now. You don't object? Good." After lighting up, he continues. "You know, I never drink. Drinking and driving is dangerous. Someone could get killed. Smoking, on the other hand, kills no one. Well, in the long run, it will probably kill me. But it won't contribute to a driving accident. Now, will it?"

Sugar is unable to tell if this requires an acknowledgement from her, so she remains silent. The driver continues to talk. Sugar hopes that it is into his phone. The truck reaches cruising speed and the engine runs quietly. She falls to sleep, lulled by the motion of the truck. She is vaguely aware of the driver talking to his phone – 'make up for lost time', 'skip lunch', 'return load', and 'Ottawa', – as he continues to talk for the entire duration of the journey.

It is 3:20pm when they arrive at *Petro-Pass* at 3070 Regent Street, Sudbury, at the intersection of Highways 17 and 69 – where the Trans-Canada Highway splits to eastbound and southbound. From here, the truck will proceed eastbound. Sugar, on the other hand, needs to travel south.

The truck stop is a hive of activity. At first, Sugar is confused by the disorderly commotion in the lot. Truckers are wandering about; some are smoking while others speak together in small groups. The smell of diesel wafts in the air from idling engines. The oily smell of smoky exhaust triggers an unwanted image in her memory. For an instant, Sugar sees a mental picture of the flames that consumed her unfortunate homestead and her luckless father. She blinks. And shakes herself back to the present. She sizes up the truck stop and decides on her next course of action. First, Sugar avails of the *Petro-Pass* rest stop.

Sugar, dressed in her mukluks and parka, is ready to embark on the next stage of her journey. She approaches random drivers in the lot in an attempt to get a ride to Toronto. She experiences numerous rejections – 'Sorry, I'm westbound' or 'Sorry, I'm eastbound', or no response at all. By 4:00pm, she is getting desperate. She approaches one truck not as shining clean as the others. The driver is walking back from the rest-stop store with a coffee in his hand.

She intercepts him and says, "Hey!" In her anxiety, she renders her 'hey' louder than intended. The trucker hesitates. He turns his head and looks at her. He sips his coffee. Sugar continues to speak and timidly asks, "Are you bound for Toronto? I need to get there – to Toronto."

He looks her up and down. "Oh. And what if I say 'yes'?"

"If you take me to Toronto, I promise to be good."

"That's a big promise. Are you sure?"

"Yes, please."

The driver is dressed in a brown uniform with no identification insignia. He studies her, a girl dressed in a parka and mukluks and asks, "Are you an Indian girl?"

"I'm from a First Nations reserve."

"That makes you an Indian. So you want a ride to Toronto. And you promise to be good. Okay, then. Get in."

The man watches her climb aboard. Sugar is uncomfortable. She hopes that he does not notice that her mukluks are two sizes too large. He then opens the driver-side door. He reaches inside and grabs hold of a green hooded winter jacket. He puts this on, and when zip-fastened, he climbs into the cab. The cab is not heated, hence the need to wear winter coats inside. And it is noisy. Some heat enters the cab from the engine, but overall, the inside temperature hovers at around -18°C. Sugar sits with her hood up and her parka on but unfastened. She permits her mitts to dangle freely from her wrists. The driver speaks to her as he exits the truck stop and enters Highway 69 south. He proceeds to recount his list of female friends. Sugar is disturbed by his coarse descriptions of them. She doubts that any of them are really 'friends'. So as not to appear as a participant in the conversation, she leans forward and bows her head. Why can't this man be nice, she thinks, like the first man was, or friendly-indifferent like the second man? She focuses her eyes on the empty paper coffee cups that litter the floor at her feet, rolling hither and thither with the motion of the truck.

Sometime later, the man invites a response from Sugar. "Hey, Indian Girl, you promised to be good. Remember?"

From the way he said 'good', Sugar understands that it has a meaning other than 'good' – not 'good' as in 'well behaved'. She steals a glance at the man's face and reads his eyes. Eyes, she believes, reveal the mind. She shivers slightly. His look reminds her of the wolf that stalked her while loping alongside her on the ice road. What invokes a wolf to attack? – she ponders. Unlike the time when she experienced the wolf incident on the ice road, this time her brother Mark is not at hand with his rifle. She decides to fire off a warning shot of her own to ward off any possible threat to her safety. It is a calculated decision – a warning shot to a wolf either scares it away, or it enrages it to attack.

The man looks at Sugar, now with her head bent down. "Hey, Indian! You are not going to throw up in my cab, are you? I don't want an Indian getting sick on me."

Sugar speaks. "I am only 15." She tries to disarm him by expressing her young age – her sole defensive shot.

"What? You are a kid?" He pulls her hood back roughly and peers at her face. "By God, you **are** a kid."

Sugar pulls her hood back over her head and glances furtively at the man. The predator wolf look is gone from his face. It is replaced by the mien of an opportunistic bear foraging for food in the reserve's dump. Sugar prays that she is not this bear's choice of garbage. She regrets having accepted a ride with this sleazy man.

"Look here, Indian Girl. I didn't mean to frighten you. But, you know, you have yourself to blame for leading me on." Sugar is hoping to avoid harmful consequences. But so too is the man. He realizes that to make advances to an underage girl is a serious offence. What if she lodges a complaint against him? The driver regrets having accepted her to ride in his truck.

After some minutes of tense silence, the driver speaks again. "The next truck stop is the *Husky* at Bradford Exit 64. It is for the best that I drop you off there."

The man wants her gone; Sugar wants to leave. It is an agreeable resolution for both parties. Unfortunately, Exit 64 is almost an hour away. An invisible wall of silence separates the two travellers like an icy shield. By the time the truck pulls in at *Husky*, both are exhausted from the tension.

"Okay, Indian Girl," the man says with relief. "This is where we part company. I'm dashing off to the washroom. After that, I'm grabbing a coffee to go. And when I return here, you are gone. Is that clear?"

Sugar nods and exits the truck.

When the man returns, he sees Sugar attempting to solicit a ride from other truckers. He walks over to her. "No luck, eh?"

"No."

"And you **really** want to get to Toronto?"

"Yes. I need to get to Toronto."

The man looks at the pitiful Cree girl standing in the cold and is put in mind of a shivering lost dog begging for scraps. He speaks to himself. "Ah, what the hell. It's only another 40 minutes." Then he addresses Sugar. "I suppose I can endure you for another 40 minutes. Get in the truck, Indian Girl, if you want to reach Toronto." Sugar re-enters the truck. This time, the tension is gone. They travel in an unsettled peace and reach their destination at 7:50pm. The *Husky/Esso* truck stop on Shawson Road, Mississauga, is where the driver parks his truck. He has a delivery scheduled for 7:00am the following morning in Etobicoke. He gestures to Sugar to exit.

"Is this Toronto?" Sugar asks looking around in puzzlement. She sees dozens of trucks parked in the lot and more in neighbouring lots. She has never seen so many trucks at one time.

The driver speaks to her. "Look over there," pointing to Dixie Road. "See the bus stop? That's where you get a bus to Toronto."

Sugar walks towards Dixie Road. It is clear to her that the man is finished with her. At least, she has succeeded in getting this far – and safely. At Dixie Road, three young men are standing at the curb each toting a work bag – most likely workers returning home from work. Sugar inquires of them, "Is this the bus stop?"

By way of answer, they point to the sign 'BUS STOP'. Sure enough, a bus arrives. The three youths board the bus. Sugar enters last. She is unfamiliar with the protocol. The three young men drop coins into a box beside the driver. But how much? The driver looks at her questioningly. "You need to put in the fare, Miss."

"I... I don't know the fare. What is that?"

"Put $2.50 into the slot." It strikes him that the girl is

unfamiliar with Mississauga Bus etiquette. He looks at her carefully. "What age are you, anyway?"

"Fifteen."

"Then, for you, it's a 'toonie'."

Sugar is momentarily confused by the unfamiliar procedure. She hauls a handful of coins from her pocket, the coins she received earlier from 'Bread Man', and shows them to the driver.

"That one there," he says, pointing to a $2 coin. Sugar deposits the coin. She remains standing next to the driver. It registers with him that this passenger is confused. "So, where are you headed? Are you sure you are on the right bus? Oh, and stand behind the white line while the bus is in motion."

Sugar spots the white line on the floor. She stands behind it as requested. "Does this bus take me to Toronto?"

"What part of Toronto? Downtown Toronto?"

Sugar wonders how large Toronto is. Is it so vast that it has multiple parts, all served by different buses? She has no clue, but 'Downtown Toronto' sounds appropriate. "Downtown Toronto," she says.

"To get to Downtown Toronto from here, you need to go south on Dixie. This bus is going north. You need to get off and take a southbound bus to Dundas, and a Dundas bus eastbound to the subway. The subway takes you to

Downtown Toronto." He sees that his instructions fail to register with her. "Tell you what, Miss, here's a transfer," handing her a short ribbon of paper. "I'll point you to the right bus. You'll give the driver this transfer and tell him that you want to get to the subway for Downtown Toronto. He'll set you right."

Sure enough, he stops the bus and points to one on the opposite side of the street. It appears to be waiting for her. As she steps off the bus, he shouts after her, "Cross on the green light!"

Sugar boards the southbound bus and explains her dilemma to the driver. He understands that this girl is unfamiliar with the bus route. He instructs her to sit in the seat closest to the front where he keeps his eye on her. At Dundas Street, he points her to the bus to the subway. She makes the transfer successfully. Eventually, she reaches Islington Subway Station. The bus driver announces the name of the stop in a loud voice. "Islington Subway Stop. This is the last stop. Everybody out!" She exits the bus.

Sugar is suddenly overwhelmed by the large number of people dashing about. She follows the rush of passengers from the bus. She expects that they are likewise intent on reaching the subway trains. Upon entering the main station, she sees a bank of telephones. This is fortunate. She reads the instructions on how to make a phone call. She inserts 50 cents and punches in the phone number for her Aunt Rose. She is relieved that the call connects. Rose picks up and is surprised to hear from her. She is even more surprised to learn that Dorinda is in Toronto as she speaks. Alas, Rose is unable to meet Dorinda tonight. It is already 9:00pm and Rose is working on the street. Dorinda is amazed. Toronto must work around the clock if street workers are busy at 9:00pm. Rose explains that she can have a friend meet her at the *Tim Hortons* at the food court of the *Eaton Centre*. Rose explains. "There is a subway stop right there, so there is no need to come up to street level – take the 'Eaton Centre' exit at the Dundas Subway stop. There is a subway map displayed prominently in Islington Station, and in every station. And there are more maps posted in all the train carriages. From Islington, take the train to Yonge; get off and change trains at Yonge Street Station, go south on the Yonge Line to Dundas Station. Once there, you have a choice of exits from the station. Make sure to take the one marked 'Pathway to Eaton Centre'. If you get lost, find the *Eaton Centre* – everyone knows where it is. And locate the *Tim Hortons* inside at the Dundas Street entrance. Make sure that you go to the 'Dundas Street Entrance' – the shopping centre is large and is served by many entrances. My friend will be waiting for you there. Her name is 'Monique'."

"How will I recognize Monique?"

"You won't. Monique will recognize **you.**"

"But she doesn't know me and there are hundreds of people here."

"Don't fret, Dorinda. You are still dressed in your reserve clothes? Yes?"

"In Kokum's parka and Uncle Jim's mukluks."

Rose laughs. "Believe me, there is **no one** dressed like that in the *Eaton Centre*. Monique will spot you. Don't worry. Now, get to the train."

Dorinda/Sugar figures out how to get to the train. After her experience with the Mississauga Bus, the procedure is not so confusing. And this time, she consults the map to ascertain the correct direction and the names of each station. At each station, she compares the station's name to the map to confirm the accuracy of her progress. At 9:45pm, Dorinda successfully arrives at the appointed place. Fatigued, she sits down in a seat at *Tim Hortons* located at the Dundas Street Entrance of the *Eaton Centre*.

"Hi, Sugar! You must be Rose's niece. Welcome to 'Hogtown'." Sugar is addressed by a woman dressed in a fake leather cream-coloured winter coat with matching fake-fur collar. The coat is unfastened, revealing a flame-red sparkling top with a low-cut neckline and a black leather short tight skirt. Setting off the ensemble is a pair of black high-heeled shoes. In Sugar's opinion, the coat is in poor taste, the sparkly top's neckline is too low, the skirt is too tight and much too short, and the heels on the shoes are much too high. So this is Monique, she presumes. Notwithstanding the winter weather, her head is uncovered, revealing black wavy collar-length hair. The most remarkable feature is her face. It is heavily made up to hide an underlying hardness, probably the result of premature ageing. She could be as old as 50 trying to look like 20. But Sugar does not care. At this point, sleep is her primary craving.

"Oh, hello," Sugar replies. "And how did you know to call

me 'Sugar'?"

"Your name is 'Sugar'? Well, how about that? You look wiped out, Sugar. Why don't I take you to the apartment? It's not far from here – at 435 Jarvis near Carlton. We take the subway one stop north to College, and a streetcar from there – not more than five minutes away."

Sugar has no idea where this is, but if it is close by, then she is impatient to get there. They walk through the pedestrian tunnel to the subway station. At one stop north, at College Street, they walk outside and fasten their coats against the cold wind that whistles through the high buildings like a wind tunnel. The Carlton streetcar brings them two stops east, to within half a block of their destination. It has taken them eight minutes, not five.

En route, Monique informs her, "The apartment is small. But we can't afford a larger one. The landlord's rule is to limit the number of tenants to two. He doesn't know that we are three – well, four now, it looks like. So make yourself small and unnoticed. Okay, Sugar?"

Sugar awakens on the following morning. She concentrates on putting her mind in order. She determines that it is 03 February 2017 and that she is in Toronto. She is lying in a comfortable bed. She is undressed but has no recollection of having removed her parka or mukluks. In fact, she cannot remember having gone to bed at all. She is aware that she is not the sole occupant of the bed. Rose is asleep beside her. Sugar moves.

Rose stretches and turns to her. She looks into her face and says, "Dorinda."

"Yes," she replies, stifling a yawn.

"When I came home last night or, rather, early this morning, I found you asleep on the floor. You hadn't even removed your parka or mukluks. You must have been bushed from your journey. But tell me. Why are you here? Don't they need you on the reserve?"

They both sit on the edge of the bed, talking. Dorinda explains that people started to address her as 'Sugar', and since they are not familiar with the name 'Dorinda', she has adopted this new name while off the reserve. But she is still 'Dorinda' to Rose. Dorinda relates to Rose all the events that occurred on the reserve – the fire that killed her father; Jeff's visit to the hospital; the poverty that affects the family; and the wolf she encountered on the ice road. Hence, she decided to come to Toronto to work with her and send money home.

Rose realizes that Dorinda misunderstands the work she performs in Toronto. She explains that 'working on the street' refers to a 'streetwalker' – one who provides sexual services – a 'sex worker'. Dorinda claims that if Rose can do this work so too can she.

Rose looks at her cell phone and reads the time. "Dorinda, let's get dressed and go out for breakfast. It's almost noon. There's a *Timmys* at the corner of Jarvis & Carlton. Let's go there, and I'll tell you everything about my job – the good **and** the bad.

Later, sitting in *Tim Hortons*, Rose gives a full account of the work. Last year, she earned $35,000 tax-free. It's not a lot when expenses are deducted. However, she hopes to build up a clientele of repeat customers, enough to reach $50,000 in another year. Her 'spot' is at the corner of Spadina & Richmond, a block south of *The Horseshoe*. She frequently uses the *'Shoe* as a starting point to loosen up an anxious 'john'. A few girls work that corner with her. Prospective 'johns' pull up in their cars. Rose does not approach every car that prowls the area. She chooses the cars she recognizes as repeat customers, those who express a preference for her. It is safer that way and they pay extra money for the personal attention. Monique, for example, does not work the street at all. She is semi-retired. Her customers, when requesting her services, contact her exclusively by phone. Rose explains the payment scale. There is a rate for different services, ranging from $20 to $100. The technique of 'up-selling' is employed. Depending on the number of 'tricks' one can turn, weekly earnings can range from $500 to $1,000.

Rose also delivers the bad news. A new girl can get into trouble if she steals another worker's 'john'. Miffed workers can cause a lot of damage to a new girl who breaks the code – a bruised face, torn clothes, and worse. The protocol is to hold back from approaching a car until a senior worker gives the okay signal. Senior girls refrain from approaching unfamiliar johns and from those known to be unsavoury. The potential john is sized up and, if he is 'unclaimed', he is fair game. Consequently, a new girl, in choosing 'untested' johns, is thus put into a position of greater danger. Rough johns are capable of beating up girls. Some do. And girls end up in the hospital. Regardless of the danger, the job of a sex worker is also unpleasant. The only way to get through it, night after night, is by getting drunk or high. In that way, she can detach herself from the job. It is the only profession in which 'drunk on the job' is a preferred advantage. On top of that, there is a real risk to the worker's health. Precautions need to be employed. A few ploys, if deftly executed, can reduce the risk. But the risk is never completely absent. And workers constantly contend with harassment, the weather, the expense of clothes and make-up.

Dorinda-Sugar consumes a second cup of coffee. She considers the merits of Rose's account. "Rose, if **you** can do it, **I** can do it."

"Okay. Then I'll show you the ropes. First, we need to get suitable street-clothes and make-up for you, and get you to pass for 18 – 18 is the magic number, right up to 25. I'll lend you the money and you can pay me back later. So after breakfast, we are going to the *Eaton Centre*."

Dorinda is determined to go through with her undertaking so that she can send money back to the family. She chooses the street name 'Sugar', of course. Rose instructs her on poise and attitude and how to look appealing. And she braces her for what to expect. After a week – it takes a week for Sugar to master high heels – she is ready for her first encounter. To break her in gently, Rose 'lends' her one of her gentler johns. But the first experience is not what she is prepared for. It is distasteful and unpleasant. Afterwards, she is distraught. She worries that her decision may have been rash.

Rose consoles her. "It was the first time. Next time it will be easier. Take my advice, do it while intoxicated. When you are drunk, you won't care. But not too drunk that you lose control."

Sugar is a fast learner. She is attentive to her work. She is always drunk on the job. And she encourages the johns to drink plenty too. Two drunks together result in the best outcome. The johns suspect that she is underage. This is an added appeal. Sugar quickly builds up a repeat clientele and she pays back Rose what she owes. But she sends no money to her family on the reserve. It's as if the reserve is on a different world – unconnected and forgotten.

Rose continues to warn her of the risk of encountering rough or violent johns. Some are known to beat sex workers or engage in choking and suffocation. Some get a thrill from inflicting pain. Sugar dismisses the warning. She is overconfident and is indiscriminate in selecting johns.

On Monday 03 April 2017, Sugar is working the corner of Spadina & Richmond. Monday is a slow night. None of her usual johns come by. She decides to approach the first car that pulls up, regardless of who it might be. Rose is standing back, talking on her cell phone. A black *Mustang* stops alongside the curb. Sugar promptly steps inside. Rose shouts to her, "No! Not the black *Mustang*!" But Sugar is already inside and the car drives away. Rose snaps a picture of the car with her cell phone before it turns sharp right into McDougall Lane. Rose is alarmed. The black *Mustang* is reputed to be owned by one bad-ass character. Rose is anxious. She decides to wait until the following morning before contacting the police – as if that will do any good. It's no big deal if a hooker goes off with a john. Still, if she later decides to report a disappearance to the police, she has a picture of the car, with time and place.

Sugar is seated in the front passenger seat of the *Mustang*. It speeds north on McDougall Lane notwithstanding that the lane is barely the width of the car. It makes a right turn onto Queen Street West, followed by a left at the lights and speeds north on Spadina Avenue. The radio is playing rap music loudly. Two soft dice are dangling from the rear-view mirror. The driver turns to her and smiles.

"I've noticed you for the past few weeks standing at the corner of Spadina & Richmond. And I said to myself, 'now that's a cutie I should get to know'. So, tell me. What's your name?"

"My name is 'Sugar'."

He studies her for a second. "You are Canadian? Like a native Canadian?"

"First Nations."

"Ah-hah. I thought so. Real Canadian Sugar Maple. And me? People call me 'Jamaica Man'."

"And I'm 'Misty Morning'." The voice emanating from the back seat startles her. Sugar had not noticed the person sitting behind her. Misty's accent is strange. She cannot be Canadian.

"Now this is cool," says Jamaica Man. I'm from Jamaica, Misty is From Poland, and you are from 'The Great White North'."

Sugar is attempting to fathom what kind of 'trick' would involve a black man, a white woman and an aboriginal girl. This is a new and unexpected situation. Jamaica Man continues driving north, curving around Spadina Crescent, until he makes a right turn on a red at Bloor Street West.

Misty speaks again. "'Misty Morning' is my professional name. I am a choreographer and grooming manager in a gentleman's club."

From the training she received from Rose, Sugar understands that a 'gentleman's club' is a euphemism for 'strip bar'.

As if reading her mind, Misty explains. "Jamaica Man is the owner of a high-end club. I manage the entertainment. I train girls in dancing and grooming and how to interact with the gentlemen-clients. Some girls perform so well that they are engaged for private sessions."

Jamaica Man turns south onto Queens Park. He changes lanes, without signalling, to overtake a bus at the Royal Ontario Museum. "Sugar," he says, "I believe you are more suited to a club than to the street. Why choose to work outside in the weather when you can work indoors in a luxurious club?" He rounds Queens Park Crescent and enters University Avenue.

Misty resumes speaking. "Are you interested in talking to us?

We can explain fully what is involved and what your prospects are. Just talk with us at this point, and see where it goes. What is there to lose?"

The car makes another right and enters Wellington Street West. Sugar notices that the man is dressed in an expensive well-tailored dark suit. His shirt is the colour of roasted coffee and is adorned by a gold chain hanging from his neck. The brown-haired woman in the back seat is dressed stylishly in a charcoal Ula cropped twist-front satin top over a matching magnolia-satin midi skirt by Nanushka and is wearing a gold strand necklace and hoop earrings. Sugar is impressed by their show of wealth.

Jamaica Man speaks again. "Talk? Misty, this is not the place to talk comfortably. Let's go somewhere nice. What do you say?"

"Yes, Jamaica Man. I believe you are right. What do you think, Sugar?"

He drives past Roy Thompson Hall and suddenly turns right into underground parking and brings the *Mustang* to a halt at Metro Centre Parking. "Okay", he says. "Let's talk over a juicy steak and a bottle of Malbec."

Sugar does not respond. Nevertheless, she accompanies the pair up to the street level of Metro Centre. There is no pedestrian crossing on Wellington Street at this location. But this is no deterrent to Jamaica Man. He crosses the street through moving traffic, closely followed by Misty and Sugar, both of whom trot nimbly in his wake in high-heeled shoes.

Thereupon, they enter *The Shore Club.*

"Good evening, Mr Andrews." Jamaica Man is greeted immediately upon entering the club. "Mr Kenneth Andrews and party, please follow me. I will show you to your table."

Seated at the table, Jamaica Man (Kenneth Andrews) waives aside the menu and orders 'the best steak', medium rare, and a bottle of Malbec. "You must have the steak, Sugar."

Misty interrupts. "No, you won't Sugar. If you come to work with us you need to watch your diet. You'll have a green salad with vinaigrette dressing and rainbow trout. That's what I'm having."

Kenneth/Jamaica Man looks at Sugar over his raised wine-glass. "Tell me, Sugar. How much did you make last week?"

"$500."

"Well, that is what you will make **per night** at my club. If you are interested, I will pay you for tonight, right now." He opens his wallet and passes five $100 bills across the table to Sugar.

Misty grabs the bills and says, "Not yet. So far, Sugar has not agreed to work with us." And turning to Sugar, "Have you? If you choose to come with us you need to dress with taste. You look like a street hooker in your present attire. Now, listen to me. This is what you will do. Meet me tomorrow at ten in the morning at the *Eaton Centre*. We will spend this $500 on stylish clothes. Then we'll know that you are on board with us.”

“Okay. But where exactly shall we meet? The *Eaton Centre* is huge.”

“So it is. You choose the meeting point, Sugar.”

“The *Tim Hortons* at the Dundas Street entrance.”

“Agreed.”

“A word of caution,” Jamaica Man says.” Our club is very exclusive. If your friends on the street learn of this, they will be jealous of you. They may even hurt you to prevent you from joining us. So, keep this quiet.”

“If I am to keep this a secret, how will I explain my absence tonight?”

Jamaica Man selects another $100 bill from his wallet and hands it to Sugar. “This should explain tonight’s ‘trick’. A satisfied client who appreciates your services.”

Shortly afterwards, the black *Mustang* drops Sugar off at Spadina & Richmond. Rose is relieved to see her and greets her immediately. She was fretting ever since Sugar left. Now that she is back safe, she inquires about the john in the *Mustang*.

“The ‘john’ was actually a man **and** a woman – like two clients in one. I got $100 for the ‘trick’.” Sugar says it smugly and ensures that she does not mention the club that offered her a job. For some reason, she is unable to remember the name of the club. She concludes that the name was never stated. It does not strike her as strange that Jamaica Man and Misty omitted this piece of information.

Rose is satisfied with Sugar's response. The picture of the black *Mustang* is no longer relevant. And since it is a slow night for business, they both go home.

At 10:00am on the following morning, Misty and Sugar meet at the *Tim Hortons* as agreed. Monique, who is having her morning coffee, observes them. The meeting arouses her curiosity, so she follows them. The amount of clothing that she witnesses Sugar purchase is more than she can afford. This interests Monique and arouses her suspicion. She goes back to the apartment and tells Rose. Rose waits for Sugar's return, and for an explanation. She waits, and waits, and waits.

Sugar (her niece Dorinda) does not return home that day or the next day.

CHAPTER SIX

THE ELEPHANT CLUB

On Thursday 06 April 2017, Rose Cool enters the 51 Division Metropolitan Toronto Police Station at 51 Parliament Street to report a missing minor. She gives the information to a desk sergeant. The sergeant summarizes the tendered information into the record sheet:

> Dorinda Trapper, age 15 (niece and flat-mate of complainant, Rose Cool of 435 Jarvis Street, unit 206) – picture not available.

> Disappeared on the morning of Tuesday 04 April 2017 – last seen at noon in the *Eaton Centre*. No foul play witnessed.

> Note: Subject ran away from home on 03 February 2017 from Red Rapids First Nations Reserve. She left without warning and has had no contact with her family since then. Between 03 February and 03 April, she worked as a sex worker (underage minor) in Toronto.

> List and circulate description and details – 'Female Runaway Aboriginal Girl (Minor)'

The sergeant regards this as one more tragic runaway. In Canada, over 40,000 children are reported missing each year. Of these, most return home or are quickly located within two days. But after one week, 8% remain unaccounted for. These young runaways, approximately 2,500 children, seldom turn up. In Dorinda's case, she left of her own volition and no foul play is evident. Therefore, there is no 'crime' to investigate – just be on the lookout for one more runaway minor. To Rose, he simply says, "Leave it with us, Miss Cool. We will look into it." Rose departs from the police station. In her heart, she knows that a First-Nations runaway sex worker will warrant little or no attention from the police. In subsequent police inquiries, no one links the name 'Dorinda Trapper' with 'Sugar Maple'.

Meanwhile, Sugar's life encounters a major turn. After the shopping excursion in the *Eaton Centre*, Misty brings her to the *Elephant Club* at 163 Spadina Avenue – directly opposite the Toronto Dominion Bank. The ground floor of the building houses a numismatics store with street frontage and accounting/income-tax services in the back. The entrance to the commercial suites prominently displays the name of the accounting office. Below this, a small brass plate bears the name 'Elephant Club'. Sugar is surprised at the insignificant entrance to the club. She fears that it might be a rundown strip joint. Inside, Misty foregoes the stairs and chooses the elevator. Sugar, laden with her shopping bags, follows her and rides up to the second floor. Upon exiting the elevator, they walk along a corridor to where they are confronted by a steel fireproof door. Misty punches in a code on the door's keypad and the door swings open.

Misty turns to Sugar and says, "Welcome to the *Elephant Club*. We are part of a chain of related clubs in Toronto and Montreal. Let me show you around. As you see, there is no activity at this time of day. The club operates from 10:00pm to 06:00am, seven days a week. We have 30 performers and we cater to a rich clientele."

The interior of the club is furnished in luxurious furniture and awash in hidden lighting. The lighting alternates through a range of soft colours. A long curving stage snakes through the room, illuminated by ceiling spotlights and below-ground lighting. At one end is a well-stocked bar displaying bottles of liquor that Sugar never heard of. Misty continues her descriptive narrative. "This is the main room. Of course, we have several private rooms for private parties – no more need for you to ride off in a car to perform 'tricks' for cheap 'johns'. Here, let's put your clothes in 'wardrobe'. You won't need them for a while." Misty leads her into a room stocked with costumes and shoes and an array of exotic apparel. "Here is your locker. I look after the wardrobe. Your locker will be stocked with appropriate clothing for your assigned duties. As your duties change, so too will your stock of clothes. **We** tell you what to wear, and how to wear it. This is how it works here – you are an employee now, not a free agent. Do as instructed, Sugar, and we will all get along."

Sugar considers these directives. It makes sense that an operation that engages 30 performers surely requires an efficient operation. She replies to Misty, "Of course. I understand."

Jamaica Man appears from an inner office. He looks at Sugar, but he addresses Misty. "Have you explained our rules to Sugar?"

"Yes, Boss. She's on board."

Sugar claps her hands and exclaims, "Oh, I must tell this to Rose." She runs to the door with the intent to leave. She is surprised that the door refuses to open. How can it be a 'fire door' if it does not permit emergency exit? Jamaica Man walks to her and slaps her hard on the mouth. Sugar falls to the floor. Her lip is bleeding. Jamaica Man walks away without uttering a word of explanation. Confused and shocked, Sugar looks up at Misty.

Misty explains coldly. "One more thing. You are not permitted to leave the club without permission. This applies to all our girls. Now, come with me. We need to conceal that cut in your lip if you are to work." Back in 'wardrobe', Misty applies a transparent band-aid to Sugar's lip. "There. No one will notice. Now, come with me. I'll show you where you will stay when not performing."

Misty leads her down a passageway to another locked door. As with the previous door, Misty taps in a code on the keypad and proceeds through the open doorway. She leads Sugar into an apartment unit, not unlike Rose's apartment on Jarvis Street, but larger. Misty explains. "This is where you live while working here. Thirty girls live here – now 31 – sleeping eight to a room." She points to what Sugar understands are bedrooms. "Now remove your clothes, **all** your clothes. And wear these," pointing to a grey tee-shirt and boxer shorts on a table. "When off duty, these are what you wear. I will check on you daily for any other needs. You will be kept adequately fed and healthy."

Sugar's heart sinks. Is this what Rose warned her about? She realizes that she has become a prisoner in a sex-trafficking operation. She considers her options. If she should strike Misty and attempt to flee, she will be unable to exit the club through the steel door. And she fears that she will be beaten if she refuses to obey. Resigned to her fate, she complies with Misty's instructions. Sugar recognizes that she has become like livestock confined on a farm.

Once Misty leaves the apartment, the other occupants reveal themselves to Sugar. They are all young, mostly in their teens. They introduce themselves to Sugar, girls from the Caribbean, from the Philippines, from Russia, and as of today – Canada. All are dressed alike in grey tee-shirts and grey boxers as in a prison uniform. And Sugar is now one of their fellow-prisoners. Sugar tours the apartment. She discovers that there are no windows and, hence, she has no visual link to the outside world. The kitchen is stocked with simple, but adequate, food. It has a fridge, coffee maker, microwave, a hotplate, oven and eating utensils. It is better stocked than Sugar's previous home on the reserve. Sugar wonders what happens to older girls – the oldest girl here is about 22. Are they employed elsewhere? Or do they 'disappear'? Sugar resolves to formulate a plan of escape.

The oldest girl in the apartment is Katia. She is Russian and is 22 years old. Katia invites Sugar to sit with her at the kitchen table. The Cree girl accepts. Katia lights a cigarette. She blows smoke out the side of her mouth and addresses the newcomer. "'Sugar'. So your name is 'Sugar'?"

Sugar is anxious to make a friend. She answers, "Yes, my name is 'Sugar'."

"But it's not your real name. Is it?"

"Before, it was 'Dorinda'. But 'Sugar' is my name now."

"Well, my name is 'Katia', but I am called 'Cat' in the club."

Sugar nods. Then, she asks, "Are you allowed to smoke in here?"

Katia glances at her smouldering cigarette. "They provide us with cigarettes. They provide us with whatever they choose. But yes, they allow cigarettes." Katia peers at Sugar for a moment. Then she surprises her with a terse comment. "Don't think of escaping. If you try, they will hurt you. If you succeed, they will find you and kill you." The Russian takes a drag from her cigarette. Then, she continues. "How do I know you wish to escape? Let me tell you, everyone dreams of escaping. Some try. But all fail. And they are punished as a result – broken bones sometimes."

"Why are you telling me this?"

Katia declines to answer. Instead, she poses a new question. "Sugar, did you get a tour of the club?"

"Yes. And they explained everything to me."

"Ah, yes. But not 'everything'. First, you think that this is a private talk? Well, it's not. There is a control room in the club. That room listens to us and spies on us all the time. There is no private space here – not the bedroom, not the washroom, not the private entertainment rooms, not in the main room or at the bar, or on stage, not anywhere.”

Sugar is alarmed. “You mean, they are listening to us now –
to this conversation?”

“Listening and watching. See that shiny ball in the ceiling?
That’s a camera. It scans the entire room. Cameras are
everywhere. And that’s not all. Cell-phone signals are
blocked in the club. The only working phone is in Jamaica
Man’s office. There is no possible communication for us to
the outside.” Katia draws on her cigarette. She continues.
“The girls in the club, including me, are here illegally. Even if
we return home, it would be worse for us. You see, we have a
past, or a debt, that condemns us to... The club is the best that
we can look forward to. At least for a short time. And then it
is over. No one here gets out and no one here gets old.”

“No one gets old? What do you mean?”

“Sugar, don’t think about it. Just do what you’re told and
make the best of it.” Katia’s cigarette burns down. She stubs
it out, thus indicating that the conversation is over.

Sugar considers what Katia has revealed to her. Did Katia tell
her this out of camaraderie? Or was she instructed to do so?
Most likely, it was for both reasons. The Cree girl glances
furtively at the camera in the ceiling – and shivers.

*   *   *   *   *

Over the next week, Sugar learns that good performance
earns privileges. As the only aboriginal in the ‘stable’, she is a

91

popular choice for private entertainment. She is promoted as 'Sugar Maple, the Sweet Savage from the Tundra'. Sugar is not a savage and she is not from the tundra, but she enthusiastically plays her part. She strives to convey a favourable impression to Jamaica Man in the hope of gaining his trust. She suspects that what Jamaica Man told her is true – she makes over $500 a night. What he did **not** tell her is that he keeps the entire amount. She is, therefore, a valuable asset in the stable.

On Wednesday 12 April 2017, Jamaica Man summons Misty. He instructs her to provide him with a pretty black girl, a pretty white girl, and the savage aboriginal girl. And he wants them dressed for a meeting. He has an appointment and wishes to make a good impression.

At 11:00am, Kenneth Andrews (Jamaica Man) arrives at his appointment in the Toronto Dominion Bank at Queen & Spadina. It is literally across the street from the club. He and his three girls enter the office of John Maxwell, Assistant Manager Credit. Mr Andrews, as he is known at the bank, requests a line of credit. The purpose of the loan is to renovate the club. He intends to install a moving platform to snake through the main room and disappear through a wall and reappear back through another wall. He got the idea at the baggage carousel at the airport. The beauty of his plan is that all his patrons, regardless of where they are seated, are afforded a full close-up view of the performers. Furthermore, the performers do not need to walk to the platform. They appear, suddenly, in dramatic fashion through the wall.

John Maxwell explains that a line of credit for this purpose needs to be secured. He asks what collateral can be provided.

By way of response, Jamaica Man gestures to the three girls standing beside him in the office. "Mr Maxwell, you can have girls – any girl, any time – at no charge. See, here is 'Opal' a pretty black girl from Trinidad, or 'Natasha', a pretty Russian, or this gem from the Canadian North, 'Sugar Maple'."

In his exuberance, Jamaica Man knocks over the credit manager's tray of business cards, scattering them on the floor. Sugar immediately offers to pick them up and refill the tray on the desk. She kneels and gathers the scattered cards. She deftly scratches one card with her fingernails, etching it as deeply as possible, and pushes it out of sight under the desk.

John Maxwell declines Jamaica Man's offer and refuses to grant the loan. Jamaica Man is disappointed that he failed to obtain a line of credit. He expresses annoyance and leaves quickly. He and the three girls walk back across Spadina Avenue to the *Elephant Club*. Pete Harvey, Assistant Manager Administration enters John Maxwell's office. He enquires, "Who was that? And what was the noise?"

John slaps his pencil on his desk and pushes back his chair. "Oh, that sleaze-bag from the *Elephant Club* across the street knocked over my business cards."

"You didn't give him a line of credit, surely?"

"Of course not, I sent him packing."

Pete Harvey peers at the floor where the business cards had fallen. "That First Nations girl was sure pretty, but she didn't do a good job of retrieving your cards. There is one still here on the ground." Pete picks it up and looks at it. "Well, you won't be able to use this one. It's scratched."

"So throw it away. And why are you here anyway, Pete?" John is impatient to get back to work.

Pete, on the other hand, has business that pertains directly to John Maxwell. "The inspection requirements," he says bluntly. A month earlier, an inspection-audit was conducted in the branch. Where files were found to be deficient, updated authorizations are required. As each deficiency is corrected, a report is sent to Inspection Division with a copy of the relative amended form. As Pete reams off the list, John confirms the updated status – a copy of minutes received, current list of officers obtained, current list of receivables filed etc. John hands him the relevant files, now completely in order. Accordingly, Pete can finalize the report to Inspection.

John remarks, "It's a wonder that the *Elephant Club* account passed inspection."

"Well, it did. They looked at it for possible money-laundering, but are satisfied that all payments are for legitimate expenses – utility bills and the like. I'll show you the file." Pete returns moments later with the account file. Sure enough, it is stamped in green with the inspection date 13 March 2017 and initialled *'CC'*.

John quickly glances at the file and exclaims, "Well, son-of-a-gun."

Pete Harvey returns the file to the cabinet and walks to his office. When he sits down, he remembers that he still has the scratched business card in his pocket. He had slipped in there when he went to fetch the file. He looks at it. It contains a scratched doodle – 'HELF'. Disinterested, he throws the card in the wastebasket.

Later that night, Pete Harvey is at home watching the eleven o'clock news. He is idly doodling on his copy of the *TV Guide*. He doodles his name, 'PETE', but since he is using his fingernail, the 'P' looks like an 'F'. Pete looks at the paper and sees that he has scratched 'FETE'. He is suddenly struck by a portentous thought. Thereupon, he rushes out to his car and drives for 25 minutes to his office in the bank. He runs to his wastebasket, relieved that the cleaners have not yet arrived to empty the trash. He fishes for the discarded business card. He finds it and reads it with a new understanding – 'HELP'.

Pete is at work early on the following morning at seven o'clock. He runs upstairs to the second-floor units. The front units are commercial spaces, currently unoccupied. These were once a dentist's office, but the bank terminated the lease some years earlier for security reasons. The rear unit is occupied by the bank's ageing porter who lives on the premises. Pete likes old George. And Pete discusses personal concerns with him and avails of his wisdom. Pete stops at George's door and listens. He hears the clinking sound of a spoon stirring in a cup. Satisfied that George is up and about, he knocks at the door. George answers the door promptly. He is surprised to see Pete Harvey.

"Good Lord, Mr Harvey. Is there a problem?"

"George, your grandson is a cop in 11 Division. Right?"

"That's right. So?" George sees that Pete is distraught.

Pete shows the scratched business card to George and gives him an account of the previous day's occurrence. "You see, I don't know if this is important, or if I am unduly alarmed over nothing. What do you think? Should I report it to the police?"

"Sit down, Mr Harvey. I'll phone Greg right away." A few minutes later, George announces, "Greg goes off duty at two. He will come by here at two-thirty. You can explain all to him when he arrives."

Officer Gregory Landers meets with Pete at 2:30pm. Pete relates the story a second time. Greg tells him to retain the card safely. Then he promptly leaves. Pete wonders what is next. He does not wonder for long. At 3:00pm, a burly detective comes to the branch. Straight away, he interviews Pete. Pete gives him the business card containing the First Nations girl's scratched message for help. When he finishes with Pete, the detective interviews John Maxwell. By 3:30pm he has obtained both collaborating accounts. Detective Sergeant Alex Crouse notes the description and names of the three girls that had accompanied Ken Andrews into the bank. He underlines the name of the First-Nations girl – 'Sugar

Maple' – the writer of the 'help' message. John and Pete are unable to give an accurate estimate of the girls' ages – their make-up is deceiving. Their guess is 'young, perhaps 18' – since 18 is the minimum legal age.

Detective Crouse dwells for a moment on the information he has thus garnered. Then he comes to a decision. He asks for Pete's assistance. He requests permission to place surveillance devices in the TD Bank, directed at the *Elephant Club* across the street. Pete guesses that the police have no permission to plant surveillance devices directly on the club's property, but this does not apply to the bank building. The detective informs him that because of the close proximity to the club across the street, their listening devices can pick up conversations as if they had an ear to the window. The devices would be installed on the second floor, above the street noise and with an unobstructed view of the subject building. All they need, now, is the bank's permission. Pete considers the required protocol. It could be a challenging task to get Head Office to agree. Pete discusses the situation with George and makes a decision. Dispensing with Head Office's approval, he grants permission to the police. Furthermore, he engages George to accommodate them by granting access through his private entrance rather than through the banking floor.

At 5:00pm, a 'cable-company' truck parks on the street outside the bank. These are common sights where cable repairs and maintenance are conducted. The police establish surveillance without disrupting the business of the bank. To ensure secrecy, their presence is concealed from potentially curious staff. Except for Pete and George, no one in the bank knows about the police operation. Pete prays that the operation goes well and undetected. And he hopes that in due course, the police will remove their equipment surreptitiously.

On Sunday 16 April 2017, Jamaica Man summons Sugar. Her 'jailor', Misty, escorts her to his office. Upon entering, Jamaica Man smiles at her. Sugar detects that he is pleased about something. He addresses her. "Congratulations. We have a client that wishes to engage you for a private party at his home. He has taken quite a shine to our little savage. Misty will see that you are properly outfitted for the occasion. Here is the protocol. The client will come to the club to check you out – just to see how you look and to confirm his choice. He will take you to his house. Your minder (one of the club bouncers) will follow you and park at the venue to ensure that all goes well and to protect my asset." He turns to Misty. "Have Sugar ready for 7:30."

At the appointed time, Sugar is dressed in the Sigmund dress she had purchased in her shopping expedition with Misty, on the day she first joined the *Elephant Club*. She is elegantly attired in the black midi-length dress with a square neckline, slightly puffed shoulders and a high slit. She wears it with stiletto-heeled black shoes. But Misty insists that she foregoes jewellery lest it gets lost or stolen. Misty is satisfied that Sugar is suitably dressed. The 'savage from the tundra' tilts her head. Her long black hair falls loose and fans out on her upper arm. She does not look anything like a sex worker. Sugar feels like a celebrity.

Her client (she cannot refer to him as a 'john') arrives and is satisfied with her appearance. He escorts her from the club to his BMW parked at the side of the building in Lots Lane. Thereupon, he drives to a house in Mississauga, a currently fashionable immense residence on a small lot. The driveway is wide, but Sugar observes that it is shared with the neighbouring house, so it is really only half the width. The garage door opens and they enter.

Inside the house, she meets the party. It is a soccer team celebrating a win. Her host is the captain of the team. He is addressed as 'Colin'. From the talk, Sugar understands that the team plays seven-a-side soccer, hence she is expected to entertain seven men. They all get liquored-up in expectation of the 'entertainment' – all except Sugar who rations her intake of alcohol to stay alert. She looks for an opportunity to execute an escape.

Later in the night, when the men are quite drunk, Colin is relaxed. Sugar takes advantage of the down-time to speak with him. "This is Mississauga, is it not?" she asks innocently.

Colin answers with little interest. "Yeah. So what?"

She engages him in casual conversation "Why is it called 'Mississauga'"?

Colin brightens up, although his eyes remain out of focus. "'Mississauga' is Indian. There was once a reserve along the Credit River. The Mississauga Indian reserve – that's what it was called. They moved the Indians out in the 1940s."

"A reserve on the Credit River? I didn't know that. Is it far from here?"

Colin brings his eyes into focus and looks at Sugar. "There is no reserve here anymore – just a plaque on the roadside to indicate the historic site. It was located on Mississauga Road south of Dundas Street – not all that far from here."

"At the Credit River? Why not show me? It would be fun to run through the forest along the riverbank."

Colin laughs. "What? Like the Indians did 100 years ago?"

"Why not? It is smoky in here. And you could do with fresh air to clear your head."

Colin jumps up unexpectedly. "And why not? It would be a hoot. Come on, 'Tundra Savage'. Let's go."

Dorinda is working out her plan. She cautions herself to proceed carefully. "Ah. My minder is outside. I am not permitted to leave here except for him to drive me back to the club."

Colin returns to the couch. He sprawls out and resumes his relaxed position.

Sugar attempts to regain his interest. "Of course, you could sneak me out."

Colin is amused at the intrigue. And he is keen on the adventure. He takes her hand and leads her to his BMW in the garage. Thereupon, he instructs her to recline on the back seat of the car. He covers her with his jacket to conceal her. Then he takes an empty coke bottle to hold in his hand. Colin exits the garage. He spots an unfamiliar car parked at the roadside. This must be Sugar's 'minder'. He stops alongside and gestures. The occupant slides down his window. Colin indicates the empty coke bottle to signify that he has run out of soda mix for the drinks. The minder blinks at him and closes the window. Colin drives off, laughing.

"Sugar, do you know why I am laughing? Well, it cost me $500 to secure you for the evening. But I charged each member of the team $100 for your entertainment. Hah, I made $100 profit." He laughs again and drives to Erindale Park. Upon entering the park, they observe another car there. Sugar, still in the back seat, says, "Wait for them to leave. Then we'll have the park to ourselves."

They wait. A short time later, having relaxed from his previous exuberance, the effects of the alcohol induces Colin to sleep. The neighbouring car drives off and Colin's BMW is the sole car remaining in the park. Sugar sees her opportunity to leave. Alas, the rear doors won't open due to child safety locks. She attempts to reach the lock release at the driver's side door. But Colin, who is slumped against the door, is blocking access to the switch. Sugar considers an alternative method of escape. If she were in the front passenger seat she could simply exit through the front passenger door. However, she cannot risk climbing over the backrest of the passenger seat for fear of alerting the sleeping man. Sugar is frustrated. Having come thus far, she is still a prisoner. Colin's jacket is still beside her on the back seat. She searches through the pockets and locates Colin's cell phone. She also finds the

$600 he boasted of. She stuffs the bills into her elasticized slightly-puffed shoulders. Her sole chance of escape rests in her ability to phone for help. Then she punches in the phone number for her mother, Amy. True to form, Amy in Niagara Falls fails to pick up. Sugar clenches her fists in frustration. She then attempts to phone Rose. She punches in her number, but before the call succeeds in connecting, Colin is awakened by the sound.

He shouts threateningly at Sugar. "Hey, you thieving Indian. Let go my phone!" Colin gets out and opens the rear door. He drags Sugar from the car and flings her roughly onto the ground. Then, unconcerned for her wellbeing, he drives off, leaving her sprawled on the grass of Erindale Park.

When Colin pushes her to the ground, Sugar twists her body to avoid hitting the concrete curb of the parking space. She lands heavily on the grass verge in a rolling fall, bruising her right shoulder blade. She is momentarily winded. She hears the roar of the BMW engine as it exits the park. She waits until the sound fades into the distance. Satisfied that Colin is gone, she regains her feet. She composes herself and determines that she has suffered no broken bones. She is bare-footed. Her shoes had fallen off in the fall. She concentrates and quickly takes stock of her situation. Sugar is done with the sex-trade industry. No more 'Sugar'. Her name is 'Dorinda'.

At this juncture, she must act fast. At some point, Colin will discover that his $600 is missing. He could come back at any moment. Even if he doesn't, her minder will surely come looking. Should she go to the police? Dorinda is distrustful of the police. Would they believe her story? Would they arrest Jamaica Man and lock him up? Even if they do, would not Dorinda herself be arrested for her work as a sex worker and for the theft of $600? Regardless, she is still vulnerable to exploitation by Jamaica Man's associates who also traffic in the sex trade. She knows how they mistreat their girls and how none of them is over 22. She would undoubtedly be fingered by them for payback and fears that they may likely kill her. She decides to return home to Red Rapids.

Dorinda spurs herself into urgent action. She taps her shoulder and confirms that Colin's $600 is still secure in the elasticized shoulder pad of her dress. She gathers her shoes from where they had fallen and carries them in her hands. She runs barefoot away from Erindale Park. The high slit in her dress affords her freedom of movement. She jogs east along Dundas Street, determined to retrace her original journey back to Red Rapids from whence she came. She is headed for Dixie Road and thence to *Husky/Esso* on Shawson Drive. Although she has money, she is reluctant to get the bus to Sudbury. The express bus to Sudbury departs from Bay Street, Toronto. She cannot risk going back to Downtown Toronto. If they are looking for her, a bus terminal is the one place they would expect to find her.

A Mississauga bus passes her. This indicates to her that Dundas Street has a night-time bus service, but she needs exact change for the fare. She maintains a steady pace until she encounters a 24-hour *Tim Hortons* at 144 Dundas Street West at the corner of Confederation Parkway. The drive-through is open. And it provides a counter service for takeout. Dorinda, breathless from her run, enters the shop. Inside, she tenders a $100 bill for a coffee. The cashier looks at her in a Sigmund dress, carrying her stiletto-heeled shoes and deduces that this must be a sex worker. Notwithstanding, she permits Dorinda to sit inside on the window ledge, but prevents her from accessing the taped-off darkened dining area. Dorinda asks her the time. It is 5:15am. She then asks if she knows when the buses run. The next eastbound bus is due to stop outside the *Tim Hortons* at 5:22am, in a few minutes. Dorinda, having broken the $100 bill with the purchase of the coffee, has the exact change for the bus fare. She has no pocket for the coins, so she remains barefooted and secures the coins inside the toes of her shoes. She thanks the cashier and goes outside. She sees the bus approach in the distance and crosses Confederation Parkway to the bus shelter to await its arrival. When she boards, the driver raises his eyebrows at her and says, "For me, it's early morning; for you, it must be a late night."

Dorinda sits and thinks out her plan. She is attracting undue attention in her attire. She considers a change of clothes. Looking out the bus window, she sees *Mark's Work Warehouse* clothing store beside *Canadian Tire* at Arena Road on Dundas. She exits the bus one stop shy of Dixie and walks back to the clothing store. She is disappointed to find that *Mark's* opens at 10:00am. She mentally debates if she should proceed to Shawson in her Sigmund dress, carrying her shoes, or wait for the store to open? She spots another *Tim Hortons* on the north side of Dundas. She decides to wait it out in *Timmys* at a secluded table. The time is well spent. She fortifies herself with breakfast and permits herself to doze off for a period. The staff tolerates her. After all, she is a paying customer who is no bother to anyone.

As Dorinda sleeps, she is unaware of events unfolding back at the club. At 6:40am, the police raid the *Elephant Club* at 163 Spadina Avenue, Second Floor. They are prepared for the locked steel door. They wield axes and quickly break through the wood-and-plaster interior walls. The tactical unit enters the club with guns in the assault position. They shout warnings as they rush through the broken wall. "Police! Police! Everyone on the floor! On the floor – now! Show your hands!"

The inside of the club is in turmoil. The bouncers push against the steel door to prevent it from opening, not realizing that it is a futile exercise. Jamaica Man dashes to his computer in an attempt to delete files. He is intercepted before he enters his password. The bouncers initially protest loudly, more in panic than in defence. Within seconds, they and the staff of the club are overwhelmed and subdued. The police sweep the entire premises. Five people are taken into custody, including Kenneth Andrews (Jamaica Man), Misty Morning (real name unknown), the barman and two bouncers. The lead detective compels Jamaica man and Misty Morning to open all locked doors. They comply. Thirty sex slaves are found in an adjoining apartment. Detective Sergeant Alex Crouse guesses that these girls are undocumented non-residents. It will take some time to identify their status and return them to their families. He looks for, but is unable to find, the brave aboriginal girl who triggered the police raid. He wonders where Sugar Maple might be.

Dorinda consumes a few more coffees and avails of the washroom. At 9:55am, she walks back to *Mark's* clothing store. She is the first to enter the store when it opens. Straight away, she chooses comfortable boots for walking – not the heavy construction kind with the reinforced toecaps. She also chooses a winter coat with a hood. Being late in the season, winter wear is offered at 50% off. Dorinda ensures that her chosen articles qualify for the end-of-season discount. She pays for the items and walks across the parking lot to the adjoining *Canadian Tire* store. She spots 'sporting goods' and makes one final purchase – a hunting knife with a belt and sheath 'ideal for gutting fish'. At last, she is properly dressed for her journey to Red Rapids. She decides to hang on to her stylish shoes, so she stuffs them into the spacious pockets of the coat.

Dorinda reaches the *Husky/Esso* truck stop at 11:00am without incident. It does not register with her that it is Easter Monday, hence truck traffic is light. Most trucks have already departed by this time. Of those on the lot, none is going as far north as Sudbury. She convinces a driver to take her as far as Parry Sound for $50. She arrives in Parry Sound at 1:30pm. Thereupon, she goes to the bus station intending to get a bus to Sudbury. The next bus is scheduled to depart at 3:00pm. Unfortunately, the bus is filled due to the holiday demand. She waits for the next bus – scheduled to depart at 5:05pm. That too is full. The last bus is due to part at 11:50pm. Armed with this information, Dorinda attempts to hitchhike. Unluckily for Dorinda, holiday traffic is not accommodating to hitchhikers.

Later, Dorinda returns to the bus station. This time, she succeeds in getting a seat on the 11:50pm bus. She boards an Ontario Northland bus to Sudbury for $43. By coincidence rather than design, *Greater Sudbury Health Science North* is the preferred bus stop. She arrives at 1:45am on Tuesday 18 April. Unsure of where to go at such a time, and being fatigued, Dorinda falls asleep on the bench in the bus shelter. She awakens at 5:11am to the sound of traffic. She shakes herself and takes stock of her situation. She has $300 remaining of Colin's money. She realizes that it could have been stolen from her while she slept on the bench. She is a few days away from reaching Red Rapids and fears that she might be accosted and robbed en route by a malicious person. From her recent experience, she knows all too well that such people exist. She considers the possibility that someone from the club might be tracking her. Dorinda is anxious about losing the money and decides to do the one thing she has neglected since leaving Red Rapids – send money to her mother's account in the reserve's credit union. In doing so, she will have one less thing to worry about.

Having come to this decision, Dorinda leaves the bus shelter at *Science North* and walks on Paris Street in the direction of a familiar place – to *Petro-Pass Truck Stop*. She is halfway to the truck stop when she spots a *Canada Post* sign on Paris Street at Regent Street. Immediately, she walks to the post office in *Shoppers Drug Mart*. She waits until it opens at 8:00am, whereupon she purchases a postal money order for $300 and mails it to her mother at Red Rapids. She hopes that Mark will check the mail and ensure that the money is deposited into the appropriate account.

With only $20 remaining in coins in her pocket, Dorinda has no option but to hitchhike to Elliott Lake. The bus fare is $50. Notwithstanding this, she does not regret sending the money home. It is a small sacrifice to make. Anyway, hitchhiking is her preferred way to travel, and she regards bus fares as too expensive. She exits the post office and resumes her walk. At this point, she favours Regent Street and reaches *Petro Pass*, 40 minutes later.

Upon reaching the truck stop, Dorinda sees a 19-year-old Ojibwe girl sitting on the ground at the perimeter fence. The Ojibwe girl looks at Dorinda and recognizes a fellow hitchhiker. Both girls are dressed alike except for the legs. The Ojibwe girl is wearing blue jeans on her outstretched legs. Dorinda is wearing what appears to be an old-fashioned long dress under her parka. Her once-elegant dress is wrinkled and scuffed. To the Ojibwe girl, it looks like a hand-me-down dress from a grandmother.

The girl address Dorinda. "On your way to Toronto? Are you?"

Dorinda approaches her. She notices that the Ojibwe girl has a handwritten cardboard sign resting on her outstretched legs – TRANS-C WEST. Dorinda responds, "No. I am going to Elliot Lake."

"That's westbound on the Trans-Canada, same as me. I am going to the reserve about an hour west of here." She points to her sign. Then she makes a surprising statement. "You'll hafta wait out here for your turn." Dorinda is puzzled by the unexpected remark. Seeing her confused look, the Ojibwe girl explains. "Too many people going on the same route turns them off – truckers, you know. If you want to get a ride in a truck you need to be alone. Two other hitchhikers are ahead of you, so you'll hafta wait your turn."

"What happens if I don't wait my turn?"

"That ruins it for everyone, including yourself. And someone might teach you a lesson." She sees that Dorinda requires further explanation. "You see, you need to increase your chances for a ride, not lessen your chances. I travel this route every week and I know what works best. Truckers offer rides to one person at a time."

Dorinda accepts this advice from the experienced hitchhiker. She sits on the ground beside the Ojibwe girl and waits her turn.

Moments later, the Ojibwe girl offers more advice. "You want to increase your chances for a ride? Well, make a sign. Go to the waste bin inside the lot and find some discarded paper. I'll lend you my marker so you can write a sign. And don't worry. You'll make it to Elliot Lake before nightfall."

It is mid-afternoon when Dorinda eventually succeeds in getting a ride in a delivery van travelling westbound on the Trans-Canada Highway en route from Sudbury to Sault Ste. Marie. At 7:20pm, she reaches the intersection of Highway 109. She alights from the van and walks the 100 metres to the *Gas and Hot Food* store. It has not changed since she last visited. Grouchy Man is still there. She buys a coffee and listens to him talk by phone to Nate (Greasy Man) to give him an update on his parking lot.

Dorinda walks back outside. There is a modest amount of northbound traffic on the road – 7:30pm is a popular time for people to return home to Elliot Lake from working in

Sudbury and the Soo (Sault Ste. Marie). Chances are good that she will get a ride to Elliot Lake. After that, she has a long walk to Red Rapids. It is Tuesday 18 April 2017. The ice road should still be sufficiently intact for walking – and she has a gutting knife as a defence against preying wolves.

A vehicle pulls up alongside the gas pump – a potential ride to Elliot Lake. Dorinda approaches it.

CHAPTER SEVEN

AMY TRAPPER

Amy Trapper's life is ordinary in many ways. It is not an easy life. She is 37 years old, 5′ 6″, stocky but not plump. Her hair is neatly tied back in a bun. Although life is trying, she is thankful. Her circumstances are better than many other women working in the hospitality industry in 'housekeeping'. The hotel, where she works, attracts a lot of U.S. and international guests who come to visit Niagara Falls – Canada's most famous natural attraction. She works a 44-hour week for minimum wage – $14 per hour. Her shifts are broken up into segments of a few hours at a time, never a straight eight-hour day. She realizes that her work-week usually exceeds 44 hours, but she is thankful for the money she earns and has no complaint. A few years ago they went on strike for improved working conditions, mostly with regard to the broken shifts. Danny Glover, the actor and activist, joined the picket line and explicated the righteousness of their cause on TV. Afterwards, the workers were given a copy of the labour codes educating them on their rights – a shift must be at least four hours straight and contain a mandatory 15-minute break. In practice, some workers, like Amy, waive this so long as they maintain sufficient hours to maximize their earnings. Unlike restaurant servers, hotel housekeepers rarely receive tips. Amy appreciates the occasional monetary gift she finds on the bed pillow placed there by departing guests. She is thankful for American guests. They are the best tippers by far.

On Friday 07 April 2017, as Amy polishes a bathroom mirror

in a V.I.P. suite, she pauses to examine her reflection. She looks older than her 37 years.

She remembers growing up in Red Rapids Reserve. As Amy Cool, she was a skilled dancer and eagerly participated in the annual pow-wow in the women's Jingle Dress Dance. Amy prepared for each event many months in advance. Her jingle dress was made of velvet and adorned with 700 jingles of shiny metal. The Jingle Dress Dance was always colourful and energetic, requiring a fast drum beat and fancy footwork. Amy's eyes water as she reminisces about her childhood. She shuts her eyes to visualize it in her mind – the white plume she wore in her hair and the red-and-green tail fan she waved. Her dress was a bright flash of multi-coloured appliqué designs.

At 17 she earned her Ontario Secondary School Diploma (OSSD) thanks to the online courses available at the reserve school. Afterwards, she obtained her Canada Social Insurance Card, her Indian Status Card (Certificate of Indian Status) and prepared for adulthood. She married Paul Trapper. She had known Paul all her life. He was humorous and fun-loving and was a skilled hunter. She gave birth to Mark and Dorinda within two years. Life took a turn, not a sudden turn, but a slow turn. Paul fell afoul of demon whisky. Whisky made him lethargic and sapped his motivation to work. By the time Amy turned 25, Paul's income from hunting and guiding had dried up. As a result, the family needed an alternative source of income. Prompted by the urgency of the situation, Amy availed of the reserve's services to search for jobs online. She succeeded in obtaining employment off the reserve. Thereupon, she made the difficult, but necessary, decision to leave her children under the care of her mother, Kokum Cool, and her 15-year-old sister, 'Wild' Rose Cool. Amy left the reserve and started work in a hotel in Niagara Falls. Thereupon, she commenced her weekly practice of mailing postal money orders home to the family.

Amy shakes her head and comes back to the present. She rushes to make up for the time spent day-dreaming. She completes the checklist of tasks. Finally, she restocks the mini-bar and concludes her duties in the suite.

Later, during her 15-minute break, Amy checks her cell phone for missed calls. At 4:11pm she notices that Rose had called her. Rose seldom phones her. Amy considers that it must be important. She hopes that it is not bad news. She returns the call. Rose picks up. Amy's intuition is correct. Rose quickly relates to her that Dorinda had recently come to Toronto and was staying with her. She gives a brief summary of events. Sadly, the events conclude in tragedy. Dorinda went missing on 04 April and the police are investigating her disappearance.

After concluding the phone call, Amy sits in silence. She contemplates what she must do in light of this shocking news. She comes to a decision. Amy resolves to return home to Red Rapids. If only there was some way to replace her weekly financial remittances to her family on the reserve – money sorely needed. She phones Rose to advise her of her decision.

Rose answers the phone. She sees that the call is from Amy. It is less than 10 minutes since the previous call. She guesses that it is important. "Amy? What is it?"

"I have come to a decision."

"Oh. And what is it?" Rose senses the concern in her older sister's voice.

"I must go back to Red Rapids. I must go right away. The family needs me at this time."

Rose is supportive. "I understand. Is there anything..."

Amy interrupts. "Yes, Rose. The only thing that is holding me back is the money I send home. We need that money. And if I return to the reserve, what then?"

Rose offers to help financially. "Sis, let me look after that."

"Oh, Rose, would you?" Amy is thankful, and yet, surprised.

"Amy, I know that I have been neglectful up to now, with Jeff and the family and all." 'Wild' Rose, who never sent a penny home, promises to take over that responsibility. "But now, it is different. You can rely on me. How much should I send?" Undoubtedly, she feels guilty for failing to protect Dorinda while she was under her wing in Toronto.

"Try to send $100 every week. Can you manage that?"

"$100 a week? Consider it done as of today."

They conclude the phone call. Amy hopes that Rose will follow through on her commitment. So putting her faith in her 'baby sister', Amy goes to the hotel's personnel office and tenders her notice to quit.

On Monday 17 April 2017, Amy Trapper looks out the window of the bus from Sudbury to Elliot Lake. She recognizes the truck-inspection station at the Serpent River intersection of Highway 17 (Trans-Canada) and Highway 108. The bus slows and turns right off the Trans-Canada Highway and proceeds north on Highway 108 to Elliot Lake. As the bus rounds the corner and picks up speed, she identifies the familiar *Gas and Hot Food* store on her left. It is a solitary building on an otherwise empty highway. The road sign displays 'Elliot Lake 30'. She checks the time on her cell phone. It is 8:10pm – 20 minutes to Elliot Lake. She glances at the familiar roadside aspens that crowd the conifers in this region. It is beginning to look like home. "Home", she thinks aloud. But is it 'home' without Dorinda? As the bus speeds past the vacant truck parking lot on her right, she sighs. "Where oh where are you, Dorinda Trapper?"

CHAPTER EIGHT

OKWAHO'KÓ:WA

Louis David Riel surrendered to Canadian forces after the Battle of Batoche on 15 May 1885. He was hanged for treason on 16 November 1885 at the North-West Mounted Police barracks in Regina. Following the failed rebellion, a small group of his followers formed a secret society, 'The Hand', and vowed to continue to fight for the rights of indigenous peoples. The Saskatchewan Métis land grants were honoured by the government in 1887. This turned out to be a short-lived success. The Métis people (who have a mixed heritage of European and First Nations) were increasingly forced to live on undesirable land or in the shadow of Indian reserves as they did not have treaty status.

The Hand instituted a policy of manipulation, in which members infiltrated native and non-native organizations. Active members secretly operated under the banners of these entities. They formed two operating wings, the 'Black Hand' and the 'White Hand'. Today, the Black Hand is still active. Its members confront non-native incursions into native lands and are active in protests and acts of civil disobedience to defend their rights. Some members are not averse to violence and sabotage as a medium of protest. And where an unfair law is encountered, they advocate a duty to break that law.

Rather than employing aggressive confrontation, the White Hand operates as a beneficial component within non-native institutions. Today, members seek education as a means to assume positions of influence in society, in business and in politics. Members of the White Hand are active in law practices; they represent electoral constituencies as MPs (Members of Parliament), MPPs (Members of Provincial Parliament) and MLAs (Members of Legislative Assemblies); they sit on governing boards of industry and commerce. They promote and strengthen the entities they serve while working to protect and support native rights. They address infringements of these rights and tender workable resolutions.

Okwaho'kó:wa considers himself to be a true disciple of Louis Riel. He alternates with ease from Black Hand to White Hand – from intimidating agitation to diplomatic lobbying. He is in constant touch with the member cells of the society. He maintains a nationwide network, discipline, and a sense of order and unified purpose to their mission.

On Tuesday 15 November 2011, Okwaho learns from Peggy Echum, his Black Hand contact on Cornwall Island, that one U.S. agent is causing them grief. He is a troublesome investigator who operates outside official channels and uses questionable tactics. He crosses and re-crosses the international border with impunity, interfering with the local band's conduct of commerce (cross-border smuggling). He is attached to Homeland Security Investigation division. The band could report him to HSI for his unorthodox behaviour and have him censured or even removed from service. But this course of action is imprudent. It could draw excessive attention to their activities and, hence, result in a more intense U.S./Canadian investigation of their activities.

On the following day, Okwaho meets with Peggy Echum in *Tim Hortons* at Brookdale Avenue & Vincent Massey Drive in Cornwall. Peggy is dressed in a black tee-shirt and jeans. She looks about 16. He wonders how she got here. He did not see her drive into the parking lot. Notwithstanding her young age, Peggy speaks with a great deal of self-assurance. She appears to be well-informed on the commercial activities of the reserve. After the initial introduction, Okwaho asks, "You want me to deal with a thorn in your side? So, what do you expect of me? Make an anonymous protest to Homeland Security?"

"Just get him off our backs."

"I cannot counsel anything extreme. And don't expect me to have him knocked off. That's out of the question. So, tell me, what's his name? And I will see what can be done."

"Jack Doyle."

"Jack Doyle? Oh, I know Jack Doyle. He is an anti-First-Nations individual who targets us exclusively and relentlessly. Upon my word, he needs to meet his comeuppance. Leave it with me. I'll get in touch with you later."

On 08 December 2011, Peggy contacts Okwaho by phone. "Okwaho," she says. "Have you arranged anything yet for our mutual friend?"

"Yes. A lesson is in place. We need an opportunity to deliver it."

"Well, hold off. We need 'the friend' to do us a favour."

"Really?"

"We have a complaint against another party. If we can manipulate 'Mutual Friend' to address the complaint and move against the offending third party, the outcome will be to our benefit."

"When?"

"Tomorrow. That's when we make our presentation. Our agent has the details. His operative name is 'Tom'."

"I am familiar with the agent. Thanks. I'll check with Tom. I have the means to contact him."

On Friday 09 December 2011, Okwaho executes Jack Doyle's 'lesson'. The lesson ought to serve as a warning that, notwithstanding his position, he is not beyond the reach of 'the troublesome Indian'. To execute the lesson, Jack is lured to a 'meeting' where Okwaho marks his forehead with a branding iron. Unfortunately, the lesson emboldens Jack Doyle to greater resolve and determination in targeting First Nations communities in his investigations. Their ploy, to use Jack Doyle to knock the encroaching Mexicans down a notch, is a victory. The Hamilton drug-bust is executed successfully. But it does nothing to endear Jack Doyle to the First Nations.

Seven years later, in 2018, Okwaho'kó:wa continues to work in the interests of indigenous people. The attitudes of the previous centuries' policy of 'Civilizing Mission' is so deeply ingrained that well-meaning non-native Canadians still believe that westernization is the most effective way to improve conditions on reserves. Whereas, in actual fact, the poor conditions on reserves are the result of these very policies and practices that were initially enforced to 'civilize' the native peoples. Notwithstanding, the notion persists that indigenous people must break from their old culture as a prerequisite to socio-economic progress. The result, when implemented, is to alter their collective psychology and mental attitude, philosophy and way of life. The physical poverty, so prevalent in many native communities, is the direct result of the cultural poverty inflicted upon them. The way forward is to restore indigenous culture, and respect native rights, and have these rights recognized and respected by the Canadian government. But this in itself is not enough. It is perilous to ignore the capitalist consumer society of the outside world. Hence, native communities need to bridge both worlds in a delicate balance.

Okwaho, notwithstanding his extreme nationalism, holds a Bachelor of Arts degree in economics from McMaster University. He works within the Secretariat of the Assembly of First Nations in lobbying MPs and Cabinet ministers on economic matters. He currently carries a Certificate of Indian Status card identifying him as 'Mohawk – Six Nations of the Grand River'. To circumvent the requirement of a surname, and to comply with his birth registration, his legal name is rendered as 'Okwaho'kó:wa, Okwaho'.

*   *   *   *   *

Thursday 08 November 2018. Okwaho enters the corporate offices of Brax Mining in Sault Ste. Marie. Sam Caldwell, the Senior Projects Manager, is expecting a representative of the

Assembly of First Nations. The meeting is swift and to the point. Brax is shutting down its Gold Mine operation near Sultan, Ontario. They are obliged, by law, to clear the site to permit natural regeneration of the forest. Okwaho offers to purchase the site's modular buildings for a nominal price of $10. For Brax, this is a good deal. The alternative is to dismantle the modules and attempt to resell them. Transporting and storing the modular buildings is an expensive and cumbersome exercise that the company would rather avoid. Okwaho proposes that the Cree First Nations Band of Red Rapids will undertake the work of clearing the site, including dismantling and removing the modular buildings. Okwaho promises to have the agreement signed by the band and delivered back to the corporate office with payment by Monday 12 November. When executed, the agreement is expected to render a favourable outcome to all parties.

Friday 09 November 2018. Okwaho arrives early at the Red Rapids Reserve. He requests an immediate meeting with the elders to address the band's recent request for emergency funds from the federal government. Lobbying the government is a skill in which Okwaho excels. But he is also highly skilled in getting quick results from unexpected sources. He had previously lobbied against the Brax mining operation at Sultan, but now he is quite content to do business with them for a win-win outcome.

Okwaho questions the hastily-convened meeting of elders to fully explain the basis for their recent request for emergency funding. To substantiate such a request, he requires supporting evidence that demonstrates a justification for emergency funding. The elders describe the conditions of the Cool family's uninhabitable abode and the fire-gutted house alongside. Okwaho insists on conducting an on-site inspection. In total, he identifies four houses most in need of replacement – three in the 'B' section and one in the 'A' section of the reserve. Next, he points out to the elders that, in successfully lobbying for funds, he practices discrimination. It is frequently prudent to conserve a 'favour' in the short term for a more pressing need in the future. Pressing for government assistance at this time is not the best way forward. The procedures can be exhausting and frustrating. Where funds are approved and released, they pass through bureaucratic red tape and legal opinions at both ends – the Canadian government and the band council. This is further aggravated by petty disputes within the reserve and the band's inability to exercise prudent judgement in bidding for contracts. And then there is the question of the integrity of the contractor. In the end, the actual value of the goods and services received may amount to 50% of the funds originally allocated.

The elders object to Okwaho's harsh judgment of them. They protest. The chief exclaims defensively, "Are you suggesting that we are unable to manage our finances?"

One elder remarks to the chief, "I think Okwaho is implying that the allocation of funds is not always carried out fairly."

"Or efficiently," the second elder comments.

The chief stares at Okwaho while addressing the two elders. "Perhaps the 'Wolf' is suggesting misappropriation of funds for personal gain?" He directs his next comment to Okwaho. "I can assure you that your unfair generalization does not apply to the judicious administration of the Red Rapids Reserve. Corruption may occur elsewhere, but not here." The chief slaps the table to emphasize his point. The passion of his denial reinforces Okwaho's suspicions.

Okwaho's dark stare silences them. When he has regained their attention, he informs them, "Be that as it may, but there is a better way to proceed. For $10, we can acquire four modular buildings, built and ready for occupation within one week. However, the band is required to fulfill conditions."

This last comment arrests their attention. Four buildings ready for occupation within a week for a mere $10 is an unexpected windfall. This is too good to pass up. They have sufficient respect for Okwaho that they agree to follow his instructions. Immediately, and in Okwaho's presence, they select and clear four sites in preparation for the new buildings. Okwaho makes it clear that this must be executed today for his inspection and approval. This is to ensure against any subsequent dispute or delay in allocating the sites.

Under Okwaho's direction, they assemble all able-bodied men and women and instruct them to travel by water to the Brax mining site where they will dismantle the site's modular buildings, clear the site, and transport the dismantled buildings back to the reserve by water and portage. The buildings will be easily reassembled on the reserve. The entire operation should take five days to complete.

Normally, the band would not be able to execute a project of this nature so expeditiously. Members would find a reason to delay until the following year – the frost is coming, the water might freeze, wait for the ice road, and multiple other excuses to procrastinate. But Okwaho inspires the elders. And the entire band is motivated to accomplish the project. They view the undertaking as the labour of their own hands, a project to be proud of. They get down to following Okwaho's instructions.

Okwaho leaves the reserve later that day. Wet snow begins to fall. Okwaho's choice of floatplane is fitted with Full Lotus Floats – it can land on water or snow or solid ground. Thus, the approach of winter is no deterrent for him. According to weather predictions, the lakes are not expected to freeze for another two weeks, thus permitting sufficient time for the Red Rapids Reserve to accomplish their mission. As the departing floatplane gains altitude, he looks down at the reserve diminishing in size. He sighs in relief. The signed agreement and $10 for Brax Mining are safely in his possession for delivery on Monday.

The building project is accomplished without a hitch. Four new houses are constructed and inhabited before the onslaught of winter. Okwaho later flies over the abandoned Brax mining site and is satisfied that the site has been adequately cleared for natural regeneration by the boreal forest.

On Thursday 03 January 2019 Okwaho arrives at the Red Rapids Reserve for a follow-up visit. The floatplane lands successfully on the snow at the shoreline of Red Fox Lake, thanks to the Full Lotus Floats. He walks the short distance on the trampled pathway of snow to the Red Rapids Reserve. He desires to see if the families are accommodated comfortably in their new homes – at least, that is the reason he tenders. His true purpose is to get an understanding of the circumstances that gave rise to the request for emergency funding. He understands that a fire destroyed a house. Was it an accident? Or was it due to negligence? Or is the reserve suffering from a social malaise?

The chief is expecting him and deduces from the appearance of the floatplane that it heralds the arrival of Okwaho. The chief greets him and escorts Okwaho on a tour of the reserve. Okwaho is pleased with the chief's initiative in redefining the new buildings. What was once the mining company's cafeteria is now the new schoolhouse situated in the 'A' section. The previous one-room schoolhouse was too small to accommodate the reserve's entire student population. In the past, two buildings were utilized – one in the 'A' section for all grades and one in the 'B' section for primary grades. Today, the 'A' section boasts a fine two-room schoolhouse that accommodates the entire body of students. In summer, a school-boat ferries the pupils from the 'B' section daily. Today, of course, they walk to school across the frozen river. The two previous schoolhouses now accommodate two families, one in each section of the reserve. As a result of the chief's good judgment, the four new modular buildings, indirectly, provide five new homes for the reserve. Okwaho congratulates him on his wise leadership.

The Cool-Trapper clan reconfigures their families over three buildings. Six remain in the old house, down from 12. Jim Cool and Mark Trapper occupy the smallest house. Kokum

Cool resides in the third house with three of her grandchildren and Amy Trapper. Jim and Mark make an efficient trapper team. They store their traps and hunting gear where they live. Mark earned sufficient money during the summer season that he recently obtained a new hunting rifle. Previously, he and Uncle Jim shared the same gun. There is less income in the winter. Whereas they act as guides for non-native hunters in the summer, only a few fishermen arrive in winter for ice-fishing – an activity that does not require a hunter-guide. Come summer, he expects to be employed profitably once more. And next year, he hopes to obtain a snowmobile to replace the one destroyed in the fire.

Okwaho is introduced to the residents of the third building, the one that replaced the house destroyed by fire. He meets Kokum Cool, Amy Trapper and five-year-old Jeff Cool. Rose Cool, the fourth member and mother to Jeff, is absent – currently working in Toronto. The chief points out the excellent flat-topped wood stove in the home. It came with the buildings. The chimney-pipe was already in place in the structure at the mine and was easily reinstalled upon reconstruction on the reserve. And that is not the only item of importance. When the tribe cleared the mine site, they scavenged everything of value. Everyone who contributed to the effort obtained some prized item. Transporting the stove presented a particular challenge. It could not be loaded onto a canoe for fear of damaging it – resulting in the loss of both canoe and stove. Fortunately, there were sufficient bits and pieces of debris in the mining site to fashion a raft. They floated and dragged the stove the entire distance back to the reserve on a raft-sled, utilizing sticks as rollers on occasion. And quite a lot of grunt work too. Thanks to Okwaho's deal with Brax Mining, and the band's own labour, the Red Rapids Reserve has benefited greatly.

Okwaho looks for an excuse to delay in the Trapper home. He is afforded the opportunity when Amy invites him to partake of herbal tea. He accepts. Ever since a boil-water advisory was introduced in 2007, flavoured tea is a popular way to consume drinking-water. Minutes later, Okwaho is drinking a mug of *kâkikêpakwa* tea with Amy Trapper. Mark Trapper and Kokum Cool are also present.

Okwaho addresses Amy. "So, tell me about the fire, Amy – the one that destroyed your home."

"I can't tell you anything. I was not here at the time."

"No? Why not?"

"I was working in Niagara Falls at the time of the fire. Had I been here, it would not have happened. Had I been here, a lot of things would not have happened." She turns to her son. "Mark, you were here at the time. Can you tell the man about the fire?"

Mark is hesitant to speak. "There was a fire. I don't remember anything. Just, that there was a fire." With that, Mark exits the house.

Amy shouts after him. "Mark! Where are you going? Are you not going to stay?"

He responds with a lame excuse. "The pelts. I need to scrape the skins and..." Mark continues on his way without finishing the sentence.

Amy looks at Okwaho. "Mark blames himself for the fire that destroyed the house. His father, Paul Trapper, perished in the fire that day. His charred body was later recovered from the burned-down house. I don't know if Mark truly has no recollection, or if he is too ashamed to remember. It appears that he and his friends were smoking and sniffing gas where Paul had stored gasoline."

Okwaho is disturbed by this admission. "In the house? Gasoline stored inside a house with people smoking?"

Amy sighs in acceptance. Irresponsible behaviour is common here, even when it is prohibited. "That's right. I suspect that Paul was hiding the gasoline. Well, for whatever reason, the house went up in flames when the gasoline ignited."

Okwaho pictures the scene. Paul Trapper stored gasoline in the house. That was reckless and dangerous. He was likely concealing stolen gasoline.

Amy continues. "Kokum was next door at the time. Perhaps she can tell you about the fire."

Kokum struggles to follow the conversation. She speaks to Amy in Cree. Amy relays to Okwaho. "Kokum says that she was sitting in her house. She saw the red glow of the fire through her window. That's all she can tell you." Kokum speaks again. Amy translates. "She says that it is a pity Dorinda is not here. She could tell you a lot." Amy's voice drops to a whisper.

"Dorinda? So where is Dorinda? Could I speak to her?"

"Dorinda is my daughter. She's not here anymore. She left the reserve soon after the fire. The fire was in June 2016. Dorinda left by the ice road in February 2017. She arrived in Toronto and stayed with Rose – her aunt, Rose Cool. Then she disappeared. Rose reported it to the police. But the police..." Amy's voice trails off.

Okwaho places his mug on the table. He leans forward in his chair. He looks at Amy's face and sees the anguish. This news disturbs him. He was not expecting it. But it also arrests his attention. Okwaho has a mission to improve the lives of indigenous people. At the top of his agenda is the 'Missing and Murdered Indigenous Women (MMIW) Epidemic' that affects indigenous peoples, including First Nations, Inuit and Métis (FNIM). A large number of young underage girls disappear each year from reserves. They are regarded as 'runaways'. Where do they disappear to? Perhaps they disappear among the nameless street people. Okwaho fears that many are enslaved by sex traffickers and eventually killed. Police investigations seldom meet with success, largely because First Nation runaways are difficult to identify and locate. In Okwaho's opinion, this is exacerbated by the police's failure to treat indigenous runaways with due seriousness. Within a few seconds, Okwaho's visit to the Red Rapids Reserve has taken on a new urgency. If he understands the situation correctly, the disappearance of Dorinda Trapper warrants his committed attention.

"Amy," he says gently. "Tell me about Dorinda. Tell me all you can. I will drop everything and adopt this as my primary mission – to find your lost girl."

Amy looks up at him. "Find Dorinda? You can do that? How, if the police can't?"

"I have resources and contacts in high places. I can press them for help. Now, I need information – one piece at a time."

"If it helps."

Okwaho delays his departure from the reserve by one day. He questions Amy, Kokum, Mark and members of the reserve. He establishes the sequence of events leading up to Dorinda's trek to Elliot Lake.

Dorinda Trapper, age 15, left the reserve on 01 February 2017. Mark was the last to see her. He observed her walking toward the outskirts of Elliot Lake on the following day about an hour before noon. She was on her way to Toronto, to her aunt, Rose Cool. She intended to find work there and send money home to the family.

Armed with this information, Okwaho resolves to contact Rose Cool. He ascertains her address and phone number from Amy. Then, at noon on Friday 04 January, Okwaho departs from the Red Rapids Reserve. The floatplane bumps over the snow, struggling to gain speed, and eventually rises off the ground. Once airborne, it makes rapid progress. He is in Elliot Lake a half-hour later and arrives at Sudbury Airport

(YSB) in time to catch a Porter Dash 8-400 flight to Toronto Island at 4:30pm. He arrives at Billy Bishop Toronto City Airport (YTZ) at 5:30pm.

At 6:30pm, Okwaho checks into the *Bond Place Hotel* at 65 Dundas Street East, Toronto. The hotel is a 15-minute walk from 435 Jarvis Street. Okwaho enters the dining room and orders dinner. While waiting, he phones Rose Cool.

Rose answers the call. "Yes."

"Hello. Is this Rose Cool?"

"Ah, you must be Okwaho."

"Correct. I arrived from Red Rapids. I'm here in Toronto as we speak."

"I was expecting to hear from you. My sister, Amy, told me about you. You are coming to see me, I understand. And you have questions about Dorinda. That is what she told me."

"That is correct. Could we meet, say, at 7:30? I'm just a short walk from your place on Jarvis."

"No. That won't work. How about 10:00 tomorrow morning at the *Tim Hortons* at Jarvis & Carlton – southwest corner?"

"Okay. That will work. I don't believe we will have any difficulty identifying each other, being both First Nations."

"Really? Not like the other Indians wandering the streets of

Cabbage Town? Anyway, I'll be wearing a red parka and dark glasses. Oh, and I may not be alone."

"That's okay. And I'll be wearing a leather broad-brimmed hat and buckskin jacket. See you tomorrow."

On Saturday 05 January 2019, Okwaho has no difficulty in meeting up with Rose. She is dressed, as she promised, in a red parka and dark glasses. Her parka is flung open to reveal a navy-blue sweater over jeans. Notwithstanding the wintry weather, she is wearing high-heeled shoes. The Toronto sidewalks are clear of snow, so walking is not a problem, but high-heeled shoes on a wintry morning? Seated beside her is another older woman dressed in a fake leather cream-coloured winter coat with matching fake-fur collar. The coat is unfastened, revealing an orange-coloured sparkling top with a low-cut neckline and a black leather short tight skirt. She too is wearing black high-heeled shoes.

Rose looks at Okwaho as he approaches. "I like your hat. So you are Okwaho. And this here is my friend, Monique".

Okwaho is dressed in his signature leather hat. The brim is pulled down to his eyes as if he needs to shade his eyes from the sun. He is wearing his buckskin jacket over blue jeans and ornately beaded mukluks. "Hello, Rose. Hello, Monique."

"Sit down, handsome. And no, you don't look like any of the other Indians around here."

Okwaho gets down to business. Rose explains that Monique was the last to have seen 'Sugar', Dorinda's street name.

Monique describes the shopping spree in the *Eaton Centre* on Tuesday 04 April 2017. No, she did not recognize the woman in Sugar's company. She never saw her before or since. The woman companion looked affluent.

When Monique finishes her report, Rose continues to narrate additional information. When Dorinda failed to return home, she filed a Missing Persons Report with Toronto Police 51 Division on 06 April 2017.

After the meeting with Rose and Monique, Okwaho takes a 15-minute TTC ride to 51 Division for an update on the investigation. The police inform him that they conducted a thorough investigation but were unable to locate Dorinda. One year and nine months have elapsed and still no leads. It does not look promising that the investigation will meet with success.

It is close to noon. Okwaho walks back to his hotel. He thinks while he walks for 25 minutes. Upon reaching the *Bond Place Hotel,* he realizes that it is only a further two-minute walk to the Dundas entrance of the *Eaton Centre*. He makes his way to the *Tim Hortons*. He lingers over a coffee and thinks. He finishes his coffee and walks through the *Eaton Centre*. This is where Dorinda was last sighted. Okwaho learns nothing new from his walkabout. At this point, all he knows is that Dorinda was last seen in the presence of an affluent woman in the *Eaton Centre*. And she was observed spending a lot of money. How does this add up to a disappearance?

Okwaho is stymied. If he is to succeed in finding Dorinda

Trapper, he needs to engage the services of an expert –
someone skilled in tracing and locating people. He resolves to
contact the most capable person he can think of.

CHAPTER NINE

JACK DOYLE, PRIVATE INVESTIGATOR

JACK DOYLE INVESTIGATOR

Find Jack Doyle

And he finds the person you're looking for

On Wednesday 09 January 2019, Jack Doyle is seated at his desk in 101B, 1660 North Service Road East in Oakville. It is a good location for a private investigator – low-key and conveniently located. The parking lot has ample free parking (a rarity today) and he is located at the entrance ramp to the QEW/403. The QEW (Queen Elizabeth Way) links Toronto to the U.S. border at Niagara Falls and Buffalo; Highway 403 connects to southwestern Ontario. Unit 101B is located on the upper floor at the rear of a two-story building. This also suits him. He considers a ground-floor location with street frontage to be ostentatious, not 'private' enough for a private investigator.

Yes, Unit 101B is ideal. It affords him a business address and mailbox. In the interests of privacy, his current office has no identifying name other than 'Unit 101B' and is tucked behind the 'Electrical and Telephone Room'. For anyone arriving at the first-floor offices, Jack's unit is not visible from the top of the stairs. Unit 101B is around the corner of an apparent dead-end where the corridor bends to avoid the Electrical and

Telephone Room. Access to the kitchenette/lunchroom and washrooms is farther along the corridor, a short distance past Jack's office. There is no walk-in traffic. In the course of a day, only three people walk past his office – the insurance broker from Unit 101C and the Marriage Counsellor and her assistant from Unit 101D. Although the Electrical Room blocks Jack's view of the stairs, his ears are alert to activity. His office is situated over the stairwell. Hence, Jack hears everyone who enters the building from the moment the front door opens to the footsteps ascending the stairs.

In keeping with his low-key appearance, Jack dresses in a modest navy-blue jacket over grey pants with a white shirt and burgundy tie. His hair has receded to the point that he now admits to himself that he is bald. Once, he wore a baseball cap to conceal his receding hairline. Or was it to conceal the mark on his forehead? Regardless, he has gotten to like the mark on his forehead – a striking snake. People regard it as a cool tattoo.

He idly looks out his window at the westbound traffic where the 403 merges with the QEW. He peers once more at the business card in his hand. He is pleased with the new slogan after his name – 'Find Jack Doyle and he finds the person you're looking for'. After all, this is what he specializes in – skip tracing. Since leaving HSI (Homeland Security Investigations) on 31 August 2018, Jack has embarked on a new business. Actually, it is his old business, only now he is self-employed, beholden to no one, and no longer deals with risky operations. He smiles as he considers what possible dangers he risks in locating 'deadbeat dads'.

The wet parking lot is only half full. There was a light snowfall overnight, but at +3°C it has already melted on the blacktop surface of the parking lot. He sees a *Toyota Camry* arrive at the lot. He immediately recognizes it as a rental car from the licence plate frame. It drives slowly through the parking lot and past his unit. Perhaps the driver is searching for a specific unit number or a suitable parking spot. Disinterested, Jack checks his watch. It is 10:00am. He walks to the shared kitchenette and pours himself a coffee. Thereupon, he strolls leisurely back to his office. Upon entering, he deliberately leaves his door ajar. The door self-locks when closed – the normal and prudent state to ensure privacy. But the office is too hot for Jack's comfort. He occasionally leaves his door ajar for short periods to improve the air circulation. And this is one such occasion.

Jack is now 39 years old. His separation package from HSI was generous. He is not short of money and his frugal lifestyle puts little financial demands on him. Mary Liz is employed as a dental assistant at South Oakville Shopping Centre. Their combined income ensures them a secure, comfortable life. He briefly calls to mind the accident he suffered at Cornwall Island in an encounter with the Black Hand Warriors. It was the turning point that convinced him to change his life. Today, he sits comfortably with his feet up on his desk and lifts his coffee cup to his lips in a toast. Never again will Jack Doyle encounter a Mohawk or have any future dealings with Indians. They were never anything but trouble.

Just then, a man enters Jack Doyle's office. Jack is taken aback. The newcomer appears stealthily without forewarning.

Jack had neglected to shut his office door. And he had not heard the sound of anyone ascending the stairs and approaching his unit. Jack looks up in surprise. It is an Indian, And not just any Indian – it is a Mohawk. And not just any Mohawk – it is the last person Jack expects to see, or **wants** to see.

"Okwaho'kó:wa!" Jack exclaims in surprise. His cup tips over in his hand. Fortunately, it is empty.

"Onyare!" The man looks at Jack's forehead as if to confirm his remark.

Jack is in no doubt. Okwaho is dressed in his distinctive garb, from his leather hat, to his buckskin jacket and jeans, to his feet. No, his feet are different. Instead of hand-stitched moccasins, Okwaho is wearing beaded mukluks.

Okwaho speaks again. "The last time I was in your office, you ordered me to sit down. Do you remember?" And with that, he sits in the guest chair uninvited.

Jack has yet to recover from his surprise."Why are you here? Is there no end to the trouble you inflict?"

"Trouble? I frequently **bring** trouble, but I seldom **cause** it. You, on the other hand..." Okwaho waves his hand in the air and turns his head. Then he continues. "But not today. I bring you no grief today. This time, I need your help."

Jack, by now, is over the shock of seeing the 'troublesome Indian'. He stands up and leans on his desk. "Well, you've come to the wrong place. I'd be much obliged if you leave."

Okwaho nudges the brim of his hat up a fraction to look into Jack's face. He speaks in his quiet commanding voice. "Dorinda Trapper, age 15, disappeared on Tuesday 04 April 2017. She was never located." Okwaho studies Jack's face for a reaction. There is none, but neither is there a follow-up to his command to depart. Okwaho continues. "I see your business card states that if I find Jack Doyle, he finds the person I'm looking for. Well, I've found Jack Doyle." Okwaho hesitates. Jack remains standing, staring at him in a hostile manner. Okwaho takes advantage of the pause and continues to speak. "On 04 April 2017, Dorinda Trapper was last seen at noon in the *Eaton Centre*. She had previously run away from home at the Red Rapids Reserve on 03 February 2017." He pauses to gauge Jack's reaction. Jack raises an eyebrow but remains silent. Okwaho poses the expected question. "Are you interested?"

"You are asking me to conduct a skip search?"

"Yes."

"Why not go to the police?"

"The police came up empty-handed. Twenty-one months have elapsed since her disappearance."

"Do you expect to find her?"

"Not without expert help."

"Indeed."

"So? Will you help me?"

Jack Doyle remains on his feet. He stares down at Okwaho seated before him. "Help you, Okwaho? I'm afraid not."

After a moment's tense silence, Okwaho rises from the chair and departs from Jack's office. He runs down the stairs, but before he reaches the exit door he hears Jack shout from his office. "How do I get to Red Rapids Reserve?" Okwaho stops midstride and slowly re-ascends the stairs back to Jack's office.

Jack repeats the question. "How do I get to Red Rapids Reserve? You said that the missing girl is from Red Rapids. So, how do I get to Red Rapids?"

"What? You are taking the assignment?"

"Understand this, you troublesome Indian, whether I take the assignment or not, I will not help you in any way. As far as I am concerned, you can be damned. But the Trapper family – now that's different." Jack considers the significance of this task. The number of missing and murdered indigenous women has reached epidemic levels. Indigenous women and girls account for 16% of all female homicides, yet, they constitute only 4% of the female population.

Okwaho presses Jack to clarify. "So, you are taking the assignment?"

"Not so fast," Jack answers. "First I need to meet with the Trapper family. Then I'll decide."

Okwaho is unsure if Jack is serious. "The Trapper family in Red Rapids Reserve?"

By way of answer, Jack asks, "If we leave now, will we get there by tonight?"

"Do you mean to go right now?" Then, to test the sincerity of Jack's intent, Okwaho queries him. "And how much is this going to cost?"

Having made his decision, Jack is impatient to proceed. "Don't worry. I'll bill you later. First off, I need to conduct the initial consultation. Now, how do we get to Red Rapids from here?"

"I am familiar with getting to Red Rapids. Let's see..." Okwaho taps the Air Canada app on his cell phone as he speaks. "There is an Air Canada flight from Pearson to Sudbury at 12:30pm. It arrives at 1:45pm. Then, by car to Elliot Lake. If the roads are clear, we reach Elliot Lake, say, by 4:00pm. Charter a floatplane that can land on ice or snow... We could arrive in Red Rapids by 5:00pm. The reserve is 47° north, so we have daylight until 5:25pm, and usable daylight/twilight until 6:40pm. Yes, it's feasible."

Jack walks towards the door and exclaims, "Okay, then. Let's go."

Okwaho looks at Jack and laughs. "Dressed, like that, you're not."

Jack is offended by the remark. "What's wrong with how I'm dressed?"

"The temperature up there ranges from -11°C to -23°C, and the snow is over five feet deep. You'll need to pack heavy winter clothes."

Jack Doyle analyzes his options. "You are right. I need to change and pack."

Okwaho interrupts. "Snake-man, I know where you live. Drive to Huron Park in Mississauga, and pack an overnight bag."

Once again, Jack is taken aback. He remembers the note he found on his windshield on the day he left Buffalo. He is unnerved by this stealthy Indian who knows too much about his personal life. Jack utters defensively, "You know where I live?"

Okwaho responds calmly, "The wolf knows the snake's lair."

Jack swallows. He recovers quickly. "Okay. Huron Park is on the way to the airport. I'll grab a change of clothes. You can drive us both from there. And you can drop off your rental car at the airport."

"What makes you think I have a rental car?"

Jack chuckles at getting one up on the 'Wolf'. "I'm an

investigator. I saw a *Camry* enter the parking lot with a rental sticker... Oh, never mind." Jack grabs his laptop and they both exit the building.

*   *   *   *   *

Wednesday 09 January 2019, 12:45pm, Jack and Okwaho are sitting side by side on a De Havilland Dash 8-300 operated by Air Canada Express Jazz, en route to Sudbury. Okwaho reclines his seat and relaxes. Jack, on the other hand, sits erect. He opens his notebook and prepares to write. He accepts a coffee from the flight attendant and fumbles to accommodate a cup, a jotter and a pencil simultaneously.

Jack addresses his travelling companion. "Tell me, Okwaho, about the Trapper girl's disappearance. Bring me up to speed on what you know." Jack flips his tray into the open position, taking care not to spill his coffee.

Okwaho is relaxed. His hat is pulled down over his eyes. "I spoke with everyone in the Trapper family – Amy (the mother), Mark (the brother) and Kokum (the grandmother). I also spoke with the chief in the reserve. In Toronto, I spoke with her aunt, Rose, and to her friend, Monique. They were unable to give me anything helpful."

"First off, I need the following:

> a first and last name

> a last known residential address

143

> last known phone number, email
>
> date of birth
>
> recent photograph
>
> Social Insurance Number
>
> last known employment
>
> information on relatives, friends, associates

Do you have all that?"

Okwaho tilts the brim of his hat and looks askance at Jack. "Ah."

"I take that for a 'not-so-sure'. And I need to conduct a proper search:

> phone number databases
>
> credit bureau search
>
> job application information
>
> utility bills
>
> driver abstracts
>
> public databases and internet searches
>
> leasing inquiries

Personal Property Security Registration (PPSR) searches to identify a lien associated with an individual, or collateral for payment of a debt

loans and bank affiliations

"Have you checked any of these – with the consent of the reserve and the parents of the missing minor?"

Okwaho grunts another "Ah."

"I see. So I am starting from scratch."

"Ah."

They reach Elliot Lake as predicted. Okwaho knows where to go. He drives his newly-rented car to the floatplane charter company and negotiates a flight to Red Rapids. Shortly after 4:30pm, they are flying over the forest. They are almost a half-hour ahead of their estimated schedule. This relieves any anxiety the pilot may have regarding the return flight to Elliot Lake. He ought to be back in base a few minutes past sundown in ample daylight.

Jack remarks to Okwaho, "One thing I neglected to do."

"What's that? Lock your door when you left?"

"I just realized how hungry I am."

"You'll eat at the reserve."

"Lord, I hope it's more than burnt bannock, wet and doughy in the centre."

"Don't worry. The reserve is scarce in many things, but not game. You'll probably eat hare."

It is a bumpy landing. The landing strip is trampled snow, flattened along the edge of the lake. Jack and Okwaho exit the floatplane. It takes off immediately to return to its base at Elliot Lake. Jack and Okwaho make their way to the reserve, towards the hotel in the 'A' section. The snow is five feet deep. And where it has drifted, it is twice that height. Jack pulls his toque further down his head until his ears are fully covered. He notices that Okwaho has lowered the inner flaps of his hat to cover his ears. Jack feels as if he is walking through an open-top tunnel. Although the snow is removed to clear a pathway, it is still deep enough to cover Jack's boots. The freezing breeze brushes his cheeks. Fortunately, the high snowbanks afford shelter from the cruel wind; otherwise, a temperature of -15°C would have hit Jack with a shocking wind-chill of -20°C.

After 10 minutes of walking and trudging, they reach the hotel at 5:15pm. By this time, Jack's cheeks are stinging red, his nose-hairs have frozen into needles, and his feet are wet from the snow that entered his boots. Jack wonders if the hotel is closed for the season. Who would come here in winter? He need not worry. The hotel is open to accommodate visiting fishermen for ice fishing. Today, Jack and Okwaho are the sole guests.

After checking into their rooms, Jack changes into dry socks, his only spare pair. His head is still cold; his nose is running. He sensibly decides to retain the toque on his head to cover his crown. They eat dinner at 6:00pm. Bannock is on the menu. So too is hare stew. But Jack opts for freshly caught lake trout.

Usable daylight wanes at 6:40pm. By the time they have completed dinner, night has fallen. The chief and two elders enter the hotel and welcome Jack to the reserve. Okwaho had forewarned them of the visit. They offer to escort them to meet Amy Trapper and her family. Jack accepts graciously. It appears that his visit is being treated with importance.

Jack bundles up for another foray through the snow. When he steps outside, he stops in astonishment and subconsciously raises his hand above his head. The clear black sky is bejewelled with stars, more than he has ever seen before. They appear so close that at first Jack feels that they are within an arm's length. They are bright enough to illuminate the landscape. It is colder since their arrival. The temperature has dropped to -18°C – too cold for the snow to enter Jack's boots. The powdery snow dislodges from his legs with each step. The party of five walks across the frozen river. The Trapper/Cool clan meets them on the other side, on the bank of the 'B' section. Okwaho conducts the introductions according to traditional protocol. Jack notes the names – Amy Trapper, Kokum Cool, Mark Trapper, Jim Cool and Jeff Cool. They are invited to Amy Trapper's house. Jack views the houses in the 'B' section. He observes them in the starlight reflecting off the snow. He wonders how any of these small houses could accommodate the entire party of 10.

Okwaho whispers to Jack. "If you are offered food, eat it. If you are offered a beverage, drink it. Do not question what it is, or make a face when you consume it. Don't worry. It will not kill you. And you may even like it. Oh – and keep your toque on."

Upon reaching Amy Trapper's house, the elders depart and return to the 'A' section. Inside, Jack is treated to food. A table is laid out like a buffet and he is invited to partake of the food. He chooses some sticks of dried meat like jerky. It tastes good, whatever it is. The scones are a variety of soda bread/flatbreads. Okay, that's good too. A teapot is whistling on the flat-topped stove. Amy pours some of the hot liquid into a mug and proffers it to Jack. The tea is unrecognizable. He drinks and struggles not to make a face. Fearing that he might lose the struggle, he speaks. "Perhaps we should get down to business."

This is an unexpected interruption. Nevertheless, it is welcomed. Amy and Mark arrange six chairs in a circle. They sit facing inwards, except five-year-old Jeff who sits on Kokum's lap. Jack addresses them. "So tell me about Dorinda. What were the events in her life before she left home? Do you know what may have prompted her to leave the reserve?"

Amy looks at Mark and signals him to speak. Mark relates the incident of the fire. "Opâpâmâw (Paul Trapper) perished in the fire that destroyed our house. This event upset Dorinda. Later, she attempted to look after the family, but she was overburdened by the task. Then on the night of 31 January 2017, or rather, the early morning 01 February, I heard the crunch of footsteps in the snow outside the house. It did not sound like a bear or any other animal – it was definitely a person. I got up to see. That is when I saw the items missing from the porch – Uncle Jim's mukluks that had been there on the previous night, and Kokum's heavy coat. Since losing everything in the fire, it was customary for us, me and Dorinda, to avail of borrowed clothes. At that point, I realized that it was Dorinda I heard outside. To be certain, I checked her bed. And yes, she was gone for sure. I dressed quickly and got Uncle Jim's hunting rifle, the one he lent to me. We know that it is reckless to wander away from the safety of the reserve on a winter's night unarmed. Well, I tracked her easily through the snow, but I kept well back and out of earshot. I decided not to confront her or restrain her. If she was leaving the reserve, how could I fault her? I determined to safeguard her until she either returned to the reserve or until she reached an inhabited region. She walked through the night and into the following day. After saving her from a wolf attack, I escorted her safely to Elliot Lake. Dorinda walked out of sight at the outskirts of the town. I never saw her ever afterwards."

When Mark finishes his account, the family members look at each other in acknowledgement. They concur. They have nothing to add. Jack is jotting notes in his notepad. He pauses. He rubs his pen on his brow in thought as he formulates a remark. Before he can utter a word, he is aware of a sudden chilling silence in the room. Everyone has their eyes on Jack, actually on his forehead where he has disturbed the position of his toque. He realizes, too late, that in rubbing his brow he has exposed the mark of the snake. Jack holds his breath, whereupon everyone looks at Okwaho – presumably for elucidation.

Okwaho tenders an explanation. "'Onyare' – 'the snake'. It is true. Jack Doyle is a 'snake-man'. Yes, he is not deserving of our hospitality; he is not worthy of our respect. Do I know Jack Doyle? Yes, more than most people. For years he has been a curse to me." Mark stands up in protest. Okwaho speaks to him with calm authority. "Mark, remain seated and hear me out." Mark yields. He defers to Okwaho, a respected elder. Okwaho continues to address the family. "Notwithstanding 'Snake-man's' faults – and Lord knows he has serious faults – he has one unrivalled attribute. He is a resolute and meticulous investigator – the best I know."

There are vocal protests from the assembled family. Jim Cool expresses, "Never in the history of the reserve have we ever welcomed a 'snake-man'. I never thought I would live to see the day…" Jim attempts to say more but is lost for words.

Mark adds, "And we fed him too – wasting our scarce food on a snake."

Okwaho brings order. "Let us talk this through." He turns to Jack. "Jack. Wait outside. We have matters to discuss in here." Jack bundles up once more. He ensures that his toque is secured on his head, low enough to protect his ears. He steps out through the porch. Outside, the temperature continues to drop. It is -20°C – too cold for Jack to endure. He arches his back against the cold. He is undecided whether to move or stand motionless. Neither option brings any relief from the bitter chill. He considers that his meeting with the Trapper family has come to an abrupt and ignominious end.

Unable to bear the cold, and accepting defeat, Jack decides to jog back to the hotel. He trots to the river but, after passing the last house, he realizes that he is lost. Did he miss the river, or is he travelling in the wrong direction? Jack has no clue. He curses the Indians, whom he regards are so inept that they are unable to position their houses in an orderly straight line. All the houses look alike and are arranged haphazardly without conforming to any recognizable plan. He alters course. Shortly, he sees a white expanse. Taking this to be the river, he runs onto it and sinks in a snowbank. Jack is panting. He estimates that he has been running for five minutes. Is it true, he speculates, that when fatigued a person could freeze to death in 10 minutes in these conditions? Jack decides, as a last resort, to present himself at the closest house to gain shelter and beg for assistance. He readies himself to knock at the first door he reaches. Before he knocks, the door opens unexpectedly.

"Onyare, you may come back in now." Okwaho is standing in the doorway addressing him.

Jack is taken by surprise but, more than that, he is relieved. He is too numb to remove his coat. He staggers through the porch and into the house. At a glance, he sees that the food platters have been removed – no surprise. However, the steaming teakettle is still positioned on the stove. With clumsy frigid hands, and uninvited, he pours a measure of the hot liquid into a mug. Thereupon, he hugs the mug between his frozen hands until the comforting warmth permeates through to his body. Whereupon, he downs the distasteful beverage to savour its reviving heat. At this point, Jack looks at the assembled family. They regard him critically but acknowledge that a 'snake-man' cannot be expected to behave with decorum. They look at him in silence. Jack recovers his sense of propriety. He returns to the porch and removes his coat. He checks that his toque is correctly positioned on his head to cover the mark of Onyare. Okwaho gestures to him to be seated. Jack complies.

Amy breaks the silence. "Mr 'Snake-man', we have come to a decision – **my** decision. If I must deal with the devil to get results, then so be it."

Jack surveys the assembly. Everyone nods. Amy's decision is accepted. Jack acknowledges Amy. "Very good."

"Now what? How do we proceed from here?"

Jack gets back into his stride. He takes charge of the meeting. "I will ask you some questions and request information. I urge you to be open with me. To hold back anything would only frustrate the investigation. It could delay it or even render it futile."

They agree to cooperate. Amy pours him a refill of tea.

Jack opens his notepad and readies himself for recording pertinent information. "Dorinda Trapper. Is that her legal name? I would like to see her birth certificate."

Mark responds. "It was burned in the fire."

Amy interrupts. "The reserve must have a copy. They need it for the band's own internal government."

"And the same goes for the Certificate of Indian Status and Social Insurance Number."

"I don't know if Dorinda carried her status card on her person. She seldom needed to present it while on the reserve. I suspect that it was also lost in the fire. However, the band's administration office would have a record, perhaps even a photocopy of it. And concerning Social Insurance, Dorinda did not have a SIN card. Why would she, unless she applied for employment or for government benefits? Birth certificate and status card are all she needs."

"So, may I see both of these? Or copies of them?"

"Why?"

"It's as you say. Birth certificate and status card are all she needs. She would be obliged to present one or the other of these in many circumstances."

"What circumstances?"

"That is part of the investigation."

"And if they are lost or destroyed, she won't have them. So, then what?"

"Both are replaceable. We don't know if she obtained a new copy of her birth certificate or if she succeeded in obtaining a replacement status card with identical data and 10-digit number. I need to see those documents."

"Well, tomorrow…"

"Why not now? Surely the chief or a reserve administrator has access. They cannot be far away. Are they not here on the reserve?"

Amy considers this request. She is unfamiliar with the practice of urgent haste that Jack demands. She turns to Mark. "Mark, go to the chief. Tell him this, and ask him to help." Mark departs from the house to request assistance from the chief.

Jack continues. "Could you give me a picture of Dorinda, one taken about the time of her departure from the reserve?"

"Dorinda's pictures were lost in the fire. There are no pictures of her anymore." Kokum speaks to Amy. Amy corrects her statement. "Kokum has a picture of her at her First Communion. She was seven at the time."

Jack nods, although a picture of a seven-year-old isn't any help. "Did she have a cell phone, iPad, laptop? Anything like that?"

"No. Nothing like that."

"Then, she did not have an email address."

"No email address. Dorinda lived on the reserve. She had no contact outside the reserve. What need would she have for anything like that? If she needed to speak to someone on the reserve, she just walked over to them."

"She never contacted anyone off the reserve? Ever?"

"No. She contacted me by phone, and I contacted her by phone. And she contacted Rose in Toronto. But she used the phone in the administration building."

"I see. Let me understand. You used your cell phone to communicate with Dorinda via the administration building on the reserve?"

"Yes. Perhaps Rose did so, as well."

Jack considers this information for a moment. Then he asks Amy, "May I see your phone?"

Amy gives her cell phone to Jack. He scrolls through her calls. They go back for two years. He pays careful attention to all activity within two months of either side of Dorinda's disappearance. He asks Amy to walk him through the list of phone calls. Amy identifies each call as Jack scrolls through them. She identifies the reserve's number and Rose's number. There are no calls from Dorinda after the day she left the reserve. Jack now focuses on the displayed numbers that Amy is **unable** to identify. There is only one. It is a missed call on 17 April 2017 at 4:48am. Jack calculates that this is 13 days after the Cree girl disappeared in Toronto. Jack notes the number, date and time. He is interested in the source of the unidentified phone call.

Jack queries Amy about the number. "Amy, did you attempt to phone the 'missed call' number?"

"Yes, I phoned. It was a wrong number."

Did he/she explain? Like, who they were? A name? Anything to identify them?"

"It was a man. I said 'hello'. Then he said 'hello'. I asked him why he had phoned me. He said 'sorry, wrong number'."

"A man. Young, old? Accent? Rude or polite? Anything unusual?"

"No. He sounded… well, neither young nor old. He was matter-of-fact. I did not notice an accent. But, he said so little. Is this important?"

"Every little thing, no matter how insignificant it may appear, could be of major importance. I will not know until I piece it all together."

Amy looks at him hopefully. "But you say that it **could** be important?"

At this point, Mark returns. The chief is with him. The chief has photocopies of Dorinda's birth certificate and status card. He tenders them to Jack. Thereupon, he takes a seat at the meeting. Mark stands behind his mother.

Jack continues questioning Amy. "Dorinda's life on the reserve was wholly taken up in the reserve. Is that correct?"

"Yes."

"Tomorrow, I will speak to her friends. Someone may be able to shed light on what she intended to do."

Amy speaks to satisfy Jack's remark. "She went to Rose in Toronto. We know that."

"Yes. I will visit Rose next. But first I need to get a complete picture of Dorinda's life here on the reserve – who she interacted with, and why. She may have expressed aspirations other than a desire to visit her Aunt Rose."

The chief speaks. "Tomorrow you will speak to everyone on the reserve. I'll see to it."

"Okay. Thanks." Jack addresses the family. "We can pick this up tomorrow. I still need more information."

Amy looks at him quizzically. "What 'more information'?"

"That depends on what I learn tomorrow."

Okwaho looks at Jack with a puzzled expression. What possible additional information could there be on Dorinda Trapper? Surely, we have learned all there is to know as it pertains to her disappearance. He speaks to Jack. "Are we finished here? Then, let's return to the hotel."

Everyone stands in acknowledgement. The meeting is concluded. Jack and Okwaho prepare to leave. Jack questions Okwaho. "How cold is it outside? I nearly froze to death the last time I went outside."

Jim Cool approaches Jack. "I see that your boots are not lined. And your pants are…" Jim shakes his head. He reaches into the porch and talks back to Jack. "Here, put these overalls on over your pants. And wear these mukluks in place of your boots." Jack does as he is bidden. When dressed, Jim inspects him. "Now tie up your neck with the collar up to meet your toque. And tie your cuffs to cover your gloves. And those gloves are no damned good – stick your hands into your pockets. There. Now you are set." Then he turns to Mark. "Go with this 'snake-man' to the other side and bring back my stuff when he reaches the hotel."

Jack feels stuffed and tied up. He is unable to move with any dexterity. Nevertheless, he is insulated from the cold much better than before. The chief parts from them upon reaching the 'A' section. They continue to the hotel where Jack disrobes and returns Jim Cool's belongings to Mark.

Before retiring for the night, Okwaho asks Jack, "How much more information do you expect to collect?"

Jack removes his notepad and papers from his pocket – the photocopies he received from the chief – and waves them at Okwaho and says, "I haven't penetrated the surface yet."

CHAPTER TEN

JACK DOYLE AT RED RAPIDS

Thursday 10 January 2019. Jack Doyle is eating pancakes and sausages for breakfast. He fortifies himself with a second cup of strong sweet coffee and checks that, for a second time, his toque is positioned to conceal the mark of the snake. Okwaho is nowhere in sight. He decides to proceed on his own. Sunrise is 6:20am. He estimates that the temperature should rise in the first two hours of sunshine. He dresses securely against the cold and goes outside at 9:00am. He braces himself against the cold. He is relieved to find that it is a tolerable -18°C. He plans to limit his time outside by conducting his investigation indoors as much as possible.

His first stop is at the administration building. This building is the location of the reserve's government office, the post office, the credit union and the general store. The chief greets him as he enters. Jack feels that the entire reserve is aware of his presence and is attentive to his every move. The chief escorts him and ensures that everyone helps in the investigation. Jack is thankful. Although everyone is keen for Jack to succeed, he fears that some may hold back information out of a sense of loyalty to the band. A nod and a wink from the chief is all that it takes for the people to open up.

Within two hours, Jack has compiled interesting data on Dorinda. Her school attendance was sporadic following the death of her father, Paul Trapper. The few times she attended, she appeared to be distracted or preoccupied. The teacher is sympathetic, considering the tragic circumstances of the Trapper/Cool clan.

Dorinda was a weekly visitor to the post office and picked up the family's mail. Her routine was to go from the post office to the credit union and thence to the general store to purchase goods against the balance in the account.

The credit union confirms that Dorinda deposited money into the account comprised exclusively of postal money orders she received in the mail. The money orders were always payable to Amy Trapper. Dorinda never withdrew money. Only Paul Trapper or Amy Trapper has signing authority. After Paul's death, Amy remains the sole signing authority on the account. From the period of the destructive fire to Dorinda's departure from the reserve, there were no withdrawals from the account. Unless someone gifted money to her, Dorinda was not in possession of any cash when she departed from the reserve. Furthermore, as far as Jack could ascertain from the reserve residents, no one on the reserve ever presented her with money.

The general store has a standing order from Amy Trapper to charge her credit union account for her family's purchases. Thus, Dorinda purchased goods from the store by presenting her status card. From 20 June 2016 (the date of the fire) to 01 February 2017 (the date of her departure), Dorinda routinely purchased goods from the store up to the limit of the available account balance.

At 12:00 noon, Jack returns to the hotel for a quick lunch. He is anxious to continue collecting data while the band members are convivial. Seated in the dining room, he consults the menu and decides on the quickest thing – coffee and bannock. When the bannock arrives he immediately regrets his choice. The fried dough-bread looks as if it was resurrected from the morning's leftover oatmeal cereal. Upon consuming the meal, Jack throws himself into his work with renewed energy and resolve. He crosses the frozen river and proceeds to Amy Trapper's house. He is confused as to which house is which but eventually decides on the one most likely. Fortunately, it is the correct house. Okwaho is already present in the house when he arrives. Amy Trapper invites Jack inside and offers him food. Okwaho gives him a knowing wink. Okwaho, it appears, spent the morning with the Trapper/Cool family convincing them of Jack's value to the investigation. Jack consumes the proffered food – bannock and more of the unpalatable hot beverage. He proceeds with his inquiries. He speaks while eating in order to conceal his reaction to the food.

Jack directs his first remarks to Mark Trapper and Jim Cool. "Dorinda neglected school prior to leaving the reserve. Why was that?"

Mark responds. "She was busy in the house."

Jim corroborates. "Yes, 12 in one house that could only fit six. Two hunters – myself and young Mark here. And Kokum and eight children."

"Could that have precipitated her departure?"

Mark replies. "There was never enough money in the account

and never enough food in the house. And the growing children needed new clothes. Dorinda believed that she could better provide for us by going off the reserve to find work."

Jack turns to Amy. "I spoke with the chief. He introduced me to the credit union and the general store. I learned of your account in the credit union and your shopping arrangements with the general store."

"Yes?" Amy wonders where this is leading.

"I would like to see your account statements from two months before Dorinda's departure from the reserve, to two months past her disappearance in Toronto."

"I don't keep the statements after I read them."

Jack hides his frustration. "Then request duplicates from the credit union. Or even obtain activity reports on your account for the period."

Amy balks. "Is this necessary? How does this help find Dorinda?"

This time, Jack's frustration is evident. "You want me to find Dorinda. To do that, I must **investigate**. What I am doing now, here in the reserve, is conducting the rudimentary but vital stage of the investigation. This stage – Phase One – takes about a week of research. The difficult part comes later – but its success could be determined on how productive the initial investigation is."

Okwaho interjects to press Jack's point. "What Jack Doyle 'Snake-man' is saying is that he is thorough. The reason that Dorinda is still missing is because the investigation up to this point has **not** been thorough. Isn't that what you want, Amy – a thorough investigation?"

Amy sighs and acquiesces. "I suppose you are right." She turns to face Jack and says, "You want statements from the credit union for..."

"For the period April 2016 to May 2017. They will release this information to you, but not to me. Judging from my visit there this morning, I believe they will expedite your request."

"And when do you want it by?"

"Within an hour."

Okwaho speaks. "Amy, I will accompany you to the credit union and explain to them how urgent it is."

"That's not all." Jack resumes speaking. "I want to see the detailed receipts from the general store from 01 December 2016 up to 01 February 2017. I don't suppose that you kept those receipts either. If the store charged your account, it should be able to cross-refer from the transactions in your credit union account."

"Detailed receipts?" Amy says this as if fatigued.

"Amy, this is important. I need to see what Dorinda purchased in the two months prior to leaving."

Okwaho takes Amy's arm. "Come, Amy. Let's get on with this." He turns back to Jack. "And will there be anything else?"

"When you return, I will need Amy and Mark to go through the information with me, item by item."

Okwaho is not familiar with the amount of detailed research that basic investigation entails. "This will take hours."

"So? It takes what it takes. And it needs to be done. Actually, you should have copies of the statements and receipts within an hour. Whereupon, we should be able to analyze the details over the succeeding hour. And then we'll see."

Jack turns his attention to Mark. He questions him and continues to compile data on Dorinda. He inquires about Dorinda's state of mind at the time of her departure and what she expressed to him on her trek from Red Rapids to Elliot Lake. Jack writes in his pad – 'Did Dorinda leave to better her family? Or did she just simply run away from an intolerable situation?'

At 3:00pm, Amy, Mark, Jim and Okwaho are seated with Jack. Amy hands the requested documents to Jack. Jack peruses the purchase receipts from the general store. "Now Amy, and Mark, scan your eyes over the items. Did Dorinda purchase anything inconsistent with day-to-day provision for the family? Anything that is out of the ordinary?"

After a few minutes, Amy hands the receipts back to Jack. "No. Nothing unusual."

Mark adds, "Well, she wasn't hoarding food. I remember how hungry she was on the ice road."

"Okay." Jack is satisfied with the information. "Now let's look at the activity in the savings account." He hands the credit union statements to Amy. "Amy, can you identify these deposits into the account?" Jack observes that all the deposits are encoded 'deposit'. According to the information key listed at the bottom of the statement, these are teller transactions. There are no transfers, EFTs or wired funds listed.

Amy squints at the statements. Jack directs her to inspect each deposit in turn. Amy speaks. "Those are the postal money orders I sent home every week. After Paul's death, Mark or Dorinda would deposit them into the account at the credit union."

Mark is also looking at the statements, but not as intently. He corrects Amy's remark. "Not me. Dorinda did all that – the mail and the credit union. It was only after Dorinda left that I picked up the mail and made the deposits at the credit union. That would be from the first of February 2017."

"Until I came home." Amy looks at Mark and Jack. "I returned home to the reserve in April last year. That was after Rose phoned to tell me that Dorinda went missing in Toronto."

"What day was that?" Jack is scribbling notes in his notepad.

"I don't remember which day... But it was the day after Rose went to the police to report that Dorinda was missing. I think it was a Friday."

Jack mentally calculates, 'Dorinda went missing on Tuesday 04 April' and writes in his pad, 'Amy advised of D on Friday 07 April 2017'. Then, he speaks to Amy. "May I check your phone history?"

Amy hands him her phone. Jack scrolls to 07 April 2017. He sees a missed call at 10:22am, and a return call made to the number at 4:11pm. "Is this the call – the one in which Rose informed you of Dorinda's disappearance?" he asks.

Amy looks at her phone. "Yes. That's Rose's number. She seldom phoned me, so that's got to be the call."

"So, Rose phoned you and told you that Dorinda went missing. And that was on Friday 07 April 2017. When did you return to the reserve?"

"I gave a week's notice at work. And I came home on the following Monday. But it was a day later when I arrived here"

"On the Monday, after you worked your week's notice?"

"That's right. I gave notice. I worked for a final week. After that, I left Niagara Falls on the first Monday and reached Red Rapids Reserve on Tuesday."

Jack notates 'Tuesday 18 April 2017' in his notebook. "Why not make the journey all in one day?"

"I left Niagara Falls on the first bus, at 6:45am – a 'Greyhound' bus to Toronto Bus Terminal. Then, I took the Ontario Northland bus from Bay Street at 11:00am. It arrived in Sudbury in time to get the 5:30pm bus to Elliot Lake. I knew when the bus turned off the Trans-Canada Highway at Serpent River onto the road to Elliot Lake at 8:10pm that I would not be able to get a floatplane charter before nightfall. I arrived at Elliot Lake at 8:30pm. I stayed overnight and got a flight at 8:00 the following morning with the company that is chartered to make routine deliveries to the reserve."

"I see." Jack continues notating. "Back to the activity in your account, do you recognize the deposits?"

Amy resumes examining the statements. "All these deposits," she says, indicating to the entries before 18 April 2017, "correspond to the money orders I sent home. I earned minimum wage, working 44 hours per week. I well remember what I could afford to send home every week – $88. And this one here, on 18 April, is where I deposited the contents of my purse when I arrived home."

Jack observes a deposit of $305. "That's a lot of money."

"I got holiday pay with my final pay. And the last week's rent was prepaid. I had almost $800 when I left Niagara Falls."

"It cost you $500 to get to Red Rapids?"

Amy looks critically at Jack. She wonders what relevance these intrusive questions could have to the investigation. She answers curtly. "The temperature drops to below -40°C here in Red Rapids. Even in April, it is below -20°C. Are you aware of that? Anyway, the bus from Bay Street was due to depart Toronto at 11:00am. I had arrived from Niagara Falls at 9:20am. That gave me enough time to walk across to *Mark's* in the *Eaton Centre* and buy a winter coat and boots and a few things to bring home. I spent about $300 in *Mark's*. Is there anything wrong with that?"

Jack feels chastised. "Sorry, Amy. I am attempting to get a full picture. Details like these may seem irrelevant now, but they put the entire picture into focus and strengthen the integrity of the inquiry."

Amy responds unconvincingly. "Very well, then."

Jack brings her attention back to the account statement. "Subsequent to the deposit of $305 you made upon returning home, how do you account for the following deposits?"

Amy scrutinizes the statement, taking up where she left off. "After Dorinda's disappearance, Rose started to send us money orders. I pick up the mail every Friday. And if any money orders arrive, I bring them to the credit union. The first money order arrived on 21 April 2017."

Jack takes the statements from Amy. He draws a line under 18 April 2017, separating the deposits that originated from Amy's money orders from those subsequently received from Rose. The first deposit appearing below the line is for $300, made on 21 April 2017. Jack appears satisfied with the information. "Okay, Amy. Now, look at the charges. Do you recognize them?" It is a non-chequing account and, clearly, there are no cash withdrawals. All the debit entries are authorized charges.

Amy identifies each charge in turn. She interprets the abbreviated remarks notated at each entry. She recognizes the general store, the reserve administration – that would be for phone calls – and so on.

It is past 5:00pm when Jack finishes his inquiries. He and Okwaho return to the hotel. Nightfall is approaching. It is too late to arrange a charter flight to Elliot Lake. They decide to spend one more night on the reserve.

Back at the hotel, Okwaho asks Jack "Well, tell me. How is the investigation going, so far?"

"It is more fatiguing than I expected. But I believe I have established a sound starting point. Over the next hour, I will construct a profile of Dorinda Trapper and tabulate the collected data according to relevance. At that point, Okwaho, the actual investigative part of the investigation begins."

"What? You require all this information **before** you can even **start** your investigation?"

"Precisely."

"Oh, Jack." Jack notices the absence of 'snake' when Okwaho addresses him. "I was with you the entire time you were with Amy Trapper. I don't remember you referring to your fee. Surely, your 'initial consultation' has been concluded."

"Correct."

"Well, don't you think you should give her the heads-up on what this is likely to cost?"

"Okwaho, I don't expect this will be a normal skip-trace situation. Usually, missing persons leave a trail that is easily followed. They can't help but leave a trail – purchases on their credit card, financing for a car purchase, a store card like *Canadian Tire*, email address, Facebook and social media, traffic violations, etc, etc. I fear Dorinda lived in a different world. This task, I suspect, will need an experienced Indian tracker."

"What do you mean?"

"To succeed, the 'troublesome Indian wolf' and the 'snake-man' need to combine their skills and work together."

"And the cost to Amy Trapper for this 'snake-and-wolf' venture is...?

"Let's say I have a non-mercenary interest in the assignment."

"No cost?"

"No **monetary** cost."

*   *   *   *   *

Later, Jack Doyle composes a profile on Dorinda Trapper.

Legal Name: Dorinda Trapper

I.D: Certificate of Indian Status
          (in possession of – probably)

          Birth certificate (in possession of – unsure)

Age: DOB 02 July 2001
          15 at time of her disappearance – now 17

Skills: Not skilled for life outside the reserve

Means: No financial means

Phone databases: None – searched

Credit bureau: Search pending

Job applications: Search pending

Driver abstracts: None – searched

Internet/public databases: Searches pending

Leasing/rental: Search pending

Utility bills: Searches pending

Bank/credit affiliations: Searches pending

Jack decides to wait until he returns to Oakville, where he benefits from high-speed internet, to begin the standard searches. Dorinda's legal name is unique. It is unlikely that he will encounter another 'Dorinda Trapper' with a birth date of 02 July 2001. He wonders if he will encounter **any** 'Dorinda Trapper'. Jack visualizes the wolf attack on Dorinda on the ice road. He fears that, outside the reserve, 15-year-old Dorinda Trapper (now 17) is a lamb among wolves.

CHAPTER ELEVEN

SNAKE-MAN AND WOLF

Friday 11 January 2019, Jack and Okwaho depart from Red Rapids. They travel by floatplane to Elliot Lake where Okwaho has parked his rental car. Two hours later, they enter Sudbury airport where they avail of the Air Canada Express Jazz flight departing at 11:36am. They arrive at Toronto's Pearson Airport at 12:49pm. Okwaho picks up his car and drives Jack to his house at Huron Park. Thence, Jack drives to his office in Oakville.

At 2:00pm, both men are working together on the assignment. Jack executes searches on Dorinda Trapper. In most instances, he gets the response – 'no data found'. The remaining searches will return results within three days. This will establish if Dorinda had any traceable dealings since leaving the reserve. Jack spends five hours conducting searches online. Meanwhile, Okwaho, now an integral part of the investigation team, contacts Rose by phone. He gives her an account of the investigation to date and a progress report. He impresses upon her the importance of compiling all relevant information on Dorinda and her life in Toronto. They are determined to meet everyone who interacted with Dorinda prior to her disappearance. A meeting with Rose and Monique is a top priority. Okwaho prepares her for a lengthy meeting ASAP. They agree to meet at 10:00am on the following day at *Tim Hortons* in the *Eaton Centre* at the Dundas Street entrance. Monique will also attend.

*   *   *   *   *

Saturday 12 January 2019 is a snowy day in Toronto. Snow blows through the wind tunnels between the high buildings. Snowplows rumble through the main arterial roads to clear the snow and road-maintenance trucks spray brine in their wake. Smaller plows carve a walking path on the sidewalks. The temperature is -13°C, but, with the wind chill, it feels more like -18°C. The sidewalk on Yonge Street north of Dundas is taped off on the west side due to the risk of falling ice from the glass-fronted buildings. Pedestrians, familiar with the city, choose to navigate throughout downtown Toronto via the confusing network of below-ground shops and walkways. Notwithstanding, several professional men and women in business attire dart quickly at ground level between buildings – men's ties fluttering like pennants in the wind and women's high heels clicking noisily on the frozen pavement. The requirement for professional dress trumps the need for weather-appropriate clothing. Jack and Okwaho, having parked their cars at Kipling subway station, travel to the *Eaton Centre* via TTC subway. Thus, they access the agreed meeting place via the underground pathway directly from the Dundas subway station.

Jack and Okwaho arrive at the coffee shop ten minutes early. Being Saturday, the shopping centre is open from 9:30am. They order coffee. Jack purchases a maple-dip doughnut and they locate a suitable table large enough to accommodate four customers. Shortly, Rose and Monique arrive. Coming from Jarvis Street, they would have travelled by surface on Carlton Street to the subway line. They immediately order coffee for its warmth. Rose and Monique are dressed in the same clothes as on the previous Saturday when they met with Okwaho. The 'Wolf-man' is dressed in his signature buckskin and leather hat. He has prudently layered two tee-shirts under his red-checkered fully-fastened work shirt. Jack, the newcomer to the two women, is in his usual blue work shirt over dark-grey cargo pants and snow boots. His green parka is unfastened and flung open and his baseball cap is pulled low to his eyebrows. The two women join them at their table.

Rose addresses Okwaho. "Hello again, handsome. I see you brought your *Blue-Jays* buddy with you this time."

The 'Wolf-man' accepts 'Wild Rose's' brash greeting. "This is Jack Doyle, the investigator". In turn, he introduces Jack to the two women. "Jack, this is Rose Cool, Dorinda's aunt. And this is Monique... Monique..."

Monique interrupts. "No, love, there is only one of me. And it's just 'Monique'." She smiles at him and lifts her cup to her lips. As is her manner, one cannot tell if her smile is sincere or if she is simply accommodating her lips to sip from her coffee cup. She turns to Jack and studies him for a moment. Then she speaks to no one in particular. "A private eye. He doesn't look like much. I hope he performs better than he looks." She takes another sip of coffee.

After this bizarre introduction, Jack comes to the point. He addresses Monique. "Monique, as I understand, you observed Dorinda shopping here in the *Eaton Centre* on the day she disappeared – about noon on Tuesday 04 April 2017." He hopes that his voice is more impressive than his appearance. He wonders what Monique's reaction would have been, had she noticed his hidden snake tattoo. He subconsciously tugs the peak of his cap.

"That's correct. And Sugar hasn't been seen since. Rose here went to the police…"

"Sugar? Who is 'Sugar'?"

Rose interjects. "Dorinda went by the name 'Sugar' while in Toronto. She used it as her street name."

Jack nods in understanding and turns his attention back to Monique. "That's okay, Monique. I don't want you to tell me what Rose did, just what **you** did. Walk me through the shopping centre and identify the stores where you saw Dorinda-Sugar. Can you do that? We can talk as we walk."

"Very well, if it does any good. But I'm taking my coffee with me."

All four walk from the north end of the shopping centre through to the south end. Jack instructs Monique to describe Dorinda's actions prior to her last sighting of her. "Point out to me which stores Sugar entered. And who she spoke to and interacted with."

"It did not appear that the stores were Sugar's choice at all. The woman with her seemed to be leading her to them."

"There was a woman 'leading' her? Tell me about this woman. Can you describe her?"

"Sure. The woman was with her all the time. She was thirtyish, brown hair collar-length, about my height (5′ 6″), very well dressed. She had a long maxi dark-green overcoat –

expensive looking. The pants were the same colour but a shade lighter. She wore a black light-weight turtleneck sweater. Oh, and she wore stiletto-heeled black boots. And she walked as if she was a somebody."

Monique identifies *M Boutique, Reitmans, Club Monaco, Babaton* and *Nordstrom* – stores in which Dorinda or her partner purchased clothing. Jack enters these stores in turn and inquires from the respective store managers regarding purchases made on 04 April 2017. As expected, the stores refuse to divulge the information on their purchasers. Monique had observed Dorinda and partner tendering cash for their purchases. Jack understands that personal data is not provided for cash transactions, so there is no point in pressing the issue. If Dorinda identified herself for the purpose of obtaining a store's card, it would appear in a credit-bureau search. And in Dorinda's case, Jack knows that this did not occur. Jack explains to the store managers that he is tracing a missing person, last seen in their store. The store managers are understanding but are unable to help. When Jack asks about security cameras, he learns that security footage is purged after one year. After speaking with the store managers, he next visits the shopping centre's central security office. He ascertains that the centre's security-camera records are purged after one year – and that includes the parking areas and exterior camera footage.

They return to the north entrance of the shopping centre. Monique has no further information to impart. Jack thanks her and excuses her. Seated once more in the coffee shop, Jack questions Rose. "Rose. You did not see Dorinda at all on Tuesday 04 April. Is that true?"

"On that Tuesday, I was still asleep when Dorinda left the bed. I didn't awaken until after ten. She had already left the apartment by that time. I figured that she had stepped out for breakfast – that's the usual thing she would do."

"So, when **did** you see her last?"

"It was on the previous night. We had been working together. We got home simultaneously before midnight and went to bed."

"Tell me about it. Give me a detailed account of your time together that day."

"Okay. As I said, Dorinda and I worked nights – you know what line of work it is. Our 'corner' was, still is, at Spadina and Richmond northwest corner. The sidewalk is wide there, and in the middle is a huge statue shaped like a thimble. We can dodge in and out from behind the statue as it suits us. There were four of us girls working the corner that night. It was a slow night. None of our regular johns showed up. And we don't like approaching strangers unless we are hard up for money. Dorinda approached a black *Mustang*. Word on the street was that this car, the black *Mustang*, was bad news and we should avoid it. But before I could warn her, Dorinda entered the car and drove off in it. I was concerned at first. But after a couple of hours, Dorinda was dropped off, safe and sound, back at our spot."

"And did Dorinda enlighten you about her experience in the black *Mustang*?"

"She told me that it was a man **and** a woman and that she got $100 for the encounter."

"What about the man and the woman? Did Dorinda tell you anything about them?"

"Dorinda was tight-lipped about that. But that in itself was not strange. I really can't tell you anything about the man or the woman. You know, I was so concerned at the time she went off, that I took a picture of the car as it drove away. I still have that picture somewhere on my phone. Here, I'll show you."

Rose scrolls through the pictures on her phone. She stops upon identifying her selection. Jack examines the picture of the black *Mustang*. The licence plate is legible. "Rose, send me a copy of the picture. I am interested in the owner and the occupants of that car."

"Here. Take the phone and message it to yourself."

Jack takes Rose's phone. He sends a message to his own phone with the picture attached. While holding Rose's phone, he asks, "Rose, may I look at the activity on your phone? I need to compare it to Amy's account of phone calls made and received."

Rose is agreeable. "If you think it helps, go ahead."

Jack examines the call history for the period one month prior to Dorinda's disappearance to one month later. He identifies Amy's number. Jack asks Rose about the remaining numbers.

She states that the calls are to, or from, her 'clients'. Jack hesitates. He scrolls back to 17 April 2017. One particular call strikes a chord – a missed call at 4:48am. Jack flips through his note pad, to his interview with Amy. There it is – a missed call at 4:48am on 17 April 2017. And this call displayed on Rose's phone is the same number. Two missed calls from the same number within the same minute – one to Amy's phone and another to Rose's phone. "Dorinda," he exclaims aloud.

Rose puts down her coffee and queries Jack. "Why did you say 'Dorinda' just now?" Okwaho comes closer to Jack and peers at Rose's phone.

Jack responds. "Dorinda made this call, I warrant." He points to the display on Rose's phone.

"Dorinda didn't have a phone," remarks Rose.

Okwaho looks from Rose's phone to Jack's notes. He instantly comes to the most likely conclusion. "It's Dorinda. Who else would attempt to contact Amy **and** Rose at the same time?"

Rose looks at both men and speaks with emphasis. "I told you, Dorinda did not have a phone."

Jack looks at her and quietly says, "Unless…"

Rose grasps the significance of the point. "Unless she borrowed someone's phone."

Jack continues. "This is important, Rose. Do you recognize this number? Do you know where this call originated?"

Rose is agitated. "I don't know. I don't remember ever attempting to reply."

Jack confirms that there was no outgoing call from Rose's phone in response.

Rose is distressed. She is moaning. "Oh, my God. It was Dorinda. She called me and I did not get her call. She was probably calling for help. Oh, God."

Okwaho asks Jack, "Surely you can trace the call?"

"Locating a cell phone's owner can be challenging. Cell-phone numbers are not public domain. If you ring up a cell-phone service provider and inquire about a specific number's owner, you will not be provided with the information as it is confidential."

"Then, it's impossible?"

"Not impossible. It is difficult. And even then, the user's name may not be recorded." Jack taps a number into his cell phone and signals the others to be silent. When the call picks up, Jack speaks. "Hello. Is that Michael?

"I'm sorry. I thought I was phoning Michael Brown.

"So, you are not Michael Brown? I must have the wrong number. Please excuse me.

"Okay. Good-bye."

Okwaho smiles at Jack's wily ploy. "Who is 'Michael Brown'?"

"Well, the phone number is still active. A male voice – could be anywhere between 20 and 50. There was no background noise. I kept him speaking for as long as I could. He sounded educated and polite. He could be a professional man or someone in the hospitality industry."

Okwaho is impressed by Jack's action. He asks, "Would you be able to recognize his voice if you heard it later?"

Jack nods his head slowly in thought. "A pretty good chance. Yes, I believe I could."

They sit in silence for a few moments. Jack coughs and drinks his coffee. Then he addresses Rose once more. "Rose, I have Amy's statements from the credit union. Here they are. Now, take a look at them. Pay attention to the deposits made into her account. See where I have drawn a line? Amy identified the source of all the deposits above the line; you, I understand, are responsible for the later deposits. Can you confirm which deposits originated from you?"

Rose examines the statements. "I only ever send sums of $100, usually once a week."

"This one here, for $300 made on 21 April 2017. Is this not one of yours?"

"No. I did not mail any money to Amy until she arrived home. And that would have been the first Monday after 18 April."

"24 April 2017."

"If you say so. Look, Amy sent postal money orders by Canada Post. It takes anything from two to nine days for mail to arrive at Red Rapids. And Mark was likely tardy in picking up the mail there. The deposit of $300 was probably from a money order purchased early in April and was not deposited into the account until Amy picked up the mail after her arrival home. Or maybe the mail was uncollected for a time and this deposit was comprised of several money orders, not just one."

Jack nods. This is a reasonable explanation. The money order, or money orders, could have remained in uncollected mail for weeks. He makes a note to check later with Amy.

*   *   *   *   *

Saturday 12 January 2019. At 1:00pm, Jack and Okwaho are back in Jack's office. Jack is working on his laptop computer. He studies the displayed information. Then he speaks to Okwaho, "I ran the plates – you know, the *Mustang* that Rose saw."

"Yes? The one she photographed on her cell phone?"

"Yup. The one that drove off, with Dorinda inside, on the eve of her disappearance – **that** one."

"And?" Okwaho is alert in the expectation of some news.

"I just received an email confirmation to check the search results. And here it is. I now have a name and address."

Okwaho waits for Jack to continue. Jack hesitates. Okwaho is impatient for Jack to impart this important information. He asks, with some irritation, "So spit it out – the name and address."

Jack frowns. After a second, one long second, he says, "I'm not permitted by law to share this information. The Privacy act..."

"To hell with the Privacy Act. Who is, was, the owner of the *Mustang*?"

"Kenneth Andrews of 200 - 163 Spadina Avenue, Toronto."

"Great work, 'Snake-man'. We are making progress. Let's check out this 'Kenneth Andrews'."

"Yes, let's." Forty-five minutes later, Jack and Okwaho are standing at the corner of Queen & Spadina. Jack points to number 163 Spadina Avenue. "There it is."

Okwaho looks up at the signage on the second-floor windows. "It's a tattoo parlour."

At 163 Spadina Avenue, they locate the entrance to the office suites and upper-floor units. They ascend the stairs to unit 200 and speak with the owner-manager of the tattoo parlour.

The manager is suspicious of anyone asking questions. He replies curtly to Jack's inquiry. "Kenneth Andrews? Never heard of him. When did you say he was here?"

"In 2017."

"2017? Hah. That's long before my time. I've been here only three months. I don't know who was here before that. As far as I know, this place was vacant for over a year."

"So, you are unable to help?"

The man shrugs in disinterest. "Try the tax accountant downstairs at the back. He's been here forever. Ask him if he knows." The manager turns away to indicate that the conversation is ended.

Jack and Okwaho descend the stairs and seek out the tax accountant. Ted Wong, the elderly accountant on the ground level provides a tax-filing service. He is willing to help Jack with his inquiries. He remembers the man from upstairs who once availed of his tax-filing services. Ted Wong rubs his brow to stimulate his memory and says, "Kenneth Andrews, also known as 'Jamaica Man', operated a club on the upper level – the *Elephant Club*. In April 2017, the *Elephant Club* was shut down by the police. The space remained vacant after that, until three months ago. Now it is a tattoo and body-piercing place."

Jack remembers the case. It was front-page news at the time. In April 2017, the operators of the *Elephant Club* were arrested and tried for sex trafficking and are currently serving prison sentences. This information does not bode well for the fate of Dorinda Trapper.

Jack's next visit is to Toronto Police Division 52. He leaves a message requesting a meeting with the lead officer in the *Elephant Club* investigation. The desk officer informs him that the lead officer in the case was Detective Sergeant Alex Crouse, now Detective Inspector.

Alex Crouse was never totally satisfied with the outcome of the *Elephant Club* case. He fears that some of the captive girls were never found. And now a private investigator is asking about the case. The police detective contacts Jack at 9:30am on Monday 14 January 2019. Jack explains his interest in the case – that he is following a lead on a missing underage girl, Dorinda Trapper. And it may have a connection with the *Elephant Club* case in April 2017.

The detective asks, "A missing underage girl? And you believe it may have a connection to the *Elephant Club* case?" His voice denotes interest.

"Dorinda Trapper, a 15-year-old Cree girl..."

Detective Crouse interrupts. "Did you say 'Cree girl'?"

"Yes. Does that mean something to you?"

By way of answer, Alex responds, "Let's meet. How about today at 11:00am at 52 Division?"

Later, Jack and Okwaho exit the University Line subway train at St Patrick Station. They walk west on Dundas Street to the next block. Police Division 52, located at 255 Dundas Street West, takes up an entire block on the south side of Dundas, stretching from Simcoe Street to St Patrick Street. There is a *Tim Hortons* on the east side of Simcoe & Dundas. Jack wonders if it is a coincidence that this *Tim Hortons* is only a short doughnut's throw from the police station.

At 11:00am, Jack and Okwaho meet with Alex Crouse in one of the interview rooms at the police station. Jack introduces Okwaho as a 'representative of the family'. Alex directs Jack's attention to his laptop computer. It displays an open file. He invites Jack to look at it.

As Alex speaks, he scrolls down the file. "This is the file on the missing person Dorinda Trapper – 15 years old at the time of her disappearance on Tuesday 04 April 2017. We have had no leads and no positive results in this investigation. And now you tell me that she may have had a connection with the *Elephant Club*. How so?"

"First, her street name was 'Sugar'." This point appears to register with the police detective. Jack continues. "She was observed entering a black *Mustang* on the evening of 04 April 2017. The registered owner of that *Mustang* was Kenneth Andrews."

"That is significant." Alex downloads a second file to his computer. "Please, go on."

"She turned up later that evening, safe and sound. But here's where it gets interesting. She went shopping in the *Eaton*

Centre on the following morning. She was seen in the company of a well-dressed woman and she spent a lot of cash. After that, she simply disappeared. She never returned to her apartment or contacted a friend or family member."

Alex has the file open on the computer. Referring to the file, he says, "On Monday 17 April 2017, at 6:40am, we raided the *Elephant Club* at 163 Spadina Avenue, Second Floor. Five people were taken into custody, including Kenneth Andrews. And 30 sex slaves were rescued." Alex turns to face Jack and Okwaho. "Here is where your information strikes a chord. Our original tip-off that young women and girls were being held captive came from 'Sugar Maple'. Let me explain." Alex consults his on-screen file. "On Thursday 13 April 2017, Kenneth Andrews applied for a line of credit at the Toronto Dominion Bank at Queen & Spadina. He met with John Maxwell, the credit manager. To induce John Maxwell to comply, he offered sexual favours. His enticement included Sugar Maple – a Canadian aboriginal girl and one of three girls that accompanied Andrews to the meeting. When he failed to obtain a line of credit, he left the bank. Later, the office manager, Pete Harvey, found a business card that had fallen on the ground. Here, I'll show you." Alex scrolls to an image of John Maxwell's business card. "If you look carefully, you see where a message was scratched on it."

Jack peers at the image, 'HELF'. "Helf?"

"No. The writing was shaped by a fingernail. The 'P' is rendered as 'F'. Try writing on a card using your fingernail as an etching pen and you find that curves are difficult to execute."

"Sugar Maple wrote 'HELP'?"

"Exactly."

"Are you sure that the message was from Sugar?"

"No doubt. Andrews knocked over the card stand on Maxwell's desk. The business cards fell to the ground. Sugar Maple picked them up and replaced them in the card stand. Except for one card which she pushed out of sight under the desk. Maxwell's colleague Pete Harvey discovered the card moments after Andrews left the office. Pete contacted the police on the following morning and we set up surveillance on the *Elephant Club*. You understand that the club was under suspicion, but we needed something substantial to proceed. This was it. The surveillance yielded positive results. We acted with great urgency in the belief that Sugar Maple and others were being held captive in a sex trafficking operation. We executed a successful raid on the club and rescued 30 captive girls, most of whom were underage minors. I looked high and low throughout the club, but I was unable to locate Sugar Maple. In fact, there were no Canadian indigenous girls among the 30 rescued. I never set eyes on Sugar Maple – not then or ever. Nor have I seen a picture of her. The only description I received of Sugar Maple was from the two bank officers. They both described her as an 18-year-old First Nations girl. Failing to rescue Sugar Maple was my one disappointment in an otherwise successful operation."

"You said 'an 18-year-old First Nations girl'. Dorinda was 15 at the time." Jack experiences a momentary comedown. There is nothing to substantiate that the club's 'Sugar Maple' is

Dorinda 'Sugar'. He realizes that he must establish a link lest his investigation veers off course.

The detective echoes the same uncertainty. "That was how the two bankers described her. If, in fact, it is the same girl, you can see how we failed to connect the missing 15-year-old Dorinda Trapper to 18-year-old Sugar Maple. The missing-persons file is still open. But, to be honest, I don't expect a successful result. Dorinda/Sugar has truly disappeared."

"That may be so. But we are giving it a shot. May I ask a favour?"

"If it helps, sure."

"Were you able to capture any video or pictures in your surveillance?"

"In the hope of seeing an image of Sugar? Of course. But let me tell you, I have gone through it a dozen times or more. There is no picture of Sugar. There is one picture that I considered briefly, but... Let me scroll to it." Alex quickly scrolls through the file. He is familiar with the contents and stops at the precise spot. "Look at this."

Jack and Okwaho scrutinize the picture. Alex enlarges it, sharpens it, brightens it and alters the contrast.

Alex describes the picture. "This was taken from across the street – from the TD bank, actually. It is a view of the entrance to the club at ground level. The view of the street was obstructed by the moving traffic. Notice the date and time."

Jack reads '2017-04-16 – 19:34'. "Sunday 16 April 2017 at 7:34pm."

"Correct. That was the evening before the raid. Now, look closely. What do you see in the picture?"

Jack and Okwaho peer at it intently. Jack describes what he sees. "A young woman or girl with long straight black hair. Her face is hidden by her hair. She is dressed in a long black evening gown. There is a man beside her, partially facing her. He is dressed semi-formally in a stylish dark-blue suit with a burgundy tie and burgundy shoes. He appears to be in his early twenties." Jack turns to Alex and asks, "Is there another shot in the next or preceding frame?"

"I'm afraid not. The next shot has a streetcar, and the previous shot shows a truck. This shot is squeezed into a fraction of a second in between."

"And this might be Sugar/Dorinda?"

"Upon scrutiny, I don't believe it is. What do **you** think?"

Jack observes and remarks, "The clothes are wrong. That is not how a sex worker dresses – at least not on Spadina Avenue. It is more likely that this person is on her way to some event, or is a singer from a performance in the *Horseshoe*."

Okwaho expresses his opinion. "There is no indication that

she even entered or exited the club. That couple may have been walking on the street and just happen to walk past the club. That can't be a 15-year-old in the picture. That's a stylish young lady."

Alex tenders his opinion. "And there is nothing to suggest that she is an indigenous Canadian. She could be south-Asian, oriental or Filipina. It's Toronto, for God's sake. Chinatown starts right there at the corner of Queen & Spadina. Hundreds of young Chinese women walk by that intersection every day, many of whom have long-hair and are fashionably dressed."

"Or just maybe..." Okwaho peers at the picture until his eyes water.

Jack addresses Alex. "Could you run off a copy of that picture? I would like to show it to those who interacted with Dorinda."

"And to those who met Sugar Maple," adds Alex. He prints off a copy of the picture and hands it to Jack.

Armed with this new information, Jack and Okwaho exit the police station. Jack proceeds to walk west, not east as Okwaho expects.

"Jack, where are you off to?"

"Come this way. I'll explain as we go. It's a 15-minute walk."

"Perhaps we should have come by car."

Jack tenders no answer but continues walking. Okwaho falls into stride beside him. They walk past the *Art Gallery of Ontario* and reach the perimeter of 'Chinatown' at Beverly Street. They continue walking west until they reach Spadina Avenue. They pass numerous restaurants. Okwaho wonders how much food Chinese people eat. He smiles at seeing a *Tim Hortons* sharing space with *CIBC BANKING*. He speculates that by walking for two blocks in any direction, he will encounter a *Tim Hortons*.

"So Jack, are you going to enlighten me?"

"Do you remember the pledge I made? I told you that I needed to speak to everyone who interacted with Dorinda."

"Ah. The two bank guys?"

"Exactly. We are over half-way there."

*   *   *   *   *

At 1:15pm Jack and Okwaho stand at the intersection of Queen & Spadina.

"There's the 'TD'", says Jack pointing to the Toronto Dominion Bank.

"And there's what used to be the *Elephant Club* across the street," says Okwaho pointing.

"And there's the *'Shoe* behind us," says Jack, turning around and indicating to the *Horseshoe Tavern*. "Let's grab a burger and fries. I'm starving."

Forty-five minutes later they enter the TD Bank. They approach the front counter and request a meeting with Pete Harvey and John Maxwell.

The friendly counter officer responds, "Mr Maxwell has an appointment at 2:00pm. But I see that Mr Harvey is free. What is this in regards to, if I may ask?"

Jack displays his business card and says, "The *Elephant Club*."

The counter officer raises her eyes and repeats, "The *Elephant Club?*" She is clearly at a loss as to its significance.

"Yes. They'll understand its relevance."

She walks to the back office. Moments later, a man in a three-piece grey suit approaches them. "Good afternoon. I'm Pete Harvey. You are inquiring about the *Elephant Club*? Is that correct?"

"Just a moment of your time, if you don't mind. I'm Jack Doyle – as you see from my card. And this is my colleague Okwaho."

"If this about the *Elephant Club*, then come into my office."

Seated in Pete Harvey's office, Jack asks, "Is it possible to include John Maxwell in this meeting as well?"

"Hold on." Pete keys a number into his phone. He speaks. "John. I have two detectives in here in my office, They want to talk to us about the *Elephant Club*. Can you come in here?"

Before Pete replaces the telephone in its cradle, a tall 35-year-old man enters Pete's office. He remains standing in the doorway. He is dressed in a blue three-piece suit sans jacket. His shirt sleeves are folded back to his elbows. And he is holding a pen in his right hand. "You don't need to use the phone, Pete. I can hear you through the wall. Anyway, what's this about?" He addresses the two visitors. "My 'two o'clock' is running late. I'm here for you until he shows up."

Jack comes to the point. He shows the picture to John – the one that he obtained from the police an hour earlier. "Do you recognize anyone in this picture?"

John looks at the picture. "No. I don't recognize either of these people. You say it's about the *Elephant Club*?" He takes the picture from Jack and scrutinizes it more closely.

Jack prompts him. "Do you remember 'Sugar Maple' from the *Elephant Club*?"

"Yes. I remember. Why do you ask?"

"Could that be her in the picture?"

"Sorry. I don't recognize either person in the picture." He returns the picture to Jack. "Look, I have to go. I see my 'two o'clock' at the counter." He proceeds to adjust his shirt cuffs as he speaks and enters the adjacent office.

Jack now turns to address Pete, seated across from him behind his desk. "You heard that?"

"Yes. I remember 'Sugar Maple'. She came in here once with Kenneth Andrews of the *Elephant Club.* I remember her well. She was a native Indian..." Pete looks at Okwaho and rephrases. "She was a young First Nations woman. She left an appeal for help scratched on one of John's business cards. I found it immediately after they left."

"Did you get a good look at her at the time, sufficient to recognize her if you saw her again?"

"I only saw from behind and in profile – never face-on."

Jack places the picture on Pete's desk. "Take a look at the picture. Could that be her?"

"I cannot say. Sorry."

Jack retrieves that picture. He is about to leave when Pete asks a surprising question.

"Are you not asking about the **man** in the picture?"

"The **man** in the picture? Do you recognize him?"

"When you came here at first, you said that you were inquiring about the *Elephant Club*."

"And is this man associated with the club?" Jack points to the man in the picture.

"No. But he knew the club. That is a picture of one of our bank inspectors. Actually, at that time, he was a junior member of the inspection team."

"What is his connection to the club?"

"Let me explain. He inspected the current accounts in the branch back in March 2017. He examined the *Elephant Club* account closely. He was looking for money laundering or illicit activity. He was satisfied that it was a 'clean' account. He gave it a 'pass'."

Okwaho comments to himself, but loud enough to be heard. "Perhaps not totally 'clean', but he gave it a 'pass' nevertheless."

Jack continues. "So, tell me his name, and how we do contact him?"

"I never learned his name. But hold on..." Pete hastily exits his office. Moments later, he returns with a manila folder. "This is the account file – its status is 'inactive' now." He opens the file entitled *Elephant Club* and shows it to Jack. The file is stamped in green with the inspection date 13 March 2017 and initialled *'CC'*.

Jack regards this with keen interest. He reassembles his papers. Then, he asks Pete, "May I have a photocopy of the file – just the part with the inspection stamp. In colour, if you don't mind?" Pete complies. At 2:22pm, Jack and Okwaho depart from the TD Bank at Queen & Spadina.

Outside, Okwaho speaks to Jack. "You didn't expect that, did you?"

"I need a moment to sift through this information. Let's go into the *'Shoe*."

Moments later, in the *Horseshoe Tavern,* Jack considers the relevance of the information recently obtained. He explains his reasoning to Okwaho. "Dorinda had a connection to the *Elephant Club*; 'TD inspector' had a connection to the *Elephant Club*; Dorinda's failed phone call was on 17 April 2017 at 4:48am; TD inspector was at the entrance to the club on 16 April 2017 at 7:44pm – nine hours earlier. Okwaho, this is a connection that warrants investigation.

"Are you sure they are connected?"

"Sure? No, far from it. But I intend to **make** it sure. Should I confront the TD inspector? If this inspector has something to hide, he will not be forthcoming. We need to devise a strategy to penetrate him."

"Why not scare him into opening up?"

"Or a bit of both." Jack thinks for a few minutes. He consumes his black coffee. When he empties his cup he says, "Let's leave. We will confront this inspector tomorrow morning."

"Why not now? He can't be all that far away."

"At this time, we do not know his name, or where he is

located. He could be conducting a branch inspection anywhere in Canada. Tomorrow morning, we will start at the TD Bank Inspection Division."

CHAPTER TWELVE

JACK AND OKWAHO PURSUE A LEAD

9:00am on Tuesday 14 January 2019. Jack and Okwaho exit the subway train at Union Station. They access the Toronto Dominion Bank Tower on 66 Wellington Street via the pedestrian underpass. Jack selects '22' in the elevator and they quickly ascend to the requested floor.

Okwaho asks, "How did you know to hit '22'?"

Jack answers smugly. "I did my investigative research."

True enough, upon stepping out of the elevator, they see the TD Inspection Division. They walk through the glass doors and enter the reception area. The decor is grey carpeting and grey walls – precise and functional, but dull. The two men approach the mahogany reception desk. The 40-something-year-old receptionist in a crisp white blouse with padded shoulders greets them as they enter. She steadies her glasses firmly on her nose and peers at them with lizard-like eyes. The gesture conveys 'I'm looking at you, and you deal with me.' Her voice is friendlier than her looks. However, the voice may deceive when looks are true. "Good morning, gentlemen. Who are you here to see? I don't appear to have you on the appointment calendar." She interrupts her greeting to attend to the switchboard. She answers an incoming call promptly and transfers it to the appropriate person. Notwithstanding, her focus remains firmly fixed on the two visitors.

Jack is prepared to fake his way in. "Good morning. My name is Jack Doyle. Here is my card. I am investigating an insurance claim. Each party asserts that the other party is at fault. I wish to speak with a bystander witness who agreed to come forward if requested. Unfortunately, my client lost his business card. All she remembers are the initial letters 'C C' and Toronto Dominion Bank Inspection Division."

The receptionist looks at Jack incredulously. "You request to see Mr 'C C'? I'm afraid I would need a precise name in order to help you. Are you sure you don't remember? Perhaps you are here by mistake." She is dismissive of Jack and turns her attention to another incoming telephone call.

Okwaho leans on the counter of her neat clutterless desk. He appears to be disinterested in Jack's conversation with the receptionist. He stares blankly at the switchboard on the desk and interjects a single word. "Clark".

The receptionist is taken aback by the unexpected comment from the 'quiet' man. "I'm sorry, sir. What did you say?"

Okwaho leans on the counter with his chin resting on his upturned hand. He fixes his eyes innocently at the receptionist and says, "The man's name is 'Clark'. That's who we wish to see."

She grudgingly concedes. She considers that perhaps these two men have a legitimate reason to meet Mr Clark. "Yes. We have a Mr Colin Clark. I'll tell him that you are here. Please have a seat."

Jack and Okwaho sit in the chairs indicated. Jack whispers to Okwaho. "How did you know to ask for 'Clark'?"

"I didn't. It was the first name displayed under 'C' on the row of buttons on the switchboard."

"Excuse me, gentlemen." The receptionist speaks to catch their attention. They acknowledge her. She continues. "Mr Clark apologizes. I'm afraid he is too busy to see you today. Perhaps..."

"Perhaps I should tell him how he is connected to my client. I believe he will recognize her from the 'Elephant Club'. Please tell him that."

The receptionist is upset by Jack's rude interruption. She clicks her tongue in annoyance and says, "Very well. The 'Elephant Club' you say?"

"Yes please, if you don't mind." It is clear to Jack that she **does** mind. Nevertheless, she complies begrudgingly.

A moment later she announces, "Mr Clark will see you in his office. Please follow me."

She escorts them down a short corridor to an interior windowless office. She announces her arrival. "Mr Doyle and Mr..." – not bothering to ascertain his name – "to see you, Mr Clark." Thereupon, she turns sharply on her heel and marches away, every movement of her body signalling disapproval of the 'abrasive American' and the 'uncouth Indian'.

Colin Clark invites the two men to be seated. "What can I do for you, Mr Doyle and..."

Jack hands him his business card. "... and my colleague Mr Okwaho."

Colin Clark reads Jack's card. "You are a private investigator I see. And you are investigating an insurance claim I understand? Someone connected to the *Elephant Club*?"

Jack is certain that this is the man in the police picture, the man seen with the long-haired woman outside the club on the evening before the police raid. Instead of answering directly, he places a copy of the picture on the desk. He gestures to it. "Mr Clark, this is you in the picture, is it not?"

Colin Clark moves his chair closer to take a look. Upon viewing the picture, he pushes his chair back an inch as if repelled by what he sees. He opens his mouth to speak, but changes his mind and remains silent. His eyes, however, betray his surprise.

Jack pretends not to notice. He taps the picture with his forefinger and says, "This picture was taken outside the *Elephant Club*. That is you in the picture, Mr Clark, is it not?"

Colin Clark glances at the picture and averts his eyes immediately. He is unsure of what to say. Instead, he asks, "And this is about an insurance claim?"

"It is about a charge of injuries sustained from a physical

assault." Jack pauses. He looks at Colin Clark for a reaction. Then, he continues. "My question pertains to this picture." Jack taps the picture with his forefinger. "But of course, it's you in the picture. We are in no doubt. The question is, 'who is the woman'? Look at the picture, Mr Clark. Who is the woman you are with?"

Colin Clark recovers somewhat. He is sufficiently recomposed to lie. He peers at the picture and then glances to his left and rubs the side of his nose with his forefinger. "I don't know that woman. I wasn't even **with** that woman. That's just a picture of me on the street. And a woman, a stranger, happens to be there at the same time."

"Do you know the *Elephant Club*? You are standing at the entrance to it in the picture."

"I have heard of that club. But that's all. Why do you ask?"

Jack produces the photocopy of the inspection certification he obtained from the TD branch at Queen and Spadina. He shows it to Colin Clark. "You inspected the *Elephant Club* account at your Queen and Spadina branch a month before this picture was taken."

This time, Colin fails to hide his surprise. He recognizes that the photocopy displays a file entitled 'Elephant Club' and is stamped in green with the inspection date 13 March 2017 and initialled *'CC'*. He recovers sufficiently to exclaim, "This is a confidential bank file. How did you obtain it?"

Jack ignores the question. He takes advantage of Colin's

surprise and probes at the resulting chink in his armour of defence. "So how well did you know the *Elephant Club?*"

"That is how I know the name – from inspecting the current accounts at the branch. Nothing more. Now, I must ask you to leave." Colin's request betrays his anxiety.

Jack suspects that Colin Clark is hiding relevant information. However, he is sure of one thing – this is the voice that answered the 'Michael' phone calls. Jack employs a different tactic. He changes his tone and appears to have exhausted his inquiry. "Very well, Mr Clark. Let me understand. You never had any association with the *Elephant Club,* and you are unable to identify the woman in the picture. Then, we are finished. I'm sorry to have taken up your time. Thank you for your cooperation." Jack gathers his papers and sorts them into his folder. "Mr Clark, sorry to be a nuisance, but could I avail of your washroom before I leave? Then, we'll be on our way. And once again, thanks."

"Well, the washroom is next to the elevators."

"Oh yes. Of course, it is." Jack turns to Okwaho and gives him a signal to delay. "Okwaho. Here, sort my papers into my folder. I'll meet you by the elevators in a few minutes."

Okwaho fumbles with the papers. He adjusts the bank file and rearranges the sheets. Colin looks at him impatiently. Nevertheless, he is glad to see that the two men are leaving.

Colin's cell phone rings. He ignores Okwaho and answers it. "Hello.

"Who?

"I told you before, I'm not 'Michael'.

"No, I am **not** Michael Brown." Colin disconnects the call. He looks impatiently at Okwaho, annoyed at his delay in leaving. Without forewarning, he sees a fast-approaching fist, so fast that he has no time to react. The fist impacts his face full-on. His chair rolls back from the impact and topples over. He falls noisily onto the floor. When Colin looks up, he is aware that blood is flowing from his nose. Jack is standing in the doorway holding a cell phone. He points it at Colin, who is sitting with legs sprawled on the ground.

Okwaho, on the other hand, leans over the desk and speaks intensely down to Colin. "You low-life scumbag. She was only 15 at the time – an underage minor."

The commotion attracts attention. The lizard-like receptionist appears. And on her heels the chief inspector, Samuel Barker, appears. Barker shouts in through the open doorway. "What's going on here?"

Jack, who has remained standing at the doorway, turns to Barker and says calmly, "Mr Clark received some disturbing news quite suddenly. It appears that the shock knocked him off his chair."

Barker strides past 'Miss Lizard' and Jack, and stands over the fallen Colin Clark. "Is this true, Clark?"

Colin Clark is unable to come up with an answer. His instinct for self-preservation wins out and induces him to lie. "Yes. I must have fallen off my chair. It rolled unexpectedly and I hit my nose on the desk."

Sam Barker does not believe him. He looks at the two visitors and addresses them. "You are finished in here, I understand? And you are leaving." This is clearly rendered as an order, not as a question.

Jack looks at Colin, who has managed to regain his composure and is sitting at his desk once more. He holds his nose to stem the flow of blood and waves away any attempted assistance. Okwaho remains leaning over him in an intimidating manner.

Jack responds to Barker. "No. We are not quite finished. I believe Mr Clark has some more information to impart to us before we leave."

Barker looks disapprovingly at Colin Clark. He addresses him coarsely. "Is this true, Clark?"

"Yes, yes. Just give us a few minutes."

It is apparent to Barker that Colin would prefer the visitors to leave, but is compelled by some obligation to have them remain. There is something unsavoury about this encounter. "Very well. But make it quick." He strides away and signals to Miss Lizard to accompany him.

Jack and Okwaho are seated once more. Jack speaks calmly and gravely. "Colin Clark, let me bring you up to speed.

Currently, five former members of the *Elephant Club* are serving prison sentences. Of course, you know that – it was front-page news back in 2017. You remember that 30 young women were rescued from a human trafficking operation in the *Elephant Club*." Jack opens his file once more and extracts the unwelcome picture. "This picture is from the police file on the case. Be assured, we have no interest in you other than to connect with the girl in the picture. Don't play games with us. Help us find the girl and we will be out of your hair. Anything less than full cooperation and we will advise Detective Crouse of the Toronto Police of your connection to the *Elephant Club*."

Colin swallows hard and nods. He is still holding his nose. Miss Lizard walks past the office. Jack is aware of her in his peripheral vision. He sees the crisp white blouse and black below-the-knee flared skirt and one-inch high-heeled pumps stride past – the sentinel on active duty.

Colin manages to speak at last. He chooses his words slowly as he assembles his thoughts. "'Sugar'. That was her name. She was my escort that evening."

"Her name is 'Dorinda Trapper'. 'Sugar Maple' was her name while enslaved by the *Elephant Club*." Colin winches visibly as Jack utters 'enslaved'. Jack continues. "The picture was taken on Sunday 16 April 2017 at 7:34pm. Is that the evening you are referring to?"

"I guess so. There was only one such engagement."

"Tell us about the evening."

"As I say, Sugar was my escort for the evening. It was a private event."

Jack refers to the picture. "A formal event?"

"A celebration. I wanted to impress my friends by bringing an attractive escort."

"And did you impress?"

"I believe so."

Jack directs his attention to a critical point in time. "Pay attention. There were two calls made from your cell phone at 4:48am on 17 April 2017. That is nine hours and 14 minutes later. Tell us about that."

"I don't remember at what time anything occurred that night. I certainly didn't make any phone calls."

"Where is your phone now?"

"It's right here on my desk." Colin motions to where his phone is located.

"The same phone?"

"I have one cell phone. I have had this phone for three years."

Okwaho lifts Colin's phone and scrolls through the call history. He stops at a selected spot and shows the display to Colin and Jack in turn – two calls made at 4:48am on 17 April

2017.

Jack looks at Colin intently. "I didn't say you made the calls. I said that two calls were made. Dorinda Trapper made those calls. Explain how she had your phone."

Colin raises his eyebrows questioningly. Just then, it strikes him how Jack knew about the calls. He mutters, "The 'Michael' calls. That's what they were about. You were tracing the source of the calls."

"And when you answered my call a few minutes ago, we were certain. And so, the penny dropped." Or in this case, for Colin, the 'fist' dropped.

Colin concentrates to jog his memory and form his reply. "At one point during the night, I discovered Sugar stealing from my jacket. I retrieved my phone from her and I insisted that she leave."

"Where was that and in what manner did you 'insist'?"

"It was in a park."

"The 'event' was in a park?"

"No, it was late and the event was winding down. We were driving away from it at the time. We stopped at a park. It was Sugar's idea to stop there."

"Let me understand. You left the venue of the event and you drove to a park. And it was Sugar's idea?"

"That's right. But she tricked me. She only wanted to rob me."

"And did she rob you?"

"Yes. She took my phone but I wrested it from her. She also took the $600 I had in my jacket pocket. I did not notice the loss of the money until some minutes later. But when I returned to the park, she was nowhere to be seen. She had disappeared with my $600."

Jack and Okwago exchange glances. They are getting somewhere with their questioning. Jack continues to press Colin while he is talkative. "So, which park was it?"

"I don't know. It was in Mississauga."

"There are many parks in Mississauga. You say you drove back to it. What street were you on at the time?"

"It was the Dundas."

"If I understand, you drove on Dundas Street to return to the park?"

"Yes."

"Was it a large park, a small park, a road-side park? What do you remember about the park?"

"It was a large park. I remember a river. There was a river in the park."

"A big river, or a creek?"

"The river was wide. It was a big river."

Jack recognizes the location. "Dundas Street West at the Credit River. That's Erindale Park. It has vehicular access and parking."

Okwaho addresses Colin. "You didn't answer how you 'insisted' that she leave. Did Dorinda choose to leave of her own free will? Or did you use forceful encouragement?"

Colin replies defensively. "She was stealing from me. I took my phone from her and I pushed her away. When I drove off, she was lying on the grass in the park. She wasn't hurt or anything. I just drove away to teach her a lesson."

"You 'taught her a lesson'?"

Colin has no reply. But the inference is clear. Okwaho is suggesting that Colin roughed her up before departing.

Jack sums up. "Just to be clear. The last time you saw Dorinda Trapper (Sugar) was shortly before 5:00am on 17 April 2017. And she was alive and well at that time. Is that correct?"

"That is correct. And she **was** alive and well."

Jack notices Miss Lizard make another sortie past the office. Their meeting is being monitored by the guardian lizard. Jack and Okwaho stand. Jack assembles his papers and secures the file. He concludes the meeting with a parting shot. "Colin Clark, if what you tell us is false or misleading in any way, we will meet again. And next time, you will contend primarily with Okwaho here. And you can expect a follow-up visit from Detective Crouse. Let's hope, for all our sakes, that we are done."

When Jack and Okwaho enter the reception area, they observe Miss Lizard at her station. Sam Barker is standing beside her desk. He scowls at them. Two bank security guards stand on either side of the exit doors.

Barker addresses Jack and Okwaho. "I must ask you to leave. I insist. To ensure that you comply, you will be escorted out of the building by security officers."

Jack shrugs. He has acquired the information he sought. Okwaho is expressionless. Jack walks to the exit doors. The guards move closer together to compel the two men to exit in single file. Okwaho follows closely behind Jack. The burly officer on the right shifts his weight a little to the left. Jack turns his body sideways to avoid making contact and walks past him. The officer scowls menacingly at Okwaho, who is following close behind. He diminishes the gap by a further inch. Okwaho stumbles against him, requiring the officer to step back to maintain his balance. Unfortunately for the security officer, Okwaho's toe snags the burly man's heel. The security guard trips and falls heavily to the floor. Okwaho's mukluk-bearing foot lands firmly on his chest and presses against the man's Adam's apple thus rendering him immobile.

Security man number two springs to his partner's aid. However, Jack's reflexes are faster. Jack deftly grabs the second man's right thumb and twists it. The man winces in a combination of pain and surprise and discovers that he is also rendered immobile with his arm held fast behind his back and his face pressed to the wall.

Okwaho speaks quietly and solemnly. "Heed this, 'Kenraken', lay your hand on me at your peril. When I release you, you will stand clear. Say 'yes' if you accept."

Man number one, whose face is pressed to the ground, mutters a muffled 'Yes'.

Simultaneously, Jack whispers a calming 'Easy' to man number two. Thus cautioned, they release the two subdued security officers who resume a dignified stance. They carefully observe an acceptable distance beyond an arm's reach.

Meanwhile, Sam Barker is taken by surprise, stunned by the suddenness of the commotion. He stands at the reception desk open-mouthed. By the time he is fully cognizant of the situation, a tense calm pervades the area. He shouts at Jack and Okwaho. "I am calling the police!"

Okwaho strides purposefully back to the reception desk and lifts Miss Lizard's phone. He keys in '911' on the board and hands the receiver to Barker. "Your call, sir."

Okwaho and Jack exit the suite shoulder-to-shoulder through the double doors. The security officers afford them adequate space.

While awaiting the elevator, Jack looks back through the glass doors. The two security offers appear chastened; Barker hangs up the phone without speaking; Miss Lizard observes the entire scene critically with a mocking smile; Colin Clark peers around a distant corner like a timid mouse.

Moments later, inside the descending elevator, Jack checks that he is in possession of his valuable files. Thus assured, he remarks to Okwaho, "Good move back there – befitting a wolf."

Okwaho shakes his shoulders to adjust his jacket. He touches the brim of his hat and speaks sideways to Jack. "And the snake displayed a nifty trick too."

'Snake-man' and 'Wolf' depart from the TD Centre with a satisfying sense of accomplishment.

CHAPTER THIRTEEN

JACK AND OKWAHO ALTER COURSE

Tuesday 14 January 2019. It is 1:00pm. Jack and Okwaho exit the subway train at the end of the line at Kipling Station. They walk to Jack's car, parked in the south parking lot. When Jack departs from the lot, instead of heading south on Kipling Avenue as expected, he turns left and loops around to Kipling northbound. The intersection at Dundas Street is under reconfiguration construction. Jack fails to navigate to Dundas westbound. He snorts in disapproval. He makes a quick lane change and takes Bloor eastbound for one block. Jack is annoyed at having to circle around. Thereupon, he drives to the corner of Dundas Street West and Joplin Avenue South at the perimeter of Six Points Plaza. He brings his car to a stop at *Apache Burgers*.

Okwaho looks at Jack critically and asks, "Is this a joke?"

Jack steps out of the car and responds to Okwaho. "No joke. These are the best burgers in the GTA (Greater Toronto Area). Come on. Let's eat in celebration."

Ten minutes later, Okwaho admits that Jack is correct. He finishes his *Apache Burger* which is double the size of Jack's hamburger. The two men are pleased with the rapid progress of the investigation. Okwaho asks Jack, "Okay, 'Snake-man'. So what's next?"

"Now we visit Erindale Park." Jack travels along Dundas Street rather than take the QEW. Thirty minutes later, the two men stand in Erindale Park. The park is snow-covered. A small section of the car park is clear of snow. Jack observes that the park is open to cross-country skiers who trek the trails along the riverbank. He walks through the trampled snow to the river. He peers at the rapidly-flowing water for almost a minute. It shows no sign of freezing. Satisfied with his observation, he returns to the car. He rotates his body and scans the area. Then he declares, "This is where Colin Clark would have parked his car. The river, as you see, is quite close. Dorinda, if she were fleeing from him could have crossed the pedestrian bridge to *The University of Toronto Mississauga Campus* and thence to Mississauga Road." He turns to face Dundas Street. "Or, she returned the way she came..."

"...and would have proceeded either east or west on Dundas."

"There is one other option. She could have jumped into the river." Both men look somberly at the swift-flowing current of the Credit River and at the straddling snow-encrusted pedestrian bridge devoid of footprints.

Thereafter, Jack embarks on the slow, but methodical, dogged work of investigation. He is hampered by the absence of a clear photograph of Dorinda. The one picture he possesses, the one with Colin Clark in the shot, fails to display her face.

He contacts the Peel Police for reports on any dead bodies found in the region since April 2017. All deaths had been identified and none of the victims on file fit the description of Dorinda Trapper. He rules out suicide.

He contacts refuge centres for the homeless and speaks to the staff and residents. He widens his investigation to inquire of panhandlers who stand at highway ramps. He checks out charity kitchens and other places frequented by street dwellers. None recalls seeing an indigenous girl answering to the description of Dorinda Trapper.

Jack considers the activity and nature of Monday-morning traffic. 5:00am is a quiet time. There would have been little traffic on Dundas Street at the time of Dorinda's departure from Erindale Park. However, the Dundas bus runs 24 hours. Jack next contacts Mississauga Transit. The shift managers are sympathetic and cooperate attentively. He inquires if any bus driver on the Dundas route remembers observing anyone resembling Dorinda in April 2017. The shift managers refer him to the appropriate drivers, but no one recalls anything of significance.

The only stores open at 5:00am would have been 24-hour fast-food stores, 24-hour food markets and 24-hour pharmacies. Jack investigates all possible stores within a radius of an hour's walk from Erindale. He even includes the *Tim Hortons* at Dundas and Confederation, but the staff have changed in the past year and are unable to help.

After an exhaustive two weeks, Jack Doyle draws a blank. The Toronto cop was correct – Dorinda Trapper has disappeared. Jack is deflated. Until now, he has never regarded a person 'missing without a trace' as 'disappeared' – as if vanished into thin air. He was full of optimism when he walked out of the TD Centre on the morning of 14 January. Fourteen days later, on Monday 28 January 2019, he sits alone in his office drumming his fingers on the surface of his desk. He has had no contact with Okwaho since Monday 21 January when 'the Wolf' phoned for a progress report. At that time, Jack reported a disappointing lack of progress. Okwaho grunted in displeasure and disconnected the call. Today, Jack is reluctant to contact him with another empty report.

He continues to drum his fingers. A heavy snowfall descends. Jack listens to the thundering noise of the convoy of plows on the QEW. Rather than go home through the snowstorm, Jack waits for the plows to clear the streets before venturing on the road. North Service Road is not a priority road for snow removal. Jack prepares for a long wait.

At 7:47pm, the building is thrown into darkness. The streetlights extinguish. It is a storm blackout. Jack walks blindly to the kitchenette to make a coffee. He is half-way there when he realizes that it is a futile exercise. There is no electrical power for the coffee-maker. He feels his way along the wall and navigates back to his darkened office. He locates his chair and sits heavily.

Jack is aware of commotion in the corridor. He listens to the marriage counsellor and her assistant as they make their way from unit 101D.

"Thankfully, the exit sign is visible," one voice proclaims with noticeable relief.

"Yes. Let's make our way towards it."

Jack follows the sound of their conversation. The two women

proceed from their unit to the stairs. "Ah, the stairs. Thank God for the emergency lighting. We can see our way down to the exit door."

"Blast. I left my briefcase behind. I'll go back to fetch it."

"Are you sure you'll be able to locate it in the dark?"

"Yes, Rita. I'll find it with the help of my cell phone. The glow from the screen will give me sufficient light."

"Okay, Connie. I'll wait for you at the exit door."

Shortly thereafter, Jack hears the two women finally leave the building. The entrance door opens and shuts with an audible sound. The door self-locks when closed and only a keyholder has access to the building. Jack relaxes. And then, the building is ghostly silent. He remains seated and waits for the power to return.

Jack falls asleep. He awakens later when the heating furnace roars back to life and the lights flicker on. His phone chirps and beeps as it powers up. He is surprised to see Okwaho standing before him on the other side of his desk. Jack is taken aback. "Okwaho! How long have you been here? And how did you get in? I did not hear you enter." Jack surmises that the cunning Indian sneaked in as the two women exited.

Instead of a response, Okwaho leans across the desk and swings a punch at Jack. Had Jack been as slow as Colin Clark, he would have suffered a broken nose. But he deftly dodges the blow.

Jack shouts at Okwaho. "What the hell is the matter? Why did you throw the punch at me?" Jack stands up and walks to confront Okwaho face-to-face. This time, Okwaho slaps him hard on the cheek. "Damn it, Okwaho. That hurts. What's the matter with you?"

"I'm attempting to locate Jack Doyle." He slaps him again.

Jack's Irish roots rise to the surface. He punches his fist at Okwaho. 'The Wolf' ducks successfully. Both men engage in throwing punches. Both are equally adept at blocking and dodging. Neither lands a serious blow. Finally, they lock arms and wrestle to the ground.

Jack snarls to Okawo, "You damn Indian..."

"That's what I want to hear." Okwaho lessens his grip on Jack. Jack accommodates by reciprocating.

Jack sits on the ground with his back to the wall. "So, tell me, Indian, what is this about?"

Okwaho stands up. He retrieves his hat from where it fell during the struggle. Once he composes himself, he sits in the guest chair. Jack returns to his chair behind the desk. He maintains a watchful eye on Okwaho lest he resumes his attack.

'The Wolf' regains his breath and speaks. "I know Jack Doyle – 'Onyare, the snake' – for many years. On Wednesday 09 January 2019, I came to visit you. But **that** was the real Jack Doyle. This," pointing at Jack, "is not Jack Doyle. Where is the wily tricky snake?"

"What do you mean 'This is not Jack Doyle'?" Jack is offended. He did not suffer any ill effects from the scuffle, but this remark wounds him.

"You have lost your edge."

"I have lost my edge?"

"Yes. It comes down to how you regard Dorinda Trapper."

"I am committed to finding Dorinda Trapper. You have been with me since 09 January. You know how committed I am."

"What do you care?"

"That's not fair. I care. I care that Amy is suffering from grief. I care that Dorinda is lost, maybe even dead. I **care.**"

"And that's your weak point. You show sympathy and concern. You have developed an emotional attachment to the case. You are afraid to look to where the hard answers lie."

"You are suggesting that I have lost my objectivity? That I am hindered by emotion?"

"No. You are hindered by the **wrong** emotion. You were at your best when you hated us. You need to find your hatred for us again."

Jack ponders on this. He remembers when he previously

worked on an investigation. He was like a dog on a bone. He frequently outwitted cunning savages and successfully entrapped them. His adage was, 'Think like a savage and act like a savage to catch a savage'. Perhaps Okwaho is correct and Jack needs to employ this maxim to the current investigation. He addresses 'the Wolf'. "You want me to catch a 'savage Indian'?"

"That's right, 'Snake-man'. Catch a 'cunning savage Indian'."

Jack nods. He thinks aloud so that Okwaho hears. "At 4:50am on 17 April 2017, a young feisty savage is lying on the grass in Erindale Park. She is dressed in an elegant dress (presumably) and has $600 in her possession. Would she go to the police? No. They would learn of her line of work – she must know that it is illegal to sell sexual services. And she has other reasons to distrust the police. So, where would a savage go? Back to its lair to lick its wounds and recover. Could Dorinda have considered returning to Red Rapids Reserve?"

Okwaho interjects. "You're slipping again. You referred to her as 'Dorinda'. Get back to the 'young cunning savage'. Bear in mind how much you despise us."

"What would a savage with $600 do, if she resolved to journey from Erindale Park to Red Rapids? Obtain travel attire – that's what." Jack shifts his chair to access his keyboard and googles an internet search of outdoor clothing stores. He favours a location east of Erindale – westbound is the wrong direction. His first choice is *Mark's* on Dundas near Dixie. He looks at Okwaho and says, "*Mark's!* That's where she went. 1180 Dundas Street East at the corner of Palston. They are open 10:00am to 7:00pm." Jack's alternative choice is *Dixie Outlet Mall*, the location of a flea market and a *Nike Clearance Centre,* which is a half-hour walk south from *Mark's* on Dixie Road.

"You think she went to *Mark's* at Dundas & Dixie?"

"Yes. Either there or to *Dixie Outlet Mall* further south." Jack checks the time displayed in the computer's toolbar. "Hey, look at the time. It's late. *Mark's* is closed now, so, let's meet tomorrow morning."

*   *   *   *   *

On Tuesday 29 January 2019, Jack and Okwaho enter *Mark's* clothing store at 10:00am. Both men are wearing winter jackets. Okwaho is dressed in mukluks and his signature hat. Jack is dressed in cargo pants (obtained from *Mark's*) over snow boots. His *Blue Jays* cap is positioned securely on his head. Jack engages the cashier in conversation. She recognizes him from a previous purchase. The store is empty of customers. She is friendly and talkative and is willing to speak with Jack. Her employee ID pin displays her name.

Jack addresses her by name. "Sandy, have you worked here long?"

"Say, I remember you. You've been in here a few times."

"And so I have. But tell me, were you working here in April

224

2017?"

"I've been here for almost four years. And in April 2017, I worked the same hours as now – opening the store at ten o'clock Monday to Fridays. I don't work weekends, though."

"Really? Well, perhaps you remember a peculiar customer. By 'peculiar', I mean a memorable customer. She is an acquaintance of mine."

"And how 'peculiar' is your 'acquaintance'?"

"Well, at the time. She was 15, but she looked a few years older."

"She?"

"Yes. She would have been dressed in a black evening gown, totally unsuitable for day wear. She required more rugged clothing. And she favoured cash payments."

"You realize that I am not permitted to divulge our customers' personal information."

"I understand. I'm not inquiring into her private data. I'm just curious if you remember her."

Sandy is talkative by nature. Fortunately for Jack, she opens up without any further coaxing. "You know, I **do** remember that person. It was right at opening time. She was already waiting outside when I arrived. She came in here in her bare feet, carrying her shoes. Now that's 'peculiar'. This dress thing she was wearing didn't have pockets or anything. She carried her money in her shoes for want of a purse or bag. Who uses their shoes as a purse? – I asked myself. Anyway, the dress thing had a long slit up the side. It wasn't actually a dress but a short-pants outfit that flowed like a dress. It was very expensive looking. It was a pity about the dirt on the back at one of the shoulder blades. Otherwise, it was flawless. I figured she fell in her high heels. Maybe that's why she took them off."

"You know, Sandy, that's exactly the person I know." Jack shows her the picture of Dorinda taken outside the club. "And is this the dress?"

Sandy looks at the picture. Her eyes widen in recognition. "Yes. That's the dress. And that's the long hair. But I'm not too sure about the face from the way it's hidden."

Jack nods in understanding. He asks, "So, she would have purchased boots?"

"Yes. How did you know? They were better suited for walking than her high-heeled shoes, I'll say."

"And a coat?"

"Yes. A winter coat with a hood."

"Yes, that's right. Now, my friend is very frugal. I can't imagine her spending a lot of money. What would her stuff cost? $400, $500?"

"You certainly know your friend. She chose the end-of-season items that were selling for 50% off. $500 worth for half-price."

"Did she do anything else 'peculiar'?"

"Well, it was funny to watch her, you know. She pulled dollar bills out of her shoes. And she had more stuck in the elastic of her shoulder pad. She didn't want her newly-purchased clothes wrapped; she dressed in them right away. She jammed her high-heeled shoes into the coat pockets. I don't blame her, really. They were very stylish and expensive shoes. I would have given her a bag for them had she asked. Anyway, off she went."

"Which way did she go?"

"She turned east. I don't think she went to a car. There wasn't any car parked here at the time."

Jack thanks Sandy. He purchases a pair of socks and leaves the store. Outside, he and Okwaho turn left towards Dixie Road. They spend the next two hours speaking to the staff of other shops in the area. They fail to obtain any more information on Dorinda.

"Okay, 'Snake-man'. Where do we go from here?" Okwaho poses this question to Jack over a coffee in *Tim Hortons*, at the corner of Dixie & Dundas, at the same table where Dorinda sat on 17 April 2017.

"Here we are at Dixie & Dundas, in the very spot where

Dorinda..."

"...the young 'savage'..."

"...where the young 'savage' posed the same question to herself." Jack, in saying 'in the very spot', is speaking figuratively, unaware that he is sitting where Dorinda literally sat. "There are four possible ways to get from here to Red Rapids. Via Rail from Toronto Union Station to Sudbury Junction, 16 kilometres from Sudbury City Centre."

Okwaho qualifies the comment. "A Dundas bus eastbound from here to the subway. And the subway to Union Station."

"That's one way. The other way is by bus from the *Toronto Coach Terminal*. That has the advantage of greater frequency and a choice of stops in Sudbury."

The 'Wolf' nods in understanding. "*Toronto Coach Terminal* is next to the *Eaton Centre*. It is also accessible by subway. Dorinda would be familiar with the location."

"Another option is to fly from Toronto to Sudbury. This is unlikely. Judging from how 'savage girl' was dressed and how controlling the *Elephant Club* was to her, she would not have possessed ID at the time. And all airlines require a government-issued photo ID to board a flight."

"So, that's out."

"Lastly, hitchhiking. There is a major truck facility a 15-minute bus ride north of here on Dixie at Shawson Drive."

"Of the four options, you consider the bus to be the most promising choice?"

"No. Think about it. Our little 'savage' is running **to** Red Rapids. But she is also running **away** from her previous subjugation in captivity. Hence, she would avoid downtown Toronto. Come on, Okwaho. Waken up. If you were tracking an animal en route to its lair, would you expect it to travel through dangerous territory?"

"No. It would skirt around it."

"Precisely. And that is how we track our fleeing 'savage'."

Later, Jack and Okwaho conduct inquiries at the *Husky/Esso* truck facility. It is a fruitless quest. No one at the facility has any recollection of seeing Dorinda. She could have been any one of numerous anonymous hitchhikers that hit on truckers. Furthermore, truckers are transient. If Dorinda interacted with truckers on 17 April 2017, their current whereabouts could be anywhere in North America. One thing is for sure, they are not at the facility today.

Jack and Okwaho drive to the *Tim Hortons* one block north of *Husky/Esso* at Britannia Road East. Jack orders his usual coffee and maple dip doughnut. This location no longer provides maple dip. It is relegated to 'optional doughnut' and is available only at a limited number of locations. Jack considers this to be 'un-Canadian'. In protest, he declines to choose an alternative.

When they are seated, Okwaho asks, "Is this a dead-end to

your inquiry?"

"Okwaho, Okwaho, you disappoint me. Once, you were a hunter-wolf. Now, look at yourself. Let me ask you. Do you really need to track your prey when you are certain of its destination?"

"Well, if I know where it is going, I would go to its lair and intercept it en route."

"And in this investigation..."

"Go to Red Rapids and intercept... I see what you mean. Work backwards from Red Rapids to here. That's how you expect to locate Dorinda."

"Somewhere in the reverse trail, we should encounter a sign – in the reserve, in Elliot Lake, in Sudbury, back to this point if necessary. 'Wolf', we conduct the next stage of our investigation in the Red Rapids Reserve."

CHAPTER FOURTEEN

THE REVERSE INVESTIGATION

Wednesday 30 January 2019. Jack concludes his inquiries in the GTA (Greater Toronto Area). He consults his files, inserting updates and checking his emails and internet sites to confirm the accuracy of his findings to date. He looks up from his desk at Okwaho. "Do us both a favour. Book us a flight for first thing tomorrow morning and arrange transportation to Red Rapids. I'm going home to pack my things. Phone me later to confirm the departure time."

Like a sleeping wolf that springs into action in a split second, Okwaho immediately undertakes the assignment with serious determination.

Thursday 31 January 2019. Jack and Okwaho disembark from Air Canada Express Jazz flight AC8605 on a De Havilland-Bombardier Dash-8. It is 8:30am in Sudbury. A half-hour later, Okwaho picks up his rental car.

"Good God," Jack exclaims in the rental-pickup lot upon seeing Okwaho's choice of vehicle. "Did you rent a tank?"

"A *Chevrolet Tahoe Premier RST* 355 horsepower SUV with six-speed automatic transmission."

"What? Do you expect to drive to Red Rapids?"

"Okwaho replies matter-of-factly. "Yes."

Jack looks at him with skepticism. "Are you serious?"

"Deadly serious."

"How...?" Jack shakes his head, unable to comprehend the wisdom of Okwaho's decision.

At 11:30am, Okhawo navigates the corner at the intersection of the Trans-Canada (Hwy 17) and Hwy 108. He turns north onto Hwy 108. Thereupon, he drives into the snow-encrusted parking lot of the sole visible building ahead. Okwaho exclaims, "'Gas and Hot Food'. That's what the sign says, and that's what we need."

"Good thinking. This might be the last palatable food I taste for a few days."

"You don't like bannock and moose?"

Inside, Jack orders peameal bacon with eggs and home-fried potatoes. Okwaho shrugs and mouths 'What the hell' and orders the same. The grouchy old man who takes their order shouts through a hatch in the inner wall. An equally grouchy-looking woman, in what must be the kitchen, undertakes to prepare the food. Jack leans across the table to Okwaho. "Welcome to your friendly country family-run business."

Okwaho glances around. He spots the sign at the checkout counter – 'Cash Only'. The grouchy man places two cups on their table. Then without asking, he brings the coffee pot from the hot-plate and fills both cups. Okwaho says, "Thanks. But I did not order coffee."

The man walks away in disinterest and speaks with his back turned. "Coffee comes with breakfast. If you don't want it, don't drink it." He stops and turns back to face the two customers. "And don't ask for decaf or tea. You get coffee here that tastes like coffee."

Okwaho acknowledges him and responds. "Coffee that tastes like coffee is just fine. Thanks." He winks at Jack in amusement.

Notwithstanding the owner's irreverent manner, the coffee tastes good and likewise the food – freshly made with generous helpings.

Shortly after, Jack and Okwaho observe a beaten-up pickup drive up to the gas pumps. A scruffy man in a greasy boiler suit and oil-stained baseball cap gets out of the cab and fills his gas tank. Thereafter, Greasy Man parks his pickup alongside the pristine SUV and enters the store. He sits at a table in a corner partly obscured by shelves of merchandise. No greeting passes between Greasy Man and Grouchy Man, nor any gesture of acknowledgement. Grouchy Man places a cup on the newcomer's table and pours him a coffee. Neither man looks at the other. Grouchy Man slaps a slip of paper on his table. He then returns to his seat behind the counter and Greasy Man stares out the window. The entire encounter occurs without any apparent communication.

Jack leans over to Okwaho. "One of his 'regulars' I bet."

Okwaho studies Greasy Man. Ten minutes elapse. Greasy Man takes his slip of paper and whacks it on the checkout counter with some money and walks out – probably tendering exact change. At no time do Greasy Man and Grouchy Man acknowledge each other. Not a word is spoken. Okwaho observes the greasy-looking customer leave in his dilapidated pick-up truck. Grouchy Man takes the slip, scribbles on it and skewers it on a dangerous-looking spike file.

Okwaho attempts to make conversation with Grouchy Man. "One of your 'regulars'?" He asks.

"Yup."

"From around here?"

Grouchy Man turns his head and nods east. Okwaho follows his gaze. He sees a vacant lot with a parked trailer and trees beyond it. Grouchy Man mumbles, "Fortunately, you can't see his washed-out place from here."

"So what does your friend work at? Is he a mechanic?"

"He's not my friend. And he doesn't work neither. Nate is a lazy waster. Never worked a day in his life. He owns a piece of worthless land. He makes a bit of money on his parking lot – charging for overnight parking. Trucks, you know, that stop near the inspection station. He also hauls away junk for a fee – and then lets it sit on his land. He rents his property for outdoor events – barbeques and raves and the like."

Okwaho peers intently at the landscape. "Who would hold an outdoor event in a place that that?"

"Bikers. They come up the Trans-Canada twice a year." Grouchy Man takes the coffee pot and goes to the table. He refills the two cups without an invitation. He looks closely at Okwaho and says, "You're not Ojibwe."

"I'm Mohawk Haudenosaunee."

"Not connected to Serpent River then?"

"No. Why do you ask?"

"I get them in here quite often – Ojibwe from the reserve down the road." Once more, Grouchy Man points by nodding his head. "It's just out of sight beyond the inspection station at the T-intersection. Three or four hundred live there. I get a few Cree too, but not so many. I never see a Mohawk come in here, though."

"You see Cree come in here? Where do they come from?"

"There are three reserves just north of Elliot Lake. And three more just north of that. And God knows how many more are north of that again. Yes, sometimes I get Cree in here."

"And you can tell the difference?"

"Of course." Grouchy Man gives him an offended look and returns to his counter position.

Okwaho leans towards Jack and says, "See? Some people can distinguish between us. We are not all simply 'Indians'."

At 12:30pm, Jack and Okwaho pay for their breakfast in cash and leave the *Gas and Hot Food* store. Okwaho glances at the front of the SUV before stepping into the driver's seat. Jack queries him. "Checking for scratches or dents made by the pickup, are you?"

"Did you notice that when we paid for our breakfast back there, that the man scribbled on our slip and stuck it on a spike file?"

"Yes. So what? He also did it for the greasy-looking customer in the boiler suit. I'd say it's his customary filing system."

"He scribbled this SUV's licence plate number on the slip. I wonder if that's customary."

Jack is only mildly interested in the old man's archaic accounting system. "Okwaho, start the car and get some heat moving. It must be -40 in here."

Okwaho starts the car and responds bluntly. "It's only -22°C. Be prepared for -34°C"

They reach Elliot Lake 20 minutes later. Okwaho drives through the town to the north side. He stops at the outskirts of town on Hwy 108 at the intersection of Timber Road. At this location, Jack is confronted by two significant sights. The first one is no surprise – the roads are not clear of snow beyond this point. The snow is hard-packed and the road is negotiable by cars with appropriate winter tires. But, the second sight amazes Jack. The area is a hive of activity comprised of First Nations men and women.

Jack turns to Okwaho. "It looks like the entire Red Rapids Reserve is here in Elliot Lake. What's going on?"

"I see 16 here from the reserve. In addition, I see six non-indigenous people. Plus you and me. As to what is happening? This is the first convoy to travel on the ice road this year. Traditionally, the ice road is ready to accommodate wheeled vehicles starting from 01 February. Of course, snowmobiles ply the route from earlier."

"It's 31 January."

"So it is. I better tell the chief to wait 12 hours."

The site is noisy and smelly. Engines are idling, men and women are shouting to each other over the noise, and the smoky smell of gasoline and diesel hangs languidly in the air. Jack observes a *Ford Expedition Max* SUV and a *Dodge Ram 1500 TRX*. Both vehicles are brand new. And both have boat trailers hitched to them. Each trailer is loaded with an aluminum flat-bottom skiff boat. For winter conditions, the trailers are fitted with skids beside the wheels. The helpers crank down the skids to meet the ground so that they will glide over the snow when pulled. There are 10 snowmobiles parked alongside and three local delivery trucks. Each snowmobile has a rudimentary flat sled hitched at the rear, designed to transport hunted game. There is no kill today. Instead, the sleds are employed to carry equipment for ice-road maintenance. The one vehicle that is out of place is the gasoline tanker truck parked in the adjacent yard.

Okwaho parks his car close to the group. He jumps out and

shouts instructions to Jack. "Get into the driver's seat and keep the engine running. The inside temperature is not to drop below 4°C."

Jack is puzzled but is content to comply. Even with a winter coat and a toque, Jack is keen to keep the temperature at his level of comfort – significantly above freezing.

Jack observes Okwaho and the other men unload the contents of the delivery trucks and transfer cargo to the *Ram* pickup and the *Ford X*. And they continue to load additional goods into the boats. Okwaho opens the rear door of his rented SUV and loads crates of food inside. He hurriedly slams the door shut. Moments later he throws sacks of food onto the back seat. Whereupon, he resumes his place in the driver's seat. Jack returns to the passenger seat and queries Okwaho for an explanation.

Okwaho peers ahead as if checking for cues. He describes the activity. "Two snowmobiles lead the convoy. Three on the right and three on the left. And two follow in the rear."

"Why?" Jack asks in puzzlement.

"To check the integrity of the road and the safety of the loads."

"What 'integrity'? Do you mean it's not safe?"

Okwaho looks askance at Jack. "This is the first convoy to traverse the ice road this year. It is just past one o'clock. We need to be on our way if we are to reach the reserve before dark. By travelling at a modest safe speed, we expect to arrive in Red Rapids by six – a half-hour before nightfall. There is sufficient partial light from 4:30pm to 6:30pm – the period of 'usable daylight'. The men and women on the snowmobiles look for weak areas in the ice surface and warn us to avoid them. You'll see some red cone markers in places."

"How do they recognize 'weak areas'?"

"Colour is the clue. White is a sign of danger. An auger is used to confirm."

"That can't be easy. Isn't all ice white?"

Okwaho shoots a mocking smile at Jack. "To one who knows ice and snow, there are over 20 shades of white. These people are experienced. They know which white to avoid."

"And if, or when, they find faults in the ice? Then what?"

"Faults are caused by air pockets in the ice. They are speedily fixed by boring holes and pouring melted snow into the holes. At this temperature, the pockets are filled and frozen in minutes. A subsequent bore confirms the strength and thickness of the ice."

Jack sees the convoy move forward. Two snowmobiles are in the lead, followed by the Red Rapids Reserve's chief driving his new *Ford Expedition* and its trailing cargo of boat laden with goods. Next in line is the *Dodge Ram*. Both vehicles are flanked by snowmobiles. Jack expects Okwaho to join the departing convoy. But he remains stationary with the engine running. Jack looks at him enquiringly. Why is he waiting? The answer lies in the gasoline tanker. The tanker – all 13 metres of it and 2.5 metres wide – edges out of the parking yard and shifts gears as it catches up with the departing convoy. It too is flanked by two snowmobiles. At this point, Okwaho proceeds forward and joins the convoy behind the tanker truck. The final two snowmobiles take up the rear. The remaining vans and trucks are local. Having delivered their assigned merchandise to the convoy, they depart back to Elliot Lake.

On Hwy 108 north, the convoy reaches a speed of 60kph. Where the highway terminates, they continue on Secondary Highway 639 north, still maintaining a constant speed. During this leg of the trip, Okwaho explains to Jack. "I knew about this convoy from when it was planned a week ago. It was a fortunate coincidence that you decided to visit Red Rapids at the same time. So, I arranged our participation." He glances at Jack for a reaction. Jack nods and signals for more information. "You realize that it is not prudent to travel the ice road alone. Two or more vehicles at a time are recommended. Or have a snowmobile escort."

"Okay. But what about all the stuff I saw loaded?"

"This is the only way to transport cars and boats into the reserve. The SUV and the pickup will have magnetic lettering affixed later and will be employed in the reserve's administrative services. The boats, understandably, will be employed in the reserves guest-fishing business."

"And the tanker? I suppose that is the reserves yearly supply of gasoline?"

"Correct."

"So what's in the back seat that needs to be kept above 4°C?"

"Onions and potatoes. And in the back, there are crates of tomatoes and oranges. The chief, up front, is transporting six new laptop computers for the school, along with eggs and dairy products. Oh, bacon and pork and other foodstuffs, which will not suffer from freezing, are loaded inside the two aluminum boats. The pickup is loaded with maintenance and construction supplies – timber, bags of cement and power tools. Even the snowmobiles are carrying some goods. However, the trailer-sleds are very unstable on a bumpy surface. You see how the items are strapped down securely to prevent them from falling off."

After 45 minutes, they reach the entrance to the ice road. The entrance is rough. But once settled on the ice surface, they recommence the journey at speeds alternating between 40 and 50kph. Okwaho falls silent and Jack nods off to sleep.

Jack is awakened at 4:22pm by a momentary blast of cold air. He realizes that they are not moving. The *Chevy Tahoe* is stationary. The engine is running but Okwaho is gone. That would explain the short blast of cold air. Jack opens his door to step outside, but the frigid air convinces him to remain inside. There is a group huddled at the side of the ice road and the entire convoy is stopped. Some of the men bore augers into the ice and others are in discussions with some disagreement. After some minutes, the chief makes a decision. The entire convoy is required to reverse for 50 metres. This requires skill to execute safely. Jack sees that some more testing is being conducted. Finally, after 10 minutes, the road is marked with red traffic cones to define a passable route.

There is sufficient space for the first vehicle to pass through safely. The men check the ice and wave the second vehicle through. Another debate ensues. Then they indicate to the tanker to move through. The tanker knocks against the marker cones and scatters them as it moves forward. The men wave frantically to the driver to increase speed. A loud cracking noise emanates from the ice. A 9-metre-long fracture appears along the middle of the road. One side of the road separates and shifts outwards towards the weak area. The rear of the tanker shifts with the moving ice. The tanker appears to stagger drunkenly for a moment and then successfully clears the area. Shouting erupts. But the meaning is clear – keep moving. The lead vehicles are stopped a short distance ahead. They both recommence their journey in time for the tanker to catch up without losing momentum. Okwaho's *Chevy Tahoe* remains stationary behind the cracked section of road. Jack looks gloomily at the convoy disappearing steadily into the distance.

Okwaho consults with the group of men and women that remain behind with their snowmobiles. Jack has three choices on how to proceed. First, wait half an hour for the road to be fixed. It will take that time to fill the air pockets and seal the crack with melted snow – the team is already lighting portable stoves and filling pails with snow. The second option is to clear a path through the snowbank and drive around the fault. The third option is to gun it and drive across the crack at high speed before the ice shifts any further.

Okwaho walks to the snowbank and kicks a swath parallel to the road. The snow is high, but it is also soft. He enlists some help to trample a pathway. He then estimates how much width is available for a safe passageway. He determines that he could drive with one set of wheels on the ice road and the other set on the trampled snow. The total bypass distance is 10 metres. He determines that an SUV with all-wheel drive, large rims and high clearance should successfully navigate through the bypass. He returns to the vehicle and sets it in motion. He drives in first gear. The SUV lurches and bumps on the uneven surface and, after a few tense moments, it successfully regains level ground. The men and women cheer at his success. He waves to them and continues on his journey. He turns to Jack with a self-satisfied smile. "It is fortunate that the chief is transporting the eggs and not us. I don't think they would have survived the jolting back there."

Okwaho increases speed to 55kph. In a short time, he catches up to the convoy. And an hour later, they are joined by the remainder of the snowmobile team. The team shouts to the chief to indicate that the road repairs have been executed.

The convoy reaches the reserve with 40 minutes of usable daylight remaining. From this experience, Jack is certain of one thing. He would never undertake such a journey on his own.

At 5:50pm, Okwaho halts the SUV at the hotel in Red Rapids. He turns to Jack and says, "Check yourself in, Jack.

I'll join you in half an hour. Let's say we eat at seven?"

"Where are you going in the meantime?"

"Oh, just to assist the volunteers in sorting the recently-obtained purchases. It won't take more than 30 minutes to store and shelve all the stuff."

"Okay." Jack prepares to run from the SUV to the hotel entrance. It is a distance of only 10 metres but at -26°C it is a punishment for Jack.

As Jack departs the SUV, Okwaho shouts after him. "Keep your toque on."

From his previous visit, Jack has learned some of the local practices. He stops upon entering the hotel porch. There is a pigeon-hole shelving unit in the unheated porch. Jack removes his snow-encrusted boots and knocks the snow off. Then, he places his boots in one of the storage spaces and extracts a pair of house shoes from his overnight bag. He enters the hotel and approaches the front desk. He looks back proudly at the absence of wet footprints on the floor and proceeds with the check-in formality.

At 6:30pm, he enters the dining room/bar and sits on a stool at the bar counter. He looks at his reflection in the bar mirror and admires his choice of appropriate clothing. He is wearing a multi-pocket blue denim jacket over a flaming red check shirt and his preferred dark-grey cargo pants. His head is clad in a blue-and-red *Canadiens* toque with a red pom and is accompanied by a long matching scarf wrapped loosely about his neck. Jack feels comfortable in his attire and is certain that he fits in with the local surroundings. He orders a coffee at the bar and awaits the arrival of Okwaho. The barman places a cup in front of Jack and takes a second look at the strangely-dressed guest.

At 7:00pm, Okwaho joins Jack. They both sit at a table. A waitress approaches and offers them a menu. Okwaho winks at Jack and talks to the waitress.

"I see from your nametag that you are 'Sara'."

"Yes. And you are 'Okwaho'. I know who you are; everyone knows. And your associate is 'Snake-man' who keeps his head covered. We know all about him too and what he is doing."

"Well, Sara, you are well-informed. Instead of consulting the menu, let me ask if you have any surprise items available today?"

"What kind of 'surprise'?"

"I was thinking of pork chops. And potatoes, And fried onions."

"That's not on the menu. But let me check with cook." Sara enters the kitchen and returns almost immediately. "Well, would you believe it? Cook has the very things you request. So, is this the choice for both of you?"

The two men consent. Jack decides to play along. "Excuse

me, Sara, could I request a desert? Vanilla ice cream with segments of orange."

Sara suppresses a smile. "You want segments of orange? How about tinned peaches with ice cream?"

"No. I prefer segments of orange. And not tinned mandarin oranges – fresh oranges."

"Very well, I'll see what I can do." Moments later, Sara returns to their table. "I don't believe it. A consignment of fresh oranges just arrived..." Okwaho and Jack attempt, but fail, to stifle their laughter. Sara realizes that the two men are playing a prank. She playfully swats Okwaho on the head with her menu card. She considers similarly assaulting Jack but refrains from friendly interaction with a 'snake'.

At 8:00pm, Okwaho drives the SUV across the frozen river to the 'B' section of the reserve. Jack is thankful that he chose to travel by this method. It is night-time and the temperature has fallen by two additional degrees since their arrival. Okwaho manoeuvres the SUV through the 'B' section and stops at the Trapper house.

Amy Trapper hears the SUV approach. She opens the front door and gestures to Okwaho and Jack to enter. Jack is attentive to his manners. Upon entering the porch, he removes his green hooded parka and hangs it on a hook. He removes his boots and replaces them with clean shoes. He checks that his toque is secure on his head. Thereupon, he enters the interior of the house carrying his leather-bound document case.

Amy courteously offers food to the two visiting men. Jack politely accepts. He is pleasantly surprised with the raisin bannock. He was expecting stodgy dough bread, but this fare delights his palate. Unfortunately, he still regards the *kâkikêpakwa* tea with distaste – unpleasant but tolerable.

Amy's family is assembled. Present are Mark, Jim Cool and Kokum Cool. They eagerly gaze at Jack for good news. Jack swallows and chooses his words carefully. He strives to be truthful and positive. "We have made some progress – Okwaho and I – in reconstructing Dorinda's movements in Toronto at the time of her disappearance. We still have a long way to go before completing our investigation. It is prudent, at this point, to maintain a sense of balance – accept hard truth instead of improbable expectations. Even if, or when, we succeed in locating Dorinda, it may not be the conclusion you are hoping for. Do you understand?"

Amy looks hard at Jack. Then she casts her eyes downwards and murmurs. "Just find Dorinda. Find her alive or find her dead. Just find her."

The entire company falls silent. Jack coughs and gives a summary report. The assembled family members listen without comment. Jack ends by producing Amy's credit union statement of account. He addresses her, "Amy, take a look at this statement here. I noted the deposits made to the account. Here, you see the deposits that were comprised of your money orders – you sent them to the reserve by mail. Lower down are the deposits that are the result of Rose Cool's money orders – also sent here by mail."

Amy views the statement in Jack's hand and nods in agreement. Okwaho, on the other hand, appears to have no interest in viewing the statement. He rises and leaves the room without comment.

Jack speaks to Amy. "This deposit, made on 21 April 2017, for $300, is not from any of Rose's remittances. She did not mail money until 24 April 2017. I checked with her. She is certain."

Amy looks Jack in the eyes. She wonders where this line of inquiry is going. She comments, "It's not one of mine."

"Is it possible that one or more of your money orders sat in uncollected mail at the reserve's post office for a time, and were deposited late?"

Amy rises from her chair and walks to a small dresser. She opens a drawer and extracts a small pocket-size notebook. She returns to her chair. "Look at this," she says as she opens the notebook. "I record every money order I purchase and the date I mail it. Check them off."

Amy and Jack cross-check the deposits in the statement against the records in her notebook. In the end, all deposits are accounted for, except for the one in question.

Amy shuts her notebook and thinks for a moment. "I remember that deposit. It was a single money order for $300. It came in the mail. There was no note attached. At the time, I believed that it could only come from Rose. After all, she promised to send money in units of $100. She missed two payments from earlier in the month. This looked like she just made up for the ones she missed." She looks at Jack for an explanation.

"Look, Amy, I will inquire at the credit union tomorrow morning. I will request them to put a trace on the item deposited."

Amy is pensive for a moment. She sits with her palms on her knees. She whispers to herself, yet loud enough for the benefit of those present. "If that money order did not come from me or Rose..." She places a hand on Jack's hand. Mark and Jim avert their eyes at this lapse in acceptable conduct. A Trapper/Cool does not display familiarity to an outsider. And touching Jack in this manner is a breach of decorum. Considering that Jack is an alien 'snake', by so doing, Amy is breaking a respected principle. Kokum also averts her eyes, but she does so with an intuitive understanding.

Jack is aware of the breach in decorum. He breaks the silence. "I think we have exhausted our inquiry for today." Amy quickly draws her hand back to her lap. "Let's reconvene tomorrow after I receive feedback from the credit union." This is agreeable. Jack excuses himself and prepares to return to the hotel.

Moments later, Jack exits the house. Within a few seconds, he knocks at the door for re-admittance. Amy enquires of him, "Why have you returned so quick? Did you forget something?"

Jack is embarrassed. "I did not realize it. But Okwaho left in the SUV. I don't believe I can find my way back to the hotel in the dark. And the cold is too intense for me."

Mark and Jim find this amusing. They laugh at Jack. Kokum approaches Mark and Jim. She speaks angrily to them. Since she speaks in Cree, Jack is unable to understand her. Amy translates. "Jim will drive you to the hotel on his snowmobile." At this, Jim departs from the house, presumably to get his snowmobile.

Kokum continues to speak to Mark. She points to Mark's winter clothes hanging in the porch. Then she walks to Jack and removes his gloves. She looks at them and shakes her head. She stuffs them in Jack's parka pockets. Mark is holding his large windproof fur-lined parka. She gestures to Jack to put it on. She slaps him on the shoulder until he turns his back. Then she directs Mark to place the parka on Jack back-to-front.

Mark explains to Jack. "Kokum says that you are to wear this over your parka. And you should wear it back-to-front with the hood up to protect your face." Jack permits Mark to dress him. He checks that his house shoes are securely packed in his parka. And he hangs the document bag across his shoulder. When Jack is fully attired, Mark says, "Here, put on these windproof mitts. Now, hop up behind Jim out there on the snowmobile."

Jack is thankful. His movements are inhibited by the amount of clothing he is wearing. He blindly waddles, rather than walks, to the snowmobile and struggles to mount the seat behind the driver. He shouts to Mark in the hope that he is heard through the upturned hood. "What else did Kokum say?"

"She says that you are too soft to survive here. You would die if left on your own."

Jack agrees. Before he can compose a response, the snowmobile takes off unexpectedly. Jack is thrown backwards. He flails blindly and flings his arms around. Thankfully, he manages to grab hold of Jim's body. By the time he determines how to safely maintain his seat, he arrives at the hotel. Jim retrieves Mark's parka and mitts and drives off speedily. Jack dashes to the hotel porch and quickly enters. He checks that his shoes are still within the voluminous pouch on the back of his parka. Thankfully, they are. And he confirms that his leather document bag is still strapped securely over his shoulder. Thus satisfied, he changes his shoes and enters the warmth of the hotel. He proceeds to the bar and orders a coffee. He looks around and wonders where Okwaho might be. On a hunch, he runs to the hotel entrance and looks to where the SUV was parked earlier. The spot is vacant. There is no sign of 'Wolf-man's' rented *Chevy Tahoe*. Jack shuts the door against the biting cold and returns to the bar. Where is Okwaho? His penchant for appearing and disappearing like a shadowy predator is unsettling for Jack.

CHAPTER FIFTEEN

THE WOLF LEADS

It is Saturday 02 February 2019. Jack experiences a restless night. He is awake at 6:15am. He views the first line of light that scores the horizon at Red Fox Lake. An hour later, he determines that it is time to rise. It is daylight outside but not yet dawn. He shivers, not because he feels chilly, but because the view from his window threatens him with the promise of the cold that awaits him once he steps outside. It is as if the northern winter is taunting him – daring him to venture outside.

Jack makes his way to the dining room. He is planning the day's schedule in his head. His first task, after breakfast, is to visit the credit union. He wonders if the credit union is open on a Saturday. If not, he will remain in the reserve until Monday. He trusts that he will survive the Red Rapids' chilling cold.

He sits at a table. He looks for Sara, the cheery waitress. He spots her. But he is mistaken. Instead, it is an older Sara-look-alike girl that approaches his table. Jack peers at her name tag and addresses her. "Karen, where is Sara this morning?"

Karen responds. "My sister Sara works evenings. She is still asleep. And she told me about you last night. So, would you like to order breakfast, or shall I waken Sara to come here to serve you?" Droll humour to start the day.

"Tell me, Karen. Is the credit union open today – this being

Saturday?”

“The credit union is open from nine to twelve. It’s just gone eight o’clock. Shall I take your order now?”

“Yes, of course. Coffee, pancakes and sausages. No – pancakes with crisp streaky bacon and syrup.”

“You know, you can have sausages **and** bacon.”

“Very well, then – pancakes with sausages and bacon.”

Karen goes to the kitchen to place the order. She returns with the coffee pot. As she pours the hot liquid, Jack queries her. “Karen, do you know if Okwaho is here this morning? I don’t see him.”

“I guess he is. His car is here for sure, so he must be here.” Jack nods in thanks and she leaves.

Shortly thereafter, Karen places the plate of pancakes on Jack’s table. As he commences eating, Okwaho walks in and sits opposite him. Jack speaks to Okwaho through a mouthful of pancake. “Okwaho. Where were you last night? I need to talk with you.” He wipes a dribble of maple syrup off his lower lip and takes a sip of coffee. He is not finished speaking, but Okwaho replies during the pause.

“At nine o’clock last night, I escorted the gas tanker truck back to the 639...”

“What? You went back to Elliot Lake?”

"No. Just as far the highway."

"Just the two of you?"

"Yes. And I returned alone. The round trip took seven hours. I got back to the hotel before four this morning."

"Did you not tell me that it is imprudent to travel the ice road alone?"

"Imprudent, but not prohibited. The tracks were still fresh from the convoy. We travelled over the same tracks, thus we were assured of identical surface conditions on the ice road."

"And what about the cracked portion?"

"We crossed that portion gingerly. The surface checked out. It was solid and bore the weight of the tanker without a problem – the empty tanker is lighter. On the return trip to the reserve, I sped past that area. The potential danger was not from the road surface, but from wildlife wandering onto the road. I made sure to have all lights on full beam and I was especially alert for hazards." Karen approaches the table to take his breakfast order. Okwaho glances at her quickly and says, "I'll have whatever he's having." Okwaho is not finished speaking to Jack. However, this time Jack effectively intrudes.

"Listen, Okwaho. This is an important development. I'm giving it top priority. You know the lead I'm talking about – the deposit of $300 into Amy's account?"

"What important lead? Did you not confirm all the deposits

and found nothing of substantial significance?"

"Good God, Okwaho. You were there last night when Amy and I crosschecked the deposits to her records. And we found... Wait. You left before that, did you not?"

"I don't know what significant material you discovered. So, fill me in." Okwaho is anxious for Jack to explain.

Jack shifts in his chair and leans across the table to emphasize the importance of what he is about to reveal. Suddenly, he hesitates and stands up. "It is easier if I show you." With that, Jack rushes away from the table and leaves the room.

Okwaho's breakfast has not yet arrived. He helps himself to Jack's unattended pancakes, bacon and sausages. Karen brings his breakfast plate and is momentarily confused. She places the second plate beside Okwaho and leaves with a mixed expression of puzzlement and amusement. Okwaho replenishes Jack's missing food – almost. He claims an extra pancake. Jack returns with Amy's account statement and resumes his seat.

Jack is panting from the exertion. "Look at this, Okwaho," he says. He points to the deposit of $300 dated 21 April 2017. "This deposit was comprised of one postal money order. It did not originate from Amy. And it did not come from Rose. It did not come from inside the reserve – it came in the mail. Now, if you eliminate Amy, Rose and the reserve, who else..." Jack leaves the sentence unfinished.

Okwaho comes to the only logical conclusion. He ceases

chewing and whispers one word. "Dorinda." He pushes his plate to the side. He has lost interest in eating. He lifts the statement and reads the line for himself. "This can only be from Dorinda."

Jack slaps the table and says, "Exactly. And that is why we will be at the credit union when it opens at nine. I need them to put a trace on the money order in the deposit."

"Ah, that brings me to what I was about to tell you. The chief has requested a progress report from you. I made an appointment for nine this morning."

"Well, he'll have to wait."

"Not necessarily." Okwaho points to the statement. "Let's bring him in on this."

At 8:50am, Okwaho and Jack enter the administration building. Jack recognizes the office of the credit union, so he goes to the door and waits for opening time. Okwaho, on the other hand, proceeds to the upper level, to the office suites, and enters the chief's office. The office secretary greets him. She is expecting Jack Doyle for a nine-o'clock meeting. She also knows why the chief has requested the meeting and that Okwaho is Jack Doyle's associate.

"Mr Okwaho, is it not? Will Mr Doyle be joining us? Chief Kataquapit will be with you shortly. Please, have a seat."

Okwaho responds. "No 'mister', if you don't mind. It is an alien title form of address to us. I am 'Okwaho'kó:wa'. But it is okay if you address me simply as 'Okwaho'."

"My apologies…"

"Oh, and Jack Doyle is downstairs. We will meet with him later."

"Very well. I'll inform Chief Kataquapit."

"And tell Chief Brenden Kataquapit that I have news. He'll want to hear this, immediately."

"Very well, Okwaho. I'll tell him right away." Rather than utilize the phone on her desk, the receptionist enters an inner room, presumably to speak to the chief and forewarn him of Okwako's abrasiveness.

Okwaho shouts after her, hoping that he is heard through the open doorway. "It is a new development in the investigation."

The chief recognizes the exuberant urgency in Okwaho's voice. He comes to the doorway and meets him. Okwaho's excitement is infectious. The chief asks, "A new development? In the Dorinda Trapper investigation? So, tell me. What is it?"

"Jack Doyle is looking into it. Come with me to the credit union. We believe that Dorinda sent a money order to Amy. It was deposited into her credit union account on 21 April 2017. Jack Doyle is at the credit union as we speak. He wants to put a trace on the money order."

Okwaho is already walking towards the credit union. The chief hurries to catch up. They both reach Jack as he enters the savings bank. Jack approaches the teller wicket. He displays Amy's statement to the teller.

Jack explains his purpose. "I would like to trace the item in this deposit." He points to the item of interest.

The teller is startled by Jack's direct approach. She observes that the account is in the name of Amy Trapper. She responds apologetically to Jack. "I'm sorry. This is Amy Trapper's account..."

The chief intervenes. "We need to speak with the manager on this." He strides into the manager's office unannounced. He gestures to Jack and Okwaho to follow.

The manager is taken by surprise at the sudden burst of bodies into her office. However, Kelly Moore recognizes the chief and the look of concern on his face. "Chief Kataquapit, is something the matter?" She gestures to two guest chairs in her office. The chief sits down in one. Okwaho and Jack remain standing.

The chief responds. "This is an urgent matter. And we need your help." He signals to Jack to explain.

Jack places the account statement on Kelly's desk. He points to the deposit of $300 on 21 April 2017. "This deposit," he explains, "was comprised of one item, a postal money order. I need to see a copy of that item."

Kelly seeks clarification. "You request a copy of the money order that was deposited to this account on 21 April 2017? Is that correct?"

"Yes," says Jack impatiently.

"Very well. I'll send a request to the data clearing centre to run off a copy and..."

"When?" Jack interrupts impatiently.

Kelly is ticked at Jack's impoliteness. She responds, "I'll send the request immediately." She reaches to her computer keyboard and commences to tap.

Jack looks into her face to get her attention. "I mean, when can I **see** a copy?"

Kelly answers brusquely. "On Monday. I expect to receive a reply with the copy attached."

Jack's impatience increases. "Don't you scan each item when it is deposited?"

By this time, Kelly is visibly annoyed. "Of course. The teller scans each deposited item when executing the transaction."

The chief intervenes. He says gently, but firmly, "Kelly, this is important. Is there any way to display the item to us here and now?"

Kelly ponders for a moment. "The teller," she exclaims. "The computer at the teller station can recall past transactions.”

“Then let’s go to the teller station.”

All four proceed to the teller station. Kelly takes control of the teller’s computer. She speaks as she taps in a request. “Let’s see. No, that’s not it. Ah, here it is.” She swivels the monitor so that the three men read it. The screen displays five cheques, obviously part of a scroll of items. Each item is displayed left and right in a double-column to show the front and back. Kelly indicates to the uppermost item. “There it is. A postal money order for $300.”

Jack squints at the monitor. “That’s a bit small. Can you enlarge the picture of the first item?”

Kelly responds, “No, sorry.”

“Okay, then print me a hard copy.”

“Sorry. This is not a printable file.”

Jack’s frustration is rising again. “Okay. Then ‘print screen’ and send the image to my cell phone.”

Kelly is forming another refusal when Okwaho leans over the counter and takes a picture with his cell-phone camera. Okwaho shows the captured image to Jack. Jack spreads his fingers on the image to enlarge it. He states undecidedly, “I can just about make it out...”

The chief peers at the image and says, “Come back to my

office. I will download that image to my computer. I have photo-smart software that can enlarge and crop pictures."

The three men depart from the credit union. They are so intent on their finding that they neglect to thank the manager. Some minutes later, they view a clear picture of the money order on the chief's computer. They observe that the money order is dated 18 April 2017 and is issued by a post office in Sudbury.

Jack exclaims, "Send that image to my phone. And print me a full-size copy."

Okwaho adds, "And me too."

The chief complies. Next, Okwaho requests him to conduct an online search of Canada Post locations in Sudbury. They identify the location of the issuing office. It is the Post Office in *Shoppers Drug Mart* at 1935 Paris Street, Sudbury. The website gives details and directions. Jack notes that the hours are '8:00am - 8:00pm'.

Jack thanks the chief for his helpful assistance. Then he turns to Okwaho and says, "Okay, 'Wolf', let's go to Sudbury."

As they turn to depart from the chief's office, they see Amy Trapper in the reception area. She explains her presence and speaks directly to Jack. "I heard about your visit to the credit union. You found out something, did you not?"

Jack speaks to her. "Amy, I believe we have tracked Dorinda to a *Shoppers Drug Mart* in Sudbury on Tuesday 18 April

2017. That would be the same day you returned home to Red Rapids.”

Amy walks slowly to Jack. She rests her left hand on Jack’s right shoulder and leans in slightly. “I trust you, ‘Snake-man’, to find her.” She turns on her heel and walks away.

Jack follows her out of the room. Okwaho and the chief exchange glances. Okwaho whispers, “That is not what I like to see.”

The chief raises his eyebrows and looks to Okwaho for clarification. “What? You don’t approve of an aboriginal woman placing her hand on an outsider – on the shoulder of an offensive snake? You consider it inappropriate?”

“No, not that. Amy’s gesture is understandable. It is a moving gesture of appeal. What I do not like is ‘Snake-man’s’ reaction to it.”

“Explain.”

“Let’s catch up with Jack. I’ll show you.”

When they reach Jack, he is standing at the top of the stairs watching Amy descend and walk out of sight. Jack turns at the sound of footsteps and faces the two men. Thereupon, Okwaho throws a punch at Jack’s face. Instinctively, Jack dodges, but his reflexes are slow. Okwaho manages a glancing blow to Jack’s cheek. Jack staggers and drops to one knee. Okwaho immediately extends a hand and helps him up. Jack has suffered no ill effect and does not attempt to retaliate. Somehow, he understands the message.

Okwaho turns to the chief and says, "See. Last month, my fist would not have landed. Jack here has become emotionally close to the Trapper clan. His feelings slow him and his edge is blunted."

"You say so? But surely, he demonstrates fortitude and integrity. You just witnessed it moments ago."

"But not with sufficient ferocity." Okwaho puts his arm on Jack's shoulder and says to him, "Come on, 'Snake', sharpen your fangs and let's be on our way to Sudbury."

At 10:30am, Jack and Okwaho depart from Red Rapids destined for Sudbury. The 'Wolf' guns the *Chevrolet Tahoe Premier RST* 355 horsepower SUV over the ice road as if the ice surface were a paved highway. Two hours and thirty minutes later they enter Elliot Lake. And at 3:00pm Okwaho drives into the parking lot of *Shoppers Drug Mart* at 1935 Paris Street in Sudbury.

Inside the drug store, Okwaho and Jack stride up to the Canada Post counter. The clerk views them with interest. Okwaho shows her a copy of the money order and inquires regarding its fate. The clerk is helpful. She understands that this is an inquiry into a lost money order – not an unusual inquiry. She confirms that the money order was purchased from this location – the issuing office is stated on the money order itself. She conducts a search on her computer and states, "The money order is not lost. I can confirm that it was paid a week after the purchase date."

Okwaho informs her, "Indeed the money order is not lost. However, the purchaser of the money order is lost. She disappeared immediately after mailing it, presumably at the mailbox here."

"The purchaser disappeared at the mailbox here?"

"No. She disappeared shortly after mailing the money order. It arrived safe and sound. But the purchaser has not been seen since then."

The clerk expresses sympathy. "Are the police looking for her? I sure hope they find her."

"The police are certainly looking for her. But after a lapse of a year and nine months, they have not had any success in finding her. We, my colleague and I, are retained by the family to investigate her disappearance and locate her."

The clerk is genuinely concerned. "You understand that I am not authorized to divulge confidential information on a transaction with Canada Post. But, outside of that, is there anything I can do to help..."

"Yes. Perhaps you remember the purchaser. She was 15 at the time, a First Nations girl?"

"I'm afraid that does not help much. We have many customers..."

"Were you working that day? Could someone else have served her?"

"I am the only full-time clerk here. And I would have worked that shift alone that day – Tuesday 18 April 2017 at 8:09am. But, I'm sorry I am unable to help."

"What about security cameras? Surely, you have those?"

"Of course. But records for April 2017? No, sorry." She tries to be helpful and asks, "Perhaps you have a picture? It might jog my memory."

Jack shows her the picture taken from the bank on Spadina Avenue in Toronto. "This was taken by a security camera. It is the only recent picture we have of her."

The clerk looks at it. She looks at Jack with a puzzled expression. "I can't see her face in this picture. How..."

"Yes. It is a challenge. But this picture is the best we have. Perhaps you recognize the clothing."

The clerk looks at the picture once more. "I'm really sorry. I am unable to help you."

"Here is another picture. It is a copy of her Status Card. But this picture was taken four years earlier when she was 11 years old. Take a look." Jack continues. "And here is an artist's rendering of how she would have looked at 15 years old when she went missing." Jack is stymied by the lack of clear pictures – the result of the fire that destroyed the Trapper house and its contents. The grey picture he tenders is of 11-year-old Dorinda. It is a copy of a copy from the reserve's administration files. And it is not a true likeness of

Dorinda at 15 years old. The artist's rendering is the closest resemblance.

Once more, the clerk shakes her head and apologizes. "I'm sorry. I have no recollection of this girl. I am unable to recall her."

Jack and Okwaho thank the clerk and leave. Outside, Okwaho states, "I must think about this. But first, I need to gas-up." He drives to the rear entrance of the parking lot and fills up his gas tank at *Petro Canada*.

When he re-enters the SUV, Jack points to the west side of Regent Street. "Look over there. There is a *Tim Hortons On The Run* at the *Esso* station. Let's go there and discuss our next move."

On The Run caters to drive-through customers and is not equipped for seating. The two men enter the store and purchase two coffees. Fortunately, the store area has a narrow pub table located between the rack of road maps and the 'special' on windshield-washer fluid. They avail of the tall table and stand drinking their coffee.

Okwaho speaks to Jack. "You imparted some wisdom to me, the other day."

"I did?" It is not like Okwaho to proffer a compliment. "And what was that?"

"When you said 'intercept' as a preference to 'pursue'."

"I said that?"

"I'm paraphrasing. But that is what you meant." Okwaho hurriedly drinks a mouthful of coffee and resumes speaking. "Work with me here, Jack. Why did Dorinda come to this particular post office? Is there some significance in its location? Or is it en route to her destination?"

Jack wrinkles his forehead in thought. "Let's think. If she were to choose between travelling by bus to Elliot Lake or by hitchhiking... Considering that she had $600. And she spent $250 in Mississauga and $300 in Sudbury. Would she have $50 remaining? I don't think so. She probably spent some money along the way – small amounts here and there."

"I see what you mean. And if she was considering the bus from Sudbury to Elliot Lake, she would have chosen a post office near to the bus station. This location is almost a two-hour walk from the bus depot. If she were taking the bus to Elliot Lake she would have no reason to pass by here. There are several post office locations much closer than this one – like the one on Bancroft Drive, for example, only a 20-minute walk from the depot. I agree, Jack. She did not take the bus to Elliot Lake."

Jack mentally pictures the layout of Sudbury from the perspective of a pedestrian. In considering the geography of the town, he puts the location of the post office into context. "You know, this location is close to *Greater Sudbury Health Sciences North*."

"A place Dorinda was familiar with."

"And *Health Sciences* is also a bus stop location for the bus from Toronto."

"But not for the bus to Elliot Lake."

"Correct."

"We speculated that she did not get the bus from Toronto. Are you saying we presumed incorrectly?"

"No. I still maintain that Dorinda did not board a bus in Bay Street, Toronto. But later, en route to Sudbury, who knows? Regardless, she arrived here either because it was convenient or familiar."

"Or for both reasons."

"Consider this, Okwaho. Draw a line from *Health Sciences North* to the *Petro Pass Truck Stop* at the Trans-Canada Highway..."

"...and this is right on the line at the halfway point."

"Which brings us to the second and most likely conclusion."

"Dorinda hitchhiked to Elliot Lake."

"Or, she intended to."

"Then, we go back to Elliot Lake."

"Yes. But first, let's swing by the truck stop and make

inquiries."

Jack and Okwaho conduct an investigation at the truck stop. It is no surprise that they come up with zero results. It is 5:10pm when they depart from Sudbury.

En route to Elliot Lake, Okwaho slows the car to make the right turn from the Trans-Canada Hwy to Hwy 108. The time is 6:30pm. An aboriginal girl with a dog is standing on the south side of the road, close to the truck inspection station. Okwaho observes them as he completes the turn and drives into the snow-encrusted parking lot of the *Gas and Hot Food* store ahead.

Jack is pleased to see the *Gas and Hot Food* store. "Ah, good decision, Okwaho. I haven't eaten a proper meal since this morning's pancakes. I'm starving." Okwaho parks the SUV. Jack exits the vehicle and quickly enters the store. Okwaho, on the other hand, walks south to the Trans-Canada Highway.

Okwaho crosses to the south side of the highway and approaches the aboriginal girl who is standing at the roadside ramp from the truck inspection station. She is Cree, about 14 or 15 years old. A black mongrel puppy – perhaps a one-year-old – is lying at her feet. The dog is snarling and chewing on a piece of frozen roadkill.

He greets her. "Hello, Kid. On your way to Sudbury, I see."

The Cree girl looks at him but tenders no response.

Okwaho continues. "You don't recognize me. That means you

are not from Red Rapids."

She retorts. "Red Rapids is Cree. You're not Cree. You can't be from Red Rapids."

"True. But I am well known there."

She turns her head either in disbelief or disinterest. This non-Cree First Nations man is on foot. Where is his car or truck? He is of no benefit to her.

Okwaho resumes talking. "I see your dog has something to eat. But how about you? Are you hungry?" She looks at Okwaho with curiosity but remains silent.

Okwaho reads her expression. He turns towards the road and faces north. "Come on," he says and proceeds to cross the highway. "I'll buy you dinner," he shouts back. The girl and dog fall into step behind him. They enter Hwy 108 at the T-intersection. Thereupon, they walk on the roadside three abreast – 'Wolf-man', Cree Girl and the dog with the road-kill in its mouth.

They enter the store. The grouchy man eyes them with disapproval and says, "No dogs allowed. Leave it outside."

Okwaho walks to the counter. The girl and dog stand in the doorway. Okwaho orders two hamburgers and fries and two coffees. He turns to the girl. "You drink coffee? Or some other drink?" She makes no reply. Okwaho takes her silence as acquiescence. He concludes the order with the grouchy man. "We'll eat outside."

The man shouts at the girl in the doorway. "Shut the door. The cold is blowing in." He goes to the kitchen hatch and places the order with 'Grouchy Woman' for a 'take-out'.

Back outside, at the side of the building, Okwaho clears snow off the picnic table. The girl knocks snow off the seat and sits. The dog lies at her feet and resumes chewing its roadkill. Minutes later, Grouchy Man shouts from the doorway that their food is ready. Okwaho enters the store and picks up the food. It is wrapped 'to go' in Styrofoam boxes and cups. He pays for it and Grouchy Man writes up the customary slip which he spears onto the spike file. Back at the picnic table, the girl eats and drinks in silence.

The side of the building is sheltered. Cree Girl pushes back the hood of her green parka and stretches out her black mukluk-covered legs. Okwaho talks to her and warns her of the dangers of hitchhiking in this manner. He cannot help but think that he is talking to another 'Dorinda' – one more potential future 'disappearance'. The girl's attention is on the food she is eating and not on Okwaho's advice. She quickly consumes her hamburger well before Okwaho has taken three bites.

Okwaho draws $20 from his pocket. "Here, Kid. You need some food for the road. Buy something to stick in your knapsack for later on. I'll stay here with your dog." He points her to the store. She tentatively takes the bill from him lest he is playing a prank. Once she has it firmly in her hand she quickly enters the store. Moments later, she exits the store. She checks the security of her knapsack on her back and walks away from Okwaho and the store, back to her spot on the highway. The little black dog, with the roadkill in its mouth, walks beside her. Okwaho watches them for a moment. Then, he shakes his head sadly and enters the store.

Okwaho saunters to the counter and addresses Grouchy Man. "That girl, there," pointing to the highway.

"The Cree girl? What about her?"

"She is 14 or 15 years old."

"So?"

"Is it usual to see Cree girls, as young as that, hitchhiking alone on the Trans-Canada?"

"I see it all the time. Most go east towards Sudbury. A few go west to the Soo (Sault St. Marie)."

"What about north?"

"No. I seldom see them going north. I suppose whatever reason they have for leaving, is reason enough not to return." He thinks for a while. "Or, maybe if they ever come back they are much older or can afford the bus fare. But a Cree girl, that young, hitchhiking north? I haven't seen that in well over a year. Would you believe that?"

Grouchy Man's comments put Okwaho on high alert. "Hold on. Did you say that the last time you saw a young Cree girl hiking north was a year ago?"

"I said **over** a year ago. I remember one that looked like that girl there," nodding towards the Trans-Canada Highway. "She was Cree, all right. She bought a coffee but no food. I figured she was short of money. Anyway, she was going north towards Elliot Lake."

Okwaho is tense with excitement. He speaks calmly as if only mildly interested. "Hmm. Could that have been around Easter 2017?" He produces the two pictures of Dorinda – one with her face obscured, and the other of the 11-year-old. He also presents the artist's rendering of her as she would have looked at 15 years old. "We are attempting to find a missing girl. See. Here is a picture of her. And here is another. And here is an artist's depiction of her. She is Cree, and was 15 at the time."

The man peers at the pictures and shakes his head. He looks up at Okwaho and shrugs his shoulders. He makes no further comment. Okwaho peers around. He sees Jack seated at a table. He joins him and sits opposite.

Jack is curious. "So what is all that about? You come in here with an indigenous girl. Then you leave. And you come back. How many times did you enter and leave in the past half-hour? And just now, you have a tête-à-tête with old Grouchy Man back there?"

"Jack, we need to investigate."

"And that is what we are doing – 'investigating'."

"I mean here in this, this..." He leans forward to speak low to

Jack. "Grouchy Man just told me that he remembers a young Cree girl hitchhiking north over a year ago – just one Cree girl in all that time."

"One Cree girl? I don't think that can be accurate. Surely, a hitchhiking Cree girl is a common sight here at the intersection of Hwy 108 and the Trans-Canada."

"That's just it. It is a common sight – true. But not hiking northbound."

Jack is about to query this, but Grouchy Man places a cup in front of Okwaho and pours coffee.

Okwaho looks up at Grouchy Man. "I did not order coffee."

"You don't sit here for free. You're buying coffee." Grouchy Man walks away, having made his point.

Okwaho resumes his account. Jack is unsure if Okwaho's assessment is accurate. Grouchy Man may have responded reciprocally to Okwaho's leading prompts rather than tender his independent account unaided.

Grouchy Man returns to the table. He slaps a slip of paper on the surface in front of Okwaho. Okwaho is annoyed that the man wants early payment for 'meeting time'. The man speaks to him. "7:32pm, 18 April 2017."

Okwaho realizes that he misunderstood the man's actions in producing the slip. This is not his bill for coffee. This is a sales slip from 18 April 2017. Okwaho looks at the man and asks, "Is this about the Cree girl?"

"Yes. You were asking about her, weren't you? See where I marked the slip with the date. And here, where it asks for a name, I wrote 'W'. That means that the customer was walking, not driving. And the purchase was for one coffee. So, how about that?"

"Do you write all your receipts like that?"

"So you think I am not organized just because I don't have a till? Let me tell you, I have records on every sale going back ten years. I record the licence plate number here where it says 'name'. Except where someone is walking, then I just write in 'W'."

Okwaho indicates to the slip. "Are you certain about this? Could there be another similar sale?"

"This was the only walk-in sale for a single coffee that week."

Jack takes the sales slip and examines it. He asks the man, "Could I look through your sales receipts for that period?"

The man sneers a surly laugh at Jack. "Are you the taxman from the CRA? If not, you don't snoop in my records. I'm just telling your friend here that my memory is sound and I have the papers to back it up." With that, he grabs back the sales slip and returns to his counter.

Okwaho takes his cup and follows him. He observes the man

place the slip within a bundle of other slips. He appears to be concerned with their sequence. When satisfied, he staples the bundle and places it in an envelope. The envelope contains many similar bundles, all stapled in like manner. The envelope is identified on the outside with the date. It appears that each stapled bundle represents a day's sales, and each envelope a week. The man then places the envelope in a box, taking care to place it in its appropriate place among other envelopes. He then closes the lid. The box displays the name *Star of the Sea Sardines*. Over this, written in bold black marker is the date – 2017.

Okwaho says, "Very impressive – your filing system."

"I know. And it's foolproof. So, why are you here at the counter?"

"To ask permission to post pictures of the missing person in your store." Okwaho places the pictures on the counter.

"You want permission to post a picture with no face? And another one that is too grainy to make out clearly? And one that an artist thinks **might** look like her? If you think it helps, okay. There's a pinboard by the door." The man looks at the pictures and notes the contact information. "Jack Doyle? Is that you?"

"No. Jack Doyle is my partner. That's him drinking coffee back there."

The man looks over at Jack seated at a table. Then he says, "Okay. I'll post the pictures for you. Is there anything else?"

Okwaho holds up his cup. "Ah, a top-up of coffee, please. And I'll take two of your chewy beef jerkies."

The man takes two sticks of beef jerky from the counter display and hands them to Okwaho. "I'll bring the coffee over." With that, the man enters a back storeroom. Okwaho strains to watch him through the partly-open doorway. He observes the man places the box atop a similar-sized box on a wooden shelf.

Okwaho returns to his table. He whispers to Jack, "I know what my next move will be. Let's finish up here and leave. We will check into a hotel in Elliot Lake. But, I'm not done here."

Jack and Okwaho finish drinking coffee. They settle their purchases with Grouchy Man. They watch him scribble the time on the receipt slip and record the SUV's licence plate number under 'name'. When payment is executed, he skewers the slip on the spike file and puts the money in a drawer. He turns a key in the drawer and places it in his pants pocket.

CHAPTER SIXTEEN

THE WOLF HUNTS

It is 8:30pm on Saturday 02 February 2019, when Okwaho and Jack check into a hotel on Hwy 108 at Manitoba Road in Elliot Lake. *McDonald's* is located on the south side of the hotel and a *Tim Hortons* next to that. At 9:15pm, the two men sit at a corner table in *Tim Hortons* and discuss their current situation and plan their next step. Jack is keen to conduct inquires in Elliot Lake on the following day.

"Okwaho, we know that Dorinda..." He pauses and modifies his comment. "No. There is a distinct possibility – a high probability – that Dorinda was at the store at the Trans-Canada intersection at 7:32pm on 18 April 2017. And that she was hitchhiking to Elliot Lake. Elliot Lake is the next link we need to establish."

"I disagree. We are not quite ready yet for Elliot Lake, not until I check out what the store owner told us today."

"What? You think he was lying?"

"Actually, I believe he was telling us the truth. But his memory could be spotty. And his conclusions might be faulty. Notwithstanding the value of his opinions, I believe we should qualify them, confirm them and place them into perspective."

"Are you proposing that we return to the *Gas and Hot Food* store?"

"Consider this, Jack. The grouchy old man told us that Cree girls seldom hitchhike northbound from the Trans-Canada to Elliot Lake. I doubt if that's true. And here's why. Less than 40% of First Nations people have driver's licences. There is very little opportunity to drive on a reserve. And even if there is, you don't require a driver's licence unless you drive off the reserve. Secondly, in remote areas, even immediately north of Elliot Lake, there is no bus service."

"So what's your point?"

"Hitchhiking is an acceptable part of the culture. And it is accommodated by the people who live here."

"Okay. So the people around here tolerate hitchhiking."

"No, Jack. Not **tolerate.** They accept it and are accommodating to it."

"Even if there is a bus service?"

"Jack, there is only one bus per day from Sudbury to Elliot Lake. It leaves Sudbury at 5:30pm and arrives at Elliot Lake at 8:35pm. Outside that time, it is common for local people to hitchhike – even northbound on Hwy 108. And not everyone who is hitchhiking purchases a coffee from old Grouchy Man.

"So, Grouchy Man's account is not necessarily false. It may convey an incomplete description and, hence, an erroneous conclusion. Okwaho, I tend to agree with you in this – the old man's account could be misleading. We need to substantiate it. However, you are not telling me this unless you have devised a plan of action."

"Correct. Let's meet back here at midnight. And have your cell phone fully charged."

Jack is agreeable. He is also annoyed with himself. Okwaho is correct and a private investigator should have made this decision unaided and unprompted. He worries that perhaps 'Wolf-man' is correct – he has lost his edge after all.

The *Tim Hortons* beside the hotel provides a 24-hour service. Meeting there at midnight poses no problem. The two men purchase two coffees 'to go'. Jack is curious as to why the coffees are for take-out, rather than for in-store consumption. He inquires of Okwaho. "Coffee on the go? So, where are we going?"

"Just work with me. Okay?"

"Sure." Jack is puzzled but trusting, nonetheless.

"You have your phone?"

"Yeah. Fully charged."

Okwaho drives to the Trans-Canada Highway. Jack expects him to turn into the snow-encrusted parking lot of the gas-and-food store. Instead, Okwaho continues driving. The store is in darkness and is evidently closed for business. Okwaho makes a right turn onto Hwy 17 (Trans-Canada) and immediately makes a U-turn into the truck inspection station. The station is closed and the entrance gate is shut, but

Okwaho avails of the entrance lane to park his SUV.

Jack's bewilderment increases. "Okwaho, you can't park here. MOT won't like it. And why are you parking here anyway?"

"The Ministry of Transportation will not know. And if an officer comes by, apologize and park on the road-side rest area on the north side. Here is the car key."

"Here is the car key? What do you mean..."

"You, Jack, remain in the car. I will be back in 15 minutes."

Before Jack can respond, Okwaho throws him the car key and jumps out of the SUV. He jogs swiftly away and disappears out of sight. Jack starts the engine to maintain a comfortable heat level. He guesses that it is -20°C outside. He turns on the radio and waits for Okwaho's return.

Sure enough, within 15 minutes, Okwaho returns to the car. He opens the back door and tosses a bundle of envelopes on the back seat. Jack glances at him questioningly. Okwaho elucidates. "The old man's sales receipts for April 2017. Now quickly, let's record each receipt slip with our cell-phone cameras. And keep them in sequence. I don't want the old man to learn of this. If any of his papers are in disarray, it will tip him off."

Jack is shocked at this. "What? You broke into the old man's store and stole his sales records?"

"I didn't 'break' anything. And I did not 'steal'. Just take pictures. When I put all these back, the old man will be none the wiser."

"But this is a criminal offence..."

"Stop talking, Jack. You are wasting time. Here take these two envelopes and start recording."

Within a few minutes, they record all the slips in captured images on their cell phones. Okwaho ensures that the contents of the envelopes are restored to their original state. Then, he scoops them in his hands and returns to the store. Seven minutes later, Okwaho returns to the SUV. He slides into the driver's seat and sets the car in motion. He turns to Jack and says, "Everything is back in the box. The old man won't suspect a thing. As far as he is concerned, nothing happened." They drive past the food store and its slumbering occupants and proceed north on Hwy 108.

Jack is agitated. "Nothing happened? You... we have committed a criminal offence..."

"Yes, Jack. Now, shut up. No harm was done."

"Lord, Okwaho, you could have been spotted..."

"Spotted?" Okwaho is offended by the suggestion. "There was no one around. And the store has no security cameras. It's a wonder it even has a telephone. Don't worry, Jack. This is my forte. I know how to steal around without being detected."

Jack makes no answer. But he inwardly admits that the 'Wolf' is stealthy. He knew this from the moment he found the disturbing calling card stuck in his wiper blade in Buffalo.

At 1:07am, the two men are back in *Tim Hortons* beside the hotel. They sit at a back table and scroll through the sales receipts on their cell phones. Jack makes note of significant items. A few licence plate numbers appear weekly. Judging by the amounts, he surmises these are gasoline purchases by commuters who travel the route regularly. One number is of particular interest – AW 58227. This is a commercial vehicle. It is recorded 10 times in the month of April. Strangely, the amounts vary from the price of a coffee to $80. Jack thinks aloud. "The greasy man in the boiler suit."

Okwaho hears him and queries. "What about the man in the boiler suit?"

"AW 58227 was at the store 10 times in April. That must be him. He fills up his gas tank occasionally. And other times he drops in for a single coffee or a minor purchase."

Okwaho leans over the table to view the image in Jack's phone. "Yes. That could be him."

Jack scrolls some more. "And look at this. He made a gasoline purchase on 18 April 2017 at 7:48pm."

Okwaho rises from his seat and stands behind Jack. Thus, he is better able to study the displayed image. "This is 15 or 16 minutes after the Cree girl was in the store."

"Okwaho, you said 'Cree girl'. Yes, I see that you are cautious. The old man spoke of a 'Cree girl'. At this point, we don't know if it is **our** Cree girl."

"'Nate'. The store owner said that his name is 'Nate' – the greasy man with the beaten-up pickup truck. His place is on the east side of the 108, back a ways from the road and out of sight."

"Yup. The greasy man is 'Nate'." Jack stares at his phone until the image fades to black. He places it on the table and studies the contents of his coffee cup. He consumes a mouthful of coffee and says, "This is a possible link we cannot ignore. Tomorrow – actually, today – we visit Nate at his out-of-sight abode. Let's see if his licence plate number checks out. And if it does, we determine if he remembers seeing a Cree girl at the store when he filled up his gas tank on 18 April 2017."

Okwaho stands up and drains his cup. "I agree. See you here at 9:00am."

"So, tell me. How did you get into Grouchy Man's store? Surely, it wasn't unlocked."

"A magician never reveals his secrets. Let's say, I availed of a 'window of opportunity'."

As the 'Wolf-man' walks away, Jack comments to him, "Okwaho. You did good today." Okwaho flashes a 'thumbs-up' in acknowledgement and exits the coffee shop.

It is 9:30am on Sunday 03 February 2019. Okwaho drives his SUV to Nate's place. At least, he hopes that it is to Nate's place. The road surface is rutted and potholed. It is much too rough for a coupe or a sedan. The only clue that this is an actual access road is in the snow that is packed down by vehicular traffic. Okwaho observes that it underwent some degree of snowplowing. Doubtless, Nate has a snowplow blade mounted on his pickup. He grunts at his reasoning. What pickup around here does **not** have a snowplow-blade attachment?

Jack turns to Okwaho and says, "Nate might be at church this morning."

Okwaho looks askance at Jack. "What holy-rolling grease-church would he belong to?"

Jack suppresses a smile. "True. Or he could be a late riser."

"Well, we are just about to find out. Look. There is his place. You can hardly see it behind all the mounds of snow." Thereupon, Okwaho brings the SUV to a sudden halt and exclaims, "A chain across the road. I almost ran into it." There are two gateposts, one on either side of the road, but instead of a gate, a heavy-duty chain is stretched across between them.

Okwaho and Jack exit the SUV. They stride to the chain and consider walking the remaining 50 metres to the building. Okwaho spots the pickup parked next to the building. Just then, a Rottweiler, barking aggressively, runs from the house and stops at the chain-gate a mere metre short of the two men. It paws the ground and lowers its head while staring up at the two men, baring its teeth and snarling vehemently. Its steamy-hot saliva drips to the snow-covered ground. Jack, fearful for his safety, jumps headlong into the car and slams the door shut. Okwaho, on the other hand, steps inside the chain and leans back against the gatepost. He stares calmly at the threatening dog and extracts a stick of beef jerky from his pocket. He takes a bite and waits for Nate to appear. Surely, Greasy Man will investigate the cause of the dog's alarm. A few seconds later, Nate runs from the house. He too stops at the chain.

Nate addresses Okwaho. "What business do you have here?"

Okwaho takes another bite of jerky. He chews it twice and spits the mouthful right at the dog's face. The dog snaps at the wad of chewed jerky and swallows it whole. Okwaho looks at Nate and says, "Your dog is hungry."

"So he is. It keeps him mean. So what do you want here?"

"Jack Doyle is in the car back there." He indicates with a tilt of his head and keeps a watchful eye on the dog. "He wants to ask you something."

Nate steps to the passenger side of the car. Jack lowers the window and shows him the picture of Dorinda. "We are looking for this girl. I'm afraid her face in the picture is obscured by her hair. Here is another picture. It is an artist's drawing with a description."

Nate ignores the pictures. He maintains silence and stares glassily at Jack.

Jack continues. He attempts to read Nate's body language. "We need to ask her some questions. We believe she passed through here some time ago. Have you ever seen her in the area?"

Nate displays no emotion other than contempt for the intrusion. He speaks to Jack with mocking sarcasm. "When? Today? Yesterday?"

"April 2017. We believe she might be the Cree girl who was at the store back there at the intersection on Tuesday 18 April 2017. That was the Tuesday after Easter. She left the store at 7:30pm and was hitchhiking north. I was wondering if you remember seeing an indigenous girl on that day – one who looked like this girl here?"

'Greasy-man' Nate stares poker-faced at Jack but declines to look at the picture. "What makes you think I saw her or anyone?"

"You live here. And you frequent the area. If you were around there, between 7:30pm and 8:00pm that evening, perhaps you noticed her."

Nate glares at Jack and sneers. "I see nothing that doesn't concern me; I know nothing that doesn't concern me. If there was a woman or a man or beast on the road that evening, unless I bumped into it, I would not notice it. I mind my own business. And this," pointing to the picture, "is none of my business. Now, get this. I and mine are none of your business either. Now, turn around and leave."

Jack is not finished questioning Nate. But Nate is clearly finished with Jack. The greasy man steps back from the car and returns to the chain-gate.

Okwaho and the dog are still in a stare-down standoff. 'Wolf-man' bites off another chunk of jerky, chews it a few times and spits in at the dog's face. Once more, the dog catches it deftly in its mouth. Nate walks back towards his house. The dog turns and walks after the greasy man. After ten paces, both man and dog stop and turn. They glare at Okwaho with unmistakable hostility. Okwaho stands away from the gatepost and slowly enters the SUV. Thereupon, he executes a skidding U-turn that sends a shower of snow towards the man and dog. He views them in his rear-view mirror. As the SUV departs, the man and dog turn and walk homewards.

Jack expels a sigh of relief. "Lord. That was nasty back there. Were you not afraid of that monstrous dog?"

"Somewhat. But not as much as Nate feared me."

"Nate feared you? How do you know that?"

"He saw that my hand was resting on the hilt of my knife," slapping the belt under his parka. "He is mean, meaner than his dog. But he is not stupid. He would know of the defensive technique that is employed in the wild – sacrifice your left forearm to the attacking animal coinciding with a knife thrust to the belly and, in Nate's case, the added bonus of his throat slashed. Had the dog attacked me, you would be driving me to the hospital now to have my arm treated. Nate and his dog would be dead – their hot blood melting the snow."

"Good God. And you could do that?"

"I **have** done that. One thing more, Jack. I saw Nate's pickup parked back there. The licence plate number is..."

"...AW 58227"

"Bingo!"

Jack takes a moment to digest this information. The 'Wolf' is worthy of his name.

Upon reaching the highway, Okwaho turns left and travels the short distance to *Gas And Hot Food*. It is 10:30am – time for a coffee and a talk.

Moments later, sitting at a table in the store, Jack remarks to Okwaho, "That Nate character did not answer me one way or the other."

"You are correct. He did not say if he saw the Cree girl or if he didn't."

"And I don't like the implication of 'bumping'. What if he **did** 'bump' into her? In that case, would it become his 'business'? And what business could that be?"

Okwaho is silent. He is deep in thought. After some moments, he looks at Jack. "We are doing this wrong. Do you remember we agreed to conduct this like a hunter who intercepts a wounded animal returning to its lair?"

Jack is alert to what point Okwaho is forming. "I remember. And it's working, is it not?"

"No, Jack. There are many important aspects to be considered in a hunt. The missing factor in our situation is 'conditions'."

"'Conditions'? I don't understand."

"Dorinda travelled from Sudbury to somewhere unknown en route to Red Rapids in the latter part of April. April is a pivotal month with regard to conditions. Picture this place..." Okwaho waves his arm to indicate the landscape visible from the food-store window, "...in February."

Jack leans his elbow on the table and swivels to view the scenery. "Yes. It's February now. I see it."

"Now picture this same place in the third week of April. And picture it in June."

"It is different each time. It is snow-covered now. Later, the snow melts and the ground is saturated. And in June, the trees are fully in leaf. So what's your point?"

"People behave differently and animals behave differently according to the time of year and according to the time of day. They are obliged to accommodate to the changing conditions activated by seasons and weather."

Jack tries to follow Okwaho's line of thinking. He visualizes the landscape as it changes from snow-covered to green. It strikes Jack that significant changes occur. He exclaims to Okwaho, "For example, there is no ice road in summer. Hence, travel to the reserve is restricted."

"Exactly. But there are many factors in play. How they interact and influence one's decisions and actions is complex. A hunter knows this. **How** he hunts, **what** he hunts, **where** he hunts and **when** he hunts is determined by changing conditions."

"I think you are saying that we should be hunting for Dorinda under the same conditions that she was contending with."

"That is exactly what I'm saying."

Okwaho's counsel is not a welcome contribution at this stage of the investigation. Jack states, with obvious displeasure, "That would mean postponing the current investigation for 11 weeks."

Okwaho appears to be studying the tree-topped horizon. Only the conifers are green – a dark evergreen. The deciduous trees stand naked against the winter sky. Okwaho speaks as if reading an augury in the trees. "To continue at this time is futile. But more importantly, I have a sense of the hunt now. I know **where** to go; I know **when** to go. And I know that the appropriate time to act is 18 April."

Jack expresses dissatisfaction. "The family and the chief are waiting for a progress report. What shall I tell them?"

"Jack, you had intended to conduct your investigation in Elliot Lake today. Go ahead and execute it. It can't hurt. It may even bring miraculous results. But don't pin your hopes on it."

"And then?"

"Promise a report for the end of April."

"And what will be in the report at the end of April?"

"The answer."

Jack is astounded by Okwaho's prophetic prediction. He looks at him to determine if he is speaking figuratively. He decides that Okwaho is sincere. Furthermore, he appears determined and certain.

On 5 February 2019, Jack concludes his investigation in Elliot Lake. As Okwaho predicted, nothing of substance comes to light. Having exhausted their inquiry, they drive to Sudbury. Okwaho returns the rental car and they catch the last flight to Toronto – AC 8614, departing Wednesday 05 February 2019 at 20:30 arriving at Pearson Airport Toronto at 21:45

*　　*　　*　　*　　*

Two months later, on Wednesday 17 April 2019 as arranged, Okwaho meets with Jack Doyle in his office at 1660 North Service Road East, Oakville. It is 8:00am. Okwaho peers at Jack from below the brim of his leather hat and enquires,

292

"Are you ready for this, 'Snake-man'?"

Jack stares back from below the peak of his *Blue Jays* baseball cap. "I've been waiting for this day since 05 February. Yes, 'Wolf-man'. I'm ready."

On this occasion, Jack chooses to drive. Okwaho transfers his overnight bag and personal items to Jack's *Ford Fiesta.* When seated, the two men exchange a look that denotes an agreement of purpose. Jack says, "Okay. We trace the route that Dorinda travelled on April 2017."

Okwaho confirms and adds, "Not only the route we **know** she travelled, but the onward route she **intended** to travel."

"As best we know."

"Let's go."

Jack drives north on Ninth Line. At Dundas Street, he turns east. A few minutes later, he slows the car and points to the left. "That's Erindale Park." He drives in and stops in the parking lot. They cast their eyes around briefly.

"Okay." Okwaho acknowledges the site. "This is stop number one – the start of Dorinda's journey home to Red Rapids at 5:00am on 17 April 2017."

Jack navigates the car from the park and rejoins the flow of traffic on Dundas Street. "Now for stop number two."

Fifteen minutes later, Jack enters the parking lot of *Mark's* at

Dundas near Dixie. He looks at the store and says, "This is stop number two. Same day."

Okwaho looks around and scans the area. "The traffic is heavy. Buses are running on Dundas and Dixie."

"Remember, Okwaho, 17 April 2017 was Easter Monday. The traffic would have been lighter and the buses ran on a Sunday schedule."

Okwaho nods. "Okay, onwards to the next stop."

Jack drives north on Dixie Road. He turns onto Shawson Drive and stops at the *Husky/Esso* truck stop. "This could be Dorinda's stop number three – or maybe not. We don't know for sure. Regardless, we are a block north of the intersection of Dixie & 401. Highway 401 is the most likely route."

Jack accesses Highway 401 east. Fifty minutes later, he turns north on Highway 400 and proceeds in the direction of Sudbury. At five minutes to 2:00pm, they arrive at *Shoppers Drug Mart,* 1935 Paris Street, Sudbury. Jack speaks to Okwaho. "Stop number four. And we are certain of this one."

Okwaho nods and peers at the building. "She was here on Tuesday 18 April 2017, the following day."

At this point, the two men agree to stop for lunch. They consider dining at *Fionn McCool's* next to *Shoppers*, but they choose to obtain a fast-food meal with minimal delay. Jack drives two blocks east on Regent Street and parks next to *Tim Hortons* at Algonquin Road. Inside, he orders the chilli special. He is pleased that he obtains a maple dip doughnut with his order. Okwaho orders a BLT. While eating, they decide on their next move. *Shoppers*, they determine, is a half-hour walk from the *Petro-Pass Truck Stop* on Regent Street. The location of the truck stop is also the closest access to the Trans-Canada Highway. If Dorinda hitchhiked from *Shoppers* at Paris & Regent, the Regent Street access to the Trans-Canada Highway would have been her obvious choice – whether she went to the truck stop or not.

At 2:30pm, they enter the highway interchange on Regent Street and proceed west on Hwy 17 (Trans-Canada Highway). At 4:10pm they reach *Gas and Hot Food* on Hwy 108. On this visit, the parking lot is clear of snow. Jack draws alongside the gasoline pumps. He attempts to fill the gas tank, but the pump fails to dispense. Then, he spots the sign – *CASH ONLY – PAY INSIDE*. Jack enters the store. The owner recognizes him from his previous visit and explains to him that he must first tender cash before he activates the pump. Jack tenders $80. On his next attempt, Jack succeeds in filling his gas tank. The total charge is $62.48. Back inside, Jack receives $17.50 in change. Okwaho enters and purchases a stick of beef jerky.

Jack acknowledges Okwaho and states, "So, this is stop number five."

Okwaho responds, "Stop number five – but not confirmed. Let's proceed further."

"To Elliot Lake?"

"No. Go past Elliot Lake to the ice road. I need to check the condition of that location."

Once north of Elliot Lake, Jack expects the highway to be snow-covered. He is surprised to find Highway 639 free of snow. Not quite. The paved surface of the driving area is clear of snow to the width of a single lane. The roadside is still snow-covered. At 5:15pm, Jack stops the car on Highway 639 at the termination of the ice road. He parks his *Ford Fiesta* on the roadside snow. He ensures that his outer wheels remain firmly on bare pavement and that the car is not wedged in the snowbank. He prudently determines that it is folly to drive onto the ice road itself. The two men exit the car.

The entrance to the ice road is wet from the melting ice. The surface is a mixture of rocks and mud. Twenty metres farther down the road, the ice surface is partly intact. Little rivulets of melting ice run along the ruts. There are gaps in sections of the ice where the rivulets cut at right angles to drain towards the side. The remaining ice is wet, slippery and dirty. Jack estimates that the ice surface is too fragile to bear the weight of a car. This is a moot point since the remaining ice is not wide enough to accommodate a vehicle. The patches of remaining ice are in long rectangular shapes, broken at intervals. The road appears to be surfaced with giant dismembered fingers pointing to Red Rapids. Jack questions Okwaho. "The ice road is impassible, don't you think? The road is covered by less than 50% ice. And I don't think it could bear the weight of a car. Do you not agree?"

Okwaho studies the ice road. "Hmm. The daytime temperature is 4°C. It drops to -7°C at night." Having made

this declaration, Okwaho walks back to the car. He invites
Jack to follow. "Come on, Jack. Drive back to the Trans-
Canada."

At 6:10pm Jack is approaching the now-familiar *Gas and Hot
Food* store. Okwaho directs him to turn left. "Turn left? Are
you sure Okwaho? This is the entrance to the weird man's
place and the vicious dog."

"I want to take a look at his place without the cloaking cover
of snow."

"Why on earth do you want to do that?"

"The last time we were here, he refused to answer you."

"That's right. His answers were non-answers."

"And he prevented us from getting close to his house."

"As I say, he's weird. And it's best to stay away from him and
his mad dog."

"He's the kind of creature I'm curious about. What has he to
hide, other than his objectionable self?"

Jack travels a few metres. Then he decides to stop the car. He
pulls over to the side and parks. "Lord! Look at those
potholes. I can't risk bending a wheel or damaging my car.
I'm not driving any farther on this dirt track."

Okwaho opens the passenger door and steps out. "I'm fine

with that. So, let's walk the rest of the way to his decrepit place."

Okwaho strides off in the direction of Nate's house. Jack follows grudgingly. Some minutes later they confront the chain across the road. Without hesitating, Okwaho lifts the chain and walks under it.

Jack is alarmed by Okwaho's disregard for safety. The chain implies 'no entry'. Okwaho walks steadily towards the house. Jack implores him to be cautious. "Okwaho. I don't think you should be doing this. What if the dog..."

Okwaho shouts back, "What's keeping you, Jack? Don't fall behind."

Okwaho stops long enough for Jack to catch up. He scans his eyes around the property. The low house is visible. The pickup is parked beside it. There is a second low building attached to the house – either an extension of the house or a separate attached building. It could be a workshop or a garage or a storage shed. The area around it is littered with piles of junk. The piles appear to be segregated into categories of junk: there is a pile of household furniture, a pile of kitchen appliances, a pile of playground equipment, and many random piles of metal. These were not visible on their previous visit due to the snow.

They are less than 10 metres from the house when the dog is alerted to their presence. It rushes up to them barking and snarling. The greasy man calls it to heel from the doorway. Okwaho continues walking at an even pace, apparently unperturbed by the threatening dog. Jack, on the other hand, ensures that Okwaho separates him from any possible direct canine assault.

The man challenges them. "You again? I told you last time that I have no business with you. So, what do you want?"

Okwaho answers. "Jack Doyle here requires clarification of the information you tendered to him at the last visit. Me? I want to look at your stuff to see if anything is worth buying."

The man is skeptical. "You buying? What would you be buying from me?"

"Well, the last site I purchased from was the Brax mining site up near Sultan when they shut down the place."

"What? The gold mine?"

"Yup. I had the reserve come and scavenge the place. When we were done it was as clean as a whistle."

"A reserve, you say?"

"Oh, we look for deals wherever we can." Okwaho strolls over to the pile of playground equipment. "This chain here?" He points to a broken swing set. "How much do you want for it?"

"$20."

"$20? I can get it for that price at *Canadian Tire*."

"So, go to *Canadian Tire*."

"I'll give you $5 for it."

The man refrains from answering.

Okwaho walks farther away. He shouts back. "This furniture here looks interesting. I'll take a look at it." He turns his attention to Jack. "Jack, you require some information, don't you? So, carry on. Don't mind me poking around here."

A few minutes later Okwaho finishes his inspection of the discarded goods. Once again, he addresses the man. "There are some tables and chairs I could do with. But to cart them to the reserve would require transportation over an ice road. Alas, the weather is too mild now and the ice road is not serviceable again until next February. Why don't I come by again in January?"

"Yes. Why don't you." This is rendered with evident sarcasm.

Okwaho turns to Jack and queries him. "Are you done here, Jack?"

The man answers instead. "Your friend Jack was done before he started. You're both done, so you can both leave."

Okwaho shrugs and walks away. Jack falls into stride at his side. Jack whispers to Okwaho, "Why did you leave me alone with him and his vicious beast? I thought that I was going to become the dog's dinner."

Okwaho laughs and slaps him on the back. "Now we go for dinner. Have you ever tried the *Gas and Hot Food* store?"

A short time later, both men are dining at the *Gas and Hot Food* store. Jack queries Okwaho. "Well, did you succeed in finding the answer you sought?"

Okwaho ceases chewing his steak. He peers out the window in the direction of Nate's place. "No, no answers. But I unearthed another question back at that wretched place."

"Yes?" Jack says this invitingly, prompting Okwaho to explain.

"Greasy Nate lives alone."

"That's what the store owner says. And from what we saw, it certainly looks that way."

"So why did I see women's clothing through the window of his house?"

"He collects junk. So, he must accumulate clothing amongst all the other rubbish."

"What I saw was women's clothing – no men's clothing was present. And it was strewn around in disorganized piles."

"That is strange indeed. And why store it inside? From what we could see, all his junk is heaped out in the open to rust, rot and decay. The whole place is just one big refuse dump. I don't believe he 'stores' anything."

"And therein lies the question – what is the significance of the women's clothing stored inside?"

Jack remembers the previous time that Okwaho sought answers. On that occasion, he broke into the gas-and-food store to access the sales receipts. "Okwaho, you are not thinking of..."

"Jack," he exclaims decisively, "I will pay a visit to greasy Nate's place." He points his steak-knife at Jack. "And you are going to help me."

"To commit a felony?"

"I commit the felony. You do the other part."

"Okwaho, do you understand 'aiding and abetting'? And if you are discovered, I would lose my licence. Jeez!"

Okwaho appears oblivious to Jack's concerns. "The conditions need to be right. So, not yet, and not tonight. First I need to prepare. He smiles at Jack and resumes eating his steak. "Lighten up, Jack. This could be progress."

"I see that we are going to spend the night in Elliot Lake."

Later, they check into the hotel at Manitoba Road in Elliot Lake. Afterwards, Okwaho induces Jack to embark on a night venture.

Jack questions him. "It's nine o'clock. Where are we going? Surely, not to Nate's Place."

"To the ice road, Jack. To the ice road."

"We already went there today."

"But not at night-time when the temperature drops to -7°C."

At 9:15pm and, as before, Jack parks his car on Secondary Highway 639 at the entrance to the ice road. Okwaho invites him to walk on the ice road once again. This time it is different. The wet ice has refrozen and is easier to traverse. The night is dark but the starlight illuminates the frosty surface of the ice. Jack studies the elongated white patches of ice stretching into the distance like giant stepping stones through a black quagmire. Jack now understands that Dorinda would know this. The ice road in mid-April is traversable when the temperature drops below freezing. He is satisfied that they are on Dorinda's track – or, at least, on her intended track. He appreciates Okwaho's attention to 'conditions'.

On the return trip to the hotel, Okwaho requests Jack to drop him off at *Shoppers Drug Mart*, behind the *Bank of Montreal* across the road from their destination. Jack does as requested. They arrange an 8:00am meeting for the following morning. Then, Jack drives into the hotel's parking lot.

*   *   *   *   *

On Thursday 18 April 2019, the two men meet in the hotel lobby as agreed. Jack expects to eat breakfast in the neighbouring *Tim Hortons*. Instead, Okwaho insists on going to the *Gas and Hot Food* store. At 8:25am, they are seated in the familiar store overlooking the intersection of Hwy 108 and the Trans-Canada. In addition to bacon & eggs and home fries, Okwaho selects a frozen chicken breast from the store freezer and requests the owner to defrost it. He complies.

A few minutes later, Grouchy Man sets the defrosted chicken breast on a plate and brings it to the table. He queries Okwaho with undeniable sarcasm. "Do you need any ketchup for your chicken, or will you eat it as is?"

"Thanks. It is fine as is. It's for later."

Jack speaks to Okwaho. "How did it go at *Shoppers* last night? Did you obtain whatever you needed?"

"Oh, I acquired all my supplies for today."

"Really. Now, don't tell me it goes with that lump of raw chicken there?" Jack looks critically at the raw chicken. He would prefer it to be out of sight. "And what's the reason for raw chicken anyway?"

"The chicken is for the dog." Okwaho says this casually. Then, he tenders additional information. "I will prepare it nicely for him. Watch."

Okwaho takes a pill bottle from his pocket. He spills the contents on a plate and crushes them into powder with his knife. Then, he stirs in bacon grease until the powder becomes a paste. Thereupon, he slits the chicken breast to form a meat envelope which he fills with the paste. When finished, he pats the chicken meat into shape. He looks at his works and appears satisfied. "Behold, the chicken is ready to be served to Nate's dog."

"Good God, Okwaho. Do you intend to poison the damn dog?"

"Nope. This is enough to distract him from biting me. With this," pointing to the chicken piece, "his mind will be on other matters."

Jack understands the 'Wolf's' wily plot. Under the circumstances, he approves and intends to help. "'Wolf-man', if you plan to enter Nate's property... come with me to the trunk of my car."

As the two men exit the store, Grouchy Man shouts, "Don't leave without paying."

Jack waves at him and puts him at ease. "No. We are not leaving. I need something from the car. I'll be back in a jiffy to continue my breakfast."

Grouchy Man glances at the table. He confirms that the meal is only half-eaten. The raw chicken is still lying on the plate. And Jack's jacket is slung over the back of his chair. He is satisfied that the men are returning as stated.

Outside, Jack pops open the trunk. He indicates to items stored therein. "Okwaho, take a pair of gloves from here. And dispose of them afterwards." Okwaho explores Jack's professional supplies. He selects two pairs of disposable gloves and three plastic bags from the stock of items.

Okwaho places the items in his pockets and says, "What makes me think that you are not a stranger to nefarious tactics either?"

"Just don't get caught." Jack closes the trunk lid. "Now let's go back and finish breakfast."

Back inside the store, Jack asks, "So what's next? We just sit here?"

"Yes. Until Nate shows up. Then I leave." Okwaho removes one of the newly-acquired plastic bags from his pocket. He wraps the piece of raw chicken in it and conceals it within his coat.

Jack continues with the trend of the conversation. "So when Nate shows up here, you leave. And I inform you by phone when he finishes up in here and departs, presumably to return to his run-down rubbish-heap home."

Okwaho smiles and remarks, "Are you sure you haven't done this before?"

Jack changes the subject. "You know, 'Wolf-man', I was thinking about Dorinda and her hike through the ice road."

"Yes?"

"On her first venture, she was attacked by wolves. I don't believe she would risk another trek over the same route alone."

"Unless she learned from her first experience and is prepared."

"What could she do to protect herself from a wolf attack?"

"Jack, remember she is from a hunting family – her father was a hunter; her brother and uncle still are. She would know how to fashion an effective weapon."

"She would? How?"

Rather than answer, Okwaho exits the building. A few moments later, he raps at the window for Jack's attention. Jack studies him outside in the parking lot. He is brandishing a wooden pole in one hand and a steak knife in the other. He smiles at Jack. Then he disappears and re-enters the store a minute later. When he returns to the table he clarifies for Jack. "The steak knife came from the table here. The pole came from the yard broom out at the back. I made sure to screw it back into place."

"What? A broom handle and a steak knife against a pack of wolves? You must be joking."

"Jack, Kokum is correct. You would not survive alone in the north." Okwaho leans towards Jack and speaks to him as if to a child. "Use the knife to whittle the pole and carve a slot to hold the hilt. Secure the knife to the pole and you have an effective spear."

"I see how Dorinda could easily obtain a knife and a pole. So how do you secure the knife to the pole and prevent it from falling off?"

"With black tape."

"And how likely is Dorinda to have a roll of black tape?"

Okwaho clicks his tongue disapprovingly and says, "Watch." He strolls up to the check-out counter and speaks to Grouchy Man. "My knife here has a slippery handle. I require a firm grip. Have you any black tape to wrap around it?"

The man reaches under the counter and extracts a roll of tape. "Here. Try this."

Okwaho tears off a strip and wraps it around the hilt of his knife. When finished, he hands the roll back to the owner. "Thanks."

Back at the table, Okwaho looks at Jack with an I-told-you-so expression. "How many garages and service stations are there between here and the ice road? One of them would give you a piece of black tape, enough to secure a knife to a pole. I warrant you, if Dorinda made it to the ice road, she had a formidable defensive weapon to ward off predators. And she had a pole to assist her in securing her footing on slippery ice."

Jack nods. He is content with Okwaho's explanation. So far, 'Wolf-man's' understanding of Dorinda's flight conditions is sound.

Minutes pass. They drink more coffee. The store owner is

content to accommodate them for as long as they continue to purchase his products.

An hour passes and, so far, Nate has not appeared in the store. The store owner refills their cups. Jack remarks to Okwaho, "There is only so much coffee we can drink. What if the greasy man doesn't show up today?"

"Then we come back tomorrow. And if you are tired of coffee, chew some jerky."

At 11:22am, Nate enters the store. As is his habit, he greets no one; he acknowledges no one. He is unconcerned that the two investigators are still around. He surmises that they are focusing their inquiry on the truck inspection station at the intersection – a futile exercise, just like their annoying and fruitless visit to his own place. He sits smugly at the partly-obscured table behind the rack of merchandise. Jack whispers to Okwaho. "This is 'early morning' for that lazy cuss, I'll bet."

Okwaho rises from the table. He secures his hat and casually walks out through the doorway. Once out of sight of the store windows, he jogs to Nate's place. The 'Wolf-man' is fit. He reaches the obstructive chain in less than five minutes. He halts at the gatepost. Thereupon, he whistles loudly. Instantly, the savage dog is alerted. It runs to Okwaho, snarling and baring its teeth. And just like on the previous occasion, Okwaho spits a wad of jerky in its direction. The dog is expecting this and catches it adroitly in its mouth. Thereupon, Okwaho flings the lump of raw chicken at the dog. This is unexpected. The dog is wary of the object thrown in his direction. He dodges the missile of chicken breast. He retreats a half-step. Then he pounces on the meat. He tears at it and quickly devours it. Being greedy for more, the dog sniffs the ground and licks all traces of the meat off the gravel and mud.

Okwaho waits for a reaction. The dog walks in tight circles as if attempting to investigate his rear end. Then it toddles drunkenly back to the house. Okwaho takes his cue and strides to the building. The dog snarls half-heartedly at him. After one feeble snarl, it lies down on the bald doormat at the entrance to the building on the west side. Then it turns its attention to licking its paws.

Okwaho wonders if Nate puts sufficient trust in his dog to leave his front door unlocked. He checks the door. It is locked. Undeterred, he makes his way to the other side of the building, to where he spotted the articles of clothing through a window. The window, he observes, is two-paned and opens by sliding left and right. He peers through the glass. Each pane is held in place by a plastic toggle that prevents it from moving. Okwaho places his palms on one windowpane and pushes it up. It moves a fraction. Then, while maintaining upward pressure, he jiggles the glass against the toggle. The pane is high enough to mount the toggle, but not sufficient to clear it. He continues to wiggle the pane until he achieves a small opening. Then he curls his fingers around the opening and pushes the toggle. Thereupon, the window slides unimpeded. Next, he prepares to execute the same process with the inner pane. Fortunately, the toggle on the inner pane is not engaged. Okwaho slides open the second pane with ease. Thus accomplished, he has unimpeded access to the room. He places gloves on his hands and nimbly enters.

He casts his eyes around the gloomy interior and quickly spies a black garment lying on a disorderly bundle. It is partly covered by a floral skirt. He hastily extracts the black garment from the heap of clothes. He holds it aloft. It looks like the dress he saw in Jack's picture of Dorinda. Satisfied with his find, he spreads it on the floor and takes pictures of it with his cell phone. Thereupon, he places it back as he found it and carefully covers it again with the floral skirt. When he is finished, the bundle of clothes appears as before. Nate will never know that it was disturbed.

Okwaho considers that if this truly is Dorinda's dress, there should be other articles of her clothing present. However, there is no sign of her fancy shoes, or of her boots or parka. It strikes him that this black dress may not be Dorinda's at all. He continues to search for any evidence of the Cree girl.

Stealthily, Okwaho inspects every room in the house. He takes pictures at intervals. It is an easy task. All the interior doors are wide open. There are no 'secret' rooms or locked rooms, or areas where a person could be confined or imprisoned. The 'Wolf' is not sure if he is relieved or disappointed at this discovery. He concludes that there is no evidence that Dorinda was ever here – other than the unidentified suspicious black garment. From his exploration of the house, he is certain that Nate lives alone. There is no sign that a second person has ever set foot in the creepy abode. The room with the discarded clothing is an anomaly.

Okwaho is alerted by the vibration of his cell phone. He sees that Jack is contacting him. That means that it is time to leave. He steps through the room that is littered with the scattered clothing and exits through the open window. He reaches back inside and wipes the glass to remove his fingerprints from where he had employed his bare hands to push open the panes. Then he slides both panes shut. Just then, he hears the sound of the approaching pickup. He sprints to the end of the building and rounds the corner. From there, he runs from the property unobserved, and enters the concealment of the trees. When he is out of sight of Nate's property, he phones Jack to report his success.

Later, inside the store, Jack examines the outcome of Okwaho's foray into Nate's forbidding dump. Jack scrolls through the pictures in Okwaho's phone as he listens to the 'Wolf's' account.

Okwaho studies Jack as he inspects the picture of the black garment. "This is Dorinda's dress. Don't you agree?"

"It **looks** like her dress." Jack goes silent. He studies the picture.

Okwaho expects him to continue talking. After a pause, the 'Wolf' asks, "But..."

Jack is in thought. He speaks aloud, perhaps to Okwaho, or perhaps to himself. "We should go to the police with this information. It warrants a police investigation." Then he focuses his gaze on the 'Wolf-man'. "But we can't."

Okwaho is puzzled by Jack's remark. "What do you mean 'we should but we can't'? Explain."

"I'm not sure if the police have reason enough to search Nate's place based on this alone. If they do – that is, execute a search – they would conduct a forensic examination on the black garment. And if it is Dorinda's, they would undoubtedly find her DNA evidence on it."

"And if it's not Dorinda's, we continue on our quest. Either way, we will know – the trail leads to Nate, or it doesn't."

Jack leans his head against his upraised palms. He speaks quietly and slowly. "This picture here," he points to Okwaho's cell phone, "is evidence of a break-and-enter. And likely tampering with evidence. The only certain outcome, if we reveal this to the police, is our immediate arrest. And the permanent loss of my licence."

"Are you saying that my efforts were wasted?"

"No. Far from it. However, we need to find a reason for the police to search Nate's place – a reason other than this picture here. Once inside, they will find the garment and..."

"I see. And with no indication of my being there or having disturbed potential evidence."

"Exactly. But for now, we only know that you found a black dress, one that looks like Dorinda's. Let's obtain positive identification that it truly is her garment, the one she wore when she fled from Colin Clark and the *Elephant Club*. There's no point going off half-cocked and barking up the wrong tree."

Okwaho agrees. "This means returning to Toronto."

"Yes. We check out of our hotel in Elliot Lake and head south."

"We will not reach Toronto until after 6:00pm."

"True. In the meantime, our time is not wasted." Jack keys in a number on his cell phone. He looks at Okwaho and informs him, "Detective Inspector Alex Crouse – that's who I'm phoning. I'll bring him in on our progress – Dorinda at the post office in Sudbury; and a Cree girl spotted here at 7:32pm on 18 April 2017. I'll slip in Nate's name as a local person of interest. It might trigger a response. Perhaps the OPP have something on..." The call connects. "Alex? It's Jack Doyle. About the missing person Dorinda Trapper AKA Sugar Maple..."

CHAPTER SEVENTEEN

THE TRAP

On Thursday 18 April 2019, Okwaho and Jack check out of their hotel in Elliot Lake before noon. Jack avails of the hotel's internet service to conduct an online search on his laptop. He scrolls through retail locations of *Mark's* and *Mark's Work Warehouse*. He notes the phone number of the store at 1180 Dundas Street East in Mississauga. At 12:05pm, they drive south on Hwy 108, en route from Elliot Lake to Toronto.

While driving, Jack places his cell phone in the mobile-phone car mount and places a call to Colin Clark. Colin is surprised and disturbed at receiving a phone call from Jack Doyle.

Colin speaks. "Jack Doyle again? I thought you said last time that you were finished with me."

"No, Colin. Not quite. This is one small, but important, detail. I'd like to meet with you to clarify it. This won't take long."

"And what if I refuse?"

"That would be unwise. Remember, you are a potential material witness in a missing person investigation."

Colin grunts in acknowledgement.

Jack continues. "Let me wise you up on things. Since 01 July 2018, the Toronto Police Service Missing Persons Unit investigates approximately 4,300 cases per year. Dorinda Trapper is just one of those cases and her file will not be closed until the police have verified the location and identity of the missing person. Are you listening?"

Colin responds in a defeated tone, "Yes."

"Okay. Here's what I need – confirmation on one vital piece of information. Once you comply, I am finished with you." Jack waits for a response. Colin is silent. But Jack hears him breathing, an indication that he has not terminated the call. Jack continues. "The requested meeting will not take more than a minute or two. Your cooperation is crucial to the investigation. And Colin, should you refuse, I will be obliged to inform the MPU."

"Okay! Okay!" Colin is unable to hide his agitation. He is reluctant to meet. But, faced with the alternative, he complies. "I'll meet with you. But I want this done in private. And quickly. No police. And not at Inspection Division."

"I agree. And the sooner, the better."

Jack suspects that Colin lives a short driving distance from Erindale Park – the location of his departing encounter with Dorinda. Hence, he suggests meeting in the vicinity. Jack continues to speak. "Let's meet after work at *Tim Hortons* on Mavis Road, a short distance south of the 403."

Colin is familiar with the location. "It's at the corner of Mavis and Central Parkway at the *Pioneer* gasoline station. I know it. At what time?"

Jack is relieved that Colin accepts. "Later today. Say, 7:30pm?"

"7:30pm this evening. Agreed." Colin terminates the call.

Before he can make another call, Jack answers an incoming call on his phone. It is Detective Alex Crouse. "Jack, regarding your call of earlier today. The OPP (Ontario Provincial Police) are actively working on the case of the missing person. As we speak, they are following up in Sudbury where Dorinda Trapper was last spotted."

"That's good news, Alex. Will they circulate pictures..."

"Jack, they have a team that specializes in missing persons. They know what they are doing. Have no fear on that account."

"Yes, of course, you are correct. I feel that we are getting close..."

"And you are anxious. I understand. But listen, Jack, you said that your inquiries brought you to Serpent River – to the intersection of the Trans-Canada and Highway 108."

"Yes. So what?"

"If you encounter any leads up in that area, you should contact Detective Stan Wilcox of the OPP in Elliot Lake."

"Detective Stan Wilcox? Why is that?"

"Jack, you are breaking up. I didn't catch that. Detective Stan Wilcox. That's his area..." Silence. Jack's phone displays 'no signal'.

Okwaho speaks to Jack. "I heard that. Why did he mention the OPP in Elliot Lake?"

"I don't know." Jack is silent for a moment. "Okwaho, if the OPP is interested in our progress..."

"Are you going to turn around and go back to Elliot Lake?"

Jack speaks aloud to himself. "Stan Wilcox. Why does that name ring a bell?" Then he responds to Okwaho. "I believe that we need to obtain 'credible cause' against greasy Nate."

"You are referring to a justification for the police to search his place?"

"And to do that, we continue on our present course. But I sense that we are on the right trail."

When they approach Sudbury, the cell phone displays a connection. Thereupon, Jack calls *Mark's* in Mississauga. When the call connects, Jack asks to speak with Sandy, the person he spoke with on his last visit. As it so happens, it is Sandy who has picked up the call. Jack quickly reminds her of their previous encounter. He concludes by informing Sandy that his friend – the girl he spoke about in the store – has disappeared and is the subject in a missing-person case. Sandy's response is the opposite of Colin Clark's. She is keen to help. Jack explains that he needs to confirm a piece of information vital to the investigation. She informs him that she is willing to meet him before 5:00pm today. After that, she is off work until Monday at 10:00am. Jack explains that he is currently travelling from Elliot Lake and will not arrive in Mississauga until after 6:00pm. Therefore, he requests a meeting after hours. Sandy is wary of meeting in private outside of her comfort zone. Jack understands and suggests they meet on the following morning in a busy location – the *Tim Hortons* across from her place of work. Being sympathetic to the plight of a missing girl, Sandy is agreeable, on condition that she brings a friend. Thus, the meeting is set for the following morning at 10:00am.

Upon arriving at the GTA, Jack drives to his office in Oakville. He downloads Okwaho's pictures of the black dress to his computer. After enhancing and enlarging the images, he prints colour copies. Thus armed, he is prepared for his upcoming meetings.

At 7:30pm, Jack and Okwaho sit at a table in *Tim Hortons* at Mavis & Central Parkway. Colin Clark, still dressed in his professional suit and tie, enters. Jack stands in order to be seen. Colin spots him and walks over to their table.

"Hello, Colin," he says. "I appreciate your help. We are close to locating our missing person. I need to confirm one thing to tie up a loose end."

Colin remains standing. He wants this meeting to be brief. "You say that this will not take long? So let's get on with it. I'm sick of your harassment."

Jack, also standing, replies. "No sweat. If your answers are quick and to the point, we will be gone in a jiffy." Jack directs Colin to look at the picture on the table. "You recognize this picture? Right?"

Colin glances at it. "Of course. That's me. And that's Sugar Maple beside me."

"That picture was taken outside the *Elephant Club* on Sunday 16 April 2017 at roughly 7:30pm."

"We both know that. So, what is your question?"

"I'm coming to that. Note the girl's attire. Was she wearing the same outfit when you last saw her?"

"I don't remember what she was wearing."

"Okay. Was she wearing **anything** at the time?"

"When I last saw Sugar Maple, she was dressed in the same clothes that she wore when I picked her up at the club. I cannot recall what she wore, except that it was a dark colour. I am unable to give you a description. But whatever she is wearing **there,**" pointing to the picture, "is what she was wearing later on."

"By 'later on', are you referring to when you were at Erindale Park at 4:48am on the morning of 17 April 2017?"

"I refer to the time she stole $600 from me and attempted to steal my phone. That is when I saw her last. And at that time, she was wearing whatever clothes I picked her up in."

"Thank you, Colin. This is important information. Let me confirm. Dorinda Trapper was dressed in a dark-coloured dress when you picked her up at the *Elephant Club* and she was wearing the same clothes when you left her at Erindale Park on the morning of 17 April 2017. Is that correct?"

"Yes. That is correct."

Jack produces the recent pictures of the dress – Okwaho's pictures of the garment lying on the floor in Nate's house. "I want to show you something. It is a dress. See if you recognize it." Jack looks at Colin's face to judge his reaction. "Is this the dress?"

Colin visually examines the pictures. "That could be the dress. Or one just like it."

Jack is satisfied with Colin's answer. "Thank you. You may go now."

Colin departs quickly with a closing remark. "We're done? So don't bother me again." He is relieved that nothing else was introduced and that no threatening innuendo was conveyed. He exits before Jack can respond.

Jack sits down at the table and lifts his cup. Okwaho leans across and queries him. "What was the point of that?"

Jack points to the picture on the table, the picture of Colin and Sugar. "This garment is identified as a 'Sigmund dress'."

Then he points to the recent picture. "Is this also a 'Sigmund dress'?"

"Of course. It's the same dress."

"Yes. But are you sure? And here's something to consider. What if Colin had stated that when he last saw Dorinda, she was dressed in jeans and sweater?"

"I see. But Colin **didn't** say that."

"Precisely. We established from Colin that Dorinda did not part from the dress. What she was wearing when he picked her up, is what she was wearing when they parted – the dress she is wearing in this picture here."

"And I discovered it at Nate's place up by Serpent River."

"Not so fast, Okwaho. Is it the same dress, or a similar dress? I mean to establish that it is undeniably the same dress. I have reason to believe that the dress worn by Dorinda has distinctive characteristics. Once I establish the uniqueness of the garment, we know that there can be no other like it."

"Is this why you need to meet with Sandy of *Mark's* clothing store?"

"Yes. When I spoke with her last, she mentioned a distinctive stain on the garment. If she recognizes a distinguishing mark, it establishes the uniqueness of the garment."

"'Unique'. Only one. Dorinda's dress and the one from Nate's house is one and the same?"

"Let's hope that with Sandy's authentication we establish that without a doubt."

*   *   *   *   *

At 10:00am on the following morning – Good Friday – Okwaho and Jack meet Sandy outside in the parking lot of *Tim Hortons* at Dundas Street and Dixie Road. She is accompanied by 'Doug', her boyfriend. Jack directs her attention to the earlier picture. She nods in recognition and says, "Yes, I remember that picture."

"Good." Jack hands her the new pictures. "Do you recognize the dress in these pictures?"

She recognizes the clothing. "That is the dress I saw your friend wearing – a 'Sigmund dress'. I remember the elasticized shoulders where she held her money. And see the smudge of dirt? I also remember that. I assumed, at the time, that she fell sideways and landed on her shoulder. It can easily happen when you wear high heels on soft ground and stumble." She hesitates and re-examines the picture. "But wait, there are other dirt marks. Those were not on the dress I saw your friend in. Perhaps this is not the same dress after all." She looks Jack in the eyes and says. "I'm not sure if this is the dress the indigenous girl was wearing."

"Now, Sandy, when you first looked at the picture, you were sure. And now you say that you are not sure. Look again. How certain are you?"

323

"I'm half-sure."

"Half-sure?"

No. More than half-sure."

"75% then?"

"No. More like three-quarters. 75% is exact. 'Three-quarters' is..."

"Inexact?"

"That's it. I am three-quarters inexact sure." Sandy returns the pictures to Jack. Then she asks, "Have you found your missing friend?"

"Not yet. But this will help, Sandy. I believe we are close to finding her." Jack's comment is without foundation. He prudently conceals details of his investigation. He merely tenders his remark solely to put the helpful girl at ease.

"Oh, I'm so glad to hear that. And I hope she is okay."

Sandy and Doug leave. Okwaho ambles over to Jack. He speaks quietly. "A unique garment, worn exclusively by Dorinda. Where I found the garment..."

Jack turns to Okwaho. "You discovered a dress in Nate's creepy house. You took a picture of it. It is speculation at this point to conclude that it is Dorinda's. I admit that it is highly likely and, yes, it warrants confirmation. So what is your point?"

"While you were talking with Sandy, I kept picturing the room in my mind. What is so unusual about that room? That's the question that's bothering me."

"What room are you referring to?"

"The room in Nate's house that contains women's clothing. It is so out of place. It does not conform to the other rooms." Okwaho shut's his eyes and mentally retraces his exploration of the house. Aloud, he says, "I'm thinking. Don't talk." Then he verbalizes his thoughts. "I walk from this room... I turn to the left... And back to the room. Now, if I visualize the room, not solely in the context of the house, but in the context of the house and scrapyard together..." Suddenly, Okwaho thumps his fist to his head and exclaims excitedly, "Yes! Yes!"

Jack is surprised at the Okwaho's change in demeanour. He wonders what vision the 'Wolf' is experiencing. "Yes, yes, what? Tell me."

Okwaho opens his eyes wide and exclaims, "I have come to an important realization. It pertains to Nate's place. I saw something there that only now falls into place."

Jack raises his eyebrows enquiringly.

Okwaho continues. "Come. Let's go inside *Tim Hortons*. This is best explained over coffee."

Minutes later, Jack and Okwaho sit at a table. Jack is pleased that he succeeded in obtaining a maple-dip doughnut. He settles into his chair and readies himself to learn of Okwaho's 'realization'.

Okwaho is silent. He puts his thoughts in order. He takes a sip of coffee. Then he speaks gravely. "I need to search Nate's place."

"What? You just searched Nate's place."

"I searched the **building** in Nate's place." He takes another sip of coffee. "Do you remember when we first went there?"

"Of course. How could I forget the vicious dog guarding the place? I didn't venture past the chain-gate for fear of it."

"Ah, the dog guarding the place. The dog knows the place. Consider what you just said, Jack. 'The dog guarding the place'. We were 50 metres from the house at the time."

Jack's face lights up in understanding. "Of course. 'Nate's place' is not just his house..."

"It's where he lives, and does whatever it is that he does. Now listen, Jack. When I was in his house, I went through every room – six in all. Each room was different according to its distinctiveness – a bedroom, a bathroom, a kitchen, and so on."

"That's not unusual."

Okwaho ignores the interjection and continues uninterrupted.

"But I considered one room to be an anomaly – the one with women's clothing. It was out-of-place. Or so I thought at the time."

"And now?"

"In the context of the entire property, it is perfectly in place where it ought to be – according to Nate's arrangement and sense of order."

This statement surprises Jack. He wonders what 'realization' Okwaho is experiencing. "Nate's 'arrangement of order'? His place is a dump."

"Ah!" Okwaho looks at Jack and smiles. He lifts his cup and drinks, keeping his eyes on the 'Snake-man' for his reaction. "If it were a 'dump', as you claim, would you not expect to see one big mountain of trash?"

Jack is immediately enlightened. His expression reveals his sudden and unexpected understanding. He leans forward and speaks eagerly. "The trash is segregated into distinctly different areas – a pile of furniture here, a pile of playground equipment somewhere else, and so on."

"Nate's arrangement of his 'dump' follows the same order as his interior rooms. His scrapyard is also organized into rooms, albeit out in an open space."

"But surely, you don't regard it as 'orderly'?"

"Oh yes, I do. I comprehend his structured system. I now

understand the significance of the room with the women's clothing. It is Nate's 'souvenir room'. You see, Nate organizes his possessions in a precise systematic fashion."

"He collects women's garments as souvenirs? Okwaho, is this is going somewhere?"

The 'Wolf' shuts his eyes in concentration. "I see his place in my mind. I know where to search. Not the entire property, and not inside the house, just the likely places in the scrapyard amongst the piles of junk. I know where the answer lies." He opens his eyes. "And Jack, this time there will be no 'break-and-enter'; there will be no 'contaminating the evidence'. This time... This time..."

Okwaho's confidence is infectious. Jack feels that the investigation has reached a crucial point. But there is no spark of victory in his voice. "Okwaho, let's re-visit Nate's dump. I believe we are on the brink of success. But alas, not on the brink of triumph."

Okwaho agrees. They speak not a word. Yet, each knows the other's innermost thoughts. After a moment's silence, Okwaho speaks. "I'll drive. I need to employ my hunting skills. And I carry my tools when I hunt."

Jack breaks his reverie and looks at Okwaho. "'Hunting skills'? I'm afraid that the hunt is almost over."

"The hunt is not over until the kill is executed."

Jack nods in agreement. "Let's swing by Huron Park. I'll

transfer my stuff to your car."

*   *   *   *   *

At 11:30am, Okwaho is driving north on Hwy 400. Jack sits in the passenger seat consulting the investigation file. The traffic is dense. It is the start of the Easter long weekend. Where normally they travel at 100kph, the traffic is stop-and-go until they reach Barrie. Thereafter, it improves progressively as they proceed north. Notwithstanding, what should be a journey of five hours and 15 minutes takes them six-and-a-half hours to complete. Finally, they reach their destination at 6:09pm. Okwaho drives onto the parking lot of the now-familiar *Gas and Hot Food* store. At this point, they avail of both services – a gas fill-up and a steak dinner.

Jack and Okwaho review their plan. Questioning Nate at his abode is not likely to yield a positive result. They tried this before. Nate will simply not communicate and order them to leave. And worse, another encounter with the greasy man could warn him of Jack's relentless attention to him. It is best to play it cool with Nate and show no apparent interest. As to Okwaho's proposition to stealthily search Nate's property, Jack agrees that the sneaky Indian, true to form, will succeed in snooping around the scrapyard undetected – provided that the greasy man is absent and that the dog will not devour him.

Jack is unsure what Okwaho expects to discover. "So, tell me again, 'Wolf'. What do you expect to find?"

"Expect? Or reasonably hope for? It's more like solving a puzzle. I hope to fit the missing pieces together. And thus form a roadmap to locate Dorinda. She is either there, or she is elsewhere."

"Okwaho, you know that **if** Dorinda is there, at Nate's place, she is not alive."

"And that's my fear. But this is where the compass points. And so I follow the trail."

"In the meantime, we wait for Nate to leave his property."

"And we will know that, when he comes in here as per his daily custom."

They wait until nightfall for Nate to appear at the *Gas and Hot Food* store. He fails to show. Thereupon, Jack and Okwaho drive to Elliot Lake and check into the hotel. Next day, Saturday 20 April 2019, they arrive back at Grouchy Man's store at 9:00am. They commence another day of waiting for Nate to appear. After multiple coffees and numerous sticks of jerky, they conclude a fruitless day. They depart from the store when the owner closes for the day at 10:00pm. Jack is concerned that Nate might be aware of their presence and is avoiding them.

On the drive to the hotel, Jack considers that perhaps it is time to go to the police with his suspicions. "Okwaho, I'm thinking that our plan is stalled. Perhaps it is time to report to the OPP in Elliot Lake."

"And tell them what?"

"We are attempting to locate a missing person. We have traced her to Sudbury."

"The police already know that."

"And that a person answering to her description was seen on Highway 108 at the Trans-Canada Highway."

"They know that too."

"And that we are suspicious of Nate, the owner of the scrapyard."

"And you are suspicious of Nate, why?"

"He lives in the area where she was last seen. At least, he ought to be questioned by the police."

"Jack, let me understand. You tell the police that a Cree girl was observed at the *Gas and Hot Food* store around the time that Nate filled his gas tank? The Cree girl may, or may not, be our missing person. Why focus suspicion on Nate? Everyone in the area should be questioned by the police. Okay, so let's say they question Nate. Then what? He throws his arms up and admits to a crime? Hah. Not likely."

"I know it's not much." Jack realizes that Nate would deny any knowledge of seeing Dorinda, or any Cree girl. And even if he admits to seeing an indigenous girl, how unusual is that? Especially if he claims to be unable to distinguish between Cree and Ojibwe. The Serpent River First Nation Reserve is located on the south side of the Trans-Canada Highway right at the T-junction of Highway 108, less than a kilometre from Nate's place. First Nations people are a common sight here.

Okwaho continues with his line of argument. "You said it before, Jack. We need to give the police reasonable cause to conduct a search of Nate's property. What? Tell them about the suspicious black dress in the house?"

"No. We can't do that."

"So, we are back to our plan. We find something that will arouse their suspicion, sufficient for them to conduct a search of the property – and that includes house **and** yard."

"I know. But we need to find something without incriminating ourselves. And remember – no unlawful entry, no tampering with evidence."

"Trust me, Jack. I know how to sneak around unseen and undetected. However, how about 'no **apparent** unlawful entry'?"

Jack sighs. He is unsettled. He remembers how he had been successful in the past, back when he was up against the Black Hand Warriors. At that time, he was a scourge to them, and risks paid off handsomely. Jack accepts the risk of his current venture and prays that it will be as rewarding as his decorated past. He puts his trust in God and in the 'Wolf'. He responds to Okwaho's question. "We stick to the plan for one more day. Then we re-think our strategy."

On Sunday 21 April 2019, Okwaho and Jack arrive at the *Gas and Hot Food* store, as before, at 9:00am. They are surprised to find it closed. There is a piece of ripped cardboard stuck to the door. They read the scribbled writing on it – 'EASTER SUNDAY OPEN AT 11'. With two hours to kill, Okwaho decides to study Nate's place from a distance. He walks to the greasy man's house via the woodland and views the wasted property from the edge of the trees. While maintaining cover, he circles the entire property. He notes every bump and hollow in the lot. Upon completion, Okwaho has a mental 3D image of the entire property embedded in his memory. He returns to the store in time for the 11:00am opening.

At 11:05am, they order breakfast from Grouchy Man. At 11:32am, Nate enters the store. As is his habit, he greets no one. But this time, he acknowledges the two men with a sneer. He sits in his usual spot. Okwaho rises and departs from the store.

First, he moves his car as if driving away from the location. He returns and re-parks it at the rear of the building, thus hiding it from the road and concealing it from view of the customers in the store. Then, he jogs quickly to Nate's property. He checks that his phone is switched on. On this occasion, he has no edible treat for the under-fed dog. Should the dog attempt to assault him at this visit, Okwaho is determined to kill it.

When he reaches the chain, he rattles it noisily. The dog runs to him barking and snarling as usual. But when the dog recognizes him, it retreats to a distance of 10 metres. It continues to bark – not menacingly this time, but irritatingly. The dog remembers the ill-effects of their previous encounter and keeps a safe distance away from its tormentor. Okwaho ignores the annoying dog and casts his eyes around the property. On the previous occasion, he noticed that there is no farming activity on Nate's land. And the place shows no evidence of planting. So why are low mounds visible at intervals on the land? It is unlikely that these are Nate's abandoned vegetable plots. Did Nate have a sinister reason to dig? Okwaho grunts calculatingly and considers the mounds in the context of Nate's logical arrangement.

The 'Wolf' disregards the foul odours released by the thawing conditions – the stink of decay and dog feces – and concentrates on his mission. He settles on one mound of soil. It is a short distance from the house, located behind a pile of discarded kitchen appliances. He breaks off a stick from a nearby shrub and prods the ground with it. The soil on the mound is soft. It is recently thawed and has not yet settled from being pushed up by the frost. He probes with the stick. The ground is still frozen four inches below the surface. The 'Wolf' is careful. He avoids stepping on the soft soil. He walks slowly around the perimeter of the mound. The dog ceases barking and follows after Okwaho 10 paces behind. The dog is curious and studies the 'Wolf-man's' activity with its ears perked up. Okwaho spots a depression in the side of the mound. He scrutinizes it and decides to investigate. So as not to leave evidence of his intrusion, he selects a washboard from the pile of kitchen junk to use as a kneeling board.

When he returns to the spot, the dog is scratching at the depression. The dog backs off when he approaches. Okwaho scratches at the surface of the depression with his stick. The dog returns. Man and dog scratch side by side. Okwaho breathes deeply from exertion. He ignores the strong smell of wet dog that assails his nostrils. He wonders what is of interest to the crazy half-starved dog that has distracted it from its hitherto menacing behaviour. Four inches down, they hit frozen soil. Considering that the depression is over a foot deep, Okwaho estimates that this is 18 inches below the original surface of the mound. The dog whimpers excitedly and scratches vigorously. As it brushes more soil back through its front legs, a bone appears exposed in the frozen ground. The 'Wolf' hunter is familiar with bones. He instantly identifies it as a human bone. Okwaho hurriedly take pictures. He considers leaving his gruesome find exposed, but fears that the prying dog may damage it. And worse, what if Nate investigates the dog's interest in the site? He remembers Jack's warning – 'do not contaminate the evidence'. Short of disturbing the find, how is he to secure it?

He comes to a decision. He carries a broken kitchen sink from the neighbouring pile and lays it across the depression. This should protect the site until the dog succeeds in digging around the obstruction. Okwaho records more images on his phone to identify the location of the site relative to the house. He views the captured images and, being satisfied, he transmits them to Jack's phone. Okwaho slowly walks away. The dog resumes its barking until the 'Wolf-man' passes by the chain-gate, and then it falls silent. Okwaho deliberately walks in the middle of the potholed-rutted road in the hope that he meets Nate returning home. The 'Wolf-man' rests his hand on the hilt of his knife and considers that it would be a welcome encounter.

When Okwaho reaches the *Gas and Hot Food* store, Jack is

standing outside, waiting for him. When he is within earshot, Jack addresses Okwaho. "I received your message with the images. Do you know what you found?"

Okwaho comes closer and whispers. "A human bone."

"I concur. It is probably a humerus – an upper-arm bone. To be certain that it is not an animal bone, a forensic examination is required."

Okwaho grunts. Next, he places his right hand on the hilt of his knife and asks Jack, "Is he still here?"

Jack understands that Okwaho is referring to Nate. He also knows that Okwaho sees Nate's pickup truck parked at the store. The 'Wolf-man' deduces that the greasy man is still inside. Jack blocks Okwaho's entrance into the store. "Don't go in, Okwaho. Don't do it this way. Killing Nate would be folly on your part. And to frighten him or threaten him may drive him into hiding. He is trapped. Although, at this point, he is oblivious of the trap. We need the OPP (Ontario Provincial Police) to step in at this point."

Jack gently pushes Okwaho's shoulder. He turns him around and directs him to his car. Jack speaks softly to Okwaho. "Drive. Drive away from here."

Okwaho enters the car and sets it in motion. Jack directs his progress. "Drive. Turn left and go north on the 108."

Some moments later, Okwaho's emotions have calmed somewhat. He asks, "Where are we going?"

"To 47 Hillside Drive North in Elliot Lake, to the East Algoma Elliot Lake OPP. It is beside the *Shoppers* across from the hotel." Okwaho knows the location. He drives in silence. Jack fears that he may be plotting an execution of his own justice. Jack breaks the silence. "The OPP. They will investigate and conduct forensic analysis."

"And if they fail, I will conclude the hunt with the traditional kill."

Jack decides that it is unwise to argue. "Very well."

Jack considers phoning 911. He decides against it. By the time he explains the reason for the call and provides descriptive details, he will have reached the police station. The fastest way to impart the relevant information is to display the image on the cell phone – a picture is worth a thousand words. At 1:10pm, Jack and Okwaho enter the OPP station. Jack nudges Okwaho and says, "Let me do the talking." They are greeted by a young constable at the front desk. Jack identifies himself and asks to speak with a criminal investigator. "I understand that you have a Detective Stan Wilcox. Perhaps he is available."

The constable studies the man wearing a *Blue Jays* baseball cap and a denim jacket over a blue shirt and dark-grey cargo pants and brown city shoes. He is accompanied by a First Nations man with a severe expression. The second man is wearing a leather cowboy hat and a buckskin jacket over jeans and moccasins. The constable regards this as an unlikely duo. He clarifies Jack's request. "You wish to speak to a detective. And what, may I ask, is this concerning?"

"My name is Jack Doyle, a private investigator. I'm working on a missing-person case. I wish to report a suspicious find. I believe we have stumbled upon human remains near Serpent River, on a property at the intersection of the Trans-Canada and Highway 108."

"I see. This is quite serious. And you say that you are 'Jack Doyle'?"

"Yes. Here is my card."

The constable accepts Jack's card and reads it aloud. "Jack Doyle Investigator – Find Jack Doyle, and he finds the person you're looking for." The constable selects a number on his telephone board and engages a connection. "Please have a seat, Mr Doyle. Someone will be with you shortly."

"Jack Doyle! Lord, if it's not Jack Doyle." Jack turns and sees a burly plainclothes officer approach. The man smiles and extends a hand. "You probably don't know me. But I know **you**. The name's Stan Wilcox. I was with the team that was at Hamilton Airport back in..."

"...10 December 2011."

"That's right. Alex Crouse said that you were in the area and that I might hear from you concerning a missing-person case. Is that why you are here?" The detective turns to the young constable at the desk and says, "Meet Jack Doyle, the man responsible for the greatest drug bust in Ontario." He notices the First Nations man next to him and asks Jack, "Have things changed much?"

The constable interrupts. "Detective Wilcox, I was dialling your extension. Mr Doyle is here to report a... He says that there might be human remains."

Jack is impatient. He activates his phone and displays a picture. "Stan, take a look at this."

Stan's face alters from cheerful to serious. He looks at the image. "When was this taken?"

"Twenty-five minutes ago."

"Why didn't you phone 911?"

"We were not sure at first. We are still not sure. That's why we need to show you the picture."

"Where was it taken?"

"In a yard dump just north of the Trans-Canada. The owner's name is 'Nate'."

"That would be Nathaniel Carson. I know him. Come let's go inside." He gestures to Jack and Okwaho to follow him.

Moments later, Jack and Okwaho are seated in Stan Wilcox's office. Stan rests his chin on his upraised hands and says, "This is one of your investigations, I take it. So bring me up to speed – the 10-second summary."

"Missing person – Dorinda Trapper." Stan is tapping his computer keyboard as Jack speaks. "I traced her movements to Serpent River. A Cree girl answering to her description was spotted at the *Gas and Hot Food* convenience store located at the Trans-Canada Highway and Highway 108. Fifteen minutes after that, Nate filled up at the gas pump there. She was never seen again. That was on 18 April 2017.”

“And how were you able to ascertain this information?”

“The store owner disclosed it to me. Actually, I deduced it from what he told me. I showed him pictures of the missing girl and we got to talking. I don’t think he realized how much he divulged.”

“The store owner was talkative? That doesn’t sound like Jimmy Sweeney.”

Okwaho interjects. “It was like a wager – ‘I bet you can’t remember’ kind of thing.”

“Indeed.” Stan suspects that there may have been some sort of trickery involved. But he lets it go. The detective speaks. “I have the missing-person case displayed. ‘Dorinda Trapper, Female Runaway Aboriginal Girl age 15 at the time of her disappearance on 04 April 2017.’ Is that her?”

“Yes. That’s her.”

“Show me the picture on your phone once more.”

Jack unlocks his phone and hands it to the detective. Stan asks permission to transmit the image. Jack complies. Moments later, the three men view an enhanced image of the picture on Stan's computer.

Stan whistles in astonishment as he sharpens the image. He whispers, "Human remains." He looks at Jack and Okwaho and asks, "And you say that this picture was taken at Nate's place a half-hour ago?"

Okwaho answers. "I discovered it in a mound of dirt amongst the piles of trash close to his house. Don't worry. I made sure to conceal it before I left so that Nate would not know that it has been discovered."

"Really? And how did you manage that?"

"I covered the site with a broken sink from an adjacent pile of junk."

"What I mean is, how did you manage to find evidence of human remains in Nate's scrapyard? You say that Nate is not aware of your discovery. So where was he at the time? From what I know of Nate, he would not leave his property unguarded – he would either prohibit you from entering, or his dog would stop you."

"I went to Nate's place on Wednesday 17 April, on the pretence of purchasing furniture for a First Nations reserve. It's something we do to get stuff cheap."

"And Nate let you snoop around?"

"Jack kept him distracted by asking questions about the missing Cree girl. Nate ignored me as I poked around the pile of furniture. His dog kept watching me, though."

Jack interjects. "I went to visit Nate in the course of my missing-person investigation. I questioned him about the Cree girl that was observed in the area, the one that we believe could be Dorinda Trapper. Unfortunately, he provided no information."

The detective nods while jotting notes on a pad. "That visit was four days ago. My question pertains to your visit today when you discovered human remains. How come you were in Nate's scrapyard and he did not know of your presence?"

"I walked to his place from the highway. When I reached the chain-gate, I walked towards his house via the scrapyard."

"That's not a straight line. Why did you deviate? And what reason would you have to be there?"

"I reconsidered buying scrap furniture. Perhaps I could purchase some of it cheap for Red Rapids Reserve. Nate was not at home when I arrived. So, I proceeded to leave. But first, I wanted a closer look at the quality of the furniture. I examined a pile of kitchen stuff on my way out."

"And that's when you saw the human remains?"

"No. That's when I saw the dog scratching a hole in the ground."

"Let me understand. Nate's dog was there? And it let you wander around freely?"

"Nate's underfed dog is afraid of me. All dogs are afraid of me. Anyway, I looked at what the dog was scratching at. And that's when I saw it."

"You saw the exposed bone out in the open? Just like that?"

"Yes. It was the dog that discovered it. I merely took pictures of what the starving dog unearthed."

"And then, you concealed your find? Isn't that what you said?"

"Yes. I covered it with a sink. Hey, I didn't want greasy-man Nate to learn of it."

"And what else did you do?"

"I came here. We both came here as quickly as possible."

"I mean, at the location of your find. Did you touch the bone?"

"No."

"Kick it. Or move it. Or disturb it in any way?"

"No, no and no. I saw it. I took pictures. I left. And here we are."

Stan suddenly stands up. He says, "Wait here," and rushes out of the room. After a lapse of 15 minutes, he returns. He is panting from exertion.

Jack asks, "Are you going to start an investigation?"

Stan sits and leans across the desk towards the two men. To Detective Stan Wilcox, Jack Doyle is 'one of us'. His respect for Jack Doyle induces him to reveal more information than is customary. He speaks in a low voice and imparts some interesting information. "As a result of the evidence you just showed me, we are acting on it – seriously." Stan sits upright and resumes speaking in a normal voice. "Is there any other information you wish to share?"

Jack responds. "Yes, actually. Here is a picture of Dorinda Trapper wearing a black dress." He hands a picture to Stan. "This was taken outside the *Elephant Club* on Sunday 16 April 2017 at roughly 7:30pm. Dorinda, we have reason to believe, was wearing this dress when she was at Nate's property. Find it, and you will have a DNA match."

"'Reason to believe'. How sure are you?"

Jack attempts to point him to the presence of the black dress in Nate's house. "I am gut-sure, but not evidentiary-sure."

"I see. You are 'gut-sure' that Dorinda was in Nate's house and that she was wearing this particular black dress. 'Gut-sure' isn't enough. But I'll note to give it special attention." Stan writes on his pad. He looks at Jack again. "Anything else?"

"I don't know the extent of the information in your files. So, here is my card. It has my cell-phone number. I would be pleased to share whatever information I have from my investigation. Oh, one thing more. Dorinda Trapper was reported missing by her aunt, Rose Cool. However, her next of kin is her mother, Amy Trapper. If perchance you don't have Amy's contact number on file, I'll write it on the back of my card." Jack quickly writes the information. "There – Amy Trapper of Red Rapids Reserve."

Stan takes the card from Jack and says, "We are on top of it. This is our investigation from here. There is one thing I need you to do, Jack."

"Sure. What's that?"

"Nothing."

"Nothing?"

'You could stay close for another day in case I require more information from you. Otherwise, I can contact you by phone. But you, Jack, are to stay away from Nate and from the investigation. Here is my card. It displays my direct line. If you have concerns, contact me. Other than that, stay away and do nothing."

Jack understands. Unwelcome 'help' would only impede the police investigation and could have disastrous consequences on the integrity of evidence and witness statements. Jack and Okwaho leave the police station.

*   *   *   *   *

Stan Wilcox knows a great deal more than he revealed to Jack and Okwaho. Nathaniel Carson is already under police surveillance. And, as of today, the police have requested a search warrant as part of the 'Missing Women Investigation'. They expect to descend on Nate Carson's property within 24 hours.

This is not the first time the OPP have had dealings with Nate Carson. On 23 March 2009, Nate Carson was charged with attempted murder of sex worker Lana East, whom he had stabbed several times during an altercation at his property. East had informed the police that Nate Carson had handcuffed her, but that she had disabled him after suffering several lacerations. She told the police that she had disarmed him and stabbed him with his own weapon. They were both brought to hospital for treatment, still handcuffed together, where staff used a key they found in Nate's pocket to remove the handcuffs from the woman's wrist. The attempted murder charge against Nate Carson was stayed on 27 January 2010, because the woman had drug addiction issues and prosecutors believed her too unstable for her testimony to help secure a conviction.

Stan thumps the table and exclaims, "This time we will nail him."

Monday 22 April 2019 is a holiday in Ontario. But for the East Algoma OPP, this is the first day of the busiest period they have ever experienced. They descend in force on Nate Carson's property. Nate's dog goes crazy at the invasion of so many intruders. The police threaten to shoot it if Nate refuses to control it. He reluctantly consents to chain the dog to his pickup. The police team engage a cadaver dog to sweep the area. They quickly find bodily remains but are surprised that it is the remains of three bodies – not just one as expected.

The OPP determine that the discovery of multiple bodies suggests a serial murder. This investigation could extend beyond the scope and jurisdiction of provincial police. Thus, the RCMP (Royal Canadian Mounted Police) are brought in straight away, and it becomes a joint RCMP-OPP police investigation. They extend their search and, by the end of the day, they unearth the remains of three more bodies. Coincident with these discoveries, they estimate that the amount of women's clothing found in the house suggests that 40 or more women have been here at some time. They make special note of the black 'Sigmund dress'. The police also find a loaded .22 revolver with one round fired, boxes of .357 Magnum handgun ammunition, two pairs of handcuffs and a syringe with three millilitres of blue liquid inside. At the end of the day, only a small portion of the property is explored, yet they have already discovered the remains of six victims. With the potential of finding many more bodies, the police consider employing heavy digging equipment. The forensic anthropologists request mechanical shovels and two 15-metre flat conveyor belts and soil sifters to find traces of human remains.

Nathaniel Carson is arrested and charged with six counts of first-degree murder. In police custody, Nate boasts to a cellmate that he had killed 49 women and wanted to kill one more to make it an even 50. He confesses to targeting indigenous runaways and sex workers because 'no one ever looks for them when they vanish'. Unbeknownst to Nate, his cellmate is an undercover police officer.

Meanwhile, Jack is unaware of this. He obtains limited information on the progress of the police case from what he observes driving on Highway 108, and from police news releases.

After leaving the OPP station in Elliot Lake, Okwaho drives back to the *Gas and Hot Food* store. They don't require gas and they don't need hot food. They are curious to see if there is a police presence in the area. They see an OPP car parked off to the side of the road at Nate's driveway. Okwaho drives by and enters the parking lot of the roadside store.

Upon entering the store, they are greeted by Grouchy Man. (Although they now know that his name is 'Jimmy Sweeney', they still regard him as 'Grouchy Man'.) "I hope you guys drive at the speed limit. There is an OPP speed trap out there."

Okwaho acknowledges the remark. "Yeah. We saw that. It's a speed trap, all right." After consuming a few cups of coffee, the two men decide that there is nothing more to see. They return to their hotel to retire for the night.

On Monday 22 April 2019, there is increased activity in the area. Jack and Okwaho spend the day in the *Gas and Hot Food* store, watching for unusual goings-on. A black unmarked van is parked at the truck inspection station beside the MOT vehicles. Police cars drive by at intervals. About midway through the day, numerous vehicles enter Nate's driveway and drive out of sight. Thereupon, police tape is erected to prevent entry. And to be sure, a police car parks broadside to block entry. At mid-afternoon, they observe Nate's pickup truck being towed away from his property.

Jack remarks to Okwaho, "Forensic examination of the truck. They are going to take it apart and examine every filthy inch and every grimy crack."

"And I'll bet they find a lot more than dog hairs."

At six o'clock, Jack and Okwaho order steak dinners from Grouchy Man. Fifteen minutes later, the quiet of the store is assaulted by the noisy arrival of a CBC news team. Grouchy Man goes outside to inquire. He is immediately surrounded by a confusing assemblage of microphones, cameras and crew. "Who are you? What is your name? How well did you know Nathaniel Carson?"

Jack and Okwaho look at each other. The news has broken. In the *Gas and Hot Food* store, there is no radio or television available for patrons. So, they quickly finish up their meal and drive to Elliot Lake where they hope to catch the 'CBC News at Ten'. Inside the hotel, the news release is the hot topic of conversation. The two men enter the bar and wait for ten o'clock. When the news commences, it is the first topic reported. 'Responding to an anonymous tip, police are investigating the gruesome discovery of human remains at a property south of Elliot Lake, Ontario. Police confirm that they are speaking with a person of interest in the course of their inquiries.' There is a picture displayed of Nate's blocked-off driveway. Then the camera pans to the *Gas and Hot Food* store. In the next shot, Grouchy Man is interviewed. He refers to 'a quiet man'. Jack notices that the news release omits the identity of the 'person of interest', and the interview has edited out any reference to 'Nathaniel Carson'.

Over the next day, references to Nate change from 'person of interest' to 'charged under Section 243 of the Criminal Code, to dispose of a body with the intent to conceal'. At this point, his name is released. Then, on Thursday, the CBC reports that Nathaniel Carson is charged with six counts of murder. The report also adds that two bodies have been identified, and that names are withheld pending notification of next of kin.

Jack and Okwaho are sitting in the hotel bar listening to the noon news. When Jack hears 'two bodies have been identified', he phones Stan Wilcox. Stan answers and Jack speaks. "Stan, it's Jack Doyle. I heard on the news that two bodies have been identified."

"That is correct."

"Could Dorinda Trapper be one of them?"

"Jack, you know I cannot release information on the identity of the victims until the families are notified."

"Just tell me – yes or no. Is Dorinda one of the identified bodies?"

"Come on Jack. You know how this plays."

"Yeah, I know. I just thought it was worth a shot."

"Well, there you are."

"Thanks anyway, Stan."

"Oh, Jack, before you go, I must ask you something. Can you confirm Amy Trapper's phone number for me?"

Jack recites the number from memory and disconnects. He jumps up and punches Okwaho on the shoulder. "Rise up, 'Wolf'. We are going to Red Rapids."

"Right now?"

"Yes. Right now. Do you know how to charter a floatplane flight to the reserve?"

An hour later, Jack and Okwaho land at Red Rapids. The Trapper-Cool clan and the chief greet them upon their arrival at the lakeshore. They walk as a group to the meeting hall. The family has just learned that the body of Dorinda Trapper has been positively identified. A forensic autopsy was conducted on her skeletal remains, and a DNA match was conclusive. They are advised that she is the victim of a murder. However, because of the nature of the circumstances, a forensic autopsy is ordered. The resulting post-mortem examination could take a few weeks to complete. Thereupon, the remains will be released to the next of kin. The Trapper-Cool family will be advised later of the release date.

The meeting room is set up with a large-screen TV. Several band members are present. They are following the news on CBC's 24-hour news channel. There are hourly news bulletins on 'The Carson Murders'. So far, the news channel has not reported the names of the identified victims. Jack and Okwaho remain overnight in the reserve's hotel. On the following morning, Friday 26 April, the news reports the names of the two victims – Mary Day and Dorinda Trapper. Four additional victims are still awaiting identification.

Jack looks back at the progress of his task. He had embarked on finding Dorinda Trapper. He found her, even though it was Nate's underfed dog that clinched the final step. The task is accomplished due in large part to the unyielding support of the 'troublesome Wolf' at his side all the way. Suddenly, Jack is fatigued. He wants to go home and rest. Jack and Okwaho leave the reserve at noon. It is late on Friday night when Okwaho drops Jack off at Huron Park, Mississauga. The 'Wolf' continues onwards to Mohawk First Nation on the Grand River.

On Tuesday 30 April 2019, Jack Doyle completes a progress report on his investigation. Until Dorinda Trapper is returned home, his investigation is unfinished.

*   *   *   *   *

Meanwhile, at Nate Carson's place, the police conclude their search of the property. Between Monday 22 April and Sunday 02 June 2019, a total of 19 bodies are unearthed. Nate Carson is charged with additional counts of murder – 13 more are added to the original six counts.

CHAPTER EIGHTEEN

THE OWL SURMOUNTS THE SNAKE

On Tuesday 24 June 2019, Jack Doyle is busy in his office at 1660 North Service Road East, Oakville. It is close to noon. His investigation report on 'Missing Person – Dorinda Trapper' is finished. The final entry refers to the return of Dorinda's remains to her next of kin. Jack had been waiting to confirm this detail in order to conclude his investigation report. He had promised Amy that he would find her missing daughter and bring her home. Now that Dorinda is home at last and reunited with her family, Jack's mission is accomplished. He presses 'print' on his keyboard and listens to the sound of the printer. When the printer ceases, he retrieves the printed copy. He reads through it once. He is satisfied with it, so he signs it. It is customary to include a final invoice with the concluding report. Jack had decided at the beginning of his investigation that he would provide his services gratis. Thus, he places the completed report in an envelope sans invoice. Jack is undecided whether to mail the report or to deliver it personally. To simply mail the report is cold and unsympathetic. On the other hand, to present himself to the Trapper family at this time of mourning might be an inappropriate intrusion. While weighing the pros and cons, the deciding factor is presented by the sudden and unexpected appearance of Okwaho to his office. Okwaho announces his presence by means of the door buzzer. Jack grants access, thankful that the 'Wolf' has chosen an approved mode of entry.

Jack looks up as Okwaho enters his office and says, "Okwaho. I wasn't expecting you, now that our business together is concluded."

"Hello, Jack. As to the conclusion of business, yes, it's done. But I'm not here on business."

Jack is puzzled by this remark. He looks questioningly at Okwaho. "Oh. So, why..."

"Dorinda Trapper's remains were delivered to Red Rapids yesterday..."

"Yes, I know. I am aware of that. And I confirmed that fact."

Okwaho is impatient to speak over Jack's interruptions. "Dorinda's wake. Amy Trapper spoke to me about the wake and funeral. Normally, only family and friends attend. She would welcome your presence."

Jack is taken aback. "I'd be honoured to attend. But I don't know what to wear or how to behave..."

"She knows that you don't know. Don't worry about that. Just wear your 'Sunday best' and someone will guide you."

"So, are you the one to hold my hand lest I put my foot in it?"

"I would not be a good choice. In truth, I am not proficient enough in *ililîmowin* – the Cree language. Sara Jolly volunteered."

"Sara Jolly? Do I know her?"

"Remember the 'jolly' waitress at the hotel?"

"Sara the waitress? Of course, I remember. And her name is really 'Sara Jolly'?"

"I'll take that for a 'yes'. I'll phone Amy and let her know."

Jack leans back in his chair and gestures his approval. "So, I'm to spend another day at Red Rapids."

"No Jack. You'll spend seven days at the reserve. The wake and funeral take five days. And it starts later today – in the evening."

Having made his decision, Jack is anxious to leave immediately. He avails of an Air Canada Flight to Sudbury at 2:15pm. He and Okwaho travel together and arrive in Red Rapids by floatplane from Elliot Lake at 7:30pm. At 7:50pm, Jack arrives at the hotel. Okwaho, on the other hand, proceeds directly to the administration building.

Sara greets Jack as he enters the hotel. "Jack Doyle, welcome. We are expecting you, of course. You are pre-registered. Here is your room key." She hands him the key. "And your timing is perfect. Dorinda's wake starts shortly – twelve minutes from now. Leave your things here. Come. Follow me to the meeting room in the administration building."

Sara leads Jack to the band council's meeting room. Inside, chairs encircle the perimeter of the room. A solitary table stands in the centre. Jack and Sara sit side-by-side within the circle of chairs. There are over 200 people present, but only a few sit in chairs. The others sit on the floor. Sara informs him, "Most people prefer to sit on the floor in the traditional manner. Some time ago, chairs were introduced for the comfort of the elderly. Today, seating is permitted as an optional alternative available to everyone." Sara continues to explain the tradition. She informs Jack, "Over the course of five nights and four days, people visit for short periods. The entire adult population of the reserve is expected to visit at least once during the period of the wake. You notice that the men and women sit at opposite sides. Not everyone observes that custom today. Sometimes, family groups or couples sit together, except for the traditionalists who adhere to the old ways."

Sara points to the table in the centre of the room. She explains. "Dorinda is lying on the table. She is in an open casket. Because her body is skeleton remains, she is already covered in the burial blanket. See the moccasins at her feet? These were made especially for her by the women of the reserve. Normally, these would be placed on her feet. In this instance, they are placed **at** her feet. Sweetgrass, our sacred and purifying plant is placed at her right hand. Look here," Sara gestures, "you see tobacco in the centre. That is to aid communication between the Creator and us. Furthermore, anything intimately related to Dorinda is placed there too. I believe I see some of her hair ties from home. These are 'part of the person' and will be buried with her."

Jack recognizes members of the family – Amy, Kokum, Mark, Jim Cool and Rose Cool. The three women are seated on chairs. The two men sit beside them on the floor. Jack enquires of Sara. "Do members of the family remain here for the five days?"

"No. They take turns. At least one member of the family is present at all times up to the burial. They are all in attendance at this time because it is the beginning of the wake."

This custom is not foreign to him. Jack is familiar with a traditional Irish wake. Although, in his experience, the wake is held on the day and night preceding the funeral. He once sat in vigil at his grandfather's wake from midnight to 6:00am.

At intervals, people stand up and walk towards the table. They talk together. Or perhaps they are praying. Thereafter, they return to where they were seated or exit the room. Jack is unable to comprehend the Cree language – *ililîmowin*. He looks to Sara for an explanation.

"Although the body undergoes a physical transformation, the spirit remains unchanged. Separation from the body does not mean that ties to people are disconnected. You will see people come and go. When they speak, they relate stories of earlier days and share memories of Dorinda. Some stories are funny and evoke laughter. Laughter is considered a healing medicine. Some are sad stories and we weep. Other stories are expressions of comfort. Also, songs may be sung. And prayers are offered. Each person who visits offers something and then they leave."

Jack is apprehensive. "Sara, am I expected to say something?"

Sara smiles at him. "Not every offering is vocal. I think your presence is a sufficient offering."

After an hour, Sara says, "Unless it is to acknowledge and honour the deceased, no one crosses the room except by walking around the outside of the circle. But be at ease. Amy understands that your customs are different and that you show respect differently. Hence, you are permitted to sit beside me. Now, come with me to the table. It is permitted to do so. And I believe it is your custom to spend a moment in silent prayer. That would be an acceptable offering."

Jack does so. When he turns around, Amy looks at him and smiles in appreciation. Jack expects to return to his chair. But Sara gently takes his hand and directs him to outside the circle of chairs. In another part of the meeting room, tables are set up a short distance apart. These are laden with food. Sara explains. "Eat some food. But wait to be served. Women prepare the food; men serve it. When you eat this food, you eat with the spirits. Then we leave." Jack consumes a piece of smoked meat and a scone of bannock.

Later, in walking back to the hotel, Jack asks Sara, "I understand that most Cree are Christian. Is that correct? So will there be a Christian funeral?"

Sara looks at him and smiles. "What do you think?" She hesitates a moment and looks at Jack's doubtful expression. Then, to Jack's relief, she continues. "On the fifth day, there will be a funeral Mass. There is a chapel room in the administration building next to the meeting room. An Oblate father comes here once a month. Father Dechant will arrive for the funeral on Saturday 29 June. And he will depart after Sunday Mass early the next morning. We arranged with him to have the wake and funeral coincide with his monthly visit. I understand that he flies to five reserves over the course of one day. Oh, Mass is not celebrated in Cree. It is in English or French."

On the following morning, Jack meets with the chief. He explains that he wishes to deliver his investigation report but is reluctant to intrude on the family during their period of mourning. The chief arranges a suitable meeting. At 11:00am, Jack and Amy Trapper and the chief meet in the second-floor office above the meeting room.

Jack hands the envelope to Amy. She looks at it and says, "You promised to find Dorinda. You kept your word. She is home now."

"I'm sorry the result is not what we had hoped for."

"But it is what we suspected. Under the circumstances, this is the best result possible."

There is a moment of silence. Amy places the envelope unopened on the chief's desk. Jack gestures to it. "This is the report. You may wish to read it."

Amy shakes her head. "All I need to know is lying in repose in the room below. The report belongs to the chief and the band." She addresses the chief. "Chief Kataquapit, take the report." She stands and turns to Jack. "Thank you, Jack Doyle, 'Snake-man'. Today, and for everyday hereafter, you are welcome at my house." She departs solemnly from the room.

The chief looks at Jack. He waits until Amy is out of earshot. Thereupon, he speaks confidentially to Jack. "Amy is aware of the circumstances surrounding Dorinda's death. But she is blocking the details from her mind – too much emotional stress. The death certificate revealed that the cause of death was a gunshot wound to the head. Amy does not wish to be reminded of that. And neither does she want to know about Nate Carson. The shocking details of the relationship between murderer and victim are more than she can bear."

Jack nods sympathetically. "Of course. I understand."

The chief opens Jack's envelope and removes the contents. He notices the there is no invoice attached. He checks the covering letter and observes the reference to 'services gratis'. He glances at Jack and says, "This appears to be a comprehensive report. I will read it later and share it with the elders. As to your services, Jack Doyle, the Cree of Red Rapids thank you. It would be our honour to formally express our gratitude to you on the evening of Thursday 15 August. That is the eve of a special pow-wow we are arranging to celebrate the lives of the dead who are still with us. It is different from the annual festive pow-wow that is held on National Indigenous Peoples Day. I hope you will join us."

"Of course. I accept."

Over the next two days, Jack attends the wake for two one-hour periods. For the remainder of the time, he wanders around the reserve. He garners an understanding of the layout of the place. However, Jack is unable to cross the river to the 'B' section of the reserve to where the Trapper and Cool families reside. The Red Rapids River is in flood from melting snow, yet stretches of the river bank stubbornly retain traces of still-melting slush. Jack admires the scenery. Red Fox Lake is partially ice-covered – a crescent-shaped floating island hugs the far-away shoreline. The aspen and birch are fully in leaf. In exploring the area, Jack is discouraged from lingering in admiration for any length of time. He is obliged to keep moving; otherwise, he is assaulted by swarms of mosquitoes.

From midnight to 4:00am on Saturday, the *Round Dance* concludes the wake. Women, in traditional costumes, perform the *Moving Slowly Dance* while 16 men sit around the *Ceremonial Drum*, beating in unison. The men chant to the drumbeat. Some women stand in a secondary circle chanting behind the men. Jack wonders what the chant means. To his ear, it is four hours of 'Hi-yah, hi-yah, hi-yah.' At the conclusion of the wake, the casket is closed. The mourners carry it to the chapel and drape it in the funeral blanket. Sometime later, the funeral Mass is celebrated and the casket is interred in the reserve cemetery. At the gravesite, prayers are offered and songs are sung. The male relatives fill the grave with earth. Afterwards, the mourners congregate in the meeting room to celebrate the funeral feast. The feast honours the passing of the spirit from the body in recognition that neither the spirit nor the people ever fully depart from one another.

Seven weeks after Dorinda's funeral, the Red Rapids Reserve holds a special pow-wow to celebrate the lives of the dead. At 7:00pm on Thursday 15 August 2019, on the eve of the pow-wow, the band conducts a vigil ceremony. Jack Doyle is present by special invitation of the chief. He sits facing the head table comprised of the chief and two sub-chief elders. Sara Jolly sits on his left, wedged between him and Okwaho. She is positioned thus to interpret the proceeds for the benefit of the two men. A further 15 people, men and women, occupy the front row. Sara explains that these are invited representatives of Cree and Ojibwe bands.

When the meeting commences, the chief addresses the assembly. Jack hears his name mentioned. He turns to Sara for an explanation. She nudges him sternly. "Quiet. He is talking about you."

A short time later, the chief sits. Then each of the guests speaks to the assembly in turn. Jack looks to Sara for an explanation. She informs him. "They are reciting the list of names of the 19 victims found in Nathaniel Carson's property. Eighteen victims have been positively identified. They are all Cree or Ojibwe. These are the band members representing each victim. Each victim is addressed and remembered in her own language by a family member." The last person to step forward is Amy Trapper. After Amy delivers her address to Dorinda Trapper, the chief concludes the acknowledgements. Sara whispers to Jack. "Chief Kataquapit is addressing 'Jane Doe', the unidentified aboriginal woman. And so concludes the litany of all 19 victims."

Moments later, Sara prods Jack. She whispers to him, "Stand up. The chief is addressing you. I'll translate as he speaks. "'Snake-man'. You are 'Snake-man' no more. The council has decided to accept you as an honorary member of the *People of the Owl*. This requires the approval of the band." At this, the entire assembly rises and expresses their approval, including the representatives of the visiting bands. The chief continues to speak to Jack. "You are to be inducted into our band at Red Rapids. The ceremony will continue when you are clothed in the *Cloak of Honour*."

Sara turns to face Jack. "Come with me to the adjoining room, where we will prepare you for the induction." Jack considers this to be a lot of unnecessary ceremony. Surely, they could present him with a roll of paper with a ribbon attached and that would suffice. But he obliges out of respect for their customs. He accompanies Sara and Okwaho into a small adjoining room. Jack identifies it as a dressing room. It contains ceremonial robes, emblems and feathered headbands. Sara explains the preparation procedure for Jack. "You see a cloak of beaver skin hanging there? That is the *Cloak of Honour*. But before I put it on," she points to a bowl on the table, "we mark your head with this dye. Shut your eyes while we apply it."

Jack expects Sara to apply the dye with a paintbrush. Instead, he is jolted by a stinging burn to his forehead. He jumps in surprise and opens his eyes. Okwaho is holding a branding iron in his hand. The 'Wolf' looks at Jack with approval. Sara concurs and says, "Well executed, Okwaho. The mark of the striking snake is successfully converted to an owl's head in profile."

Okwaho looks admiringly at his work. "See, Sara, you would never know that there was ever a snake there." Then he speaks to Jack. "Stop squirming as if you are in pain and let's get the cloak and headband on."

Later, when Jack is appropriately attired in the ceremonial clothing, he is presented to the meeting. The chief addresses him by his new name – 'Ôhô' (Owl). Thereupon the chief places a white owl feather in Jack's headband. The assembly applauds in appreciation. Ôhô, no longer 'Onyare', casts his eyes around the assembly. These are family members of Nate Carson's unfortunate victims. There are no reporters or outsiders present at the solemn and private event. Jack spots just one non-indigenous person present, a man wearing a necktie. It is Detective Stan Wilcox. After the meeting, Amy Trapper presents Jack with a small hand-stitched beaver wallet. She elucidates. "This is to hold your 'mekwan' (white owl feather). There are leather straps on the wallet. You could hang it around your neck when you are not wearing the mekwan on your head. Or keep it in your pocket, or on your trophy wall." She hesitates to admire Jack's new mark. "Welcome, Ôhô." And since he is no longer an outsider, she hugs him. "And here is a band-aid for your forehead. The mark will smart for a few days. Then it will heal and appear like a tattoo – except for the scaring if you look up close." Amy hands him a band-aid and walks back into the crowd.

Stan Wilcox approaches Jack. "Congratulations, Jack. Well deserved. You know, I have encountered you twice in my career. And each occasion was momentous. First, it was the biggest drug bust in Ontario history. And now it is the largest serial-murder crime in Ontario history."

"I suppose that's true, Stan."

"It's true, all right. And you, Jack, were the prime catalyst in activating both cases. Alas, you will never get any official or public recognition. Not even a 'thank-you'."

"Well, I have this." Jack points to his mekwan feather.

"Ah, yes." Stan shakes Jack's hand. "Well deserved. Now, I'm off to my OPP floatplane, and back to the old slog." Stan departs with haste.

At the pow-wow on the following day, Jack sits with the elders during the formal celebrations.

Later in the day, Jack is preparing to leave Red Rapids. As he admires his new mark of the owl in the mirror in the hotel lobby, he turns to Okwaho and inquires. "Okwaho, the snake mark. I often wondered why the snake had no eye. Was that an oversight?" Jack places a fresh band-aid on the fresh mark and pats it.

Okwaho shoulders his overnight bag and says casually, "It was no oversight. The eye is placed there when you die."

Jack walks with him to the floatplane. "What is the point of placing an eye on the snake after I'm dead?"

Okwaho looks at Jack critically. "I didn't say 'after you're dead', I said 'when you die'. The missing eye is an invitation to kill you. It's symbolic, meaning that you are not worthy to live."

"Just symbolic?"

"Yes. For most people. However, you never know who might treat it literally." Okwaho laughs. "Don't worry. You're safe now. The Owl surmounts the Snake."

<u>Acknowledgements:</u>

Chapleau Cree First Nation – chapleaucree.ca

Chapleau Crown Game Preserve – Wikipedia

Communities of Moose River and Moose Factory

Cree words – www.creedictionary.com

Driving and walking distances – Google Maps

First Nations Housing – CBC News Report

Forest Regions of Ontario – www.ontario.ca

Highways in the Algoma District – Wikipedia

Homeland Security Investigations/ICE – www.ice.gov

Louis Riel – Wikipedia

Mississagi Provincial Park

Moose Cree First Nation – www.moosecree.com

Reserves in Ontario – by Karl S. Hele, pub June 14, 2019

R. v. Pickton, Full text of Supreme Court of Canada

ABOUT THE AUTHOR

Fergus Patrick Egan was born in 1945 in Donegal in the northwest of Ireland. He spent 20 years in retail banking, including 10 years in Toronto. Over the course of 30 years, he worked in the Canadian travel industry. He currently resides in Ontario, Canada.